THE
LINCOLN
CONSPIRACY

BALLANTINE BOOKS TRADE PAPERBACKS   NEW YORK

THE
LINCOLN
CONSPIRACY

A NOVEL

Timothy L. O'Brien

2013 Ballantine Books Trade Paperback Edition

Copyright © 2012 by Timothy L. O'Brien
Excerpt from the forthcoming novel by Timothy L. O'Brien © 2013
by Timothy L. O'Brien

Published in the United States by Ballantine Books, an imprint of
The Random House Publishing Group, a division of Random House LLC,
a Penguin Random House Company, New York.

BALLANTINE and the HOUSE colophon are registered trademarks of
Random House LLC.

Originally published in hardcover in the United States by Ballantine Books,
an imprint of The Random House Publishing Group, a division of
Random House LLC, in 2012.

Title page image of Abraham Lincoln by Alexander Gardner, 1865;
National Portrait Gallery, Smithsonian Institution/Art Resource, N.Y.

This book contains an excerpt from the forthcoming novel by Timothy L.
O'Brien. This excerpt has been set for this edition only and may not reflect
the final content of the forthcoming edition.

Library of Congress Cataloging-in-Publication Data
O'Brien, Timothy L.
The Lincoln conspiracy : a novel / Timothy L. O'Brien.
p. cm.
ISBN 978-0-345-49678-2
eBook ISBN 978-0-345-53559-7
1. Lincoln, Abraham, 1809–1865—Assassination—Fiction. 2. Lincoln,
Mary Todd, 1818–1882—Fiction. 3. Presidents—United States—Fiction.
4. Washington (D.C.)—Fiction. 5. Conspiracies—Fiction.
6. Assassins—Fiction. 7. Actors—Fiction. I. Title.
PS3615.B79L56 2012
813'.6—dc23   2012022133

Printed in the United States of America on acid-free paper

www.ballantinebooks.com

9 8 7 6 5 4 3 2 1

For my wife, Devon Corneal,
who spins the wind

"The road must be built."

—ABRAHAM LINCOLN

PART ONE

SWAMPDOODLE

CHAPTER ONE

THE PACKAGE

Rain kept the dust down.

Nothing else in Washington did, especially in early summer, when the heat started coming on and dirt in the streets began the slow broil that led into August. Fiona would hate that rain was already lashing the leather on his new boots. She was practical in these matters. But even Fiona would admit that rain kept the dust down. Temple would rather be with Fiona now, instead of gimping toward a train to fetch Augustus and Pint.

> *The small rain down can rain.*
> *Christ that my love were in my arms*
> *and I in my bed again.*

As he crossed D Street on New Jersey Avenue, he could see the dome of the new Capitol building looming beyond and above the seventy-foot Italianate clock tower that marked the B&O Railroad station. If the rain got worse, New Jersey would get rutted and rats the size of dogs would slop in the puddles and pick through the garbage floating there. Several carriages and a string of horses—far more horses than usual—were tied to posts in front of the station. Union troops, boys mostly, were milling about in their blues. Weary little boys with swords and rifles and blank stares; today they seemed slightly frenzied. Then again, everyone was close to conniption fits with Lincoln dead only a month.

Shot. Dead. Just like that, the tired man, the calm one, the seer. Dead. Dead tired. Gone.

At the corner of C Street, the rain picked up and lashed Temple's face as hard as it whipped his boots. A lashing, the Dublin priests and nuns had told him, was salutary. "Saaaluutarry, Temple. Good for you." Then, smack. Fear the Lord, learn your grammar, and obey the rules of the orphanage. If you didn't obey, smack. Pain, they thought, was an education in its own right. They knew hardly a thing about it, really. He had pain every day in his bad leg, small flashes he tried to ignore. When the pain got bad, occasionally very bad, he just leaned more heavily on his cane. Fiona could look in his face and know the singe was about to arrive in his leg. But then, Fiona looked in his face and saw everything.

Temple ducked beneath the B&O's eaves to get out of the rain. He entered the depot and glanced at the ticket and freight offices, set opposite each other inside the station. A small group of women were huddled and chatting outside the ladies' waiting room, while three men, their arms wrapped across one another's shoulders, pressed toward the gentlemen's saloon.

Temple looked beyond the entry hall to the car house, where the train to Baltimore waited. The railroad tracks cut diagonally through the car house, sheltered by a dozen granite pillars that supported an iron roof with a three-hundred-foot-long glass window set inside it. Rainwater smeared the glass. Even the sky can't stop mourning the president, Temple thought.

The B&O tracks continued through the station, winding along C Street and First Street before crossing the mall in front of the Capitol, picking up Maryland Avenue and making their way to the Long Bridge. Virginia was beyond the Long Bridge. Baltimore and New York were the opposite way.

Temple scanned the platform near the Baltimore train. There—there now. There's something unusual. Stump Tigani, the most deliberate capper in the District, was actually off his heels and in a rush.

Stump's always a surprise, Temple thought. Amid the Union blues, the black long coats, and the crenellated, bell-blossomed hoopskirts of passengers waiting to board the train to Baltimore, Stump—small, muscular, and flinty—was darting along.

Like every newly minted Washington police detective ("You mean 'defective,'" Fiona would laugh. "You have a limp and a cane, my love. You're a police defective"), Temple was well aware of Stump's calling card: courier for Northern spies and the Union army during the war, may have taken money from Secesh when it suited him; connected and resourceful; inscrutable; dangerous, very dangerous.

Finding Stump at the B&O wasn't unusual. Stump had carried packages back and forth from this station many times before, sometimes twice in a single day, and all of his parcels had pedigrees: dispatches from powerful men, wealthy women, and furtive lovers. Transactions and messages; the daily push and pull. Stump hurrying, however, was quite odd. Stump was never invisible—no one in Washington was during the war—but he was paid well to be quiet, reliable, and discreet. He escorted clients' secrets from one place to another with all of the devotion and circumspection of a father helping his toddler navigate the ruts across Pennsylvania Avenue. Everyone and everything got safely to the other side, but Stump never rushed.

Stump's right hand was stuffed inside his overcoat. Looked like Old Boney. A gun? Or maybe Stump's gut hurt. Bad food at the Willard? Stump could manage paying for his own fixin's at the Willard now that he was working the carriage trade, that was for certain.

Stump was weaving and pressing forward, heading toward the Baltimore train; clinging to something, afraid of something. Stump liked to leave town at night, not in the morning. Why was he here now?

Well, none of this was Temple's concern anyhow, was it? He had come to meet Augustus and Pint, secure their cargo, and get on his way. He needed the money, Augustus needed the money, and he would get his cargo even if his right leg continued to send flashes up his side.

Washington brimmed with the wounded and crippled, but Temple was probably the only twenty-five-year-old in the city who hadn't earned his stumble in the war. And his cane—a thick, dark span of polished hickory—punctuated his limitation. Old before your time, Fiona would tease. He smiled to himself and sat down on a bench to stretch his leg while he waited.

Temple was pulling his timepiece from his waistcoat pocket when a shift in the patterns of the bristling swarm of it all made his head snap up and his eyes sharpen. A quiet, violent struggle was unfolding at the entrance to Stump's train.

Two men were on either side of Stump, their hands on his shoulders. Another was in front of him. They were murmuring something to Stump, and from dozens of feet away their lips looked as thin and dark as pencil drawings. One of the men tried peeling off Stump's coat and then spun him around, so Stump faced Temple. Stump's eyes were cast downward. The courier was concentrating. Temple saw a flash of metal as Stump slid a stiletto from inside his sleeve. Then things stopped. Stump stopped. The men around Stump seemed to stop. For a moment, all of them looked like props on a stage set. Stump lurched forward and fell to the platform, dark blood spurting from a long slice on the side of his neck. The skin on Stump's neck parted a bit more as he slumped, his eyes growing moony lickety-split and his fingers spidering up to his neck as if he were hoping he could just press the life back into his throat before it all poured out. As he flopped down to the ground, a greasy puddle of blood spread wide and silently as fog around Stump's head and neck. His teeth pressed outward against his lips and his mouth tightened into a simian oval, fixed somewhere between surprise and the last, sharp twitchings of pain.

Temple pushed off the bench to his feet. Several other men rushed the group around Stump as people began screaming. A young soldier came running, his brogans smacking the ground and the edges of his blue coat flapping. As Temple scuttled toward Stump's body, he collided with the soldier, who careened off him like a toy. Temple continued hip-hopping—damn my limp—toward Stump.

The group of men around Stump were fighting with one another now. They were all dandy, crisp white shirts and tailored black coats. Gentlemen didn't do this, didn't mix it up in gangs. Still, eight men and they were fighting like boys from his orphanage. Some of them had brass knuckles; one had a knife. One had a gun. As they scrapped, they moved a few feet away from Stump's body, leaving the courier unattended. When Temple reached the body, he rolled it over and Stump's coat flopped open, exposing the borders of a thick belt wrapped around his torso and swelling up from beneath his shirt. Temple popped the buttons and loosened the strap that was squeezing a brown paper package against Stump's sternum. This was what made Stump so anxious, this little package. And now Stump's life was oozing from a surgical tear across his throat, mucky with blood and already attracting flies. As Temple yanked the package from beneath the belt, a shadow slipped along the pavement next to Stump's body.

One of the gents was standing over him and he had a long metal rod, of all things. "Leave it alone," he said to Temple. "Take your hands off the package."

Temple pulled out his detective's badge, flat and heavy with an image of the Capitol building stamped upon it, but the gent ignored it, raised his rod, and sliced it down toward Temple's neck.

Ah, well. Temple was grateful for his cane at times.

He swept his cane from the ground and blocked the rod; a few quick turns of his wrist and he spun the rod out of the gent's hands. Still crouched, he whipped his cane across the gent's knees and, as the man crumbled, Temple gave him a solid whack across the side of his head. He looked up at the group of men, who had parted and put down their knives and knuckles to consider him. The gent with the gun turned toward him and raised his pistol. He looked delighted, his eyes dancing beneath a high, sloping forehead. That one enjoys it, Temple thought. He enjoys killing.

"Corporal," Temple shouted over his shoulder to the soldier. "I'm a Metropolitan Police detective. Charge that man."

Good boy: He did as he was told. He raised his rifle, bayonet shining at the end of it, and shouted at the gent with the gun, telling him to disarm. The gent smiled, pointed his gun, and fired. One shot. The boy's eyes widened in surprise and then he dropped like a sack, the black brim of his little blue cap crumpling behind his head. Temple drew a knife off his ankle and readied it, but now the men—as startled as everyone else in the station by the sound of a gunshot—scrambled, separated, and ran. Temple was alone with Stump, who, like the boy nearby, was limp and lifeless. And it would seem that everyone here today wanted the package more than they wanted poor Stump.

Temple loosened the package from the brown leather belt securing it to Stump's torso and wondered: Take it in or open it now? Fiona says my sin is impatience. Temple tore open the package. There was a black leather diary and a smaller red leather journal that was also a date book for the previous year. The larger of the two was written in the small, careful script of a woman; the other, on long, narrow pages filled with exclamation points and long lines of discourse, was written by a man. Temple scanned the pages: "Mr. Lincoln" and "railroads" and "New York" appeared several times in the woman's writings; "Lincoln" and "traitor" and "Lord War" in the man's script. The man's pages also contained another word, forcing Temple up on his cane: "assassination."

His leg hurt. He jammed the pages into the tops of his boots—one set for each boot, everything in order—then hurried toward the B&O's entrance to find a horse. Fiona said that theft was a sin, too, but on a morning already heavy with sin it didn't rank with murder.

Temple had to press past throngs of people twirling toward the front of the station and away from the gunshots. He could hear a baby crying to his right, a man shouting for his wife to his left. A porter had come to a full stop and was sitting on two trunks he had been dragging toward the trains. He perched on the edge, surveying the calamity around him, and then pulled his hat down over his eyes, content to wait out the pandemonium. Temple hobbled around the porter and exited the station.

Temple was large and lanky and needed large horses. Weren't many of those, 'cept for the mounts that the Army of the Potomac had. Rain was still coming down, but lighter now. First bit of luck today: a beautiful chestnut stallion, unflinching in the rain and tied to a post. Easy to spot. All of the horses that had been here earlier, and the crowd of soldiers, too, were gone. Remember that. Just this one, in the rain, waiting for him.

Temple untied the horse and it didn't buck. He stuck his left foot in the stirrup, jammed his cane between his right hand and the pommel, and hoisted himself up, stretching his gimp leg behind himself as he swung it over the saddle. Beside the pommel, burned into the leather, were two large initials: L.B.

"You should have stayed inside until the rain stopped," warned a voice to Temple's right. "We wouldn't want what you took off Stump to soak up the bad weather, would we?"

The gent who'd shot the young soldier was standing there, pointing a LeMat at Temple. Military revolver, but not a Colt. LeMats were dicey. Buckshot from the bottom barrel. The gent raised his gun toward Temple's head, eyes gleaming (He likes it, Temple thought again, he likes killing), and pulled the trigger. The hammer fell, but no shot. The horse reared.

"Powder's moist," Temple said. "The rain. You have to mind the rain, friend. Damp *pistolas* mightn't fire."

"Bastard, get off my horse and let me have the damn package."

The gent thrust his hand into the saddle and yanked a riding crop from it, then whipped Temple's right thigh. The crop tore through his pants, blood came streaming through the tear, and a flash of pain seared his thigh.

The gent brought the crop down again, but Temple jammed his cane into the middle of the man's forehead, and he stumbled back, dazed. Like billiards, Temple thought. Temple slapped the horse's neck with his left hand and the stallion skittered sideways. He slapped it again, very hard, and the horse bucked wildly into the gent, throwing him to the ground. Temple gathered the reins and galloped off, up New Jersey.

The rain began to let up, and the sun broke through in a yellow, boiling burst.

CHAPTER TWO

THE RACE

Temple leaned forward on the horse, aiming to get as far away from the station as he could as fast as possible. The gent who'd taken the crop to his leg stood nearly as tall as Temple, but he was broader, and so his horse was used to carrying a heavier man. It galloped easily, took commands. Mud flying and the horse snorting and a veil of humidity rising as the sun began to suck the rain from the ground. Impossible to breathe. As Temple hurtled forward, he cataloged places where he could take the pages crammed into his boots, his back still moist from the rain and sweat twisting tight around his collar, his leg still burning from the lash.

Temple pondered two of his best friends, Augustus and Pint, whom he had intended to meet at the B&O to complete their transaction, and he wanted to get to Fiona. She'd be fine for a bit, he reassured himself, and it wouldn't be wise to seek her out until he had stashed the pages. Augustus and Pint might have seen him at the B&O, and they would probably try to look for him around Foggy Bottom. He could ride there first and—

Temple yanked back on the reins, pressing his feet into the stirrups and arching his back. Several of the gents from the station, mounted, were facing him amid a boodle of people on New Jersey. As Temple's horse reared up, the group of them looked his way. Nothing ever registered on the gents' faces, Temple thought. Taut as rails. They recognized his horse, recognized him, and charged dead at him, drawing their guns. There were probably LeMats on the entire lot of them, too, and that's a tale. Outnumbered here. Time to dash.

Temple kicked his heels into the sides of his horse and bolted onto E Street, galloping between City Hall and the still burnt-out husk of the Infirmary as a bullet winged past his head. He raced up toward Seventh, plumes of dirty water erupting from the mud and blanketing his boots. Gardner might know what to do with the diaries, and his studio was around the block. But Alexander Gardner toyed with cameras, not guns, and Temple couldn't arrive there trailing horses and *pistolas*. Couldn't do that to Gardner. Scots had their peculiar irritations and angers, and he made it a habit never to provoke Gardner's.

The sun bore down, and Temple's hair, hanging black and damp around his ears, stuck to the sides of his head like slabs of paste.

He'd need to lose the gents, lose the horse, lose himself, lose the pages, and then get to Fiona. Once the gents from the B&O found out who he was, they might look for Fiona, too. Had to get to her first. Gardner was for later.

Another bullet whizzed past him, just below his ribs. And his leg burned. Enough, then. Temple pressed the horse onto 7th and sped past the Post Office and turned the corner onto F so that he could ride past the Patent Office, where the government still kept a hospital. Where Fiona worked. Please, Fiona, look away from your soldiers and look out one of those windows. Look away from your soldiers because I'm down here, and I'm in a race and I'm coming back to get you.

> *The fractur'd thigh, the knee, the wound in the abdomen*
> *These and more I dress with impassive hand*
> *(yet deep in my breast a fire, a burning flame).*

Temple glanced up, hoping for a glimmer of her framed in a window above him. A bolt of light bounced off some of the glass and flashed in the corner of his eye, but nothing more. He galloped straight on, bolting down F Street. St. Patrick's Church sprouted up ahead of him on the right, a handsome little mound of bricks and a steeple, on the same side of the street as the Patent Office. St. Pat's, feisty and blank, with Irish yearning dripping from every inch of it; Hoban, the Irish architect who'd designed the President's House, modeling the mansion after a grandee's pile in Dublin, had also planned St. Patrick's. They worked in cabals, his old Irish brethren. Father Walter, lord and master of St. Pat's, standing firm beside his parishioner, the Surratt woman, who'd housed the murderers. Remember that, too. Father Walter will have his thoughts.

> *I bind to myself today*
> *The power of Heaven*
> *The light of the sun*
> *The brightness of the moon. . . .*
> *I invoke today all these virtues*
> *Against every hostile merciless power.*

A decision presented itself. The biggest building in Washington, massive in granite, spread like an ancient Greek shrine across 15th Street, directly in front of Temple and corking up the end of F beyond St. Pat's: the Treasury. Like the Washington Monument—like the District itself, in fact—the Treasury building was incomplete, a notion in search of a home. But at least the Treasury functioned, and it dominated the President's House, which sat on the ruddy parkland behind it.

"Money turns the wheel in America, not votes," Fiona would say whenever they strolled near the Treasury.

Dozens of thick, thirty-six-foot-high pillars ribboned the building's exterior. Impregnable. Lincoln had converted the basement into a fortress as a last resort should the Confederates invade the city. His refuge, his last stand. Now Andy Johnson governed from the Treasury, deferring to Mrs. Lincoln until she was ready to leave the President's House. The Treasury and the streets around it were sure to be crawling with Union boys. Temple liked that fact, liked that the presence of soldiers, stoked with bayonets and rifles, might convince his pursuers to leave off. It gave him options.

Still, the gents insisted on chasing after him in their bundle, all of them waving guns and screaming. Several pigs roamed 15th Street, and dogs scurried about near puddles. The air smelled. There were dozens of soldiers around here, and confusion was always an ally. As soon as he hit 15th, Temple spun his horse around near a group of six soldiers.

"Gentlemen, that group just held up the B&O," Temple yelled. "I'm a Metropolitan Police detective, and I think they're Secesh."

"And what the hell is a Metropolitan Police detective?" one of the soldiers shouted back, looking up at Temple and squinting.

A bullet tore into the breast of Temple's horse, and the animal's forelegs buckled. Temple rolled off and away from the horse as it crumpled, staking the ground with his cane and dragging his bad leg along behind him as mud caked his side. The soldier who had just been yelling back at Temple looked down at him before he fell to the ground, too, a bullet splitting open his head. White puffs of dust burst in the air behind Temple's head and just below his feet; eruptions from rifle shots sinking into the flour sacks that the army had piled along the Treasury's foundations as added fortification against a Confederate invasion that never came.

A gray, rolling ball of smoke—a small storm cloud of it—had also formed in front of the gents and their horses as they neared 15th off F Street. All slow motion again, like the train station. The gents were simply shooting at the soldiers to clear their way, shooting so much so quickly that their posse was shrouded and smoldering, and they didn't care. They were shooting up Union boys in the middle of Washington, the sun bearing down to expose them, and they didn't care. They knew no one would take them in. Another pair of soldiers appeared to drop, but Temple couldn't be sure because a slight panic began to envelop him. One of the men was shouting, his voice ricocheting amid the shots and rising above the rest of the frenzy inside the gunpowder cloud.

"We work for Mr. Baker," the gent screamed, "and that man's a spy."

Temple absorbed the thought as he stood up, slightly dizzy.

"Lads, if I'm the spy, why are they killing you, then?" Temple shouted back.

Another bullet zipped past Temple, thigh high, before burrowing into the mud.

He wondered why they hadn't killed him yet and in the same moment knew it was because he still had the pages. They would want to know that before they killed him. They would want to find the pages—or learn if they had gone missing—before they killed him.

More than a dozen soldiers formed ranks and raised their rifles, beginning a slow trot as they moved toward the group of gents. This will slow them down, Temple thought. Slow them down, and then I'll find my trace away from here.

Temple, sweating, his chest heaving, spotted a thin, wiry gent break from the pack and swing his horse toward him. No gun out on this one. Just the crescent of a long, thin cavalry sword. He slipped to the left side of his saddle and charged toward Temple, intending to pin him with the blade. The gent was handy, comfortable on the horse and confident with his sword. As the gent bore down, Temple spun on his good leg, tendrils of mud dripping off his jacket and pants. No target left for the sword, but the gent's arm was stretched firm and rigid as the horse galloped past. Temple whipped his cane upward into the gent's wrist, breaking the bone. The gent screamed and dropped his sword and the reins as he grabbed his wrist; the horse, eyes bulging in fear, turned and then came to an abrupt stop, pitching the gent off the saddle and over its shoulder into the mud.

A leather satchel lay on the ground next to the unconscious swordsman, and Temple plucked it up and spilled out its contents: a small *pistola*, ammunition, glasses, leather gloves, a penknife with an image of a locomotive etched into the blade. Temple slung the empty satchel over his shoulder and dragged himself to the horse—yet another large, meaty one—and mounted it. Second stolen horse of the day. Temple was worn and sore. His muscles ached and his leg throbbed. He braced his cane next to the pommel and then patted his boots. High and sturdy, Fiona's boots had protected the pages from the mud and the rain and the puddles. He grabbed the diaries from inside his boots and stuffed them into the satchel, then looked back from atop the horse at the swarm of soldiers and gents behind him. Another one of the gents was dead on the ground and still more soldiers were down. Two of the gents were watching Temple from inside the melee, struggling to push through the pack of soldiers so that they could finish their work, finish Temple. They would start to regroup shortly, but now Temple knew where he was taking them. Piggies go to market.

Temple rode the horse full chisel down 15th, past a line of new three-story row houses, and he weighed veering off onto Pennsylvania Avenue. But he stayed on 15th, gathering more speed and distance from the men chasing him. He dashed down to B where it met the Tiber Creek, a finger of water that was an open sewer, just like the Potomac. The Potomac, a long, brown snake that people dumped their piss and garbage into—and then they drank from it. Even the new pipes in the President's House had Potomac water in them. Fiona thought water from the Potomac had killed the Lincolns' little boy and everyone else in Washington who got the fever; she was happy to have found a boardinghouse with its own well water. The Potomac stank when summer arrived, and it got up into your head like the humidity. Things were right in Washington only in the spring and fall. Summers were the inferno and winter never got proper. Half snows, white dustings, always the promise of blizzards but nothing more.

Galloping east on B, he was close to completing the circle that had begun that morning at the B&O: the Smithsonian was out to his right, surrounded by parkland across the Tiber, and the Capitol had come into view again, straight in front of him. But he didn't plan on going that far. The Center Market would be busy today.

As he passed 9th Street on B, Temple looked back over his shoulder. The gents, three of them, were a couple of blocks behind him. Glassworks, butchers, embalmers, tanners, and dry grocers sold their wares nearby along Pennsylvania, but the stalls surrounding the market were given over to food—heaps of food that farmers and others carted into Washington to feed the troops and the locals. Wagons were piled high with the stuff, and the Tiber stench that wafted over the market didn't stop vendors, cooks, grocers, boardinghouse owners, soldiers, and everyone else who lived in the District from crowding the weathered wooden stalls to buy yams, milk, apples, chickens, lettuce, bread, corn, pigs, and beer. The market, a yawning, single-story timber horseshoe, had its back to Pennsylvania and gaped open toward the Tiber, embracing the haze and the odors and the chaos. Temple swung his horse hard into the market's main square and jumped a pair of heavy wagons that had closed in front of him. As he and the horse landed, he spotted David Dillon next to his vegetable stall, sorting heads of browning, wilting lettuce.

"Dilly, this is for you," Temple shouted, sliding the leather satchel from his shoulder.

"What's it?" Dillon queried, his voice laced with an Irish brogue Temple had lost years ago.

"It's important. I need a favor. Bring this to Nail in Swampdoodle. I don't have any time."

"What's it?"

"Please. I'm being chased, and I have no time. Don't look inside."

"You're bloody and dirty."

"We've both seen worse."

"Well, indeed we have, Temple, indeed we have," Dillon said as he wrapped his hands around the satchel and stuffed it down into his cart, between heads of lettuce and bunches of carrots.

"Get them to Nail in Swampdoodle," Temple said. "I'll be in your debt."

Temple spun his horse around as three black stallions leapt the wagons and charged into the square, carrying the gents. His right leg was numbing, but he managed to kick his left heel into his horse's side hard enough to send both of them streaking toward the back of the square, well away from Dillon. Temple was weary now, and the reins grew heavy in his hands. A bullet grazed his left shoulder almost as soon as he heard the shot from the gun that delivered it; a rivulet of blood ran down his arm toward his wrist, dripping from his cuff like thick, warm cider. And he was quite trapped. The wooden flanks of the market surrounded him, and the gents were blocking the only way he could escape on horseback. He slipped down from the saddle as he reached one of the market's back corners and began looking for an exit beyond one of the food stalls, an exit that might take him onto Pennsylvania.

The gents, still on their horses, trotted up to him slowly. They had no need to rush now.

"Gentlemen," Temple said, leaning on his cane, his back bowed.

"The papers," one of the gents responded as the other two dismounted.

"Papers?"

Temple was too weak to get his cane off the ground. One of the gents pulled his gun from his belt and held it by the barrel—like a hammer, Temple thought. This is how death arrives. This is how death moves. The gent rushed toward Temple. A rifle shot snapped through the air, and the top of the gent's head fragmented, blood and small pieces of bone erupting in a crimson halo around his skull.

Five men—some of the same ones who had been in the scuffle back at the B&O—were striding in a phalanx across the square, all of them armed with rifles. They fired rounds jointly this time, and the two gents still astride their horses dropped from their saddles before they could turn their mounts around.

The men in the phalanx continued Temple's way, never breaking their line. His cuff hung from his wrist like a wet rag, and he wiped it against the top of his pants. A fresh stream of blood reddened his fingers again. His head drooping, his breath short, Temple watched a few tufts of green grass rise toward him from a swirl of dirt, dust, and food scraps as he collapsed.

CHAPTER THREE

THE CURES

"Most of them died from flux and diarrhea," said Springer. "They ate poorly. And the water killed many of them. On both sides. It wasn't bullets. Bullets did their work, mind you. But don't you think it shocked some of them to discover that their insides were rotting slowly, or a leg was putrid and the rot was crawling to other parts of their bodies, and that none of that seemed similar in the least to the glory they envisioned of dying in battle?"

"Don't you think it shocked them?" Springer asked again. "Mrs. McFadden?"

Fiona laid the lancet and small saw in a shallow porcelain tub of water on the stand by the table where the officer's corpse lay. A wide shaft of light slanted in through a window above her, bathing the tub in a frost that turned the rubied water a cloudy pink.

"Did we have to cut out that much of his leg this morning, Dr. Springer?"

"Mrs. McFadden?"

"Did we have to cut out that much of his leg? What were we trying to accomplish?"

"We tried to stop the rot. We always have to cut to stop the rot."

"Yes, everyone cuts."

Fiona gazed past Springer, into the airy galleries beyond him on the Patent Office's second floor. Samurai armor and swords, one of Ben Franklin's printing presses, presidential gifts from foreign dignitaries, and neatly tied rolls of state documents filled glass cases lining the museum's walls. Most of the space in the cases was given over to row upon row of unusual and largely stillborn mechanical contraptions that had won federal patents, including a model of a riverboat with inflatable devices on its hull so that it could better navigate the Mississippi's shallows. Lincoln had designed and patented the contraption when he was still a congressman. Only several months before, cots and other makeshift hospital beds had crowded the gallery's central space. Even then, many of the cots sat white and empty, floating parallel to the marble floor like a field of tumbled gravestones. Fiona, along with Springer and the other surgeons, had moved to smaller side rooms when the government renovated the gallery for Lincoln's second inaugural ball, a month before he was shot.

Though death had clung to its walls, Fiona knew that Springer felt the Patent Office to be the grandest of spaces, and in moments when they had little to say to each other, he took pleasure in reminding her of his affection for the building. She turned to find him pleased that she was contemplating the office's collections.

"President Lincoln thought our patent system a singular achievement, Mrs. McFadden, and—"

"I wish I could say the same of our medical system," Fiona said, cutting him off.

"As I was saying, we are in a building that celebrates invention. And you have an inventive, independent mind. I commend you."

"We are in a building that has been a hospital for the past four years. Very little of what we have done here has been inventive."

"May I remind you that I am a doctor and that you are here to assist me?"

"Of course you may, Dr. Springer, though, as I'm sure you know, I am a graduate of Syracuse Medical College."

"You are not a doctor."

"I have studied medicine," Fiona replied, her cheeks flushing. "I have studied medicine with men who claim to be doctors. And I have studied with a woman who actually is a very fine doctor."

"Ah, Mrs. Walker."

"Yes."

"She wears trousers."

"Mary Edwards Walker is a dedicated doctor."

"Mrs. Barton and Mrs. Dix would agree with you," said Springer, the corners of his mouth turning up into a broad grin. "But the thing remains: Mrs. Walker wears trousers!"

"As I do at times, Doctor. A dress and a corset make it impossible to work."

"I've offended you," Springer said, his eyes still twinkling.

"Please, sir, make your rounds in a corset for a day. You'll understand."

"What I don't understand is your aversion to amputation."

"I fail to see what it accomplishes. We probe the wounds with dirty fingers, and we operate with pus and blood on our gowns. We scrape the bone and tissue away and pack the abscess with soiled cotton. It's all so . . . septic."

"A minié ball tears flesh like a reaper. If we don't cut, the rot sets in."

"We don't try anything else, Doctor. How do we know?"

"Inventive, Mrs. McFadden, always inventive. As I said, good that you are toiling here, surrounded by the promise of innovation. You are averse to pus, but some pus is laudable. It means the wound is curing."

"Then why do they die? Why did this one die? Pus seeped from his leg four days ago, then stopped; the poor man went into a fever, and now he's dead."

Fiona turned away from the table. Springer's favorite cures were lined along a shelf on the wall—carbolic acid, bichloride of mercury, quinine, sodium hypochlorite, Dover's powder—next to bottles of anesthetics such as chloroform, morphine, and laudanum that Springer dispensed generously whenever he felt compelled to slice into soldiers' limbs.

"The war is over," Fiona said softly, still facing the wall. "The only ones we treat now are the occasionals, the ones that Secesh snipers and other holdouts fire on. We could do better than this. They deserve to get home alive now that the war is done."

"You and your fellow Sanitary Commission members shouldn't be overly fond of your own prescriptions on hygiene, Mrs. McFadden. It got General Hammond into trouble, didn't it?"

"I believe that Secretary Stanton got General Hammond into trouble. The secretary seems to share your views on medical practices in our military."

"I'll let the secretary of war know your displeasure. I'm sure he'll find it of utmost importance."

Fiona wheeled around. "Dr. Springer—"

She stopped. They weren't alone any longer. A Union soldier was standing in the doorway.

"There is a man downstairs to see Mrs. McFadden," the soldier said.

"Do you know him?" Fiona asked.

"No, ma'am. He is well dressed and says he is a friend. His name is Augustus Spriggs. He said it is urgent."

"Please, show him up."

"Ma'am?"

"Show him up."

"He's contraband, ma'am."

"He most certainly is not."

Springer went to the window and gazed down.

"He's a nigger, certainly," said Springer. "In a bowler. A nigger in a bowler, and your lady doctors in pants. Mrs. McFadden, you are inventive. And you choose inventive associates, no doubt."

"I'll be leaving for the day," said Fiona, picking up her bag and removing her smock. "I found our conversation today enlightening, Dr. Springer. Thank you for indulging me."

"My pleasure, Mrs. McFadden."

Fiona accompanied the soldier downstairs and pushed through the Patent Office's doors onto F Street. Augustus was pacing; despite the heat, his bowler was in place and his collar was crisp. Fiona waited for the soldier to go back inside before uttering a word.

"What's wrong, Augustus?"

A coachman sitting atop a carriage across the street was staring at them. His jacket was torn and dusty. Augustus leaned in toward Fiona, his hands trembling.

"If Pint and I had caught up to Temple at the train station, we might have protected him."

"Augustus, is Temple alive?"

"He's alive, but he's been shot. He's at Pint's in Foggy Bottom. We're to go there at once."

Fiona stared blankly at Augustus, absorbing what he had told her.

"Where was he shot? Who shot him?"

"In the Center Market. We don't know yet who shot him. We should go."

"Who's tending to him?"

"Pint is with him."

"But who is tending to his wounds?"

"He told us to wait for you."

"Where are the wounds?"

"I don't know. He's lost blood."

"Augustus, wait here a moment."

"Fiona, we should go."

But Fiona had already dashed back into the Patent Office. Augustus watched the door swing closed behind her, thinking of how many times Temple had told him that he prized Fiona's spirit in much the same way that he prized Augustus's education ("Tell me about Homer again, Augustus. We're in a time of war. You have to steer me right, you and Fiona"). Still, the longer it took Fiona, the more exposed all of them were. Whenever he came to the Patent Office before, he had always waited for Fiona with Temple, never alone. They were a threesome, and Augustus took comfort in that, in their dinners, in their small group of friends, in his books and students, in prayer, in his tiny patch of order in a place tilting mad.

Now there was disorder, the kind that Temple liked to plunge into when he became restless ("Off to figure it all out, Augustus. See you when I see you"). Disorder only made Augustus anxious, and anxiety, whenever it arose, tugged at him and made him hungry for the dens and calmer, dreamier places.

He shook off the thought and glanced at the coachman, whose eyes were still fixed on him and the door of the Patent Office. He held the reins firmly with his left hand. His right was slipped inside his jacket, where, Augustus suspected, a gun sat ready.

When Fiona returned, her bag bulged with bottles. A fine line of sweat crossed the ridge above her eyes, which, even in the sunlight, were a translucent blue.

"Dr. Springer was surprised to see me back so soon. I think I startled him. I borrowed some of his cures," she said.

"And?" Augustus asked.

"I told him I wanted to bring them home to experiment. He'll fancy it witchcraft."

They looked up at the window above them, which framed Springer's face as he looked down on them, unamused. Fiona turned toward the carriage.

"We can't ride in a carriage together, Fiona," Augustus said.

"We are *going* to ride in a carriage together. It will give Dr. Springer something more to worry about—and that pleases me."

CHAPTER FOUR

THE COMPANY

"The coachman is not a regular," Fiona said. "And he looks as if he's been brawling."

The carriage rocked along 9th Street and onto H, headed toward Foggy Bottom. Stoic brick townhouses—three stories high, shuttered, and silent—gave way to shabbier, single-story dwellings as the carriage moved deeper into Foggy Bottom, toward the lime kilns, the icehouses, the plaster, fertilizer, and ammonia factories, the breweries, the shipyards, and Camp Fry.

"The coachman's with a group," Augustus said. "Pint knows some of them."

"How?"

"I'm not sure. As we neared the B&O, Temple was struggling with a strapping ox of a man—an intense, powerful man—who was whipping him."

"Temple McFadden doesn't let people whip him," Fiona said, shaking her head. "And why were you meeting him at the B&O to start?"

"Temple didn't let himself get punished—he nearly trampled him with his horse."

"Temple can ride a horse, that he can do, but we don't own one. Whose horse did he have?"

"He was on a chestnut stallion, big enough to carry even someone of Temple's size. He forced the horse into the man who was whipping him and knocked him over. Flattened him right to the ground and then bolted away. As we got closer, Pint studied the man Temple had trampled. He said we had to get out of there right away and catch up to Temple. Then there was shooting."

"Temple doesn't carry a gun."

"They were shooting *at him*. A group of men. They looked like military. Temple turned his horse up E Street. Pint said we couldn't get through where the shooting was, but we could go back to the station and follow Temple on D. The rain slowed everything down. The streets were muddy and we just fell behind."

"But how did you find him?"

"We passed David Dillon rushing along Louisiana, coming from the Center Market. He said Temple was in trouble there, that he was being chased. So that's where we went."

"Do you know why they were chasing him?"

"No, but whatever it is, Temple's in a mix. When we got to the Center Market, there were three dead men, Temple on the ground next to them. And there was a group of five surrounding him."

"They shot him, the group of them shot him?"

Fiona unfolded her hands and then knitted them together, pressing her palms inward and then up to her forehead as she collected herself and her thoughts. Pushing panic away, as she had done so many times in the Patent Office when the wounded and the dying had been brought in from the battlefields.

"No, the group saved him," Augustus said. "When we arrived they said they would need to get Temple somewhere quiet and safe. They spoke like they owned the ground around them, which I suppose they did in that moment."

"And Pint offered them his rooms in Foggy Bottom?"

"They seemed to find that an excellent idea. They wanted to help."

"Why?"

"I don't know. But they had a ferry there lickety-split. We carried him out of the Center Market and down to the Tiber Creek. There was a small Scottish man waiting there at the dock. He didn't say much, but all of the men with the rifles took orders from him. They deferred to him. Called him Mr. Allen."

"How do you know he was Scottish?"

"He has a heavy tongue, heavier than Gardner's."

"Some keep those tongues their entire lives," Fiona said. "Temple's all but lost his. It's just an echo."

"Well, Allen's brogue is everlasting, I think," Augustus said. "It came out of him in barks: 'Move it, lads, time's a-wastin'; tend to Mr. McFadden with care.' And they all snapped to: 'Yes, Mr. Allen,' 'No, Mr. Allen.' While Allen was directing them this way and that, Temple snapped up, very chirky, as if he hadn't been shot. He asked us where he was, and Allen said we were taking him to a doctor. Temple said that his wife was the only one he wanted giving him medical attention. Then he passed out again. I told them that Pint and I knew you. They told me to find you and that they would take Temple on the ferry—to the landing off the Potomac and the canal, at Godey's Kiln, and then up to Pint's."

"You still haven't told me: why were all of you at the B&O this morning?"

"Pint had a shipment of silk, bed linens, and silverware coming in on one of the trains. He said he bought it from two Union officers in Baltimore; the soldiers took all of it from a plantation in Mississippi, and Pint plans to resell it to the vendors on Pennsylvania Avenue. He asked me and Temple to meet him there to help him receive the shipment and get it loaded onto a wagon. Pint was late to meet me, and Temple got there ahead of us."

"Helping a friend receive, transport, and sell stolen goods. Temple's a member of the police force, and you're an educator," Fiona said, shaking her head. "The things he doesn't tell me."

Augustus erupted in a full, throaty laugh that raised a vein on the side of his neck.

"Augustus?"

"Selling goods that our soldiers have rightfully confiscated from defeated slave owners isn't stealing."

"It most certainly is. It was their property."

"They said slaves were their property, too."

"Human beings aren't candlesticks. And how dare you laugh at me."

"I'm only laughing at what you said about Temple. He tells you everything, Fiona, and hides nothing from you. You're the only thing he fears, so please, don't whisper such foolishness to me again. I know Temple and I know you."

"Temple was there to help Pint sell all of that silk and silver, wasn't he?"

Augustus didn't respond.

"He wanted to help sell it so he could have cash in his pocket, didn't he?"

She turned toward him, placing her hands on his shoulders.

"Temple's gone through our cash again and he was trying to sell stolen goods to raise more, wasn't he?"

She shook Augustus and he sighed, letting his head drop into his chest.

"Temple and I both wanted money," he said.

"And for what sin were you in need of funds?"

"I'm not your husband and I don't have to reveal my wanderings to you."

They looked away from each other and sat in silence as the carriage rocked along.

"I'm sorry we didn't get to the station sooner, Fiona."

"Temple has grit," Fiona said, her hands settling into her lap. "We need to remember that."

After passing the Washington Gas Light Company at Pennsylvania and 19th Street, the carriage rattled along H to 24th and turned south on Virginia. Pint's boardinghouse stood there, run-down and defiant, like most of the German and Irish immigrants scattered around Foggy Bottom's streets. Fiona and Augustus stepped down from the carriage, the coachman behind them.

"They're all upstairs," the coachman said, lifting his chin toward the house.

"I assumed so," Fiona replied as she navigated through the mud and slop in the street.

Even with the humidity, the smell of lime wafted over from Godey's. Limestone was fed into the chimneys of the five kilns at night; lime was raked from the towers during daylight, then mixed into the mortar that was fueling the District's building boom. Several youngsters passed in front of Pint's boardinghouse wearing Emerald Athletic Club shirts, on their way to play baseball.

The front door of the boardinghouse was warped and swung inside to murk, even in the early afternoon. Augustus and the coachman climbed a narrow and steep set of stairs ahead of Fiona, to a landing that smelled musty and creaked beneath their feet. Two men were standing outside the door leading into the small set of rooms Pint kept on the second floor. Fiona reached out and put her hand on Augustus's shoulder, holding him back so she could enter first.

She pushed past Augustus, the coachman, and the two men guarding the door. When she entered, a smallish bearded man sitting in the little parlor rose to meet her. He put out his hand.

"Mrs. McFadden, I take it? E. J. Allen, at your service."

"How did you know my husband's name?" she asked.

"Whaddaya mean, ma'am?" he asked, his voice thick with the brogue Augustus had mentioned.

"Augustus told me you knew my husband's name almost as soon as you were putting him on the ferry to take him here. How did you learn his name?"

"Augustus would be . . . ?"

"The Negro gentleman. You sent him to fetch me."

Fiona left off the conversation and turned down the hallway. A dollop of light fell from a doorway to her right, where she found Temple lying on Pint's bed. His legs were too long for the frame, so they had laid him diagonally across the mattress. Pint sat at Temple's side, his fingers lacing in and out of one another as they kept pace with his distress.

"We put him at an angle so he would fit," Pint said to Fiona. "They say they had to do this for Lincoln at Petersen's the night he was shot because he stretched beyond the bed, too."

"Except Temple's not going to die," said Fiona.

She bent over Temple, laying her palm against his cheek. She stroked his forehead and loosened his shirt. There were clotted whip marks across his thigh, but those didn't concern her. The stripes could heal safely later, after she cleaned them.

"I'll need you to help me roll him onto his stomach, Pint, so I can see his wound."

A wad of white cotton was pressed against a bloody burrow at the top of Temple's shoulder, not far from his shoulder blade. The bullet hadn't penetrated very deeply—indeed, it had almost only grazed him. But it had gone in deeply enough to cause Temple to bleed profusely.

"The white gob on his shoulder is mine, Fiona," said Pint. "I tore up a shirt so we could blot the wound."

"And good that you did. Thank you. But will you bring a bottle of whiskey, please?"

"Fiona?"

"Doctors who travel with the army in the field, and my inimitable Dr. Springer, like to clean wounds with arsenic acid or sulfuric acid. Some of them even use turpentine. They are an artful lot. However, I'm going to wash this wound with alcohol, Pint, so bring a bottle, please. You, of all people, have to have whiskey in your rooms. Hurry now."

"I keep it here under the bed," Pint said. He reached beneath the bed and pulled out a heavy glass bottle of whiskey.

"Put it to the side of the bed, please," Fiona said.

She opened her bag and took out needle and thread, a long pair of slender metal forceps, and two syringes attached to a tube.

"Hello, Fi."

Temple, stomach still flat against the sheets, had turned his head sideways on the pillow so that he could see his wife. Fiona looked up from her bag and a warm rush filled her cheeks as she looked into his face. She stroked his hair.

"I came for you, Temple."

"You always do," he said, before he passed out again.

She considered him a moment longer, then set her tools beside the whiskey bottle on the nightstand, next to the bed. She pulled some linen from her bag and poured the whiskey on it. She set about scrubbing the wound and then poured some of the whiskey directly into the bullet hole.

"That's expensive whiskey," said Pint.

"And you're far too full of palaver. If you leave the room, you won't notice a drop of it disappearing."

Temple shifted slightly on the bed but remained unconscious as Fiona went about her work. Augustus entered just as Fiona was preparing to extract the bullet from Temple's shoulder. He winced.

"I've already told Pint that if any of this unnerves him, he can leave the room. I'll say the same to you, Augustus—don't stay in here if it makes you queasy."

Fiona lit a small candle on the nightstand and held the forceps and her needle in the flame. She pushed the forceps into Temple's wound and extracted the husk of a bullet, dropping it onto the nightstand. She used Pint's shirt to sop up the blood that began to trickle out, and cleaned the wound again. Then she began sewing the wound closed. Augustus and Pint left the room.

"I knew his name because it's my business to know names, Mrs. McFadden," said Allen, who was standing in the doorway. "You're deft with the needle. But you don't carry an amputation kit?"

"I don't carry a saw and a lancet and call that surgery, sir. I was just having this conversation this morning with someone who owns several amputation kits in handsome mahogany boxes. No, I don't own any. And your business is what, exactly?"

"I have a wee bit of a company."

"He has *the* company," said one of Allen's men as he entered the room and stood beside his employer.

"And what might *the* company do?" Fiona asked.

"We find people, ma'am," said Allen. "People who don't want to be found. People who are lost. People who might do harm. We find them."

"Ah, Good Samaritans you are. For whom do you find these people?"

"The government, and anyone who'll pay, ma'am," Allen replied.

Fiona kept sewing. Temple groaned softly.

"And who paid you to find my husband?"

"No one paid us to find your husband. He found us. He stumbled into a . . . into a . . . get-together we were having this morning with another group of gentlemen at the railway station. Your husband was the unplanned factor, Mrs. McFadden; he was the fly in the ointment. He found us."

"And you decided to keep him, I see."

"That we did. That we did."

"Why?"

"He left the station with the only thing everyone there wanted," Allen said, chuckling.

The man next to him leaned back against the wall, stone-faced. Fiona kept pulling the thread through Temple's wound. A heavy pair of feet bounded up the stairs outside Pint's parlor, then burst through the door. There was swearing and then footsteps in the hallway, pounding toward the room. A panting, barrel-chested man with a tangled black beard and wandering eyes forced his way past Allen's guard and into the room; he was clutching a wide-brimmed straw hat, and sweat matted his shirt.

Fiona looked up briefly from her sewing.

"Alexander Gardner without his magic camera," she said, bearing back down on her needle. "To what do we owe the pleasure?"

"What did he say his name was today?" Gardner asked, puffing through a Scottish burr even thicker than that of the man he gestured toward. "He dons and sheds new cloaks weekly."

"Allen," Fiona said. "E. J. Allen."

"'Tisn't!" bellowed Gardner. "It's Pinkerton."

"Heavens, I've been revealed," said Pinkerton, smirking.

"Allan Pinkerton," Gardner offered. "A spy for the federals, all through the war."

"No longer, Alexander. My duties from the war have ended. I'm for myself again. Pinkerton's—my company, my name, my service—is in Chicago, New York, and the District, and we're happy to be in business, thank you. And please, be kind enough to let Mrs. McFadden know that you've done work for me in the past, Alexander—socialist or not, you like your money."

Gardner mopped his brow with his sleeve and studied Temple.

"Is he all right? Word traveled from Pint, and I came as soon as I could."

"He's Temple," Fiona answered as she tied off her stitching. "We just need to give him time. Now then, I know your name and the name of your mysterious company, Mr. Pinkerton, but I still don't know why you are interested in my husband."

Pinkerton pushed off the wall, fingering a watch fob dangling from his waist.

"It's not your husband, exactly," said Pinkerton. "It's some papers he encountered at the B&O this morning that interest us. But they're nowhere to be found on him or his clothing. He has made them vanish. He's a most resourceful man."

"He is most resourceful, yes," said Fiona.

"We'll hover nearby until he can speak with us," Pinkerton said.

"Guardian angels?" said Fiona.

"Well said. Guardian angels. Of course."

"Alexander, help me roll Temple over," Fiona said.

With Temple on his back, Fiona reached over for her syringe. Pinkerton eyed the device.

"You know transfusions, Mrs. McFadden?" he said.

"You know devices that allow us to transfuse, Mr. Pinkerton?"

"I have been on the battlefield, ma'am. I worked with General McClellan. I've seen officers and soldiers tended to. The great general's father was a surgeon."

"He founded the Jefferson Medical College in Philadelphia."

"You're well informed, ma'am."

"Dr. Gross of Jefferson thought highly of the general's father— more highly than Mr. Lincoln thought of the general. I think very highly of Dr. Gross. He taught me transfusions in an afternoon at the Patent Office. I've read his *System of Surgery* and his *Manual of Military Surgery*. This syringe and tubing is his invention. He gave it to me."

"I'm duly impressed, Mrs. McFadden. You know much for a woman. Very formidable."

"I need blood for my husband, Mr. Pinkerton. He needs to replace all that you took from him today."

"'Twasn't us who took it, ma'am. He wouldn't be breathin' at all if it weren't for us."

"I still need blood."

The three men in the room looked at one another blankly. Gardner took a step backward.

"Alexander, I know blood makes you nauseous. Pint and Augustus, please—go fetch them for me."

When Gardner returned with both men, Fiona stared at them.

"Pint, you've got as much whiskey in your blood as is in this bottle. I can't use yours. We'll use Augustus's blood."

"He's a nigger!" Pinkerton exclaimed.

The room went silent, and in the quiet Fiona stared at Pinkerton. Everyone else backed out of the room but Pint and Augustus.

"He's right, Fiona," Pint said. "Bloods don't mix. What you're doing is witchcraft, not medicine."

"Leave, Pint. Mr. Pinkerton, please leave with him," Fiona said.

"I can find someone nearby, Fiona," Augustus said.

"You'll do no such thing. Temple thinks of you as a brother. Please roll up your sleeve."

Fiona closed the bedroom door and placed a chair next to the bed for Augustus. She wiped whiskey on both men's arms, then pressed the needle into Augustus's forearm. As the tube began to fill with blood, she pressed the other syringe down into Temple's arm.

"This will cause a mess, Augustus. We'll need to do it several times, and you'll be powerful tired when we have finished."

CHAPTER FIVE

THE ORPHANAGE

"Get out of your bed, boy," said one of the Dublin nuns. "The rest are up. Get out of your bed and get down to breakfast or you'll be late for prayer and lessons."

Temple rolled out of bed in a wrinkled linen nightshirt that trailed below his seven-year-old knees. He was shivering.

"Speak up, boy, you're not mute."

He slipped his feet into a pair of leather sandals. The nun smacked him on the head.

"Speak up."

"Yes, Sister."

"Ave Maria, gratia plena. Dominus tecum, benedicta tu . . ."

"In mulieribus et benedictus, fructus ventris tui Jesus," Temple replied.

"Don't forget your Ora Pro Nobis."

"No, Sister."

"Or your Confiteor."

"Neither, Sister."

He hurtled from the dormitory and down a cramped, winding flight of stone steps. There was a sliver of a window carved into the wall, and through it he could see the little synagogue that the Dubliners had blocked off from the rest of the neighborhood. They'd blocked it off, indeed, but it remained plainly in view from one of the largest Catholic churches and orphanages in the city. Temple wondered if anyone in the synagogue was looking back at him out of their very own slit in a wall, or whether any of them knew that the Oblates of Mary Immaculate, swaddled in habits and devotion, had taken an orphan from the streets but had been able to do no better with their imaginations than to name him after this very neighborhood, the Temple Bar—even though the neighborhood got its name from the synagogue! So the nuns had named him, in the end, after a Jewish house of worship, though he reckoned they'd never taken that into consideration. He was just one of many. Lord knows, a nun can't be minding everything in this world if she is to properly serve His needs and not the needs of a ratty group of beggars tossed to the streets by irreverent parents without a dime to give anyhow, Mother save us. No, simpler to name him quickly and then think about the next child. Name him after the neighborhood, after the streets whence he came. Temple called it his Hebrew christening, which won a laugh from the other boys—except, of course, from Angus.

Confiteor Deo omnipotenti, beate Mariae semper virgini . . . mea culpa, mea culpa, mea maxima culpa.

Temple slipped into his place on the bench at the breakfast table, a large vaulted ceiling opening above him and a cold, cracked floor spreading out beneath. About twenty boys shared his table, and the dining hall was lined with gray, splintering tables from end to end. A slab of stiff bread, a chipped clay bowl holding a puddle of gruel, and water sat on the table in front of him. His nose ran, and he wiped his sleeve against it. The Oblates told them all that they were fortunate to be here. True, that was, compared to the last place that had had him. There'd been no classes or latrines there, and all of them had been factory boys covered in grime. Some of the boys had worked in warehouses making matches with white phossy and their jaws had rotted away. Once their jaws started going, they didn't stay long. Yes, his old orphanage had been worse. But somehow he hated this one more.

Another rap on his head from a nun, letting him know that he was late for breakfast again. She moved along, and he began eating. If she'd had dreams like his, she'd wake in the middle of the night, too. She'd be late for breakfast herself. He brought a corner of the bread to his lips, but then he paused. Across the table from him a long, bright, almost blinding column of buttery light, like the glow between stage curtains pulling apart when a show begins, floated at eye level.

The center of the column began to form, and Temple could see the outline of a woman's face there, a beautiful woman with long auburn hair swept neatly up behind her head into a large bun. She had full lips and crystalline blue eyes gleaming like beacons.

"Hello, Fi," Temple said to the woman.

"I came for you, Temple," the pretty woman said.

"You always do."

Then the curtains were drawn and the light blinked out. The pretty woman disappeared, and Temple, still shivering, stale bread in his hand, found himself staring at Angus Mitchell, whose face was twisted into a familiar, angry knot.

"You dodgy little shit, you get out of line and I'll stomp you again outside," Angus allowed. "It will hurt. Like last week hurt."

"I'll mind the straight and narrow, Angus," Temple replied.

"Even tha' might not be good enough," the fifteen-year-old sneered. "Mind yourself."

Temple finished his breakfast and ran back upstairs to the dormitory. He opened a small wood crate at the foot of his bed and changed into a pair of wool slacks with a torn pocket hanging off the back. He pulled on a simple white shirt. His shoes fit well enough, but there was a hole in the sole that was alarming and growing ever wider.

Temple turned to go back down the stairs, but Angus was loping toward him from the doorway. As Angus neared, the odd white light appeared again, enveloping Angus; the light separated again in the middle and the beautiful woman's face appeared. She was smiling and reached a hand out to touch him.

Temple focused on her, on her face and her eyes.

"Temple," she said. "How are you feeling? Temple?"

How does she float there like that? Even the nuns can't fly. As

Temple stared at her longer, the curtains drew farther apart and he realized she wasn't floating at all. She was seated in a chair and had a moist rag in her hand.

"Temple," she said again. "How are you feeling?"

He began to recognize her. Yes, Fiona, in my orphanage. In my Dublin. Why is she here?

"You're still murmuring. You're not in Dublin," she said. "You're in Washington."

"I'm cold. My nightshirt isn't warm enough," he said.

"You're in Washington, with us. You're safe. Try to talk to me."

"I am talking to you. I just don't. Don't. I'm not."

"Think clearly now," she said. "You're in Washington."

"No, I'm in Dublin, Fi," he said. "I'm cold."

Again she disappeared, evaporating along with her column of creamy light. Angus replaced her, standing there with his fists clenched and a mass of angry pimples scattered across his forehead.

"You can't run from breakfast till I say ya can run from breakfast, laddie," said Angus. "You're the only one who never seems to mind me. I'll tell the nuns you're disobedient and they'll ship you to the Old Bailey and have you hung."

Temple nodded briskly.

"I'll be goin' now. Not to bother ya."

"But you do bother me, and mightily, Temple-without-a-last-name."

"Few of us have last names. The Oblates say we're to be unknown in the world but not in the eyes of the Lord. I'll be off now, Angus. Please let me pass."

Angus stepped forward, aiming a punch at the smaller boy's jaw. Temple, trembling, slipped beneath his arm and sprinted to the dormitory door. Angus raced after him, bouncing off the stairwell's cold walls and then down a hallway, cornering him. Tears welled up in Temple's eyes. Angus slapped him.

"Temple," he heard Fiona say. "Come back here with us."

"It stings my face," Temple said.

"No, the bullet was in your *shoulder*, not your cheek. You're healing."

A small cross dangled from a chain around Fiona's neck. Temple reached up to it.

"Your jewelry," he murmured.

"My bedrock," Fiona said. "You could use a foundation of your own."

"No, no. Got to flee. See you when I see you."

Late at night in the dormitory, and Temple was knotting sheets he had filched from a closet down the hall where the Oblates kept their bedding. Straw fell from the fabric and a roach flitted across his wrist. The other boys were sleeping, and he had stuffed his pillow, nightshirt, and towel under his bedspread to make for a proper body should the nuns take a look. He had his clothes and jacket on and a piece of bread that he'd nicked at breakfast jammed into a pocket. He pushed open one of the tall windows that overlooked the courtyard, tied one end of his makeshift rope to one leg of his bed, and dropped the other from the window. Then out and down he went. He heard the bed slide across the stone floor and crash into the wall as he slithered down, then shouting in the room. A boy's head peeked out the window, then another, shouting at him, pointing. He hung on to his sheets, unsure of what to do—up or down? He was still five yards off the ground and already found out. Some of the boys had pulled back his bedding and savaged his mattress; they had torn straw from it and were tossing wads of it down at him from the window.

Confiteor, Deo omnipotenti, beate Mariae semper virgini . . .

"Temple, stop struggling, lie still," he heard Fiona say.

He looked up again and saw Angus there, stretching down from a window, pushing a knife into one of the knots, giggling as he cut through it. Temple rushed, trying to slide down as fast as he could, but the rope went slack and he dropped through the air, all of him landing on his right leg, his knee twisting, the long bone in his thigh pressing up into him, snapping.

Mea culpa, mea culpa, mea maxima culpa.

The nuns found him crumpled and unconscious at the bottom of the wall. Several of the boys dragged him back inside, into the dining hall, where they laid him on a table. Bone stuck out from the side of his leg, which dripped with blood. Darkness enveloped him—until he felt, again, a hand on his cheek and a moist towel on his head. Not a woman's hand, though; a man's. And voices around him: the nuns and someone new. The voice of a stranger.

"Dr. McFadden, it's good of you to come. Can you save the boy's leg?"

"I can *set* the boy's leg, but I don't know that I can *save* it. What is his name?"

"Temple."

"His full name?"

"He hasn't a full name, sir."

"What will you do with him if his leg doesn't mend properly, Sister?"

"We aren't quite sure, sir."

"He shan't be able to work."

"No, sir."

"Then it's likely no one will want him."

"No, sir. Except at the match factory. They can sit there."

"The children become poisoned in the match factories, Sister. May I take him home with me?"

"That would be unusual, Dr. McFadden."

"Sister, my family gives generously to the church, as you well know. The effects of the potato blight are seeping into Dublin, as you well know. In two months, my wife and I are leaving for the States and we are childless, as you well know. The boy will be better off with us, would he not?"

I am Raftery the poet,
full of hope and love.
Having eyes without sight,
lonely I rove.

Temple opened his eyes.

Fiona was sitting next to him, slumped in a chair asleep. A man he had never seen before was sitting on another chair near the foot of his bed, pushing off from the mattress as he rocked back and forth into a corner. He was fingering a watch fob that dangled from his vest and staring at Temple.

"G'day," the man said.

"Good day," Temple replied.

"You've been in an' out for almost a week."

"Then you must care deeply to have waited all this time for me to surface. I don't recognize you, I'm afraid." Temple touched the dressing on his shoulder, where his wound was healing. "Should I thank you for this memento?"

"No, you should not. You have others to thank for that, and I'm rather certain they're anxious to hear your gratitude in person. I imagine they're looking for you."

"And they're Scots, like you?"

"No, trust the Scots, through and through. Trust us. They're Yanks, the lot of them."

"And if they knew where to look, they would have already found me, so I think I'll be safe a shade longer."

"I'm sure it helps that my men are watching the streets and this rat hole that your mate Pint calls a home. But let's quit this game," the man said as he stopped rocking and let his chair slam back into the floor with a thud. "I'm after the papers that you snatched at the B&O, and we need to speak directly with each other."

Fiona bolted upright as the man's chair hit the floor.

"Temple?" she asked, looking down at him.

"Hello, my Fi."

"You're with us now?" she asked. "Away from Dublin?"

"All yours again, I'm afraid," Temple said as he eyed the other man. "We've a new friend here."

"His name is Allan Pinkerton."

Temple struggled to raise himself up on his pillow and rubbed his eyes, still halfway between Dublin and the District, with a ripping pain in his shoulder. He stared back at the stranger, who was leaning toward him across the foot of the bed. He didn't know the man, but he knew of his notoriety.

"Ah, things make more sense now," Temple said. "*The* private eye. Hanging above the entrance to his agency in Chicago is an all-seeing eye, Fiona. An eye for hire in private business matters, and usually for the railroads. Mr. Pinkerton, it is said, never sleeps."

Pinkerton stood up and walked to the head of the bed, standing over Temple and pulling his pocket watch out to check the time.

"Oh, I sleep, Mr. McFadden. What I like to say is '*We* never sleep.' And I say that because we are many in my company and as one, united, we need no sleep. It is of value to those we serve."

"And who are your clients now, beside the railroad men? Are you still gathering information for the government and for General McClellan?"

Pinkerton's attention remained centered on his watch, his lips moving wordlessly as he tracked the movements of the hands spinning on its face. He snapped the pocket watch closed, and the wheels of the locomotive engraved on its cover chugged silently back into the darkness of his vest pocket. Pinkerton patted the watch and left his thumb hooked on the lip of the pocket.

"I don't like my time to be wasted, and I've particular interest in the papers you possess," he said to Temple. "I seek them for my own design entirely, not for any client."

"Well, I need to be with my wife now," Temple replied. "When I am fully recovered, perhaps then we can speak of these papers?"

Pinkerton, small and coiled, drew closer to the bed, his jaw trembling and his hands balled into fists as he struggled to contain himself. Temple thought the man's eyes, inky pools creased in the corners with lines, were beginning to tear in something other than rage. They were the eyes of someone who appeared to be in mourning.

"You're mucking in something quite above you. You haven't the luxury of being selective," Pinkerton said. "Please appreciate that. Give me the papers and we can end this matter."

"I need to be with my wife."

Pinkerton walked to the door. As he swung it open, he turned to Temple: "I'll return tomorrow afternoon. I expect by then you'll have reached a decision."

"Indeed, I hope we have a decision by then as well. Good day."

"Good day to you."

Fiona bent toward Temple's ear, whispering quickly, and Temple raised his arm toward Pinkerton, wincing again at the pain in his shoulder.

"Wait," Temple said. "My wife tells me I owe you my life. Thank you for that."

"Give me the papers and I'll consider your debt repaid," Pinkerton said, pausing in the doorway.

"Whose horse was I on?"

"A right strong horse, wasn't it?" Pinkerton responded, locking eyes with Temple. "You've gotten in deep, you have."

"Tomorrow afternoon, then," Temple said.

After Pinkerton closed the door, Fiona bolted it. She returned to the bed, throwing her arms around Temple and pressing him into his mattress.

"That hurts," Temple said.

"I believe I've earned the privilege, my mending defective."

CHAPTER SIX

THE HUMBUG

"Mr. Pinkerton! Mr. Pinkerton! Open up."

Pinkerton awoke to the pounding. He answered the door of his room at the Willard in a crimson dressing gown, wiping the sleep from his eyes.

"The hour's late, Mr. Walsh," Pinkerton said.

"Yes, sir, but we Pinkertons never sleep."

"No smarts now. What's your say?"

"The McFadden couple is on the move. They left their rooms in Foggy Bottom about twenty minutes ago and are headed toward Georgetown. We espied them as soon as they came down to the street. Three of us were on them; I split away to get you."

"You have a horse for me?"

"I do."

"Momentarily, then, and we'll be off. I'll meet you downstairs on Pennsylvania."

Pinkerton pulled on his clothes, stuck a pair of knives in his boots and a brace of Colts in custom-made shoulder holsters from Potter Palmer's, and descended. Even in the dead of night Washington is moist, Pinkerton thought as he walked through the lobby. The Union army was still using the Willard as its headquarters, and despite the hour more than a dozen officers were perched on velvet and mahogany sofas scattered about the lobby, some of them sharing drinks and cigars with politicians and wheeler-dealers. Several correspondents from the *Atlantic Monthly* mingled at the tables and settees, gabbing about Mr. Lincoln's murder, but Emerson, Longfellow, and Lowell weren't among them, thank the Virgin. Hawthorne was the only trustworthy one of the *Atlantic*'s abolitionist lot, and he's dead now. All the dead, tied to this swamp of a place. My Mr. Lincoln has passed, too, mercy shine upon him. First time in Washington together was here at the Willard, when the president asked me to escort him from Chicago and Baltimore, both of us outfitted in a right pair of disguises. Got Lincoln into safekeeping here for that first inauguration, and then the Willard charged him $775, no less, for only a ten-day stay! He had to wait until he got his first presidential disbursement before he could pay the bill. At least Mr. Lincoln settled his bills, unlike his missus, with her needs and her moods and her shopping debts.

Pinkerton pushed through the hotel's oak and glass doors, finding Walsh waiting for him at the corner of Pennsylvania and 14th.

"Mr. Pinkerton."

"Walsh?"

"The McFaddens were on a horsecar."

"It's two in the morning, Mr. Walsh. Horsecars don't run in the District after dark."

"They were on a car, sir. They came out of the building as a group, with McFadden propped up by his wife and Gardner. McFadden could barely walk, was bent clean over his cane, and they went up Twenty-fourth to Pennsylvania. There was a horsecar there waiting for them. They helped McFadden climb into the back of the car, and it rolled off toward Georgetown."

"And that's all the detail?"

"The woman had a shovel. And they tied a long handcart to the back of the car."

"Curious."

THE HORSE PULLING the Washington and Georgetown Railroad Company car whinnied as the driver reined it to a stop at 30th and M streets. Fiona slid off the bench inside the long green car, scooped up her shovel, and climbed down to the street. She couldn't see anyone as she looked back down M, which crested into a little hill at

Wisconsin before sloping down to where it met Pennsylvania. But she could hear hooves, just beyond the hill, and they stopped thumping the ground somewhere off in the dark as soon as she alighted from the car.

"We're certainly being followed," she whispered to the others, "so no talking until we get to the cemetery."

Gardner glanced up at the two Samuels brothers, one handling the horse from a small booth at the front of the car, the other hanging off the back near the photographer's handcart. The twins smiled back at him. He had made the two dwarves the most well-known drivers in Washington by photographing a series of cartes de visite of them in front of their WGR car. After that, the twins and Gardner traded favors. Gardner created more souvenirs, and the twins let Augustus and Temple get Sojourner Truth onto their car first when she began campaigning against the District's lily-white transit system; after Gardner produced yet another batch of mementos, the twins sometimes let him use their car in the wee hours to transport his photographic equipment. Tonight, after he got word to them, the twins came yet again, no questions asked. Gardner nodded to the pair, untied his handcart from the back of their horsecar, and pulled it behind him as he set off behind Fiona on 30th Street.

PINKERTON HAD WATCHED Gardner and the McFaddens enter Oak Hill Cemetery, but from a distance, with his horse trotting at a slow, measured gait. Once the group got inside the cemetery grounds, he had lost them. They had moved up 30th Street at a crawl, and on two occasions it looked like McFadden was going to collapse. Still, they were walking farther than they had ridden on the horsecar, so why had they bothered with the damn car to begin with? A three-story redbrick gatehouse blocked the view into the cemetery, so Pinkerton and his men moved closer. Walsh picked the lock on the door of the gatehouse and Pinkerton's group went inside, hurrying to the upper floor so that they could get a view across the entire cemetery. This perch made things easier. There was no moon tonight so Pinkerton couldn't use his field glasses to track the group. But their profiles were visible as they moved among the cemetery's obelisks and tombstones, inky figures barely outlined against tall, pale needles and thumb-shaped rocks.

"Like specters traversing among the dead," Pinkerton muttered aloud.

The McFadden woman stopped near one of the largest obelisks and paused, bending forward to examine it more closely. Then she took out her shovel and pressed its point into the ground.

"Why do you suppose these Americans picnic in cemeteries, Walsh?" Pinkerton asked.

"I think to be with their loved ones who've gone beyond, sir," Walsh replied.

"I find it passing strange. The dead at Antietam reeked of their passing, rotting in the field, and no one could have downed a bite of food around them. Cemeteries adorn the rot, but the rot is still there. The dead don't rise to sup or to commune."

Walsh stepped back, regarding Pinkerton quizzically. Pinkerton stared blankly out the window a moment longer and then turned toward Walsh.

"Walsh, I know now why the McFaddens have the horsecar here," Pinkerton said.

"Sir?"

"They are digging something up here that is going to be too heavy to carry back. That's why they have the handcart and that's why they secured the horsecar. We're going to need more people here. I want you to go back to Foggy Bottom and pull the other two men off the house where McFadden was staying. Bring them here. Hurry."

When Pinkerton gazed down again, the woman had stopped digging. She leaned her shovel against a tombstone and moved toward an ornate limestone rotunda a few yards away. The other two followed her there, with McFadden hobbling along on his crutch, and all of them sat down on the edge of the rotunda, not saying a word.

"Well, they couldn't have dug very deeply yet," Pinkerton said to the two men still with him. "We'll wait up here along with them to see who or what they're waiting for."

When Walsh returned about forty minutes later, with Pinkerton's two other men in tow, Gardner and the others were still sitting on the edge of the rotunda.

"They're silent as the dead," Pinkerton said.

"Sir, the other men here say they're afeared of this place," Walsh said. "So you might best refrain from ghoulishness, please."

"My apologies to all of you," Pinkerton snapped back. "But we'll descend into the cemetery now, so I hope you all have your manhood about you."

Pinkerton and the others wound their way among the tombstones, edging closer to the spot where the McFadden woman first began digging. No one in her group moved or said a word. The sky had turned from jet to a light purple as dawn approached, and Pinkerton could begin to see faint outlines of all the faces around him. As he neared them, the woman raised her head.

"Mr. Pinkerton, you've decided to join our dig," Fiona said.

"It's not healthy or sane to be in a cemetery late at night, Mrs. McFadden," Pinkerton said. "I felt you might all need protection."

"The sun arrives, Mr. Pinkerton. The light will keep us company."

"But it will be harder for you to get your casket or your bags or whatever you will out of here in daylight, will it not?" Pinkerton said, beaming, proud to let the McFaddens understand that he had an unusual ability to make connections. "You'll need extra hands to help you move it, yes?"

"Oh, no, Mr. Pinkerton. We've completed our digging."

"And why are you here, then?" Pinkerton asked.

"We are just here," Fiona said. "We are here to be here."

Pinkerton stepped farther forward. Gardner was staring straight back at him, amused, as was the woman. But her husband still sat slumped on his cane, his head bent toward the ground.

"This can't be a healthy place for your husband, Mrs. McFadden," Pinkerton said. "He's still recovering and he clearly lacks strength."

A loud snore emerged from beneath the brim of McFadden's floppy hat and his cane dropped to the ground. Not a cane really, but what looked like the leg of a table, broken off at its wide end. Curious.

Curious.

Curious.

"Oh, Mrs. McFadden. Your husband is not here after all."

"Indeed he's not, Mr. Pinkerton. Your powers of observation have triumphed again."

Pinkerton stepped forward and yanked the hat from Pint's head. Pint kept snoring, oblivious to everyone around him.

"Humbug," Pinkerton said.

"What do you mean, Mr. Pinkerton?" Walsh asked.

"All of this. A humbug, Walsh. We've been tricked. Mr. McFadden undoubtedly left the house in Foggy Bottom as soon as you pulled the other men off it."

"The horsecar, sir?" Walsh asked, confused.

"Temple said if we were elaborate, you would become careless, Mr. Pinkerton," Fiona said, answering Walsh's question. "You must agree, we've been elaborate."

Pinkerton didn't answer. He pulled his jacket back, revealing the Colts strapped to his sides, and he pulled one from its holster. Gardner kicked Pint in the leg, stirring him, and rose. Pinkerton cocked the hammer back and aimed his gun at Fiona's head.

"Alexander, by the time you took a step she'd be dead," Pinkerton said. "So don't wander."

The rest of Pinkerton's men spread out around Gardner, Pint, and Fiona, encircling them.

"None of us has the answers you want," Fiona said. "I have no idea where my husband's gone to, or even what exactly he has. But if one of us was to be harmed in any way, I'm certain that you'll never see a shred of what you're after. And my husband can be a determined man when his loved ones are preyed upon, Mr. Pinkerton."

Pinkerton's lips tightened. He paused a moment longer, then eased down the hammer of his Colt and lowered the weapon back into its holster.

"Your husband still doesn't recognize what surrounds him," Pinkerton replied, signaling to his men to follow him out of Oak Hill. "Humbugs or not, I have men all over the District. Your husband can't get far without being sighted, and what he is secreting is far, far beyond him."

TEMPLE WAS DRESSED and seated on the edge of Pint's bed, waiting in the dark. His boots were clean and dry—not a word this time from Fiona about getting them wet and slathered in mud—and he had a fresh shirt and trousers. Fiona had also brought along a light linen jacket she got for him from the boardinghouse before she packed their things yesterday. "If they're watching you here, then they'll follow us to our house," she warned him. "So we must decamp from there." His wounded left shoulder felt stiff, and if he moved that arm too much, he felt the same flashes of pain that always flared up in his leg. But he was clear-headed, rested, and fed.

> Take a look at me now, with my back to a wall
> Singing and playing for nothing at all.

Augustus slipped open the door and looked in on Temple. He nodded, and Temple pressed his cane into the rotting floorboards, rising from the bed. Temple no longer felt dizzy when he stood.

"The last two have gone from out front," Augustus whispered.

"Off we go, my friend."

When Augustus and Temple got to the first floor of the building, they passed down a hallway and through a small kitchen. Behind Pint's building there was a small, murky courtyard, laced with traces of the smog that clung to Foggy Bottom from the swamps and gasworks. A pile of abandoned bricks sat in the middle of the yard, and a pig was sprawled against it, sleeping. Clothes were drying on a line stretched across the courtyard, and hanging from a nearby tree branch was a large metal triangle that one of the matrons rang to summon everyone for dinner and supper. Any of the Irish or Germans who found Augustus roaming around here at this hour was likely to kill him, especially with Pint gone off with Fiona and Alexander.

None of Augustus's friends dared meet them here. But there was a safe house nearby that he knew from the Underground Railroad, at 25th and I, and they could get horses there. As they neared the barracks that the army had set up in houses around Snow's Court, Augustus paused. It was late, and two Union soldiers patrolling the neighborhood approached them.

"Who's the dapper nigger?" one of the soldiers asked Temple.

"Homo sum," Augustus said.

"How's that?" the soldier asked.

"Odi profanum vulgus et arceo," Augustus replied, looking over at Temple.

The soldier yanked at the rifle slung on his shoulder, but Temple raised his hand, waving off the soldier.

"He's an educated man, seeking greater education," Temple said. "We're late of our lessons and I'm escorting him home. We wouldn't press near your barracks at this hour if we meant harm. We'll pass now."

The soldier held them with his eyes for a moment and then stepped back. "The war may be over, but it lingers," he said. "Fighting just concluded at Palmito Ranch, and the Rebs staked their land with fury. The two of you best mind that. On your way, then."

When Temple and Augustus arrived outside the frame house on I Street, Augustus scanned the four windows on the building's façade. There was a lantern burning in the right-hand window on the upper floor, and a white handkerchief was tied to the knob on the front door.

"It's clear and safe here," Augustus said. "They'll have our horses."

Augustus untied the kerchief from the doorknob and knocked three times. After pausing, he knocked again twice on the door and stepped back. When the door opened, an old and slightly built minister greeted him. The minister was dressed in a black frock, and his face, framed by a white beard and white hair and illuminated by the lantern in his hand, almost floated above and apart from his body. Augustus handed him the handkerchief.

"I am grateful for this gift of cotton," the minister said.

"As grows the cotton, so grows our cause," Augustus replied.

"And who sends you to me?" the minister asked.

"A friend of a friend," said Augustus.

Passwords exchanged, the minister nodded and waved Augustus and Temple into the house. There was a small bundle of banknotes on the table and a bag of apples. The minister handed all of it over to them and gestured to the backyard of the house, where two black horses were hitched to a post. The minister extinguished his lantern as Augustus and Temple calmed the horses by feeding them some of the apples; they mounted and left without saying another word.

They trotted as silently as they could, taking backstreets and avoiding main thoroughfares such as Pennsylvania, New York, and Massachusetts. By the time they came out around Douglas Square, the sun was beginning to rise. All that was needed was a little more heat to bring the ground up again, and they were in a part of the city now where they would smell every foot of it: Swampdoodle. The Tiber Creek sliced through the middle of Swampdoodle, and a stench wafted up strong and clear enough to make the horses get skittish.

Augustus broke the silence as they trotted down North Capitol to H, passing by the Government Printing Office.

"They won't let a Negro into this neighborhood. I'd best go look for Fiona and the others. You'll be better off now without me."

"I want you to meet Nail," Temple replied. "And no one in Swampdoodle will move against anyone who rides with me. It's full of rounders, but I know my way about rounders, yes?"

Augustus reined in his horse and shifted uncomfortably in his saddle as he contemplated his response.

"Yes, rounders are indeed your specialty."

"Besides, a neighborhood full of hardworking Irish railroad workers can't be populated by rounders alone. We'll take the risk, yes?"

"Yes."

As the light broke across the lean-tos and little shacks that surrounded them, cows, chickens, and goats milled about, their legs sinking into the soft, damp mud that seeped all over Swampdoodle. Temple and Augustus had ridden only a few yards farther when a pack of dogs came bounding across one of the rickety wooden bridges that spanned the Tiber. They bared their fangs and bolted toward the legs of Temple's horse, snarling. Temple's horse reared and Augustus's horse retreated. Behind the dogs, a ruddy, scarred man wearing overalls and little else emerged from the morning's shadows and marched toward them. He was carrying a thick club with a blunt end that blossomed in a knotted cauliflower burst of wood; he was smacking it against his palm.

"You have to have a reason to be in Swampdoodle," he snapped at Temple and Augustus, an Irish brogue enveloping each word. As he got nearer, his pace slowed and his arms, dirty and muscular, dropped to his side. He ordered the dogs back from the horses. When one hesitated, he smacked it on its haunches with his club, and the dog, yelping, ran off.

"So it's you," he said, looking up at Temple.

"Sean," Temple said, nodding. "You're in a mood this morning."

"They said you were lashed at the B&O by a gang."

"And I was, but now I'm out for a ride."

"With the carny in tow, I see," Sean said, looking at Augustus.

"I'm here to see Nail."

"Leave the horses by the bridge."

"They'll be here when we return? And the dogs will stay off their meat?"

"Both. I'll put tots on them."

Sean whistled over his shoulder and three small boys scurried out of one of the shacks. Like Sean, they were covered in grime, their teeth rotting. Their mother, her eyes drooping in her face like saucers, looked out at them from inside the door of the lean-to. She had a tin mug in one hand and a sawed-off shotgun cradled in the other.

"Them are Mammy's boys, and she'll help them keep a watchful eye," Sean said. "She'll blast the pups if they get out of line. She'll also blast the nigger if he gets unruly."

Temple dropped from his horse, planted his cane in the mud, and walked over to Sean. Temple towered over the gatekeeper, but Sean stood his ground, looking up at him, expressionless. Temple placed his hand on Sean's shoulder and leaned down into his face, steadying himself on his cane.

"His name isn't Nigger, Sean—it's Augustus. And he's coming with me to see Nail. I want his horse looked after with special care. Am I understood?"

"You're understood, McFadden."

As he and Augustus crossed the Tiber on the footbridge, Temple noticed that his boots were already muddy again. He began to say something to Augustus, but Augustus spoke first.

"After what's happened over the last week, I don't imagine Fiona will care much about your new boots," he said. "I believe she'll let you get them as muddy as you'd like from now on."

CHAPTER SEVEN

THE COGNIACS

The B&O railroad line leaned into and then curved away from the east end of Swampdoodle, and the village clung to itself like an encampment: tough, dour, and wary, with row upon row of small shacks that immigrant and itinerant railroad workers inhabited in packs. Like the District itself, Swampdoodle had exploded in size during the war years, and its housing stock was uniformly small and flimsy—excepting a large, well-maintained rectangular warehouse that sat on stilts at the far end of the village. A dozen armed men formed a loose semicircle around the building, each with a mangy dog by his side. The building lay just beyond the last set of lean-tos, and as Temple and Augustus made their way toward it, the dogs began barking and baring their teeth.

"The pound master came in here once to round up the dogs and the Swampdoodlians hung him from a tree," Temple said to Augustus. "Nobody from the outside had the nerve to come in here and get him. He swung for two days."

With a kick, the front door of the warehouse swung open. The man who emerged from the frame wore a long cloth apron and had hands that were deeply tattooed from his forearms to his fingertips. Augustus figured he was at least as tall as Temple but far thicker, with a bull neck and heavy, muscular arms. His hair was a rusty tangle, and he smiled as he looked down from the porch at his visitors.

"I told Dilly they couldn't keep you down, Temple."

"And they didn't, Nail. I still have a weak shoulder, but it gets better by the day. Meet Augustus."

The circle of guards and dogs had tightened around the warehouse as Temple and Augustus approached, but once Nail burst through the door the group parted. Nail bounded down the stairs and held out his hand. What Augustus thought were tattoos were, upon closer inspection, ink stains.

"I bare my arms only when I'm working," Nail said, following Augustus's eyes. "A sight to behold, no? When I walk the streets, I cover my mess in shirtsleeves."

"Wouldn't want to attract unneeded attention," Temple said, winking.

"It gets harder to make a living with the war over and Mr. Stanton's boys disowning my services," Nail replied, turning his attention to Augustus. "I'm working hard to find a new art, but in the meantime—hello. I'm Jack Flaherty. Most everybody calls me Nail."

"Augustus Spriggs. Temple has mentioned you many times, but I began to think you didn't exist."

"Today, I exist," Nail said. "Getting Negroes on the streetcars is safer than taking Negroes into Swampdoodle. You're our first. Come inside."

At the top of the stairs, Temple paused and turned to Augustus.

"Mr. Flaherty, in his former pursuit, drove spikes through ties for the railroad. Better than anyone. So his mates called him Nail," Temple said. "But, as you will see, his vocation has since changed."

Nail pulled back the door and plunged into the warehouse, but before the pair could enter behind him, he turned back and put his hand on Temple's shoulder. "Everybody's buzzing about Stump having his throat cut at the B&O," he said. "Why were you there?"

"I had to meet Pint and Augustus," Temple said. "I arrived early."

"But why were you there? Why did you need to be there at all?"

"I'm a detective."

"You've been helping Pint peddle stolen goods from them plantations."

"And what if I am?"

"You make money however you see fit. This is America. You can make your money."

"Right."

"But I'm not raising a stink with you about your money. I'm thinking of something else. I'm thinking of the cards. You're selling plunder with Pint to get a grubstake together. You're gambling again."

"We should go inside," Temple said.

"You know you've got to mind the cards."

"Inside."

"I won't be caught pulling you out of a jam again because you can't control your gambling."

"And you won't have to. Now let's have a look inside."

Temple looped his arm through Nail's and pulled him into the warehouse. Once inside, it took a moment for Augustus's eyes to adjust to the shadows. There were slats in the walls, and the ceiling was arched and high. Early morning air pushed a light, lilting breeze around the cavernous warehouse, and Augustus heard the gentle, almost inaudible flapping before he was able to see anything clearly. As soon as his eyes adjusted, he dropped back a step or two, his mouth agape.

The walls to his right and left had fifty-foot clotheslines stretching across them, eight lines to a wall. Hanging from wooden pins on each line were paper banknotes, neatly spaced and numbering in the thousands, enough to fill a small bank vault. Bright pink and black on one side and a handsome blue on the other, each piece of paper moved just slightly, but their collective fluttering reminded Augustus of a deck of cards being gently shuffled or a theater audience clapping in polite measure.

"Fill your pockets if you'd like," Nail told Augustus. "Take some for the kiddies."

Augustus walked down the center of the room, gaping up at the sea of money that surrounded him. He looked back at Temple, who was grinning. When he drew closer to the wall and touched some of the bills, he discovered that they were slightly damp. All of them were Confederate States of America notes printed in Richmond,

Columbia, or New Orleans. Jefferson Davis's face looked back at him from many of them.

"You stole all of these?" Augustus asked Nail.

Nail grimaced, shaking his head.

"Each and every one of the notes is a cogniac," Nail said before pointing to the far end of the warehouse, toward a large metal machine topped by a wooden, Z-shaped press. "Homemade, with my very own bogus."

His explanation finished, Nail curled his thumbs under his armpits and rocked back and forth on his heels with pride.

"Nail is a boodler," Temple said to Augustus. "He floods the South with counterfeits."

"And our government pays you no mind?" Augustus asked.

"No, our government just pays me," Nail replied. "They wanted to dump cogniacs all over the Secesh. The more shovers I sent to the South with fake notes, the more Chase and Stanton were willing to pay me. People feel lost when they don't have faith in the money they carry in their pockets. You spread enough bad paper around the South and it's just as bad as gunshots. But the war winds down and my trade expires and they've warned me not to turn green."

"Green?" Augustus asked.

"Stanton and Chase are starting to circulate all of these greenbacks up here, these new national dollars to replace the beauties that the states made. They don't want me makin' cogniacs that pass as greenbacks. They're happy to keep the Secesh on their heels with spooky money, but they want it gone up here."

"So you won't?" Augustus asked.

"Haven't made up my mind. I've got many mouths to feed in Swampdoodle, and those lads and their pups out there aren't devoted to me beyond their next meal. Besides, do Stanton and Chase believe that all these mongrels in this Un-united States are going to magically accept a single currency just because some fookin' poliotricians in Washington tell them to?"

"Now we've got him wound up," Temple said.

"Well, one pot of money means you've got to believe in a nation, and this ain't a nation. They're set on this, though. They chased us out of New York before the war began 'cuz we were makin' more money up there than the banks themselves. Beautiful days, those. That's how I met Temple—when he was workin' Manhattan with Tommy Driscoll. They caught me and Sam Upham. But that story's for another day. I'll want to know how you met our esteemed detective as well."

Nail swiveled away from Augustus and turned his full attention to Temple.

"And, you, didn't you have Pinkerton on you at every moment?"

"Ah, so you know him?" Temple replied. "He got humbugged, I hope. Fiona, Pint, and Alexander led him to Oak Hill, and that's when we got out of Foggy Bottom. Did Dilly get here?"

Nail considered Temple, looking him in the eye. He walked toward him without a word.

"McFadden, you're going to rain down grief on all of us with whatever you have in that package. This is a purposeful, muscular lot coming after you."

"We don't even know what we have yet," Temple said. "Where are they?"

"On the table near the bogus," Nail answered, gesturing to the back of the warehouse. "They're sitting inside that pile of engraving plates—it was the easiest place to put them after Dilly gave them to me. It's my homemade vault."

"Augustus, you look first," Temple said. "I think fresh eyes will help."

The engraving plates sat in a two-foot-high pile on a table next to the Z-shaped press. Augustus lifted several plates off the top of the stack: reverse images of Jeff Davis, the Richmond capitol building, Andrew Jackson, Ceres, slaves hoeing cotton, George Washington, Stonewall Jackson, a Nashville bank, two women sitting atop a cotton bale, horses, John Calhoun, garlands, monuments, Minerva, and denominations of $2, $5, $10, $20, $50, $100, and $500 were delicately and expertly carved into the plates, each of them a mirror of the counterfeit notes drying on the lines.

"The Secesh use lithographs for their money, but in the North we print it with steel," Nail shouted from the front of the warehouse. "I used steel plates for my Secesh cogniacs, to help bring our rebellious brothers into the monetary fold. Dry them, crumple them, and dip them in tobacco juice and they can't tell the difference. Nobody trusts a crisp new note. They like 'em used and dirty."

As Augustus removed more of the plates, an opening appeared in the center of the stack and he spotted the leather satchel at the bottom. He yanked out the bag and withdrew the two diaries from inside. He looked back across the warehouse at Temple.

"Go ahead, read them," Temple said. "One of them appears to have been written by a woman. Look at that one first, if you will."

It was indeed a woman's script, each of the letters formed in careful, tight loops. It had been written by someone who had an education, an elaborate vocabulary, and was given over to random enthusiasms; exclamation points ended many of the sentences. Augustus began reading.

"Where do you get the plates?" Temple asked Nail.

"We bribed insiders at the banks in the South. Cotton smugglers helped us get them out. Once I had the plates, I published pamphlets for shop owners and bank clerks on how to spot cogniacs. We made sure the books said notes that looked like ours were tried and true and all others weren't worthy of consideration. And we sent the pamphlets back down South with the smugglers; most of the shops being vigilant for fakes were using my pamphlets."

"Well done."

"Ta."

"How do you know Pinkerton?" Temple asked.

"Those who got south during the war had to know him. He set up the first spy network for McClellan. And then Stanton came to hate him and he packed it back to Chicago."

"So he wasn't a spy for the government?"

"Of a sort. Stanton replaced him."

"With who?"

"Lafayette Baker."

"L.B."

"I heard you had his horse."

"And his riding crop," Temple said, sliding his hand along his thigh.

"Not many people walk away from encounters with Baker."

"And you know Baker from . . . ?"

"Anybody dealing cogniacs has to know him. Willy Wood has the Secret Service now out of the Old Capitol Prison, and Baker runs it for him and Stanton. Most of what he does is police the District and other cities for phony notes. And for spies. They've spent the last four years ripping the shat out of people—killing some of them—in closed rooms at the prison to get information on the Secesh. They pick up anyone on the streets they want to, and Baker has the run of it. But he doesn't surface with regularity."

Temple moved a step closer to Nail.

"You're with me, yes, Nail?"

"I have a deep debt with you, Temple. I'm with you. Tho' I would greatly like to know what exactly it is that I'm committing to."

"I would like to know that as well."

Temple looked back at Augustus and paused. He was seated near the table of plates, holding two pieces of paper in one hand and one of the diaries in the other. He was staring blankly ahead. And there was a tear running down one of his cheeks.

"Augustus?" Temple asked.

No response. Temple limped to the back of the warehouse.

"Augustus?"

Temple reached him, and Augustus handed over the sheets of paper to him. It was a letter, pulled from the back of the black leather diary.

"Read it," Augustus said.

Temple tipped the letter into a shaft of light and began reading.

"August 24, 1855. Dear Speed: You know what a poor correspondent I am . . ." He continued reading, placing the second page atop the first as he moved along.

"When you reach the last portion, read it aloud," Augustus said.

A moment later, Temple started reciting: " 'I am not a Know-Nothing. That is certain. How could I be? How can anyone who abhors the oppression of Negroes be in favor of degrading classes of white people? Our progress in degeneracy appears to me to be pretty rapid. As a nation, we began by declaring that "all men are created equal." We now practically read it "all men are created equal, except Negroes." When the Know-Nothings get control, it will read "all men are created equal, except Negroes, and foreigners, and Catholics." When it comes to this, I should prefer emigrating to some country where they make no pretence of loving liberty—to Russia, for instance, where despotism can be taken pure, and without the base alloy of hypocrisy.' "

Temple stopped, collecting himself.

"Keep reading," Augustus said.

" 'Mary will probably pass a day or two in Louisville in October. My kindest regards to Mrs. Speed. On the leading subject of this letter, I have more of her sympathy than I have of yours. And yet let me say I am, your friend forever, A. Lincoln.' "

Temple looked up at Augustus.

"The letter was neatly folded in the back of the diary," Augustus said. "The diary's owner put it there. And if you read some of these other pages, it all becomes obvious."

"I imagine it does," Temple said.

"This diary belongs to Mary Todd Lincoln."

CHAPTER EIGHT

THE SHOOTER

Nail walked slowly to the back of his warehouse toward Augustus and Temple, who stared silently at the pages in their laps. The cogniacs fluttered and Temple began tapping his cane on the floor. *Tat, tat, tat, tat.*

"This half of my find from the B&O appears to be from Mrs. Lincoln," Temple said. "Her initials, M.T.L., are embossed at the bottom of the diary's pages."

"Well, you weren't born in the woods to be scared by an owl," Nail replied.

"Joshua Speed was once the president's best friend."

"What else do you have there besides letters?" Nail asked.

"The diary goes back for four or five months, but the recent entries are of great interest. Mrs. Lincoln was fearful of the men who surrounded her," Augustus said. "She was fearful of what it meant for Mr. Lincoln, I would think." He began reading aloud from the diary's pages.

March 12, 1865: My Dear Husband is strained. He says that Northern greed will be as hard to balance as Southern bile when this great war ends. And the end comes. Mr. Stanton is with him day and night and of late all the talk is of Council Bluffs and another railway line; rebuilding the South and its railway lines; of opening the West with still more railways. Railroads to corset the country. Bankers from New York were here today and there was loud debate near his office at supper. He will not share these details with me. But he says it pains him to be at odds with Mr. Stanton, upon whom he relies so. Our Robert sides with Mr. Stanton and Father says that to be in opposition to his eldest son on any matter is a struggle. "Molly, he is our son," he says. "And our son's ambitions run deep." Mr. Stanton, of course, despises me. I despise the group he brings to father's office now, including Mr. Scott and Mr. Durant. They are all schemers. Father sees through them, but hasn't the energy to wrestle them while still wrestling with General Lee.

Augustus continued reading.

March 25, 1865: Father didn't sleep last night and he complains again of the nightmares. He has had many of a casket, surrounded by mourners, in the Executive Mansion. The casket is in the Green Room, where little Willie once lay dead. Father approaches the mourners in his dream and they tell him they are mourning for him! For him!! He is haunted. And his days remain haunted, too. My fears consume me. He and Mr. Stanton met with the bankers again today. I took it upon myself to warn Mr. Stanton that he was straining my Husband with continued talk of railroads and war and rebuilding the South. He responded with frost—withering frost! His look frightened me. I reminded Mr. Stanton that it was I who convinced my Darling Husband that General McClellan must be replaced and that he should mind his standing and his manners or share a similar fate. And no sooner had I left the room than my Dear Husband came out and warned me not to interfere—and to avoid threatening Mr. Stanton. I was taken completely aback. Three very grim-faced bankers poured out after, trailed by Mr. Stanton, who nervously pleaded with them. "This can be arranged, Sirs," Mr. Stanton, said. "Patience, please." Father raised his hand and told them all to be quiet in the presence of his wife. One of the bankers ignored him. Ig-

nored my Darling Husband! The President! The banker told Father that even in New York women know when to silence themselves, and if the President could not keep his wife quiet, then he saw no reason to be quiet, either. Father, ever slow to anger, rippled in rage and ordered the men out. "Arrangements are not the province of my War Secretary, gentlemen. And I see to arrangements as they align with the Union's needs. Do not press me beyond that," he said. "I remind all of you that our city remains defended by almost 70 fortifications and more than 800 cannon. And we still have boys dying in the fields, boys at war. Mind them—mind this war—before your purses." The bankers slinked away, but their faces remained chiseled in stone. I apologized this evening for stirring things such and my Dear Husband told me that these affairs stirred long before I became involved. I ask him to share more of this with me. "Father, I am your wife and I am here to fortify you and to support you." But he falls silent, as he has done so often in recent days.

April 9, 1865: It is a day of glory and Abraham shines! General Lee surrendered to General Grant in the court house at Appomattox. I have not seen Father so lifted in years. The railways have fled his mind. At the very least, they have fled his attention along with the New York merchants. Abraham told me that today beams celebration and redemption. Would that Willie were here with us for this day. Still, we have our Tad, our son who loves us true. And further still—the Union triumphant!

April 11, 1865: Robert has taken a stand with the bankers and Mr. Stanton in whatever dispute and with whatever forces exist against my Dear Husband. I advised him to pay it no mind. But he replies that a "mighty web" is spun. His silences are back. I ask him to elaborate. "Father, what web?" And he stares away. I need him to lighten his burdens, cast off the worries of these past four years. We may see

a play soon at Ford's and he will enjoy a proper night away from the
Executive Mansion.

Augustus paused and caught his breath. A few dogs barked outside the warehouse. The cogniacs fluttered. He pressed his hand to
the side of his head, closed his eyes briefly, and read again.

April 19, 1865: They took my Murdered Husband's body from the
Mansion to the Capitol. They are taking him from me and giving
him back to the people. Life is all darkness. The sun is a mockery
to me.

"She doesn't write very much after this," Augustus said. "Most of
the entries are brief, except for the last, and it's barely a week old."

May 11, 1865: Robert wants funds for furniture and real estate
and tells me I'm not to be disconsolate with our loss. I have
given him $1,000 this year alone and he wants more. And he
assails me for my gloves and my curtains and my other pur-
chases! I loathe my eldest son! My boy! He says he has the
Pinkertons looking after me for my protection but they drive
me to raving distraction. He says I am lunatic and unfit!! I
found some of Robert's telegrams from New York. I know of
Mars. He wants my papers. Robert wants my papers and he
wants my money. Yet nothing is worse than my Darling Husband's absence. That is my daily crucifixion. My Gethsemane.

"It ends there," Augustus said. "It stops."
Several minutes passed before Temple stood up. Nail moved
closer, bending over to examine the diary.
"You can read!" he said to Augustus.
"Negroes read," Augustus replied. "A self-taught mathematician
and Negro—Benjamin Banneker—surveyed and helped design

Pennsylvania Avenue here seventy years ago. We can read and we can add."

"You mistake me," Nail said. "I mean, you read beautifully. All I can read are banknotes. I cannot read as you read. I can't read books."

"Augustus is the son of free Negroes who fled Texas after the Alamo," Temple offered. "He is educated and he is a teacher."

Nail nodded, smiled, and extended his hand to Augustus. But Nail pulled back his hand when a fury of howling and scratching erupted around the warehouse's entry, interrupting him. Then a fist pounded against the door.

"In!" Nail shouted.

One of Nail's men opened the door a crack. The tip of a rifle peeked through the gap and the snouts of two dogs pushed through, snarling, around the man's legs. He bent his head farther inside and looked across the warehouse to where Nail and the others were standing.

" 'Sall right!" Nail hollered.

The door closed again.

"There's still the other," Augustus said.

The three men looked down at the two diaries stacked on the floor.

"You've done it once before, Temple. Open it again," said Nail.

Mary Todd Lincoln's diary was almost perfectly square, appearing as new and fresh as it was the day it was bought, and it was heavy with thick pages and a sturdy binding. The second diary, like the first, was bound in leather, but it was distinct in every other way. It was long and slender, and its red cover was faded and spotted. Some of the pages hung loosely, close to falling out. The script inside was a man's, and the writing was tight and small, with none of the looping curves that marked Mrs. Lincoln's notes. But the language, while not as florid as Mrs. Lincoln's, was just as self-absorbed.

Temple sat down and began reading aloud:

For six months we had worked to capture, but our cause being almost lost, something decisive and great must be done. But its failure was owing to others, who did not strike for their country with a heart. I struck boldly, and not as the papers say. I walked with a firm step through a thousand of his friends, was stopped, but pushed on. A colonel was at his side. I shouted Sic semper *before I fired. In jumping broke my leg. I passed all his pickets, rode sixty miles that night with the bone of my leg tearing the flesh at every jump. I can never repent it, though we hated to kill. Our country owed all her troubles to him, and God simply made me the instrument of his punishment. The country is not what it was. This forced Union is not what I have loved. I care not what becomes of me. I have no desire to outlive my country.*

Temple looked up at Augustus and Nail. Augustus didn't say a word. Nail's eyes met Temple's and Nail grimaced, shaking his head. Temple read on:

For my country I have given up all that makes life sweet and holy, brought misery upon my family, and am sure there is no pardon in the Heaven for me, since man condemns me so. I have only heard of what has been done (except what I did myself), and it fills me with horror. God, try and forgive me, and bless my mother. Tonight I will once more try the river with the intent to cross. Though I have a greater desire and almost a mind to return to Washington and in a measure clear my name—which I feel I can do. I do not repent the blow I struck. I may before my God, but not to man. I think I have done well. Though I am abandoned, with the curse of Cain upon me, when, if the world knew my heart, that one blow would have made me great, though I did desire no greatness.

Across the top of a following page, in bold, printed letters that departed from the tight script elsewhere, was the lone word that Temple had spotted at the railroad station: "assassination."

Patriot has told Maestro that I am no traitor, I am sure. Patriot says that Maestro owns Lord War. Davey, George, and Lewis are all heroes also, even if they, too, share the mark of Cain. Those that find this, those that chase me, know the cipher, and the cipher is true. I do not care that I am made a villain among those who honor the Tyrant. He wanted nigger citizenship and I ran him through.

Temple stopped.

"Temple, you've gone pale," Augustus said. "Is that all there is?"

"No, there's more," Temple said, quietly.

"Tha's the shooter," Nail said. "Johnny Booth."

Temple closed the journal and slipped it inside his breast pocket, where it sat comfortably, he thought, in exactly the same place John Wilkes Booth had probably kept it the night he shot Mr. Lincoln.

"I think Augustus and I need to move on before the morning wears long here, Nail," Temple said. "For now we best go where we don't complicate your day any further and where I can find Fiona."

"You walk through that door, Temple, you and Augustus, hanging on to those diaries, and you both walk out into a world of pain. You can't walk away from it after that."

"You told me I wasn't born in the woods to be scared of owls."

"That was before all of this reading. Those diaries are desired. They speak of a slain president. Leave them with whoever is after them and go on your way. It all smells of blood, and you'll bleed, too. You already have. More will follow."

Nail looked down at the floor in front of him. A vein pulsed on his neck, and he wrung his hands, the muscles in his forearms twitching like banjo wire.

"World of pain," he said.

"You're still with me?" Temple asked.

"I am," Nail replied. "Pinkerton and Baker hate one another, you know."

"And why?"

"Because of Stanton. Dueling allegiances."

"I want to move these diaries to a different place, and I want to set about learning more about something that's here in the second. I'll be back to you tomorrow."

"And you're off to where?"

"To a place that would be as much a mystery to them as Swamp-doodle."

"Neither of you should come back here at night, if you need to come back at all, and Augustus should never come alone," Nail said. "Those men and dogs out there recognize neighbors and nobody else. None of them will tolerate a nig . . . none of them will tolerate a Negro on his own, day or night."

Temple shoved the Lincoln diary into the satchel.

"Ta for all you've done, Nail."

"Nothing of it, Temp."

Nail turned to Augustus and paused. Then he shook his hand.

When they got to the warehouse door and flung it open, a blast of ripening heat rushed in. The dogs barked wildly outside, straining at their leashes. Temple limped down the stairs at an angle, favoring his bad leg. As he and Augustus moved past the dogs, Temple turned to look back. Nail was watching them depart, hands on his hips, the ink stains that Augustus had mistaken for tattoos now a cobalt blue in the late morning sun.

Temple closed his eyes for a moment, thinking about the queen of spades and a faro game at Mary Ann Hall's. He needn't worry about any bet he made in a card game at Mary Ann's, not when he'd have the queen of spades. No coppers in his game, no betting the turn. Just smart flat bets. Winners.

LAFAYETTE BAKER WAITED outside the tents at Camp Fry, watching the teenager tie up the back of his rucksack. Good soldier. Neat, responsible. Follows orders. Even listened to the Met at the B&O

when he told him to charge my boys. Neat, disciplined, and a little bastard.

"Son, come here," Baker said.

The soldier slung his rifle over his shoulder and walked over.

"Recognize me?"

"No," the boy replied.

"I recognize you."

"From where, sir?"

"The dustup at the B&O a few days ago."

"It was a mess there, sir."

"Your name?"

"Priston, sir. Damien Priston."

"Damien, I've been authorized to bring a reward here to you in Foggy Bottom this morning, for your bravery at the B&O, but I can't be handing out banknotes in front of other soldiers."

"The street's naked here at this time of day, sir, not a soul about."

"I know, I know, but you never can tell. Everybody is always watching somebody in the District. Follow me."

Baker walked into a nearby alley and pulled a wad of notes from his belt.

"So you don't know me, correct?"

"That's right, sir, other than you have officer's decorations on your uniform."

"Did you know the man who ordered you to draw down on some of the gentlemen at the B&O that day?"

"No, didn't know him either, sir."

"But you chose to get involved anyway—to interfere?"

"Sir?"

"You chose to get in the way, to intrude, didn't you, you little rat bastard?"

"I'll be going now, sir."

"Yes, you will."

Baker slammed his elbow into the soldier's throat. As the boy gagged, Baker brought a knee up into his crotch and shoved him into a wall. He pulled a blade out from his belt and sliced it across the boy's throat. Then he kicked his feet out from under him. The boy collapsed, gurgling through a pink mass of bubbles foaming around his mouth. Baker pressed the heel of his boot into the boy's face, silencing him until his eyes rolled back and his breathing stopped.

CHAPTER NINE

THE ARRANGEMENTS

Fiona pressed her face against the twin lenses of the stereoscope and focused her eyes on the image propped up several inches away on the other side. In three dimensions she saw a V-shaped trench filled with dead soldiers, their legs, arms, rifles, and bayonets draped willy-nilly over one another.

"It's from Gettysburg," said Gardner. "The stereos are a fine sight better than Mathew Brady's humdrum daguerreotypes. Timmy O'Sullivan and I got to Gettysburg days before Brady did."

Gardner unclasped the Gettysburg card from the clip that held it and swapped another into its place. In three dimensions again, Fiona saw another of Gardner's images from the war. Abraham Lincoln was sitting inside a tent at a small table, across from General McClellan. Even seated, Lincoln dominated the commander of the Army of the Potomac.

"That one's earlier, from Antietam," Gardner said.

"Did you ever converse with the president?" Fiona asked, her body still bent at the waist as she looked through the stereoscope.

"A fair bit," Gardner said, a note of sadness piercing his brogue. "The president was a gabber. He asked more questions than you could ever answer, and he had good, kind eyes. He was curious about photography. And he and his generals let Brady and me have the run of the battlefields. Here now, I'll show you something special, Fiona."

As Fiona straightened up, Pint hurried into her spot and looked through the lenses of the stereoscope, whistling aloud as he did so.

"Everyone can live forever in these pictures," said Pint. "It's a modern miracle. You can't be erased or forgotten."

"We'll all be erased and forgotten, just like the rotting soldiers in those trenches," said Gardner. "Maybe not Lincoln, but the rest of us aren't going to be saved by glass plates, chemical baths, and some hocus-pocus that stragglers like me perform with light and shade."

"There are other ways to be saved," said Fiona.

Gardner didn't respond to her. He reached up to a broad, locked cabinet and opened it with a key he pulled from his trouser pocket. Inside were several shelves, each filled with glass plates that were neatly ordered and alphabetized. The names on the plates offered a catalog of the celebrated and the powerful in Washington who had visited Gardner's studio to sit for a photograph: Burnside, Morse, Sumner, Hooker, Chase, Farragut, Grant, Seward, Meade, Whitman, Douglas, and, of course, Lincoln.

They all came to have Brady's protégé record their images for posterity. The high and mighty, as Gardner called them, paid him $750 for his work. For soldiers, students, and Washington's working folk he charged $10. He had earned enough to keep his wife and children in a comfortable clapboard house near Georgetown. But he spent little on himself, often slept on the floor of his 7th Street studio, and sent large chunks of money back to Scotland with relatives, earmarking a portion for writers at the *Glasgow Sentinel,* which, although he owned it, he hadn't read in years.

On a shelf of its own inside the cupboard was a mahogany box, which Gardner carefully removed and then opened on a nearby table, placing it next to *Gardner's Photographic Sketch Book of the Civil War,* an oversized compilation of his work. He had spent the better part of the last eighteen months adding and subtracting photographs from the book, and aimed to spend another year with it before he let his publisher have it. Gardner flipped open the mahogany box and removed a large glass negative draped in a piece of yellow cloth. He slipped off the cloth and then fanned the fingers of his hand toward his chest, gesturing for Fiona to have a look.

The negative had a long crack in it, which replicated itself as a thick black line across the top of the single silver and albumen print

Gardner had made from the splintered plate. He gave the print to Fiona.

"After the negative broke, I decided to make just one print," Gardner said. "He sat down for it last February, about two months before he was murdered. I think it's the last photograph anyone took of him before the killing."

Fiona was holding a photograph of Lincoln. The president had a long, skinny neck, and his left ear, slightly blurred, hung like a small saucer from an oversized head. His hair was mussed; his black bow tie was askew, wandering beneath the collar; his brow was deeply furrowed; and his beard was peppered with strands of gray. His cheeks formed two tired pouches on either side of a prominent, broad nose. He was a man who looked, and had every right to be, unwound by war, death, and the weight of the world. But there was a faint, amused smile tracing his lips, and his eyes were deep, dark, resolute, and knowing. He was his own person, a man at peace with himself. And Alexander was correct: the president had good, kind eyes.

The president's eyes would have been the most memorable feature of the photograph if it had been a clean print. But it wasn't a clean print—the crack in the glass negative scarred the photo, leaving an L-shaped fissure that plunged downward from the uppermost left corner of the photo before it sliced to the right, across the top of Lincoln's head. It could have been the shadow of a lightning bolt, Fiona thought. Or the finely grooved, gunpowder-black crease of a bullet that pierced time and justice, all of a moment in a theater balcony.

"It's like Death laid his finger across this picture," Fiona said softly.

"It was an omen, and I'm fixed to destroy this goddamn negative because of it," Gardner replied. "But I just can't rid myself of it. I put it back in the box every time."

Fiona put down the print and studied the negative on the table in front of her. She lifted Gardner's photo manuscript to eye level, then dropped the *Sketch Book* with a muffled crunch on top of the negative. When she removed the manuscript, the glass plate was webbed with cracks.

"There," she said to Gardner. "You're rid of it."

Gardner brought a small bin to the edge of the table and swept the fragments into it with the yellow cloth. He put the print back into the mahogany box and closed it, letting his hands rest a moment on the lid.

"Thank you, Fiona," he said. "I'm weary of being connected to this war."

"We're all connected, Alexander, and none of us will escape it," she replied.

Pint walked over and stared into the bin at the glass shards, tilting his head slightly as he pondered the shattered negative.

"Alexander was more connected than most, though," Pint said. "Weren't you, Alexander? The arrangements of bodies, the plums from McClellan. Those weren't accidents."

"And?" Gardner replied.

"And that's how you know Pinkerton, ain't it?"

Gardner glanced at Fiona. She knew most of this, and so did Temple, but they didn't know about Pinkerton—and with Pinkerton in all of their lives now, it amounted to more than it had in the past.

Fiona didn't say anything, waiting for Gardner to respond to Pint. Gardner brought a handkerchief to his forehead and mopped beads of sweat from his brow.

"I met Pinkerton through Mat Brady. Brady began stealing my work, putting it out under his own name, and I wanted to leave; Pinkerton introduced me to McClellan. The general had needs for his war and I met them. Once Lincoln took a shine to the photography, especially my stereos, I was granted passage with the troops."

"Why did you never tell us of Pinkerton, Alexander?" Fiona asked.

"Because they paid me well not to say a word about him. And once I got in deeper they said they'd send me to the Old Capitol for lockup if I disclosed anything," Gardner replied. "I was doing more than making images. At Pinkerton's direction, I took photographs of the terrain where battles were going to take place, or where McClellan thought they might take place. The general made military maps from them. And I took pictures of entire army units, which Pinkerton and his boys scanned with Union officers to spot Confederate infiltrators."

"You also did one other thing," Pint said. "Your arrangements."

Gardner stared coolly at Pint, as if seeing him for the first time.

"I sometimes arranged dead soldiers in more ... more ... dramatic positions for my photographs. It gave them dignity."

"No, it gave Lincoln's government powerful pictures it could plant in newspapers to curry favor for the war—and it gave you pictures that you could sell everywhere else to fatten your purse," Pint said.

"That too," said Gardner. "Yes, that too. Only the embalmers on Pennsylvania Avenue saw their businesses grow faster than mine or Brady's. But it wasn't just money. There was responsibility. Memories matter."

"None of it was real."

"It was all reality. It was a higher reality. It captured what was and what had passed. It made people care."

"You staged them," Pint shot back. "You used death as a prop."

"Then never have your photograph taken," Gardner responded. "You'll do just fine. You can be forgotten."

Gardner put his handkerchief back in his pocket. He unbundled his shoulders and sat back against a table. He pulled his hand through his black beard and exhaled.

"Pint knows Pinkerton, too, Fiona," he said.

"They know I spied," Pint said. "Temple's known that and he knows that's where I learned the codes. No mysteries about me."

"They know that Pinkerton paid you?"

Pint took his turn at gauging Fiona's reaction. Again she said nothing, waiting for Pint to respond.

"Once. Just once. I got an assignment to watch the dormitories at Georgetown College. The Secesh schoolboys there raised and lowered the shades in their bedroom windows to signal Confederate lookouts across the Potomac about Union troop movements. It was like watching signal flags on ships at sea. I figured out what the shades meant and I gave it to Pinkerton."

"The army used the information to arrest students," Gardner noted. "They went after students."

"Spies," Pint said. "They were spies. Damn them for it. I didn't care if they got rounded up."

"You see, we are all connected to the war," Fiona said. "No one in the District escapes it. Not you, Alexander. Not you, Pint. Not me."

Fiona placed her hand on Gardner's cheek, held it there briefly, and then did the same for Pint, considering his eyes before she moved toward the door.

"Time for me to walk about unescorted again, gentlemen," Fiona said. "If you'll excuse me, I need to find my husband."

As she pulled open the door she turned back to Gardner, who was slumped in a chair and staring out a window.

"Alexander."

The sound of her voice made him stir. He sat up straight and swiveled toward her.

"Fiona?"

"I take powerful delight in your stereoscopes. And thank you for showing me the photograph of the president."

"Thank you, Fiona."

"You ought not go out there all by your lonesome," Pint said to Fiona.

She raised her fingers to her lips, shushing him, then picked up her bag, still stuffed with the supplies from Dr. Springer's office, and left.

Fiona closed the door behind her and exited Gardner's studio onto 7th Street. When she reached Pennsylvania it was already heavy with midday commerce and traffic. On the avenue, just off 7th, Fiona lingered at an enormous plate glass window that featured arched bronze lettering proclaiming to visitors that they had arrived at Mathew Brady's world-famous studio of photographic portraiture (rates negotiable). The glass's expanse offered a view inside, despite the glare of the sun on the pane, where an elegant waiting room furnished with plush chairs and polished wooden tables had been arranged for visitors seeking Brady's services. A small daguerreotype of Ulysses Grant sat on a ledge inside the window, next to a larger image of Andrew Johnson. An even more sizeable daguerreotype of Lincoln, with black bunting draping its frame, rested on the opposite side of the ledge.

Brady's studio, once magical to Fiona, now felt different, blunted and farcical. As she peered inside, her reflection presented itself within the arc of the lettering on the glass, the outline of her body drawn in slightly undulating lines and shadows that were nearly overpowered by the sunlight behind her. She studied her form for a moment, wondering about the havoc the night trek to Oak Hill had visited upon her eyes, her hair, her mood. She had her overstuffed bag at her side and the midday heat on her shoulder; a poor sight, she feared, and time to come before she could address the matter.

Hers wasn't the only reflection captured by the glass. Over her shoulder, the dim reflection of a bulky man hovered behind her. Though his silhouette was largely shapeless and defined only by broad shoulders and lupine arms hanging down at his sides, the sun glazed off the white straw hat atop his head like a beacon. He appeared to be several feet away, and as Fiona began to turn, he rotated away from her. When she repositioned herself back in front of the glass, he swung toward her again.

"Quietly, quietly," she could hear Temple telling her, "that's how these things come upon you." Remember who you are, he'd advised, and respond by trying to control the pace of it all.

She stepped away from the studio and walked along more briskly than before, passing a series of dry goods dealers, tanneries, clothing stores, butchers, and all of the embalmers that Alexander had cataloged as just another perversity of the war. Bringing the little boys' corpses home to stuff them and preserve them and plant them in the ground. She stole glances into the angled windows of a barber shop (luxury shave, five cents; gentleman's haircut, ten cents), and eyed the same stocky figure trailing along behind her, floating beneath a hat that appeared as hard and white as bone.

Quietly, quietly.

Whatever doubts Fiona now had about Brady's bona fides, and about the stagings and gossamer domains of photographs, she was quite certain about something else: she was being followed.

CHAPTER TEN

THE TELEGRAMS

A scattering of Negro children played jacks and marbles; a separate pair had rolled and knotted a rag into a makeshift ball and were tossing it to each other. A brown mutt, its fur knotted and its haunches buzzing with flies, slept curled next to a puddle that was slowly evaporating against the base of a shade tree. One little girl sat alone, talking to a corn husk doll. A tall boy bobbled a baseball up and down off the tip of a crudely whittled bat and stared at the two men approaching from down the block; he didn't let the ball escape him and drop to the ground, yet he never bothered focusing on it, either.

As the men drew closer, each of the children, one by one, stopped what they were doing and also focused on the pair. One of the men was a Negro, dressed for town; the other was white and limped along, bearing his weight on a cane. Dandy Negroes rarely came to Tiber Island. White folk never came at all, except to collect rent.

Wary and bunching together shoulder to shoulder, with the dog barking at their side, the children began singing:

> *The riverbed makes a mighty fine road*
> *Dead trees to show you the way*
> *And it's left foot, peg foot, traveling on*
> *Follow the drinking gourd*

> *The river ends between two hills*
> *Follow the drinking gourd*

There's another river on the other side
Follow the drinking gourd

The air around Tiber Island was rank, with the taint of offal crawling in on the breeze off the Potomac, and as Temple and Augustus neared the children they were enveloped by it. Temple was accustomed to the odor in other parts of the District, but here, where the river melted and broke muddily into the Washington Channel, forming a bent waterfront southwest of the Capitol, the odor was so overpowering that he thought to pull a kerchief to his face. Off in the distance, the Washington Monument was all foundation, a tapering, quarter-built slab that looked as though it would never be completed. Here there were stone warehouses along the water bisected by alleys dotted and stuffed with tiny two-room huts and cabins—"alley-houses," where free Negroes lived.

Temple had been to alley-houses elsewhere in the District, each time with Augustus, but he had never been to Tiber Island before. Nor had a chorus of children greeted him.

"Do you know the song?" Temple asked.

"It's an Underground Railroad song about the Little Dipper," Augustus said. "About using the North Star on the Dipper as a guiding light, so slaves could find their way when they escaped from the South."

"And they're singing it to greet us?"

"They're singing it to warn everyone else that strangers are here. Every Negro in the alleys knows we're here now; the dice and cards are coming up, most of the doors are closing, and it will all be about watching now. Whites in Tiber Island, if they aren't unloading goods from boats into the warehouses, just mean trouble to these folks."

I thought I heard the angels say
Follow the drinking gourd
The stars in the heavens gonna show you the way
Follow the drinking gourd

Temple and Augustus walked around the children and headed into an alley directly in front of them. When they reached the back of one of the warehouses, Augustus tugged Temple's sleeve, directing him to the right. Three Negroes were sitting on stools. One of them was old, with a shock of white hair and a beard; the other two were young, broad, and muscular. They stared at the ground, their elbows propped on their knees, but they were clearly guarding the old man.

Augustus, smiling broadly, bent forward at the waist.

"I stand in humility before the right honorable former slave and wise man for the ages, Master Lexington Sparks."

"Oh, there ya go, Augustus, goddamn! Ya win me ever' time with that honeysuckle," the old man said, standing up and embracing Augustus. "I don't need the sweets from ya, son."

"But don't pretend you don't like it."

"Ha! Y'all here with a rarity, I see. A mighty tall rarity."

Lexington stepped back and eyed Temple, drawing in his cane, clothing, and bearing in a quick, wary sweep.

"I've come to ask a favor," Augustus said.

He leaned forward and whispered into Lexington's ear; as Lexington nodded, he told him about the past few days, about Temple, and about the diaries that Temple brought with him. The diaries couldn't be opened: people would die if they were. The diaries couldn't be lost: people would go unpunished if they were. And the diaries couldn't stay in one place for more than a day or two: people might find them otherwise.

Lexington would have to shepherd the satchel containing the diaries around the District, in and out of different alley-houses, for at least a week or two. He could use his grandsons as messengers; if Augustus needed the packages, he would get word to Tiber Island. Willow Tree Alley would be one of the safest places for them, but Lexington could exercise his own judgment.

"There's money in it for you," Augustus said.

"Money's good. But I be set to do it for y'all free, ya know that."

"You'll still get greenbacks. Can we use one of the houses here for an hour or so?"

"Sure 'nough."

With Lexington leading the way, Augustus and Temple proceeded down the alley. One shack looked like a small corner store; two others housed a tinsmith and a blacksmith. As they got farther along, some doors began opening behind them. More children appeared, huddling close to their mothers' skirts. Next to a cabin marked "Mt. Ararat Baptist Church" hung a small sign saying "Where Will You Spend Eternity?" A few steps beyond was another shed, with a crude banner hung above the door: "St. Matthew's Overcoming Church." Barrels and buckets lined the alley, collecting rainwater.

Lexington guided them into a cabin near the far end of the alley. Temple stooped to enter it, and once inside he had to wait while his eyes adjusted to the dim of the windowless interior. He couldn't stand at his full height inside, and he lowered himself onto one of two rickety chairs set next to a small wooden table and stretched his legs. Augustus joined him and asked Lexington to leave the door ajar so they had light to read by.

"'Fore ya start your work, I have a thing I want ya to read fer us," Lexington said. "Will ya?"

"Of course."

Lexington was only gone a moment. When he came back, he had a newspaper in his hands. There was an article in the *Washington Evening Star* that day that everyone in the alleys was buzzing about, Lexington said. He couldn't read it himself and he handed it to Augustus, who quickly scanned it.

"It's an editorial," Augustus said.

"Meanin'?"

"It's what the people running the paper think about things in the District and in the Union. They share their ponderings."

"So read me what I need to know," Lexington said.

As he had at Nail's, Augustus read aloud: " *'While willing to grant the Negro every right due him before the law, we are not prepared to make*

*a farce of the right of suffrage, by giving it to an ignorant mass of Negroes,
who know no more how to exercise it than the cattle in the field they so
lately herded with.'"*

"That sums it?" Lexington asked.

"Sums it."

"Lordy, likin' us to cows. Suffrage is the vote?"

"It's the vote. It will happen—step by step, Lexington," said Augustus. "We've got the Freedmen's Bureau, and the bureau has the army behind it, and the bureau and the army are going to make sure that Negroes get their land, their schools, and their hospitals."

"But no votes? Readin' and medicines and forty acres and a mule, but no vote? Y'all younger than this old man, son. I'd like the vote before I pass, but I ain't plannin' on seein' no vote."

"The vote will only come if free men keep their voices high and change the Constitution. The war and Mr. Lincoln didn't get us the vote, so we'll have to do that together."

"Amen," said Lexington.

"Amen," Augustus said.

Temple thumped the table in agreement, and Lexington took the *Evening Star* from Augustus and backed out of the shack.

"I'll make sure nobody bothers y'all," he said.

Temple pulled the two diaries from the satchel. Temple put Mrs. Lincoln's pages aside and flipped quickly through the Booth papers, stopping at about a dozen pages at the very end. He stared down at one page for nearly a minute, then began pulling at it, attempting to tear it from the journal.

"You can't do that, Temple," snapped Augustus. "You can't take it apart yet."

"I'll need to keep some of these pages with me before we leave these journals here. There are pages here that are odd, that read differently to me at Nail's. I didn't want to talk about it there, but here we are."

"Why didn't you speak about it there?"

"Because, as Nail suspects—and I agree—it's information that will get people killed. It's better that fewer know about the contents, particularly these final dozen pages or so. Some of it is coded, and the last page contains a cipher."

"You still can't tear it apart. You know that. It's part of a record, some proof of what's happened. It has to stay whole."

"I can't remember all of it on my own."

"I can help. Share it with me. Share it with Fiona."

"No, that won't do," Temple said, bolting up from his chair and banging his head against the ceiling. "This"—Temple flapped the journal above his head—"will kill people. They've already got Booth's accomplices and the Surratt woman in jail. There was a throat slit at the B&O over this. It can happen that quickly—to you and to Fiona, too—and I'd rather not bear witness to that, thank you."

"But I can make that decision on my own," Augustus said. "I think Fiona will want to decide for herself as well. And you have straw flakes and bits of dirt on your shoulders from your collision with the ceiling."

"I don't want Fiona to have to make that decision."

"She'll tell you that it's her choice. But I'll leave that discussion for the two of you. Brush your shoulders clean and read what you have, Temple. I want to know."

Temple sat down, straightening his bad leg and whisking off his shoulders as he resettled, and then thumbed again through Booth's journal. He stopped in the back, where a series of about a dozen telegrams, clipped down in thin strips from their original sizes, lay pasted to the pages; he showed the first to Augustus.

March 4, 1865
From: BAKBWTV
To: MVVXUJT
    FHVBS NU A ZBAM WYF DQU IG ZAKSCSCL. Q NY FFB SQOIZN
MNU WCSURMNX. HFBGJU TW EUCYWCSF WPRZ YFE VFXE
BLDAED.

"You said you wanted to read it," Temple said, the corners of his mouth lifting into a slight smile.

"And so I can't."

"All of them are encrypted like this. Except for the last three. Booth penciled translations in plain English above the last three messages. Have a look at those."

Temple handed Augustus the journal, opened to the first decoded telegram. In addition to the heavy air in the shack there was little light, and Augustus had to tilt the journal toward the door to read the pages.

April 5, 1865
From: Patriot
To: Avenger
     Maestro sends funds. Goliath and others will join you. Wise Man and Drinker should be taken with Tyrant.

April 11, 1865
From: Patriot
To: Avenger
     You will be allowed to pass at Navy Yard Bridge. Refuge at Tavern.

April 14, 1865
From: Patriot
To: Avenger
     It is Ford's. Praetorians send a Parker to guard Tyrant. He will abandon the door or let you pass.

Tucked behind the last page and the back cover of the journal was a neatly folded piece of paper, with several red flecks upon it that Augustus took to be blood. The spots could have just as well been ink or tea stains, but Augustus was content, minding the bearer, to judge them otherwise.

He pulled the page out and spread it in front of him. It was a table of letters: *A* to *Z* horizontally across its top, *A* to *Z* vertically down its left side. The alphabet repeated itself again in each row and column inside the table—though the sequence inside began with whatever letter marked the column or row.

	A	B	C	D	E	F	G	H	I	J	K	L	M	N	O	P	Q	R	S	T	U	V	W	X	Y	Z
A	A	B	C	D	E	F	G	H	I	J	K	L	M	N	O	P	Q	R	S	T	U	V	W	X	Y	Z
B	B	C	D	E	F	G	H	I	J	K	L	M	N	O	P	Q	R	S	T	U	V	W	X	Y	Z	A
C	C	D	E	F	G	H	I	J	K	L	M	N	O	P	Q	R	S	T	U	V	W	X	Y	Z	A	B
D	D	E	F	G	H	I	J	K	L	M	N	O	P	Q	R	S	T	U	V	W	X	Y	Z	A	B	C
E	E	F	G	H	I	J	K	L	M	N	O	P	Q	R	S	T	U	V	W	X	Y	Z	A	B	C	D
F	F	G	H	I	J	K	L	M	N	O	P	Q	R	S	T	U	V	W	X	Y	Z	A	B	C	D	E
G	G	H	I	J	K	L	M	N	O	P	Q	R	S	T	U	V	W	X	Y	Z	A	B	C	D	E	F
H	H	I	J	K	L	M	N	O	P	Q	R	S	T	U	V	W	X	Y	Z	A	B	C	D	E	F	G
I	I	J	K	L	M	N	O	P	Q	R	S	T	U	V	W	X	Y	Z	A	B	C	D	E	F	G	H
J	J	K	L	M	N	O	P	Q	R	S	T	U	V	W	X	Y	Z	A	B	C	D	E	F	G	H	I
K	K	L	M	N	O	P	Q	R	S	T	U	V	W	X	Y	Z	A	B	C	D	E	F	G	H	I	J
L	L	M	N	O	P	Q	R	S	T	U	V	W	X	Y	Z	A	B	C	D	E	F	G	H	I	J	K
M	M	N	O	P	Q	R	S	T	U	V	W	X	Y	Z	A	B	C	D	E	F	G	H	I	J	K	L
N	N	O	P	Q	R	S	T	U	V	W	X	Y	Z	A	B	C	D	E	F	G	H	I	J	K	L	M
O	O	P	Q	R	S	T	U	V	W	X	Y	Z	A	B	C	D	E	F	G	H	I	J	K	L	M	N
P	P	Q	R	S	T	U	V	W	X	Y	Z	A	B	C	D	E	F	G	H	I	J	K	L	M	N	O
Q	Q	R	S	T	U	V	W	X	Y	Z	A	B	C	D	E	F	G	H	I	J	K	L	M	N	O	P
R	R	S	T	U	V	W	X	Y	Z	A	B	C	D	E	F	G	H	I	J	K	L	M	N	O	P	Q
S	S	T	U	V	W	X	Y	Z	A	B	C	D	E	F	G	H	I	J	K	L	M	N	O	P	Q	R
T	T	U	V	W	X	Y	Z	A	B	C	D	E	F	G	H	I	J	K	L	M	N	O	P	Q	R	S
U	U	V	W	X	Y	Z	A	B	C	D	E	F	G	H	I	J	K	L	M	N	O	P	Q	R	S	T
V	V	W	X	Y	Z	A	B	C	D	E	F	G	H	I	J	K	L	M	N	O	P	Q	R	S	T	U
W	W	X	Y	Z	A	B	C	D	E	F	G	H	I	J	K	L	M	N	O	P	Q	R	S	T	U	V
X	X	Y	Z	A	B	C	D	E	F	G	H	I	J	K	L	M	N	O	P	Q	R	S	T	U	V	W
Y	Y	Z	A	B	C	D	E	F	G	H	I	J	K	L	M	N	O	P	Q	R	S	T	U	V	W	X
Z	Z	A	B	C	D	E	F	G	H	I	J	K	L	M	N	O	P	Q	R	S	T	U	V	W	X	Y

"It's called a Vigenère. It's a ciphering table," Temple said. "The Confederate army and Secesh spies used these. Pint's familiar with the tables and codes."

"How does Pint know them?"

Temple looked beyond Augustus, at the shaft of light spilling through the doorway. Fiona didn't know Pint's other life, either. Cipher for certain, Declan "Pint" Ramsey. As far as Fiona and Augustus knew, Pint poured beer at Jimmy Scanlon's saloon in Foggy Bottom each evening, tips in the jar, cash in the pocket, off to home, thank you very much. But where Pint actually spent most of his time was in the telegraph office on the second floor of the War Department, where he monitored the lines for the Union and unscrambled Confederate messages after the army intercepted them.

"Pint's a puzzler," Temple said. "It's one of his talents. Did you know he had a deaf sister?"

"I didn't."

"He worked out his own signs with her when they were children, and that's how they spoke, signing with their own language. I think words and letters just fluttered through his head after that, like a wordsmith. A man full of surprises."

"So, this table: Booth used it to decrypt the telegrams?"

"It would appear. They depend on a key word or phrase to loosen the secrets of an encoded message. Though Booth has given us ample guidance from the grave, I'm happy to say. Someone better versed than I in the mechanics of code breaking can help us along further; that's what has me thinking on Pint. But we have a start of our own right here: if the first message corresponds with the latter, then *BAKBWTV* converts to 'Patriot,' a code name for one of our many unknowns, and *MVVXUJT* converts to 'Avenger,' whom we can, with some confidence, assume to be Booth. I would also hazard that 'Tyrant' was President Lincoln. We can work backward from the translations of Avenger and Patriot to unravel the cipher."

Augustus understood more clearly now. The telegrams in Booth's diary could all be unscrambled, and names and associations would begin to line up. Everyone in the District would want the tell-all, some for bad purpose, some for control, some for vengeance, some for a bit of each of those things.

"I'm anticipating your question," Temple said.

"Who got this journal off Booth's body to begin with, and how did it get out into the open?"

"And another question yet?"

"How and why did it come to be bundled with Mrs. Lincoln's diary?"

"So you've configured our mission and the questions are spread before us. We only need to knit the elements together and . . ."

Temple's voice trailed off and he stopped speaking. The pain in his leg was flaring again and his head hurt. He rubbed his brow and, leaving Augustus behind, slipped away to words.

> All folks who pretend to religion and grace
> Allow there's a hell, but dispute of the place:
> But, if hell may by logical rules be defined,
> The place of the damned: I'll tell you, my mind.

No, that wasn't it. It wasn't the tricks of his imagination or his past that caused his head to throb and his leg to ache. It was spun up by Booth's telegrams, and by the swamp into which he was dragging Fiona and Augustus. He knitted his fingers behind his head and began rocking slowly. He wanted to escape into a deck of cards or a tumble of dice. Fiona would have it out with him at some point, want to know why he'd courted trouble by meeting with Pint at the B&O. He could see her now, her finger wagging and her voice sharp, taking him to task for selling plunder to bankroll his gambling. "The money serves its purpose. Then I don't take any of ours or my pay to gamble," he would argue. "That's the beauty." She would have none of it, not a word. Stealing is stealing, she would say.

"Temple?"

He let his fingers drop from his brow and looked at Augustus, who was leaning toward him and searching his face.

"Temple?" he asked again. "You still with me?"

"I'm sorry."

Temple slipped the Vigenère table into his pocket, stared at the translated messages, and then snapped the diary shut. After rebundling it, he tied it together with Mrs. Lincoln's diary and handed the package to Augustus.

"Will you call Lexington?" Temple asked. "We need to send our treasures into the alleys."

CHAPTER ELEVEN

THE VAPORS

Fiona hitched her bag higher on her shoulder and resisted walking too briskly. After all, a reflection in a shop window and a looming slab with sunbeams bouncing off its hat did not, necessarily, a predator make.

Then again, of course it did.

I should have stayed in Alexander's studio and waited there. Temple could have found me. But that's not our plan. We meet at the Castle. But slow down, now. It's midday and the streets are populated. I could just wheel on him, give him some outright jesse, and attract a crowd. But he knows his way around his tasks and he'll divert. Noise won't deter him. He'll disappear and then circle back to me again. Our boardinghouse is probably no longer safe, either, and I can't be on the streets alone after the sun sets. Only Pennsylvania between the Capitol and the President's House is lighted by gas lamps—it will be shadow and peril elsewhere at dusk.

Fiona kept on a forward path along Pennsylvania. The Willard wasn't far away, but that was where Pinkerton kept his rooms. An easy solution wasn't at hand. About twenty yards ahead, a carriage pulled out of an alley near the Willard and stopped. A driver began loading bags onto the back of it; probably a hotel guest. Fiona stepped off the narrow sidewalk onto Pennsylvania's cobblestones and walked around the horses. As she turned back to the sidewalk, she glanced over her shoulder. Her man was no longer behind her. A conundrum.

She entered the Willard, which was buzzing, as always, with activity. Only men, though, walked freely around the lobby. There were other women there, but they were accompanied by men, most likely their husbands. Fiona looked carefully at two or three of them, wondering if in fact they were adventuresses rather than wives, and decided that they most certainly must be wives—the Willard wouldn't allow women of ill repute to parade in its lobby lest its reputation become sullied. There were no other unescorted women there, and as she continued to scan the room, Fiona realized that she, too, must be drawing attention, and not only from the hotel's patrons and visitors. Her eyes moved across the faces in the room and the tendrils of cigar smoke lacing the air until she found the concierge's desk. A lean, bald man with extravagant whiskers on either side of his jaw stared at her, assessing.

She nodded in his direction, refusing to show any unease. He slipped out from behind his desk and approached her.

"Madam."

"Sir."

"May I be of service in any way?"

"None whatsoever, thank you. I'm awaiting my husband."

"I trust he's on his way or a guest, ma'am?"

"On his way. I'm most grateful for your courtesies."

The concierge returned to his post behind an ornate desk the size of a wagon. He sorted through letters and telegrams but didn't sit down, alternately gazing at the envelopes in his hands and keeping Fiona in sight. She kept her eyes on the front doors, waiting for her pursuer to push through them. The pendulum in an ornate wooden clock hanging on the wall above her head swung back and forth as the seconds passed. Expensive German clocks were appearing in all of the District's finest homes and public places, but the Gustav Becker in the Willard was the most talked about. Cherubs were carved into the casing around its face, and its pendulum was a departure—instead of a brass sphere hanging from a wooden rail, the pendulum's bottom featured two more cherubs, one riding a lion and another playing a flute. "Mother and Child" was inscribed on a porcelain insert across the front of the pendulum. Fiona found herself wondering again about when she and Temple would have a child of their own. She spoke of the topic more freely and easily than he, and they simply never spoke about it quite enough. That would have to change, she thought.

"Madam?"

The concierge had returned.

"Your husband will be arriving soon?"

"Oh, yes. Any minute," Fiona responded, trying to consider what she might do when she returned to the street. "Sir, may I ask for an indulgence, please?"

"That will surely depend on its nature, ma'am."

"The heat today bears down upon me. Might you spare two kerchiefs for me? I'd be much obliged."

He shuffled wearily back to his desk, sliding open various drawers until he found some handkerchiefs. Fiona pulled one of the glass vials from her bag and transferred it into the small purse hanging from her left wrist, nodding in gratitude at the concierge when he returned. She put one of the kerchiefs into her bag and mopped her forehead with the other.

"My thanks."

"Of course, madam."

Fiona left the lobby and returned to the street, the concierge on her heels.

"Your husband has not arrived?"

"He has not."

"Unfortunate. Then I trust we won't enjoy your company again in our lobby."

"Sir, do you consider me an adventuress?"

The concierge went pale.

"Madam?"

"A hooker? Do you?"

"No, ma'am, I only—"

"Fine, then," Fiona said. "Call me a carriage. My husband is obviously misplaced and I must run to collect him. And we will return to the Willard together, I assure you. My husband will be pleased to make your acquaintance."

A yellow splash of sunlight beamed off her pursuer's hat, lighting the corner of Fiona's eye. A patient man. She made a show of slipping her hand into the crook of the concierge's arm.

"I believe the heat is taking command of me, sir," Fiona said. "Please secure a carriage for me with due haste."

FIONA ASSUMED THAT the man in the hat was behind her somewhere as her carriage rumbled down North B Street behind Reservation No. 1. She took the extra handkerchief from her shoulder bag, bunched it up, and stuffed it into her purse. She murmured a brief prayer to herself, wondering how long it would take for Temple to meet her at the Castle.

The grounds of the Smithsonian Castle were wreathed in late afternoon shadow, and the building's nine towers rose like red sandstone circus tents above the Mall. Dr. Springer held that Renwick had designed the Castle to look like the finest British universities, but Fiona maintained that the effect was closer to a carnival. Stepping down from the carriage and giving the driver his pay, Fiona noticed that even here the stench of the Tiber snared the air around her. Its odor wasn't as thick as it had been when her carriage crossed the canal from B Street to the Mall, but it remained powerful fierce.

She anticipated seeing another carriage or a horse behind her when she stepped down to the Castle's parklike grounds, but other than a few couples strolling nearby there was nobody. Her pursuer had disappeared again.

A fire had churned through the upper story of the Castle months earlier, and its windows were boarded while workmen made repairs inside. A maze of small rooms were scattered about the Castle's first floor, containing an art gallery, a lecture hall, a library, and a chemical laboratory.

Even on warm days, the Castle's architecture kept the building relatively cool. Fiona and Temple came here at least once a month for a walk and the exhibits; they had decided that it would always be their place to rendezvous if they became separated. And when they hatched the humbug to divert Mr. Pinkerton, they agreed that this would be the best place to meet at the end of the day.

Fiona stepped inside, pirouetting in a slow circle as she scanned the rooms. Again, completely empty other than an employee by the front door. Washingtonians still preferred drink, music, and theater to their only museum. Leaving the main hallway to view the other rooms, she kept an eye on the windows as she passed them. Coming around a shelf of books in the back of the library, she waited by yet another window; moments later, the man in the white hat stepped into the window's frame outside, just feet away from her, separated by glass and the Castle's heavy walls. He was shaded now, and for the first time she could clearly see his face: he had a single thick eyebrow forming a line below his forehead, angular cheekbones, a scar across his jaw, and a plump bottom lip. He stared at her blankly and then stepped away from the window again, disappearing. Her breath quickened and she gripped her bag more tightly, trying to stave off panic.

She left the library and entered the lecture hall at the far end of the Castle, leaving her shoulder bag by the doorway. There was a single gaslight burning on one of the walls; she extinguished it, then crossed back past the doorway and pressed herself against a wall. She assumed she would have just one chance and that the opportunity would last only seconds. She pulled the extra kerchief from the Willard and the vial of chloroform from her purse and waited. Several minutes later her pursuer entered the lecture hall and picked up her bag, standing just inside the doorway as his eyes adjusted to the darkness.

A sweet smell wafted from the bottle as she uncorked it. She doused the handkerchief and held it away at arm's length, stepping toward her pursuer.

"A strong tower of defense," she said, and the man spun around to face her, looming above her and holding her shoulder bag with both of his hands. She pressed the kerchief into his face, covering his nose and mouth. He shoved her hand away and knocked her to the floor, the planks slapping Fiona's back and shoulders as she dropped.

"What are you aiming to do with that?" he asked, grabbing her wrist and tearing the kerchief out of her hand, tossing it onto the floor behind him. "I'm no harm to you. I'm just meant to be following you."

"I don't like to be followed."

"I'm also obliged to examine your bag."

He began rummaging through it.

"Please do not shatter any of the bottles that I carry. They're valuable," Fiona said.

"Don't give a shat about your bottles, missy," he said.

He crouched down next to the bag and pulled out its contents, standing the vials on the floor and patting the inside of the bag.

"I'm told you might have a book or a journal of some sort in here," he said. "Where is it?"

"I don't have a journal in my bag."

He fished around inside the bag again until he was satisfied it was empty. Scooping up her bottles and other belongings, he poured them back into the bag and stood up.

"I'm taking this with me," he said. "You stay right there."

He turned to the door but had only taken a step before his knees wobbled. He leaned against the wall.

"My mouth," he said, pawing at his lips and jaw. "It's burning."

"I'm afraid the chloroform scorched your skin. You're a large man and I had to douse my kerchief. You'll heal."

"Form-a-clore?"

He tried to pull at his jaw with both hands, his arms so rubbery that his aim betrayed him and his arms crisscrossed on separate journeys. Fiona retrieved her kerchief from behind him and the chloroform bottle from her bag and prepared another dose. She held it over her pursuer's nose and mouth again, this time pressing it into his face for several seconds.

"The vapors won't hurt you—they'll just put you to sleep," she said to him as his head began to flop. He slumped back into her arms, and she let him slip to the floor. She looked out the entrance; the hallway was still empty, and nothing that had happened in the abandoned lecture hall had stirred the guard's interest. She returned to her pursuer, grabbing his ankles and straining to slide him across the wooden planking and into the dark gap between two rows of seats.

CHAPTER TWELVE

THE BORDELLO

It was good to be free of the diaries, Temple thought. A weight lifted. Augustus was looking after the journals' transit into the alleys, and all that was left for the day was to check in at police headquarters and then meet Fiona at the Castle.

Temple had walked the entire way from Tiber Island, and by the time he reached City Center, between Louisiana and E, he was thirsty and sweating. He could stop in for a drink at a saloon, but there was always beer in the precinct house. There were always drunks in there, too. Banning drink was Sergeant Miller's monthly cause on E Street, but few of the officers had given it up.

Two policemen were stationed outside the precinct house facing Louisiana and, doing as they were told, stood rigid and in the full uniform adopted when the force had been organized four years earlier: blue cavalry hats adorned with cap plates that read POLICE; navy blue waistcoats and, despite the heat, overcoats with brass buttons; gray or navy trousers; fat leather belts with buckles that read DC; Colt Navy 6's tucked inside their belts and under their coats; billy clubs in the left or right hand but never tucked away; and badges pinned to their left breast pockets and secured with a small chain linked to a button on their overcoats.

They were municipal toughs proud of their station and on patrol, really, to keep the District in order in a way that Stanton and the other federals found comfortable and reassuring. Insurrection and dissent had already split the Union. No reason to tolerate it in the District itself.

Temple never wore the uniform and carried his badge inside his trouser pocket. Instead of a billy club he had his cane; he never carried a gun. Sergeant Miller let him follow his own course because Temple was one of the few who wasn't a drunk and who kept regular hours. And because, when Temple first arrived in the District from New York, Tommy Driscoll, the greatest detective of them all, had vouched for him.

Outside the City Center precinct, and not far from where the two policemen stood, was a tall, thick whipping post where slaves were once shackled and disciplined, either for trying to escape or for merely looking to the sky when they should have been staring at the ground. Now riders used the post to hitch their horses.

Temple would have marched right past the whipping post and into the precinct, but even at two blocks he recognized the saddle strapped atop an enormous, muscled stallion tied there. It was a rich brown saddle ornamented in silver with long stirrups meant to hoist a very large man. It was the same saddle he had sat upon when he raced away from the B&O mornings ago, but now atop a new horse equally as impressive and majestic as the one that had been shot out from beneath him.

Lafayette Baker was visiting the precinct.

A block away from City Center rose the First Presbyterian Church. Temple went inside, pulling himself along on a banister and hip-hopping—good leg, bad leg, good leg, bad leg—up the stairs to its cupola so that he could look down on the precinct. About an hour later, Baker emerged with Sergeant Miller in tow. The two men talked amiably, their heads nodding. Baker slipped an envelope into a pocket of Miller's coat, patting it gently. Well, the sergeant might rail against drink, but he cared not a jot about hard-earned graft. Temple watched Baker mount his horse, and then he descended from the cupola.

The precinct was no longer safe.

MARY ANN HALL sat in a high-backed leather chair in a corner office, her left arm entwined in the arm of a lovely Negro girl in her twenties perched on the edge of the chair and naked except for a small diamond bracelet dangling from one of her ankles. Mary Ann tipped the glass of champagne in her hand toward Temple, offering him a sip. He smiled and shook his head.

"You have faro debts with us, Detective McFadden. My dealers confide that you are twenty-five dollars in arrears. And you have thirty dollars in debts from hazard."

"The fashion now is for folks to call it craps, not hazard."

"I shall call the dice what I want to call the dice when they are rolled in my establishment."

"Your privilege indeed, Mary Ann. And I'm not here to argue with you."

"Nor are you here to pay your debts, I take it."

"I'm interested in one of your guests."

"The gentleman you scuffled with at the B&O?"

"The same."

"He beats some of my women," she said, stroking the girl's cheek and tipping her champagne flute into her mouth. "If he never patronized us again, we wouldn't miss him."

"It may get noisy upstairs."

"We shall not hear a thing, Detective."

THERE WERE HUNDREDS of registered and perfectly legal bawdy houses in the District, but few, Temple thought to himself as he limped up yet another flight of stairs, could rank themselves as bordellos. And even among the bordellos, none compared to Mary Ann's. She'd been conducting business in her three-story brownstone for more than two decades, growing independent and wealthy due to grit (word was that she had sliced the throat of a competitor who opened an establishment next door on Maryland Avenue) and location (she was only two blocks away from the Capitol and just several more from the B&O).

But in four short years the war had made Mary Ann far richer than she had ever been before, swelling the city's size and the amount of cash and men flowing through and allowing her to become one of the District's wealthiest women. She catered to Washington's elite: generals, congressmen, foreign diplomats, Georgetown tobacco traders, actors, railroad executives, and New Yorkers on weekend sprees. She also took in large shipments of Piper-Heidsieck imported from France, charging guests $15 to uncork a bottle; fed her patrons fish, fowl, beef, and berries on gilt-edged porcelain; and maintained twenty parlor girls who were healthy, conversant, and nimble and wore little more than dressing gowns.

My only books
Were women's looks,
And folly's all they've taught me.

A gleaming silver spittoon rested on a marble-topped table at the foot of the staircase leading to the third floor, and Temple paused to listen. Mary Ann had rebuilt her walls thick, and other than fragments of laughter, conversation, and occasional moans as doors opened and closed, he could hear little beyond piano strains rising from the first-floor foyer. At the end of the second-floor hallway a small, naked woman balanced a pewter tray larded with food and drink on her shoulder as she knocked on one of the doors. Temple placed his cane on the first step leading upstairs and began climbing again.

That matters had now tumbled into Hall House was his first drop of serendipity, he thought to himself. One of the sentries at City Center's entrance said that Baker had boasted to Sergeant Miller that he was on his way to Hall House for amusement, inviting Miller to join him. Ever industrious, Miller declined. Baker's choice relieved Temple. It was only a brief walk from City Center to Mary Ann's, which meant he wouldn't need a horse. More important, the madam was well disposed toward him.

When reformers had indicted Mary Ann a year earlier as a "public nuisance," Temple suggested she let slip the notion that some of her patrons' names—including those of the police superintendent and leading politicians—might find their way into the *Evening Star*. The indictment disappeared, much to the disgust of Augustus and Fiona, who regarded bawdy houses as havens of sexual slavery. Temple reminded them that Mary Ann funded the escape of slaves, including several whom Augustus had helped, but they held firm. Temple didn't tell them that Mary Ann was also one of his most reliable threads for District gossip.

Halfway down the third-floor hallway, a lone Union soldier stood outside one of the doors.

"I have a telegram for Mr. Baker," Temple said to the soldier as he approached the door.

The soldier held out his hand to receive the message, and Temple grabbed his wrist, pulling the man toward him. "My apologies," he said, driving the rounded brass top of his cane into the corner of the soldier's jaw. Temple stepped over the soldier's body and turned the knob. No locked doors permitted in Hall House. One never knew when a gentleman, fired in the loins like an Arkie, might get out of hand.

Temple stepped into a lavishly appointed suite. A red plush settee and matching chair occupied a corner, next to a mirror-fronted wardrobe that offered a reflection of a tall, tired man leaning on a cane. Against the far wall was a massive bed, adorned with several feather bolsters and a plump feather and shuck mattress. Oysters, coconut, turtle, beef, and red wine were untouched on a table at the foot of the bed.

A girl, perhaps a teenager, was bent over the side of the bed, naked except for a single feather stuck inside a band around her forehead. Lafayette Baker's pants were around his ankles and he was mounting the girl from behind.

"She's playing a squaw," Baker said, not bothering to interrupt his thrusts. "First we take the Secesh, then the army takes the Injuns. One country."

Temple didn't reply as he moved farther into the suite.

"You're not going to leave this room alive, I hope you know," said Baker, backing away from the girl and hitching up his trousers. The rest of his uniform and the LeMat were in a pile on a chair.

"You wear costumes and your adventuresses wear costumes," said Temple. "When we met at the B&O, Baker, you were dressed like a gent, and now you're wearing a uniform. Which is it?"

"Very good work—you know my name and I still don't know yours. We need to get to know each other better. If we don't, I'll have to force the information out of you."

"I think we need to converse alone. Your lady can go."

The girl pulled a blanket from the bed and wrapped it around herself, fleeing through the door. Baker eyed his gun on the chair.

"I wouldn't," said Temple.

"I won't need a gun, gimp."

"Then sit down."

"No, I won't be doing that, either."

Baker looked even larger than he had at the B&O, and his shoulders and arms were knotted with muscles.

"Why were there two groups of men at the B&O?"

"What's your name?"

"My questions first."

"We had competing interests."

"Why?"

"Have you read the diaries?"

Temple didn't answer.

"Ah, I can see in your eyes you read them. You're afeared. You know what you have and you can't contain it."

"Why did you want them?"

"My question. What's your name?"

"I don't think I'll be answering that," Temple said.

Baker charged Temple, yanking the oyster tray off the table at the foot of the bed. He had taken Temple's cane in the forehead once before and this time he was prepared, holding the tray near his shoulder like a shield. Temple swiveled to the side on his good leg and grabbed Baker by the back of his trousers as he rushed past, thrusting him along. Baker's head slammed into the mirror on the front of the wardrobe and the glass shattered.

Shaking his head to clear it, Baker touched his forehead, where blood ran out of a gash. He picked a long shard of the broken mirror from the floor and rounded again, facing Temple.

"I'll slice you up now, fingerlicker."

He charged, and Temple brought his cane up into Baker's crotch. Baker yelped, dropping the glass. But he swung an arm around Temple's neck and hauled him down to the ground with him. He tightened his arm into a hammerlock. Temple began to choke, the air in his lungs trying to escape in clipped bursts. He slammed the butt of his palm twice into Baker's throat, and Baker rolled to the side gagging.

Temple hauled himself up and retrieved his cane. He grabbed Baker's LeMat from the chair, pushed the uniform off the seat, and sat down.

"There now. If you won't sit down, Mr. Baker, I will," Temple panted.

Baker slid over to the bed and sat up against it. Temple aimed the LeMat at him.

"You'll never walk with safety in the District again," Baker hissed.

"Who sent you to the B&O?"

"I went for my own needs."

"If I used your *pistola* on your knee, then you'd need a cane like me, Mr. Baker."

Baker didn't respond and Temple fired into the rug to the right of Baker's leg. Baker flinched and wiped more blood from his forehead. A small cloud of gunsmoke filled the space between the two men.

"I work for Stanton."

"Edwin Stanton? The secretary of war?"

"None other. The other group at the B&O were Pinkertons. Pinkerton and Stanton are at odds."

"Why the diaries?"

"None of that. You've gotten what you'll get out of me." Baker stood up, blood smeared across his brow and in his beard, sweat streaming across his torso. He moved again toward Temple, who also rose.

"Sit down, Mr. Baker."

"You're not a killer. I've been with killers. You won't do it."

Baker lunged, ramming his shoulder into Temple's stomach and pressing him against the wall. Temple dropped the LeMat as the wind was forced out of him, and as he slid to the floor, Baker let go of him, reaching down for his gun. Temple sliced his cane into the back of Baker's ankles, causing the colossus to scream again and buckle backward to the floor.

"You are a dead man," gasped Baker, rolling his head toward Temple and smearing blood on the rug. "I'm looking at a dead man."

Temple slammed the top of his cane into the side of Baker's head. Baker's lips flittered as he blacked out.

"No more out of you this evening," Temple said.

He lumbered up again on his cane, pulled a billfold from Baker's jacket, and left the room.

PART TWO

MARS

CHAPTER THIRTEEN

THE CROSSING

"You're bleeding."

"You're safe."

Fiona was sitting in a pool of shade beneath a tree on the Castle grounds, surrounded by tall grass sprinkled with daisies. She had her bag beside her and a smile across her face as she looked up at Temple. His coat was draped on his arm and a magenta blossom stained his shirt at the left shoulder.

"Forced into my escapade and batted about the District, but you never waver," Temple said. "There's not a bead of perspiration on you. Have you been waiting long?"

"You're bleeding, Temple."

"Shall we stay here or shall we move on?"

"We can stay for a moment. I was followed; there's a man inside napping, and he'll stir soon. Or the guard will find him. But we have a moment."

"You were followed?"

Fiona nodded.

Temple leaned his cane against the tree trunk and dropped to one knee beside her, allowing his bad leg to splay away from his body. He placed his hands on her shoulders and gazed at her.

"I love your eyes."

"I love you," she whispered.

He tilted her chin up and kissed her, holding his mouth against hers longer than either of them would ever consider proper in public.

"I'm sorry for all of this," he said as he sat down beside her against the tree.

"What is 'all of this,' anyhow? Beyond helping you divert Mr. Pinkerton, I'm in a fog."

Fiona pulled a cloth from her bag and pressed it inside Temple's shirt at the shoulder, where the blood had matted. She ran her fingers over the shoulder toward his back and found the top of the bullet wound from Center Market. Temple winced as she pressed down slightly. Two of his six stitches had burst.

"We'll have to mend you again. Did you fall?"

"No, I was thrown into a wall at a bawdy house."

"A bawdy house?"

Temple detailed his encounter with Baker at Mary Ann Hall's, as well as their earlier dustup at the B&O. Fiona listened closely to every word, but seemed, in the end, to be much more interested in his descriptions of Mary Ann.

"She's wealthy?"

"Very," Temple replied.

"And independent of the law?"

"Also."

"Imagine that!" Fiona exclaimed. "A woman of enterprise."

"It is a mournful place," Temple replied.

"The entire District is a mournful place. Even so, I don't like the thought of you in a bawdy house. Have you gambled there?"

"Tell me about the graveyard," Temple said.

Fiona told him about the surprise on Pinkerton's face when he encountered her at dawn, which drew a chuckle from Temple. His smile disappeared when she told him about the argument between Pint and Alexander at the studio, and his face grew taut when she told him about the man in the gleaming hat who had followed her here.

"Mr. Pinkerton's reach around the District is impressive," Temple said. "It won't be easy to move without him seeing us or finding us."

"But move we must. You can't go much longer with an open wound. It will draw disease."

"Mary Ann gave me a carriage after I left Baker to her care. It's across the grounds by the Seventh Street Bridge."

"That will take us past Center Market as we go into town," Fiona said.

"I think it's best I avoid the market this time," said Temple, pulling his coat back on and picking up his cane. "It's time for us to impose upon Augustus. We'll be safer there than at our boarding-house. And I'll need your help with what we have to do next."

Fiona glanced back at the Castle, its sandstone façade dimmed to rust as the afternoon drew to a close and the light began to weaken. There was no movement at the door. No guard and no pursuer. A feathery breeze moved through the leaves and swept across the Smithsonian's grounds as Fiona and Temple made their way toward the bridge.

THERE WERE ONLY three clapboard houses on the rolling, grassy field surrounding the Campbell Hospital, and one of them belonged to Augustus. Well tended, with a white frame and black shutters, Augustus's home came into view just as Temple and Fiona's carriage neared Boundary Street, at the northern end of 7th, where the District began to end and the countryside, all thick trees and bad roads, began.

At the start of the war the hospital had been a cavalry barracks, and it still looked the part, long and low-slung with a simple peaked roof. Augustus had moved here only recently because the Freedmen's Bureau was converting the Campbell once again; this time it would become a freedmen's hospital where former slaves and free Negroes could get medical care. Fiona shook her head slightly as they neared it.

"Walt Whitman nursed soldiers here. He spoke with me once when we were tending patients at the Patent Office, and he thought the Campbell and some of the other hospitals killed just as many soldiers as they saved," she said. "He said he saw two boys needlessly die here—one because of a know-nothing master of the ward who mistakenly gave him an overdose of opium pills and laudanum, the second because they accidentally let him drink muriate of ammonia intended to clean his muddy feet."

They stepped down from the carriage and walked up a small incline to Augustus's home. Temple knocked and then looked back at the hospital.

"Augustus plans for happier days here now that the war is over," he said. "He's teaching at the hospital, and there is talk of opening a university for Negroes around the corner within the next year or two. There's already a trade school in the hospital where women can learn to sew."

The door swung open, and Augustus stood in the entrance, beaming at Temple and Fiona. Fiona stepped up and kissed Augustus on the cheek. As the two men embraced, Temple flinched.

"Are you hurt again?" Augustus asked.

"My shoulder's reopened, that's all," Temple said, his mouth curled up in amusement. "You live in a *white house*, Augustus."

"Unlike the President's House, mine wasn't built with the help of slaves," Augustus responded. "Look at all we have here. We have a hospital and a school, we'll soon have a university, and we have a growing population of free Negroes. We won't stop there—we'll have a bank, a building company, and our own businesses, too. The Freedmen's Bureau will make the District the nation's home for free Negroes, and the center of it, the very start of it, will be here, in the Shaw."

"Why here? Why not downtown?"

"Already whites don't want us there. Renters are being turned away; some Negroes looking for housing have been beaten. So they're coming here. I've gotten a loan from the Freedmen's Bureau to build my house, and others will build after me."

"It is called the Shaw now?" Fiona asked.

"The District has given our neighborhood a name, yes."

"What is Shaw?"

"Shaw is a who—the army colonel killed leading the black regiment that launched the first attack on Fort Wagner."

"Ah," Temple said. "You can live here, but they'll still name it after a white man."

"It won't be the only instance, either," Augustus replied. "Oliver Howard is one of the commissioners at the bureau. He's a good man, a general in the army, and he's raised money for the university. But there's talk that they will name the university after him. I've told the bureau that it would be a high and mighty honor to name it after Frederick Douglass, but I won't prevail in that discussion."

Augustus led them inside, to a small parlor with a table and a few chairs. As they sat down, he looked out the window at the hospital.

"Names for neighborhoods and universities are a small concession. We are still building something of our own here. It is a magnificent start. Negroes will earn a wage and get an education. Those things are where freedom lies; I've come to think that maybe they are more important than even the vote."

"Step by step," said Temple.

"Amen. But I don't suppose you came here to discuss the rights of the Negro."

"I came because it's time to share what we have with Fiona. So we will need the diaries."

"I'll have to send for them."

Augustus left the parlor and stepped outside. When he returned, he found Temple, shirtless, with Fiona fussing over his shoulder. Temple's shirt, stained with the blood from his wound, was balled up and tossed in a corner.

"You'll need a new shirt as well as the diaries," Augustus said.

"He'll also need one of your bedrooms," Fiona said as she dug into her bag. "I'll need to stitch him again. Might he sleep until we have the diaries?"

"He might," said Augustus, leading them toward the back of the house.

TEMPLE WAS ASLEEP in Augustus's bedroom, two fresh stitches in his shoulder, when there was a knock at the front door. Augustus opened it to find an elderly woman on his doorstep holding the satchel with the diaries and a fresh shirt draped over her arm. She was slightly stooped, and a white knit cap clung tightly to her head, matched by a white shawl draped over her shoulders. The cap and shawl almost shimmered against her gleaming ebony skin, and a pair of rectangular spectacles sat across the bridge of her nose. She looked up at Augustus from behind her glasses and smirked.

"Well, say something, Augustus," she said.

"Isabella Baumfree!"

"Don't you try to get my goat, boy. I stay Sojourner Truth."

Augustus turned to Fiona as he ushered Sojourner through the door.

"Mrs. Baumfree is a nurse here at the Freedmen's Hospital. It is an honorary position because the good Lord knows she hasn't a wit about her when it comes to medicine."

Sojourner reached up and slapped him on the back. Augustus, coughing and laughing, put his arm around her shoulders.

"Sojourner Truth is Mrs. Baumfree's stage name. She has used it for many years to great and wonderful effect, for she indeed blesses all of us with the truth."

"I am acquainted with your fine words, Mrs. Truth, and I honor them," Fiona said. "Elizabeth Cady Stanton and others have made market of them in pamphlets examining the plight of the woman and the plight of the Negro."

"There's a darling child," Sojourner said, reaching up to put her hand on Fiona's cheek. She shuffled into the parlor and put the satchel on the table, explaining that although Augustus had sent a boy down to the alleys to fetch the satchel, when the boy returned, she encountered him and decided to deliver it herself.

"I told him it would provide me reason for a visit and I would take it to you. So here I am."

"Will you eat with us?" Augustus asked.

"Naw, just a visit, no more."

"I heard you were speechifying downtown yesterday."

"Truly. I gave them my regular on the meanin' of this war: where there is so much racket, there must be something out of kilter. I think that 'twixt the Negroes of the South and the women of the North, all talking about rights, the white men will be in a fix pretty soon."

Fiona stepped into the parlor, her face lit with excitement.

"I know this speech, Mrs. Truth! It is your 'Aren't I a Woman?' is it not?" Fiona asked.

"It is indeed, child."

"Give us some, Sojourner," Augustus said. "Inspire and motivate."

Sojourner stood at the table, took her glasses off, and raised her right hand in the air, poking toward the ceiling with her index finger. Her voice was charged and high, and she launched into her speech with the cadence of a preacher and a passion exceeding her frame.

"Look at me! Look at my arm! I have plowed, and planted, and gathered into barns, and no man could head me! And aren't I a woman? I could work as much and eat as much as a man—when I could get it—and bear the lash as well! And aren't I a woman? I have borne thirteen children, and seen them most all sold off to slavery, and when I cried out with my mother's grief, none but Jesus heard me! And aren't I a woman?"

Augustus clapped and nodded in time with each of Sojourner's sentences, his entire body beginning to rock. Fiona joined in, her own clapping growing faster as Sojourner's speech rose to a crescendo.

"If the first woman God ever made was strong enough to turn the world upside down all alone, these women together ought to be able to turn it back, and get it right side up again!"

Sojourner's voice rose more powerfully as she concluded: "And now they are asking to do it, the men better let them."

When she finished speaking, the room was silent and still. She ran her hands down the front of her dress and sat down. She looked up at Augustus and Fiona with a broad, proud smile spread across her face.

"Mrs. Baumfree, you make us all proud," Augustus said, leaning down toward her.

She tried to kick Augustus in the shin but missed. He performed an extravagant dodge, laughing loudly again.

"There you go again, boy," she said. "As I spoke it before, I remain Sojourner Truth, and I'm set against even lettin' you have this satchel that I toiled to bring y'all. But I will gladly give it up if you introduce me proper to this delight."

"She's Temple's wife," Augustus said. "Her name is Fiona."

"She's a mercy and a gift," Sojourner said, turning toward Fiona. "Your husband is a righteous man. He aided me gettin' Negroes on the streetcars."

"He has told me and has spoken equally highly of you, Mrs. Truth."

"Where he be?"

"Sleeping in the back."

"Not even five bells yet and he's sleepin'? Not hardly. What ails your man?"

"He's just fine, Sojourner," said Augustus.

"No need for me to look in on him?"

"No need. But join us for supper? I have a root cellar and a garden here."

"No. On my way."

She got up from her chair, leaving the satchel on the table, and walked to the door. Augustus hugged her on her way out.

"It is always a pleasure, Sojourner," he said.

"Rightly, always mine," she replied. "I'm back to the hospital to ministrate. We got to keep buildin' up our new neighborhood here."

Augustus walked back into the parlor, pulled the satchel across the table, and began to open it. As Fiona sat down beside him, he told her about the diaries. While he was speaking, she reached for two thick candles in the middle of the table and lit them.

TEMPLE'S BED SWAYED, tossed about on waves, and his fingers spidered toward its edges in search of rails that weren't there, rails like those that had run across the side of his tiny bunk in the cramped first-class cabin Dr. McFadden had booked for them when they crossed the Atlantic.

Even in his dreams, the roar of the ocean enveloped everything else: the smell of the pigs and cattle packed into steerage in the bottom of the *Washington,* which they'd boarded in Liverpool; the moaning creak of wood as her timbers, three masts, and 420 tons strained against the sea; the shouts and cries of poorer passengers down below, enduring this to escape An Gorta Mór, notices to quit their land, and their families dying in droves in Ireland; and a seven-year-old's gasps of breath as he fought off nausea and fear, clutching tightly to the rails of his bunk.

Closing his eyes while he and the ship surrounding him spun atop gray-green cliffs of water that made his stomach surge; hoping the storms threatening to swallow him wouldn't expand the crossing's duration from six weeks to ten, but knowing that they would; trusting that the passage's torture was a bridge from the suffocation of the orphanage to what lay beyond Castle Garden.

Ich am of Irlonde and of the holy land of Irlonde.

Dr. McFadden's hand was on his forehead.

"There now, Temple, you were brave on the steamer from Dublin to Liverpool, and I know you can be brave again now."

"The steamer only took twelve hours," he said, a tear rolling down his cheek.

"And I will read you poetry to pass the time and we will memorize our favorites together. If you have the Lord, your family, and poems, you can overcome anything."

Dr. McFadden pulled a bucket to the side of the bed to catch the vomit that erupted from Temple's mouth.

"There's a young man from Germany in the cabin next to ours. He comes from good stock, and his parents say he fences with proficiency. They said they'd be happy for him to tutor you. And there's a teenager in steerage who is a tough; he fights for pay in Dublin. He needs money, and I've hired him to school you as well."

"I don't have a sword, and both of those boys are older."

"You have your cane. You'll learn to use it for something more than a crutch. The two of them will give you a start, so bullies can't get after you anymore, like they did at the orphanage. We have weeks on this ship—we'll find ways for you to progress."

Again Temple vomited.

The Germans were the only other family on the *Washington* with the means to secure a cabin. It cost £50 per person to book first-class passage, and with the famine spreading across Ireland, only those with estates, inheritances, or a profession could manage that sum. Most paid the £19 for steerage and shared space with animals—and disease. Four children who had died of typhus were dropped over the *Washington*'s sides during the fourth week out.

Dr. McFadden had gone down to steerage in the second week to try to treat some of the passengers there, but he was grim when he returned to the cabin. He said the planks that the folk slept on were crawling with abominations and that he was hard pressed to remain below very long because the belly of the ship breathed up a rank, wet stench. Families broke up the biscuits they were rationed because weevils were laced throughout. They tried making a porridge out of water and the biscuit powder, but some slowly starved.

"Temple, remember the wharves in Liverpool?" Dr. McFadden asked him. "How you loved the huge stone piers and the granite that laced the docks? And the view across the Mersey to Birkenhead?"

"Yes."

"I am told that the wharves in New York are horrid by comparison. They are flimsy wood things, and poorly kept."

"So we should have stayed in Liverpool?"

"No, because beyond the docks in Liverpool are muck and misery and beyond the wharves in New York are opportunity and promise. We travel for the latter."

Bridget McFadden never pushed Temple as hard as her husband did, but from the day that they plucked him from the orphanage and took him to their home she insisted he read as much as he possibly could. She corrected his grammar, worked with him on his writing, and sang to him when he was sick. She had long, lovely fingers and wide green eyes, and on the slowest days aboard the *Washington* she taught Temple how to braid her red hair and help her clip it into a bun, promising Temple that they would find their way through the water and the foam and the wind to the other side.

During the fifth week out from Liverpool, she became ill. During the sixth week out, she died.

After that, Temple could never remember any of his conversations with her, though there were many occasions later in his life when he would sit by himself and try, unsuccessfully, to recall and recapture even a few words.

For several days Dr. McFadden barely spoke to him, often burying himself in a blanket in their cabin. As the weather calmed, Temple spent hours on the deck, working with his cane and his fists as the boys hired by the doctor trained him. Initially they were patient and turned all of the lessons into games. As Temple improved, they made it harder.

He was better with his cane than with his fists because the boys were both taller than he, so he fended them off by holding his cane in front of himself with two hands, waggling it back and forth and looping it in arcs and jabs. He also began to learn how to support most of his weight on his left leg when he couldn't lean on his cane.

The German boy had found a length of wood in a small supply shed amidships and replaced his épée with it; whenever he and Temple dueled, it was accompanied by repeated cracks of wood upon wood.

When they practiced with fists, Temple was still too young and too small to gain an advantage on the fighter from steerage. If he landed a blow, the older boy would smack him back quickly, raising a small pink welt on his cheek. As he had with his fencing tutor, however, Temple stayed the course, learning to balance his weight on one leg as he protected his face with his hands and made quick jabs at the older boy's body.

During the ninth week out the storms came again, and Temple took to his bunk. One morning he found the doctor sitting on a stool, sobbing. Temple approached him and put his hand on the doctor's.

"I could call you Father now," Temple said.

Dr. McFadden wiped his sleeve across his face and pulled Temple into his arms. It was warm there. Temple wobbled back to his bunk, his stomach churning again as waves pounded the ship, and he became aware of other voices and sounds. One, familiar and clear, wasn't from the *Washington*. It came from beyond the ship and beyond Temple's dream.

"We cannot keep these. It is a violation."

He knew this voice. Fiona.

"They are not ours. They are hers."

Fiona rarely raised her voice, but now she was almost shouting. Temple slid up into a sitting position in the bed and listened more closely as his head cleared. Fiona was arguing with Augustus, who barely protested. Temple climbed out of bed, put his bloodstained shirt back on, and tucked it into the waist of his pants. He was hungry and thirsty.

When he walked into the parlor, he found Augustus and Fiona seated at a candlelit table, with the diaries open in front of them. There was a generous spread of food on the table, and a shirt was hanging off the back of one of the chairs. Augustus stared silently at a wall while Fiona looked up at Temple in anger, her face visibly flushed even in the candlelight.

"She is the president's widow, Temple McFadden, and you have no right to her particulars."

"Fiona."

"No right. They are her private thoughts."

Temple reached out and held her hands in his.

"Do you know who wrote the other journal that we have?"

"I do."

"We have the diary of an assassin and the diary of the president's wife and—"

"The president's widow," Fiona said, interrupting him.

"Yes. The president's widow. To whom might we return her diary?"

"Mrs. Lincoln."

Temple began laughing but stopped when he glanced at Augustus, who was still silent. When he looked back at Fiona, her arms were across her chest.

"Temple, these are Mrs. Lincoln's thoughts. She has been deprived of enough already."

"We'll be killed trying to return this to her."

"And why?"

Temple sat down. "Fiona, I have a hole in my shoulder. We have strangers following us. You understand why."

"I understand we have something they want. I understand that," she said. "But I don't understand why there is murder or death associated with any of this. That I don't. Do you?"

"Some things have become clearer to me, and some things are a mystery still. I intend to use part of tomorrow to clarify things. But whoever wanted these writings spirited from the Capitol—and whoever else was of the opposite persuasion and wanted to prevent Mr. Tigani's departure—all of them were willing to kill to achieve their goals."

"Your Mr. Pinkerton?"

"Perhaps. Or others."

"Well, then, read Mrs. Lincoln's papers and return them to her," Fiona said. "But you can't keep them."

"How would you get them to her?" Temple asked.

"Lizzy Keckly. She and Augustus are acquainted."

Now Temple understood why Augustus was so silent. Elizabeth Keckly, a former slave, was Mrs. Lincoln's modiste, and Fiona intended to reach the widow through her. Temple sat down and looked up at the shadows from the candles as they swam across the ceiling. Augustus was looking at him, still silent.

"You'll be putting yourself at risk," Temple said.

"I am capable," Fiona replied.

The three of them gazed at the candles and at one another without saying a word.

Temple surveyed the table as he pulled a loaf of bread toward him: there was a wedge of cheese, a bowl of peaches, pickles on a bed of lettuce, molasses, a bottle of walnut catsup, a portion of pigeon, a pitcher of water, a pitcher of switchel, and three delicacies that Augustus had gone to great expense to have for them—a tin of deviled ham and two Havana cigars. Temple avoided the bottle of nectar whiskey sitting on the corner of the table but indulged heartily in all of the food.

Save for an occasional dog barking in the woods, Augustus's home was quiet. Nearly half an hour passed before anyone spoke.

"May Augustus and I share these Havanas, Fiona?" Temple asked.

"Outside, please."

"You're angry with me."

"All I wish is that we resolve our debate over Mrs. Lincoln."

Temple pondered this, staring again at the candles. Augustus poured a glass of switchel and slowly drank it.

"I suspect all of us are a mite bit afraid right now," Temple said.

He stood up and stripped off his bloodied shirt, replacing it with the fresh shirt hanging on the chair. Then he slid his chair closer to Fiona's and put his arm around her.

"Fiona, if you return the diary to Mrs. Lincoln, it would be valuable if you did something more than merely hand it over," he said.

"And that would be?"

"Speak with her. Spend time with her. We can consider opportunities that may allow you to visit with her more than once. You can ask her what her thoughts are. You can ask her why she believes her husband was murdered."

CHAPTER FOURTEEN

THE SÉANCE

Fiona left early the next morning, before Temple or Augustus awoke. When Temple arose he found Augustus at the table, bent once more over the diary.

Temple sat beside him, placing the Vigenère table next to the pages with the telegrams. He also tossed a billfold onto the table. It was tan leather with two pouches inside and a strap holding it closed. One pouch contained greenbacks, and the other held several documents.

"Whose is that?" Augustus asked.

"His name is Lafayette Baker. He's the man I traded blows with in front of the B&O. I borrowed this from him at Mary Ann Hall's after he popped my stitches."

Temple took ten dollars from the billfold and dropped it in front of Augustus.

"This should pay for the food last night and some of your other fixings," Temple said. "Mr. Baker owes us that courtesy, I believe."

"Do you have a path into this code and these telegrams?" Augustus asked.

"I think we can both try to get a start, and then we shall show some of our work to Pint, as he is the expert in these matters."

The telegrams were in front of them on the table, one encrypted and three decrypted:

March 4, 1865
From: BAKBWTV
To: MVVXUJT

    FHVBS NU A ZBAM WYF DQU IG ZAKSCSCL. Q NY FFB SQOIZN
MNU WCSURMNX. HFBGJU TW EUCYWCSF WPRZ YFE VFXE
BLDAED.

April 5, 1865
From: Patriot
To: Avenger

    *Maestro sends funds. Goliath and others will join you. Wise Man
and Drinker should be taken with Tyrant.*

April 11, 1865
From: Patriot
To: Avenger

    You will be allowed to pass at Navy Yard Bridge. Refuge at Tavern.

April 14, 1865
From: Patriot
To: Avenger

    *It is Ford's. Praetorians send a Parker to guard Tyrant. He will aban-
don the door or let you pass.*

"As you told me when you first showed these to me, the first part
of our challenge will be easy, thanks to Booth," Augustus said. "If we
presume that the encrypted message is from Patriot and to
Avenger—like the others that Booth decrypted—then we can work
backward and learn how it might fit with the Vigenère table."

"You've done some of this already this morning?" Temple asked.

"I have."

Augustus placed a sheet of paper on the table with two of the
decrypted and encrypted words lined above each other in columns:

PATRIOT   AVENGER
BAKBWTV   MVVXUJT

Augustus pulled the Vigenère table closer to them both and pointed out on the table where the matching letters intersected. The P in *PATRIOT,* from the table's vertical axis, and the B in *BAKBWTV,* from the middle of the table, traced upward to M on the horizontal axis. He repeated this with each of the letters in each of the words, mating the vertical letters with its partner inside the table and then finding a link to a letter above on the horizontal axis.

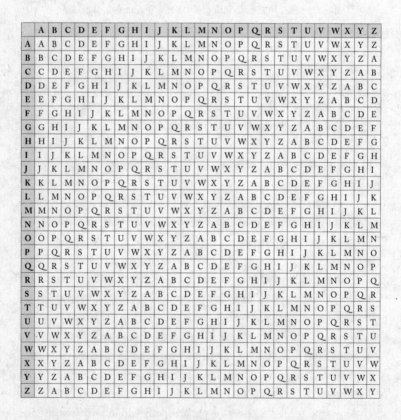

When Augustus was done, he had a sheet of paper in front of him with six words on it:

```
PATRIOT     AVENGER
BAKBWTV     MVVXUJT
MARKOFC     MARKOFC
```

"Now our challenge takes on a different shade," Temple said. "We no longer have any simple words to pair together from the decrypted and encrypted messages."

"But we do have some portion of the code," Augustus said brightly. "We have *MARKOFC*, and we could apply that to the beginning of the first encrypted message we have."

"To the point!" Temple said, squeezing Augustus's shoulder. "Do some more of your handiwork."

Augustus wrote down the first sentence of the encrypted message, with as much of the code beneath it as he could:

```
FHVBSNUAZBAMWYFDQUIGZAKSCSCL
MARKOFC
```

With the code in hand, Augustus then reversed his earlier method; he dropped down from *M* on the horizontal axis to mate it with *F* in the middle of the table, and looked across at the vertical axis to see what letter linked to it. That gave him this much:

```
FHVBSNUAZBAMWYFDQUIGZAKSCSCL
MARKOFC
THEREIS
```

"I think the single letter *A* after 'There is' is likely to be, in fact, *A*," Temple said. "So it would read 'There is a . . .' Though I am in a conundrum over what the rest of this will say."

"But we also know more of our code now," said Augustus. "The *A* in the sentence would match with *A* in the table. So our code is now *MARKOFCA*."

Temple stared at the code, nodding his head as he studied it.

"Damn."

Temple picked up Booth's diary and thumbed quickly through the pages. When he found the page he was looking for, he slapped the diary down on the table.

"Damn."

"What?" asked Augustus.

"I have it. It's right here."

FIONA WAITED IN Lafayette Park, across the street from the President's House, where Augustus had told her that Lizzy Keckly would pass in the morning. Union soldiers were still encamped in the square, and enough people were about on this Saturday morning that Fiona would have to watch sharply not to miss Lizzy. But she had an advantage: there would be few Negro women able to enter or leave the mansion freely, much less one who would be, as Augustus was quick to tell Fiona, one of the best-dressed women on Pennsylvania Avenue.

Lizzy was Mrs. Lincoln's dressmaker, and the pair sometimes shopped together, with Lizzy often forced to wait outside stores that barred her entry. While Lizzy's clothes scarcely matched the cost or elegance of those her mistress wore—few women in the District, of any means or background, could match Mrs. Lincoln's spending, after all—she took pride in the cut and quality of her garments.

"Lizzy's owner beat her and another man raped her when she was a teenager," Augustus had told Fiona. "She has scars on her back from the beatings and had a son from the violation."

"And you know of this how?" Fiona had asked.

Augustus had stepped back from the table and looked away. She'd wondered if he and Lizzy had once been involved, and she coaxed more from him about her.

Lizzy became free in 1860 when residents of St. Louis raised $1,200 so she could purchase her liberty from her owner; she made her own way thereafter as a gifted seamstress who taught classes and crafted dresses for the finer folk. Those earnings paid her way to

Baltimore and then to Washington, where, through a chance introduction, she began making gowns for Mrs. Jefferson Davis, wife of the Mississippi senator, before war made Mrs. Davis's husband the leader of the Confederacy.

Lizzy's next benefactor, Mrs. McClean, arranged a meeting with Mrs. Lincoln, who quickly grew enthralled with Lizzy's handiwork. The seamstress also became Mrs. Lincoln's confidante and traveling companion. Now, with the president dead, people said that Lizzy was the only person Mrs. Lincoln trusted.

"I am not sure of her schedule," Augustus had said. "But I can say for certain that she'll be the only handsomely dressed, female Negro that the guards usher in and out without hesitation." As the morning wore on, Fiona watched the sentries posted at the heavy gates fronting the President's House. They stood by loosely, rifles hanging from their shoulders, and occasionally took off their hats to fan themselves as the day grew warmer. She could see beyond the gates to a semicircular drive that wound around a statue of Thomas Jefferson and bore carriages to the mansion's north portico.

And out of the corner of her eye, Fiona caught sight of a singular woman preparing to cross Pennsylvania from the park. She wore an elaborate silk hat with a long, dark ostrich feather perched on the front of the brim. She also carried a fashionable tasseled parasol, and was quite clearly a Negro. Fiona sprang up from her bench.

"Mrs. Keckly!" she shouted.

The woman turned and looked at Fiona for a moment. She then turned back to the street and began to cross. Fiona bustled after her, catching up as the woman reached the mansion's gates.

"Mrs. Keckly?"

The woman stopped and turned toward her. She was much older than Fiona had expected, perhaps in her late forties; too old for Augustus. Fiona had been wrong about the reasons for Augustus's reticence about Lizzy.

"Augustus Spriggs asked me to look for you, Mrs. Keckly. I am sorely regretful if you consider this an intrusion upon your time."

The woman stared at her, then nodded at the guards, who let her pass through the gates. Fiona stepped forward, but the guards crossed their rifles in front of her. She watched Lizzy walk briskly up the drive, then asked one of the guards for the time. Shortly before noon. She crossed back to her bench in Lafayette Park.

After sitting for hours, Fiona considered departing. But after arguing with Temple about the wisdom of involving herself more deeply by trying to reach Mrs. Lincoln, she wasn't about to give up their best hope for achieving that goal. So she sat.

At around four-thirty, she saw Lizzy returning down the mansion's carriageway, her parasol swaying on her wrist. The guards opened the gates for her, and she walked directly across Pennsylvania to Fiona's bench.

"Mrs. Keckly?" Fiona asked again.

"Ma'am. It has been some time since I heard Augustus's name, and I would have preferred to hear him speak it himself."

"He has been delayed by a pressing matter, otherwise he would have come to you himself."

"I doubt that," Lizzy replied.

"Why?"

"Because I think Augustus is ashamed."

"Of what?"

"That is not for me to say, ma'am. Not for me to say."

"You are Mrs. Lincoln's seamstress?"

"I am her modiste, yes."

"Of course, her modiste."

"Why are you here?" Lizzy asked. "And why is a white woman a confidante of Augustus's?"

"Why is a Negro modiste a confidante of a white First Lady?"

Lizzy sat down beside Fiona, settling her parasol across her lap. She adjusted her cap, pulling a long pin from the back that secured it to her hair and repositioning it. Then she cleared her throat and looked directly into Fiona's eyes.

"Mrs. Lincoln and I have both lost sons," Lizzy said. "My George died as a soldier in the war. But George was grown, a young man of twenty-one years. Eddie Lincoln died in Springfield just a month before his fourth birthday, and Willie Lincoln died here in the President's House still shy of his twelfth. Those little boys died when they were just hints of what they would become one day. Mothers shorn of their children by the angel of death have much to share with one another—much more than dresses."

"I am sorry for both of your losses."

"Do you have children?"

"No, but I fancy motherhood."

"And you know my name, but I don't know yours."

"Fiona McFadden."

Fiona stood and offered her hand to Lizzy, who remained seated. Lizzy took Fiona's hand, smiling at her for the first time that day.

"Will you accompany me on a stroll?" Lizzy asked.

TEMPLE STOPPED BY Alexander's studio to look for Pint, but the doors were locked and there was no answer when he knocked. His next stop was Scanlon's.

Jimmy Scanlon's saloon occupied a generous corner at 25th and H streets, a refuge for Pint that was just a short walk from his boardinghouse. A brightly painted signboard featuring two foamy mugs and a handsome townhouse hung over Scanlon's entrance, announcing to the world the good fortune Jimmy had reaped peddling beer and whiskey before becoming an active and influential developer in and around Foggy Bottom. Large troughs of water sat out front for teamsters to cool their horses.

Inside, Jimmy gave his guests dollops of refinement as well: a piano standing firm in a corner, which was played occasionally in the day and always after ten o'clock, when four plump and diseased women—the only women allowed in the saloon—kicked up a forlorn burleycue for rowdies still at the bar; more than two dozen tables scattered throughout, surrounded by rickety wooden armchairs; large brass spittoons that absorbed cannonballs of hickory-hued treacle launched from patrons' mouths; walls adorned with random depictions, ranging from drawings of the Emerald Athletics striving on the baseball diamond to portraits of Mr. Lincoln, draped in black bunting; long gas ceiling lamps, fitted with frosted glass; and, filling a wall at each end of the saloon, a pair of haphazard reproductions of two classic nudes, "Andromache Tied to the Rock" and "Venus at Her Mirror."

The saloon's four broad windows offered views down to the Potomac, where flat-bottomed houseboats doubling as brothels plied the waters alongside steamers and schooners carrying tobacco, oysters, shad, herring, flour, sugar, and molasses. Negroes who worked as stevedores and caulkers on the docks weren't welcomed at Scanlon's; the saloon had even turned Augustus away when Temple, in a moment of delusion, accompanied him there to celebrate General Lee's surrender at Appomattox.

> *Even here beside the grand Potomac's streams*
> *The medley mass of pride and misery*
> *Of whips and charters, manacles and rights*
> *Of slaving blacks and democratic whites.*

To reach the bar inside Scanlon's, patrons navigated a floor littered with crushed cigar butts and sticky pools of spilled liquor buzzing with flies. And there, his foot firmly planted atop the brass foot rail that spanned the bottom length of the bar, was Declan "Pint" Ramsey, jotting down notes with a stubby pencil on a piece of paper. Pint was also deep in conversation with Mark McAuliffe, who served multiple roles as Scanlon's bartender, keeper of the peace, and resident sage.

Mark decided who in Foggy Bottom got loans from Scanlon's when times were tight. Within reason, he would take any legitimate currency for a drink, including shinplasters issued by nearby store owners or by sutlers working with the army.

Whenever Mark circulated a stack of free newspapers around the saloon, he first announced with unshakeable confidence what he considered the most important stories of the day. At mealtime, and that could be almost any time of day, he made sure that teamsters, Georgetown dockworkers, and coal captains and muleskinners off the C&O canal had food (salty and spicy to keep them drinking—but, Mark always insisted, at a reasonable price and nourishing). When the night grew late, Mark would put a tray of chocolates on the bar, one to a customer and not for their mouths but for the missus at home. He called the candies "wife pacifiers."

Mark spotted Temple the moment he passed through Scanlon's doors.

"Here comes Detective McFadden, due to set the world right and save our souls before the priests get to us," he shouted, grinning ear to ear and raising a glass as Temple approached the bar. "Too much time has passed since you visited us last."

"I'll have a whiskey, Mark," Temple said, resting his cane against the bar and leaning against it himself to take some weight off his leg. "Are you caring for my mate here?"

"Aye, doing the best I can. Pint's a mighty chore. He tells me that the District's nefarious elements have taken to giving you beatings."

"I'm here, Mark. I'm still here."

"I won't complain about that."

Mark walked to the other end of the bar to serve a small group of dockworkers. Pint slipped his piece of paper into his coat and regarded Temple with amusement, his cheeks offering a first, faint flush as the spirits began to take hold of him. He bent his head sideways so that he could see around Temple's shoulder and up to the print of Venus, her torso and backside luminescent as she gazed at herself in a mirror that Cupid held as he crouched upon her bed.

Pint held up his drink, tipping it toward the goddess.

"She is majestic, and I am in love."

"You're a chirk lad, Pint. What are you drinking?"

"A rascally compound: applejack and whiskey. I'll move on to a mug of flip after this."

Pint put a hand on Temple's shoulder and moved him aside so that he could get another, clearer view of the print above them on the wall.

"Venus is an inspiration and an entertainment," Pint said. "Honors to Velasco."

"Velázquez."

"Who?"

"The painter. That's a copy of his Venus up there."

"She's a beauty."

"So are you."

"And where have you been?"

"Fiona and I have been at Augustus's, in the Shaw."

"Ah. Fiona told you Gardner and I were at odds?"

"She did. You have a history with Pinkerton?"

"Once. Only once for me," Pint said, his words starting to slur. "But Gardner, your Gardner, worked for Pinkerton throughout the war. On many, many occasions."

"Why didn't you tell Fiona and me when I was laid up in your boardinghouse that you knew Pinkerton?"

"You were delusional at my house, Temple. And Fiona was utterly focused upon your care and recovery. Besides, I never knew Pinkerton directly. When he was working for Stanton—"

"Pinkerton worked for the war secretary?" Temple asked.

"Only briefly. He was really McClellan's man," Pint said, belching. "Stanton replaced him with someone else he wanted to run the intelligence service."

"Who was Pinkerton's replacement?"

"Lafayette Baker."

A loud crack rang out. Mark had smacked a thick club across the end of the bar, breaking up two men who had squared off and were about to brawl. He told them to drink or leave. Temple recognized both of them. One was a fence and the other a hoister. Their argument, he imagined, was commercial.

Temple turned back to Pint.

"Who is Lafayette Baker?" he asked him.

"He trucks a fearsome reputation. He runs the National Detective Bureau, which Stanton established to take on Pinkerton's old chores. It is said that Baker breaks teeth to get information inside the Old Capitol Prison."

"What does he look like?"

"I've never met him."

"Where does he operate from?"

"No idea."

"And your own work with Pinkerton?"

"I did it just once, and I already sorted this with Fiona," Pint wheezed, throwing the rest of his drink down his throat. "I was working in the telegraph office when Stanton began tapping into communications in and out of Washington. Lincoln himself supported listening to the wires, you know. They had me monitor things. Then I got word from one of Pinkerton's deputies that they wanted me to spy on the boys at Georgetown College who were sending signals to the Secesh. That was all I did."

Pint ordered another drink. Temple put ten cents on the bar for his whiskey and nodded to Mark that he was leaving. Then he leaned in toward Pint.

"You're my mate?"

Pint leaned away, boozy and uncertain.

"Always your mate, Temp, always your mate."

"Is your shipment still at the B&O?"

"My shipment?"

"The silk and linens and silverware. That's why I was meeting you there, after all."

"Ah, right. Of course it's still there. We'll have to get back to the B&O and round it all up. There'll be money in it for you and Augustus, Temple."

Temple stepped back, gathering his cane.

"Does 'Mars' mean anything to you, Pint?"

"Huh?"

"The word 'Mars.' When you were snooping on the telegraph messages. Did the word 'Mars' ever come up?"

"No, Temple, I can't say it did. How so?"

"As a name. Or as a code. In communications between spies."

Pint shook his head.

"What about in communications between assassins?"

Pint shook his head again, his eyes moist and pink.

"Never," he said.

Temple hugged Pint closely, something he had never done before, and the intimacy puzzled Pint. When Temple released him, he patted him on the chest.

"Old friend," Temple said, nodding.

"Old friend."

He turned to walk out the door, but Pint cleared his throat and asked him to stop. Temple turned back.

"Venus is Mars's lover," Pint said. "And Mars is the god of war."

Temple nodded to him and turned to leave, slipping the piece of paper he had lifted from Pint's shirt into his own pocket.

LIZZY KECKLY, AS Fiona discovered, took a stroll to be something more grand and lively than a tour around a park, or even a lengthy walk down Pennsylvania. She meant it to be an outing, and by the time she and Fiona had crossed onto Bridge Street in Georgetown, dusk was approaching. The streets were quieter here than in the District, and they could hear the grinding wheel of Bomford's flour mill being turned by water running off the C&O canal as it streamed down to the Potomac.

As they crossed Fishing Lane and neared the High Street, Lizzy slipped her arm into Fiona's.

"I have thought to move here to Georgetown when we leave the President's House. I have friends in Herring Hill who would take me in, and my popularity as a modiste offers me independence. I could open a shop next to Emma Brown's school on Third Street," Lizzy said. "But Mrs. Lincoln leaves for Chicago in days. She says the city's superior attractions recommend it. And while there are many of us here, I don't know how well Georgetown takes to its Negroes."

"Georgetown doesn't take well to the District," Fiona said. "Washington's stewards want to make it a part of Washington so that our city can continue its expansion, but the tobacco merchants are resisting."

"I always told Mrs. Lincoln that I felt Georgetown to be more South than North," Lizzy said. "That's why I also told her it was right just that President Lincoln had troops occupy the town, because it was teeming with rebels."

Several large livery stables were on the High Street, near the slave markets that had closed a few years earlier, and the stench of horse manure held the air, prompting Lizzy and Fiona to press kerchiefs to their faces as they continued along. When they reached 21 First Street, at the corner of Frederick, Lizzy suggested they stop. They were in front of a handsome redbrick townhouse with black shutters and a steep, eight-step stoop bordered by an iron banister.

"This is the home of Cranstoun Laurie," Lizzy said.

"And he is?"

"He is the chief statistician for the Post Office. More important, he, his wife, Margaret, and their daughter, Belle, are all the most gifted of clairvoyants."

"I am in a state of complete confusion," Fiona said.

"They are spiritualists. They can commune with the dead."

Fiona was still at a loss. She looked into Lizzy's face for something further, but Lizzy just stared back at her, offering nothing but a serene smile. Before she could ask another question, Fiona spotted curtains parting in one of the tall windows on the townhouse's façade. An old woman with high cheekbones, dark eyes, and a tightly wound bun of ice-white hair atop her head peered out silently.

"A woman is at the window," Fiona said, a small shudder running up her spine.

Lizzy turned, looked up, and nodded. The woman nodded back and the curtains closed.

"We are here to meet with her?" Fiona asked.

"No, she is the Lauries' housekeeper. She would never let me into their home unaccompanied. She resents me."

"Are we not to go in, then?"

"Of course, we will. But with Mrs. Lincoln, when she arrives."

"Mrs. Lincoln is coming here?"

"She comes here regularly. The Lauries are her friends. They help her speak to her dead sons, and it is a rare and generous comfort the Lauries provide her. When Willie appears, he speaks of the pony the Lincolns gave him on his birthday and how even in heaven the weather is changeable. He was their favorite child, but he couldn't resist the inroads of disease, and his loss still grieves Mrs. Lincoln's heart sorely. Now she wants to speak to her dead husband."

Fiona merely nodded, and Lizzy responded to her silence.

"I see in your face that you don't place faith in the Lauries' work or Mrs. Lincoln's travels to the other side. But you weren't in the President's House when Mr. Lincoln's body was brought to the East Room. Mrs. Lincoln screamed and wailed in her bedroom, and Robert tried to calm her. Tad was at the foot of her bed with a world of agony in his little face. I shall never forget the scene—the wails of a broken heart, the unearthly shrieks, the terrible convulsions, the wild, tempestuous outburst of grief."

"If it gives Mrs. Lincoln comfort, then she is more than entitled to visit with spirits or with the dead president," Fiona said.

As it grew darker, the evening cooled from the heat of the day and a fog crept onto Georgetown's streets. The gas lamps on First Street were lit and the fog curled in a light mustard swirl around the lampposts before turning gray as it spread across the cobblestone streets.

Horses passing on Georgetown's cobblestones made a distinctive clip-clop, but the sound that drew Lizzy's attention was more involved than that, and more imperial. Fiona turned to look in the same direction as a handsome black barouche, pulled by four large carriage horses, emerged from the fog onto First Street.

"Mrs. Lincoln has come for a séance," Lizzy said.

"She won't find my presence alarming?" Fiona asked.

"I will make the introduction. She has faith in my judgment."

The barouche stopped at the Lauries' house, and the driver climbed down. Mrs. Lincoln was dressed in layers of black—black silk dress, black cap, black shawl, black gloves—and she sat on the edge of her white leather seat staring at Lizzy and Fiona for several moments before she extended her hand to her driver. As she stepped to the curb, she cleared her throat and fixed Fiona with a pair of alert but careworn eyes that, in the fog and the darkness, also appeared to be black, save for fine pinpoints of light in their very middle. She was small, barely over five feet tall, and rotund, and she clutched a small black handbag close to her bosom, gripping its handles so tightly that her knuckles were turning white. She let go long enough to offer her hand to Fiona, who took it and curtsied.

"I am Mary Todd Lincoln," she said softly, barely above a whisper.

"I am Fiona McFadden. And I am honored."

"You are a friend of Lizabeth's?"

"If she considers me such, yes, ma'am."

"She is a friend, Mrs. Lincoln," Lizzy said.

"Are you here to participate, Mrs. McFadden?"

"Well, ma'am, I—"

"Yes, she will participate, Mrs. Lincoln," Lizzy said.

"Lizzy, I must tell Mrs. Lincoln my reason for being here," Fiona said, cutting her off.

Mrs. Lincoln gripped her bag again tightly and stepped away from Fiona, closer to Lizzy.

"I have had more unknown people come into my life this year to tell me things that have been all but devastating," she said. "I must ask you to bear that in mind, child, whatever you are here to say."

"I mean to cause you no fresh burden," Fiona said.

"I am my own burden," Mrs. Lincoln whispered. "I wish I could forget myself."

"Ma'am, I have your diary."

Mrs. Lincoln's hands dropped to her side and her bag fell to the pavement. She turned her head to the side, and the gaslight limned the dark pools beneath her eyes. She crept closer to Fiona.

"My diary went missing after my husband was murdered. It was—it is—a private possession."

"I know, Mrs. Lincoln, and that is why I seek to return it to you. I have it. Not here with me now, but I have it. Had I known I was to meet you today, I would have brought it with me. My sincerest apologies."

"How did you come upon it?"

"It came into my husband's possession, ma'am. I'm not at liberty to explain all of that to you, but I most certainly would like to safeguard its return."

"Have you read it?"

"I have not, ma'am. But I confess that my husband has."

"Your husband? What kind of a man is this, so lacking in chivalry?" Mrs. Lincoln asked, her voice regaining the authority and Southern cadences of a Kentucky Todd.

"My husband is an honorable man. He was uncertain of what he had until he read it. And he listened to me when I told him it was proper and decent to return it to you."

"I leave the President's House and am bound for Chicago on the twenty-second of May, two days hence. Could you be so kind as to return it to me then?"

"Of course, ma'am."

"How do you know my Lizabeth?"

"We have a common acquaintance," Fiona said.

"Who might that be, Lizabeth?"

"A man who was once a close and trusted friend of my son, George," Lizzy said.

"Is this the same man who convinced George to join the Union forces?"

"He is, ma'am."

"Yet you told me that you considered that man a murderer for convincing your boy to go to war."

"At one time I believed that for certain, Mrs. Lincoln. I most assuredly did," Lizzy said. "Augustus convinced my George to march, and now he is dead. But you know what death does to us mothers, Mrs. Lincoln. It turns our hearts and our minds around. I think I have found a different resolution for my grief, and I do believe that Mrs. McFadden comes here, today and to you, with goodwill."

"Certainly she comes with goodwill, yes, yes, yes, yes. With malice toward none, with charity for all. Of course she does," the widow said with a long, forlorn sigh, tipping her head back and closing her eyes to the night sky. "I do know what death does. Death rends one, utterly."

Mrs. Lincoln stood still, her face still raised to the moon, her arms at her side, her chest rising and falling slowly. Silent.

Fiona and Lizzy watched the widow and awaited her next word. When Fiona began to speak, Lizzy held her finger to her lips to warn her off. There was no movement on the street, just the three of them bound in the moment by Mrs. Lincoln's wanderings.

She broke from her reverie with a start, addressing Fiona.

"Have you spent time with spiritualists and mediums, Mrs. McFadden?"

"No, ma'am, I haven't."

"They are the ones—other than the good Lord—who weaken death's grip upon us. The Lauries have given me back my Eddie and my Willie, and I intend to see my Abraham again."

"Yes, ma'am."

Mrs. Lincoln sank into silence once more, shaking her head, and then engaged Fiona again.

"Queen Victoria lost her Albert at almost the same time that my

Willie passed. There are so many losses. Many, many, many. My sister Emilie knows that Willie's spirit has visited us in the mansion. On occasion he has come to me at the foot of my bed with the same sweet adorable smile he always had. Sometimes Eddie is with him, and once he came with my late brother Alec. They all love me so."

"Yes, ma'am."

"Willie was so small. He didn't damage me the way Tad did at birth," Mrs. Lincoln continued. "We did all in our power to save him. We gave him Peruvian bark, Miss Leslie's puddings, and beef tea, but still he left us. So we laid him out, properly embalmed, in the Green Room of the mansion with a laurel sprig upon his chest. And then we buried him in a little metal casket worked to appear like rosewood. It was gentle in its way. Not like my poor husband, no, no, no. Mrs. McFadden?"

"Ma'am?"

"Did you know that the blood that streamed from the bullet hole in my husband's head stained the cape I wore to Ford's?"

"No, Mrs. Lincoln, I did not."

"Yes, yes, yes."

"I am truly sorry for all of your losses, Mrs. Lincoln."

"I still have my Tad. I fear, however, that my Robert is not true. My son Robert covets my money and tells me that my emotions unravel. He says he is frightened to leave me alone, because I am . . . because he says I am . . . unwell. Tad doesn't say these things. But Robert is not truly at odds with me for my mind, Mrs. McFadden. I know his devices. He hires Mr. Pinkerton's agents to follow me, and he is in league with the railroad men and the New York bankers. His father had lost faith in him before he died. Those men all tortured the president so . . . ," she said, her voice trailing off.

Lizzy put her arm around Mrs. Lincoln's waist and guided her toward the stairs of the Lauries' house.

"Mrs. McFadden, will you join our séance this evening?" Mrs. Lincoln asked. "Invisible beings surround us like a great cloud, and the Lauries can summon them from across the river Styx. Séances can be the gayest of pleasure parties, even in a darkened room."

"I would be honored to join you, but the hour is late; I want to fetch your diary, and I need to find my husband lest he worry. I would be most grateful if we could converse but one time more. My husband has an unquenchable thirst for information about the president. He admired him so."

"Yes, yes, yes. Be on your way, then," Mrs. Lincoln said. "I will tell Mr. Lincoln this evening that you have recovered my prized journal. The news will comfort him. How will you get my diary to me?"

"You could join us on the train to Chicago, Fiona," Lizzy interjected. "If Mrs. Lincoln approves, of course. We could get it from you then, and you could have the longer conversation with Mrs. Lincoln that you have sought."

Fiona nodded.

"Yes, yes, yes, join us for Chicago, Mrs. McFadden. Mr. George Pullman is sending a private rail car for me. I insisted on such, and Mr. Stanton and the others cannot contest and complain about such courtesies now that I am no longer a captive of the President's House or Washington. I do expect my husband to scold me inside, however. He has always been wary of my extravagances."

"Yes, ma'am."

"Allow me to steer you properly to your home," Mrs. Lincoln said, as she began laboring to scale the Lauries' imposing staircase. "My driver will see you to your husband in my barouche, and I will see you on the twenty-second."

"I am deeply obliged."

"You are without children?"

"Lizzy inquired of the same earlier, Mrs. Lincoln. Yes, I am, but I am also hopeful for the future."

Fiona had to strain now to hear the widow, who, intent upon her ascent, had her back to Fiona and was speaking directly to the Lauries' townhouse. When Mrs. Lincoln finally reached the top of the staircase, she was out of breath and pulled a fan from her handbag to cool herself. Her bosom heaving, she looked down at Fiona as the door to the Lauries' house swung open.

"Lear had it exactly so, my child. Yes, yes, yes," Mrs. Lincoln said to Fiona. "Our young ones can unwind us most deeply. My Robert is the serpent's tooth. I wish you daughters when motherhood arrives for you."

Before Fiona took the driver's hand to climb into the Lincolns' barouche, she studied Mrs. Lincoln for a moment, taking stock of a woman bereft and shrouded by the fog, floating upon a sea of miseries and losses.

Fiona nodded to Lizzy and stepped up into the carriage.

CHAPTER FIFTEEN

THE MONTAUK

Temple had lingered in Foggy Bottom long enough to see if he was being followed. Satisfied he wasn't, he made his way downtown and was standing beneath a lamppost across from Alexander's studio on 7th Street, taking in the huge lettering the photographer had festooned across the building—lettering large enough to be legible even as the evening grew dark.

"Gardner's Gallery" was spelled out in foot-high letters across the top of the building, with three columns of advertisements bordering the windows right below: "Cartes de Visite, Stenographs, Album Cards; Imperial Photographs—Plain, Colored, Retouched; Ambrotypes, Hallotypes, Ivory Types." Alexander was not shy in his promotions. On the D Street side of the studio, he had attached a large billboard to the edge of the roof: "Photographs." Below that sign, another advertisement was painted on the wall: "Views of the War."

Yellow light was spilling out from the middle window of the studio's second floor. Gardner had returned.

Temple knocked on the door, but there was no answer. He pounded on it again, as loud as he could, and then backed into the street and stared up. Moments later, Gardner poked his head out the window, about to burst into a rage until he saw Temple below him, grinning.

"Why so damn noisy?" Gardner yelled.

"Why so damn hard to find?"

"Lang may yer lum reek!" Gardner shouted back in Scottish slang, as he did on the infrequent occasions when he was relaxed enough to be a wit.

Gardner had spread several lanterns around the room, but he was anxious about them. There were enough chemicals in his studio to ignite the building should any one of the lanterns tip over. For that reason, he rarely worked at night.

"Stop eyeing the lanterns and talk with me," Temple said.

Temple was sitting with his bad leg propped up on a small table. He had spent most of the day on his feet and his leg was throbbing. Before arriving at Gardner's he had contemplated going to his boardinghouse to gather fresh clothes for Fiona and himself—it was only several blocks away, at 15th and F—but he assumed that Pinkerton would be watching his home. Perhaps Baker, too, if he had already discovered Temple's identity. Maybe they were watching Gardner's studio. But he had circled the area twice before hovering across the street and observing the neighborhood and its inhabitants for several minutes. Anyhow, he needed to have this conversation.

Gardner pulled a cheroot out of a bag and lifted one of the lanterns to his face so that he could light it. His beard pressed against the lantern as the end of the cheroot glowed red, and Gardner drew deeply on it.

"You're afeared of fire and now you have one progressing in your very own mouth," Temple said. "Sitting here, in your own studio, you're surrounded by flames."

"The cheroots relax me. General Sickles gave me a dozen last week because he is still pleased with photographs I took of him."

"Everyone is usually pleased with your photographs."

"Sickles was especially pleased. I made his in New York shortly after his trial for killing Francis Scott Key's son here in Lafayette Park. He claimed that he was temporarily insane, and he had a strong, crafty lawyer who turned the judge in his favor."

"The lawyer was who?"

"Edwin Stanton. It was just a few years before he became war secretary."

"I am finding Mr. Stanton to be rather ubiquitous," Temple said. "People say Danny Sickles was a dirty sort."

"Indeed, even if he did lose half a leg at Gettysburg. When he was with Tammany Hall—workin' and givin' it laldy among the corrupts haunting your New York—he represented the city's delegation to London. In the name of the wee man! He brought an adventuress as his guest to Buckingham Palace and formally introduced her to Queen Victoria!"

Both men laughed hard enough that they rocked back in their seats. When Gardner finally settled down, he drew on the cheroot again and exhaled a thick cloud of gray smoke.

"A fine smoke is a fine smoke, no matter who gives them to you," Gardner said. "Fiona told you about my words with Pint, I take it?"

"She did."

"After Fiona left the studio, Pint just sat here ruminating, not sayin' a word. So I told him to skedaddle. Too much anger inside him, and he drinks too much."

"He's been our friend, and we all have a dose of anger inside us."

"Well, people evolve."

Temple pulled his leg down from the table and sat upright, leaning toward Gardner.

"Was everything you did in the war for Pinkerton? Every photograph?"

"Hell no!" Gardner shot back, bolting up from his chair. He sucked on the cheroot again and began walking in circles around the studio, pounding his fist against the wall—but coming to a full stop, and being careful not to do any damage, when he got near one of the cameras he had scattered about the room. Stop, start, stop, start, stop, start, until his anger slowly unwound.

Gardner sat down again, dropping the cheroot into a stone bowl to burn out. Temple waited for him to calm because, invariably, he would reveal a bit of himself after a rage, perhaps as a penance of sorts.

In addition to his equipment and his shelves and his cabinets, Gardner kept several oversized albums of his own work in the studio and the book Fiona had so enthusiastically mentioned, his *Photo-*

graphic Sketch Book of the Civil War. He walked to a table and grabbed a large, leather-bound scrapbook and brought it back to his chair, flipping through its pages until he found an article he had cut from *The New York Times* about a display of his Antietam photographs at Mathew Brady's studio. He read the clip aloud.

"'October twentieth, 1862: These pictures have a terrible distinctness. By the aid of a magnifying glass, the very features of the slain may be distinguished.'"

Gardner looked up from the book.

"I think I prize that phrase, 'a terrible distinctness.' I chronicled something horrible during the war and I recorded it with clarity, Temple."

Gardner flipped more pages in the scrapbook, closely examining a few, until he found another clip he was looking for, from *Harper's New Monthly.*

"This next one isn't about me. It's about a photograph that Jim Gibson took during the war at Savage's Station, of a field hospital scattered with the wounded and the dying. 'This scene brings the war to those who have not been to it. How patiently and still they lie; these brave men who bleed and are maimed for us. It is a picture that is more eloquent than the sternest speech.'"

Gardner looked up again at Temple.

"All of us on the battlefield were witnesses, Temple."

Gardner laid out the challenges of taking pictures in the field. He needed another photographer or an assistant with him at the same location: one to set the camera up, the other to arrange the glass plates and mix chemicals. Once the chemicals were ready, they were poured onto the plate and allowed to evaporate, and then the plate had to be dunked in a solution, in complete darkness, inside a wagon—"On a battlefield, mind you!"

When the plate was ready, it was fitted in a holder and slotted inside the camera, which had to be moved into the right position and brought into focus. After the plate was exposed, photographers had only minutes to get it back to the wagon to develop it. The plates were fragile and broke easily, so photographers had to do as much as they could to cushion them during transport—"On a battlefield!" Alexander thundered again.

Gardner told Temple that when Gibson took aerial photographs of the battlefields, he occasionally went up in one of the army's hot-air balloons. Gibson came back from his first balloon rides aglow, brimming with excitement about what he'd seen and photographed from the sky. But the army only let him up because it wanted surveillance photos that could be used to plan attacks, and when Gibson returned, the military confiscated his plates.

"By the time Jim got around to his third or fourth ride, he knew he wasn't going to keep a single thing he brought back. But I tell ya—he kept going up."

"Because that was the trade," Temple said. "They gave him access to other parts of the war in exchange for occasional reconnaissance."

"That was the trade."

"You too?"

"Yes, absolutely. And I'd do it again. I could never have gotten near the real force and terror of it without the army's help. And the army wasn't going to let me in without giving it something in exchange. So we swapped, and I gave people pictures that weren't pageantry—gave them pictures of dead Rebel and Union boys without shoes. And if that forces people to confront calamity, then I've served a purpose, and not a devilish one."

"I can't argue with that."

Gardner sat up, shaking his head, and leaned in toward Temple.

"But I also arranged bodies and rifles and swords sometimes to make the settings more appealing, so the photographs would sell. Pint rode me hard on that when he and Fiona were here, and we got to screamin'."

"We all have our unsavories."

"You've got your cards," Gardner said.

"I do."

Gardner slumped back in his chair, burying his chin in his chest and running his fingers through his beard. Temple lit up a cheroot, letting the sweet edge of it rest against his tongue while he waited again for Gardner to resurface.

"All of it makes me feel like it's time to start fresh, maybe venture to the Great Plains and acquaint myself with Indian country," Gardner said.

"We'll miss you if you go west," Temple said. "You'd better hurry there if that's what suits you, because the railroads are aiming to get there first."

"The locomotives are going to change everything. They're the future and they're progress and they'll make the country smaller, and I think for all of that, for all of their fuming and churning, I loathe them. Which means, I fear, that I'll end up being duty bound to photograph the trains as well."

Gardner pressed his cheroot into his mouth and inhaled.

"Thank you for going with Fiona to the cemetery," Temple said. "It was a helpful diversion."

"Why is Pinkerton so interested in you?"

"Can't say."

"You mean you don't know?"

"No, I mean I can't say. There's another one after me as well."

"One of Pinkerton's?"

"No. His name is Lafayette Baker."

Gardner sucked the air back in through his teeth and shook his head, gazing at Temple with a mixture of pity and fear.

"Ah, you as well," Temple said.

"Meaning what?"

"It seems so many people know of or are familiar with Mr. Baker except for me."

"Anyone who was around the war or Edwin Stanton knew of Baker. 'Tisn't so rare."

"I wasn't around the war," Temple said. "Nor have I ever been around Mr. Stanton."

Gardner went to a cabinet and pulled down a bottle of whiskey, along with two heavy glass tumblers. He filled them high and gave one to Temple. And then he explained how Baker was likely to be well known very soon, even celebrated, perhaps. Although there wasn't anything about him in the newspapers yet, not even in the *National Intelligencer*.

"Lafayette Baker led the group that tracked down Booth. People are now all jabberin' how that lad Corbett shot Booth in the barn in Port Royal—but it was Baker who tracked the assassin, and Baker who rounded up the other boys who conspired with Booth. Baker had always been Stanton's man, and when Stanton needed someone with leather on his shoes to hunt Booth, he asked Baker. And I'll tell you this: Pinkerton and Baker aren't together. They hate each other."

"Then why are they after me together?"

"I dunno."

"How do you know Baker led the group that hunted down Booth?"

"Because Stanton and the army ordered me to photograph the murderer's corpse, and when I went down to the river after they brought the body back, Baker was there telling everyone what to do. It was his show, through and through."

Temple tipped his drink, finding himself worried again about Fiona and Augustus, regretting that he had drawn them into this peril. For a moment his mouth went dry.

"Alexander, tell me about the night they brought Booth back," Temple said, putting his drink down.

Gardner told him it hadn't been night, really, but early in the morning. After Booth was killed in Virginia, they wrapped his body in a horse blanket and tied it to a wooden plank, then loaded it onto a farmer's wagon. From there they rode to the water and loaded the body onto a steamboat, the *John S. Ide*, which carried the corpse to Alexandria. Then they put Booth's body on a tugboat and ferried it across the Potomac to the Washington Navy Yard.

"It was around one forty-five in the morning on April twenty-seventh," Alexander said. "I'll never forget that date, or the day that Lincoln died."

"And that's when you first saw Booth's body? And first saw Baker?"

"I didn't arrive at the Navy Yard until just after sunrise, several hours after they brought the body ashore. Soldiers came here to the studio—a full military escort—and pounded on the door even louder than you did earlier, Temple, you rude sod. They woke me up and read the command from Stanton ordering me down to the Potomac to photograph a corpse. I couldn't have gone any earlier anyway because I wouldn't have had enough light. I brought Timmy O'Sullivan with me to help with the equipment. I didn't know until I got to the Navy Yard that it was Booth, and they told me the body had been lying there since about one forty-five in the morning."

Gardner said that by the time he reached the Navy Yard, they had moved Booth's body off the tug and onto the deck of one of the ironclads, the *Montauk*. Booth was still fully clothed, and the left leg of the corpse was wrapped in a makeshift splint and bandages. Stanton had ordered an entire parade of specialists to identify the body, and Baker had said that the war secretary wanted to ensure that they had indeed captured and shot Booth and not some imposter.

Booth's doctor, John May, had been one of the first to arrive, and he examined Booth's neck, where he had removed a large growth a few months before the assassination. Dr. May had been quite pleased with himself ("I most ably operated on a fibroid tumor clinging to the patient's neck and I find upon him now a scar marking the location on his neck in the exact position where I performed my work"). They'd also brought up Booth's dentist, Bill Merrill, who had put new fillings in the murderer's mouth a few weeks before the assassination, and the dentist found his work good and true—though Booth had been dead about a day by then, and his body had grown so stiff that they needed two soldiers to help pry open his mouth so they could look inside.

Baker had been striding back and forth on the *Montauk* like a titan and told Gardner to photograph Booth's mouth, neck, and legs, as well as his entire face and body and all of the possessions he had with him.

Two other doctors had also come aboard the *Montauk,* and they performed an autopsy that took some time. One of them was the surgeon general, Joseph Barnes, and he probed a bullet hole a couple of inches above Booth's collarbone around the base of his neck, noting that the bullet that killed him passed above the collarbone. After Barnes cut into Booth's back with a scalpel, he discovered that the bullet had smashed some of the vertebrae in the assassin's spine. He plucked the vertebrae out of his back like a farmer pulling up carrots. The entire time, he was dictating his findings to an assistant who wrote them down, and Barnes promised Baker that the report would be sent to the war secretary as soon as they were finished looking at the corpse. Barnes made sure to note in his report that Booth, though paralyzed, must have been in great pain during the two hours it took him to die, "probably from asphy . . . asphy . . ."

"Asphyxiation?" Temple asked.

"Aye!" said Gardner.

Baker, Gardner continued, had been satisfied to hear that Booth died in pain, and said that Stanton would be enormously gratified to hear that fact, too. Barnes also had pointed out that the bullet found its way back out of Booth's body on the left side of his neck, almost exactly opposite the point where it entered—probably because it bounced right off the spine after it snapped it.

The last outsiders brought on board the *Montauk* had been Seaton Munroe, a lawyer who was Booth's close friend, and Charlie Dawson, a clerk who worked at the National Hotel, where Booth had been living. Both of them said the body was Booth's, but Dawson offered the most singular identification: he pointed to the initials J.W.B. tattooed on the back of Booth's left hand, near his thumb. Dawson said he always remembered that the actor had his initials there and that Booth had told him that he'd stamped the letters on himself with India ink when he was a lad.

"Who knew to fetch a clerk from the National to identify the body?" Temple asked. "Who corralled all those people?"

"Stanton, with Baker's help. As I said, they wanted to make sure that it was Booth's body because they were afraid of scandal if they had the wrong man. But Stanton certainly didn't want anyone to find the body later—after we were all through with what we had to do, Stanton ordered the body carted away and buried anonymously."

"Why?"

"No idea."

"And you have a collection of pictures of Booth?"

"Stanton ordered them confiscated."

"Then that is that."

"No, Temple, it isn't. We came back here to develop the photographs and they had two soldiers up here with us. They didn't know a thing about photography, and O'Sullivan and I were able to make extra copies of three photos of Booth. We never gave those to Baker or Stanton."

"Which are they?" Temple asked.

"A photo of his face and two others of all that he had been carrying with him that day."

"Alexander?"

"Yes, of course I can show them to you."

"I want to keep them."

Gardner paused, then walked over to a closet at the far end of the studio. There was a small woolen rug inside, and he pulled it out. Beneath that there was a trap door in the floor, and he took a key from his pocket and bent down to unlock it. After he yanked it open, he reached down inside and pulled out a long metal box with another lock on it. Gardner slid a different key into that lock, opened the box, and then took it to a table and spilled out its contents. There were several envelopes inside, including one dated April 27. He tore it open and pulled three pictures out.

The first was of Booth's face, so pale and waxen it nearly glowed. His black moustache dripped off his upper lip and tendriled down the sides of his mouth, which was partially open in a rigid, pained grimace.

"The exposure on this wasn't quite right," Gardner said. "His face wasn't nearly that white. Because he suffocated to death, there was lots of blue in his face. But this is the way this one came out, and maybe it suits him, the ghoul."

Booth's eyelids had been pressed shut, and his hair was matted and mussed against his forehead. He had a white shirt on, torn about the shoulders and neck, and it was unbuttoned down to his sternum. The bullet wound above Booth's right collarbone was almost clean, like a tiny black orchid burrowed into his skin. Nothing more than a perforation. On the other side of Booth's neck, where the bullet had exited, the wound was larger, the flesh was torn open, and a dark, winding rivulet of blood ran to his chest. Spots of blood also flecked the left side of his neck.

"Alexander, can you remember what color the skin was around the spot where the bullet went in? Was it reddish brown or was it closer to yellow?"

"No idea. Why?"

"Just curious. If the bullet went in while Booth was still alive, the skin would be closer to an auburn color. If it went in after he was already dead, the skin would look more yellow."

"What are you gettin' at?"

"I'm not sure. Questions help me get a clearer view of matters. How old was he?"

"I'm not certain, but Baker said he was twenty-seven. A celebrated actor, of twenty-seven years. The esteemed and handsome Mr. Booth."

"He was still young."

Gardner gave Temple the two other pictures, showing the contents of Booth's pockets and other things he was carrying with him when he died. The first photo showed a pair of revolvers, a metal file, a knife, a map of the Confederate states, an ivory pipe, a candle nearly melted away, a signal whistle, and a single spur.

The second photo showed a belt and holster, several cartridges, a compass protruding from a leather case, a wad of Canadian currency, and pictures of five women.

"He kept busy with the ladies," Alexander said.

"Do you know who any of them are?"

"Only one. Lucy Hale. She was his fiancée and the daughter of a former senator from New Hampshire. Her father sat for me once for a portrait. She brought Booth as a guest to Mr. Lincoln's second inauguration. I always thought that they were an odd coupling because the senator was an abolitionist. And Booth, well, Booth loved Dixie."

"I wonder if Miss Hale knew about the other four women," Temple said. "This is the entirety of what Booth was carrying?"

"It's everything that they had spread out on the deck of the *Montauk* and asked me to photograph."

Temple lingered over the two pictures of Booth's possessions and then put them back into the envelope, sliding it inside his jacket next to the note he'd lifted from Pint at Scanlon's.

"I don't expect I'll see those again, will I?" Alexander asked.

"Probably not. You understand?"

"I don't understand what you're involved with, but the pictures are yours. And here's another thing for you: Lafayette Baker worked as a spy in Richmond for the Union before Stanton put him in charge of the intelligence services. He presented himself in Richmond as a photographer named Sam Munson—and McClellan called upon me to train him so that he could pass as a photographer."

"And?"

"I'll say it again: Lafayette Baker is the most dangerous and frightening person I think I have ever encountered. He was abusive, short-tempered, and quick with his fists."

"It must have been a fright to encounter a temper as lickety-split as yours. Was he a good photographer?"

Gardner laughed and grabbed the whiskey bottle to pour them another drink. Temple waved the bottle away and announced that it was time to get home to Fiona. He looked down at his boots to assess their condition: no mud, and just enough dust to make them look appropriately used. Spared for the evening from Fiona's wrath. He leaned on his cane and asked Gardner another question.

"Where did they bury Booth's body after all of you were done with it?"

"No one knows for certain. Stanton and Baker were in charge of that. People on the *Montauk* said that Stanton wanted it buried in an unmarked grave in Baltimore so Confederate sympathizers couldn't turn it into a memorial."

"What did you do for the rest of the day after you photographed Booth?"

"I almost set out for Memphis. The same day that they brought Booth's body to the Navy Yard, word came on the telegraph that a steamboat called the *Sultana* had exploded and sunk on the Mississippi. They said that more than fifteen hundred passengers had drowned and that most of them were Union soldiers who had been imprisoned at Andersonville. I wanted to get there, I tell you. But Stanton told the army that I had to remain in Washington because he wanted me available for other photographs."

"Such as?"

"The other people who the government says worked the assassination conspiracy with Booth: the boardinghouse owner, Mary Surratt; the one that Baker and others on the *Montauk* called Goliath, Lewis Powell—"

"Lewis Powell?" Temple asked. "They called him Goliath?"

Like Booth, Powell was an object of fascination in Washington; even among those revolted by the assassination, both men's audacity invited gossip and speculation. Powell had slashed Secretary of State Seward's face with a dagger in an attempt to kill him the same night Booth shot Mr. Lincoln. After pummeling the Seward children, Powell fled from the house and disappeared for three days before Stanton and Baker's investigators found him at the Surratts'.

"He's apparently a very big lad," Gardner said. "Thick-armed, thick-necked, with a dark mop of hair, and tall. Bigger, even, than Baker, I'm told."

"What others were on your agenda for photographs?"

"Two of the other conspirators—Herold and Atzerodt—and a doctor they picked up in Virginia who treated Booth. His name is Samuel Mudd."

Temple pondered all of the names spilling out of Gardner's mouth, committing each of them to memory.

"Baker and the others can't know that I've been here or that you and I are even in contact," Temple said. "It would be safer for both of us that way."

"I haven't seen Baker since the *Montauk* and I get my directions from Stanton."

"Can you get me to Stanton at some point? Indirectly, so you're not harmed?"

Gardner was silent, rubbing his thumb and forefinger together and stroking his beard with his other hand. He began to speak two or three times, stopping himself before he could get a word out.

"I've given you the pictures, Temple. I don't think I can arrange anything with Stanton. It unnerves me."

"Then I won't press you."

"What are you after here?"

"I'm sorry, I can't say," Temple said. "But I have one last request. Fiona said you have a splendid photograph of the president."

"Your wife did me a favor with that. She smashed the negative to wee pieces. You're married to an angel of mercy."

Gardner found the picture of Lincoln and placed it on a table, moving one of his lanterns closer so Temple could see the photograph better. Lincoln appeared just as Fiona had described him: the mild, playful smile, the deep, dark, kind eyes, and the L-shaped slash from the negative that slanted downward like a bolt in the print, cutting across the top of his head. Looking at the photograph of Booth had been a gruesome chore, Temple thought. Looking at this, looking at Lincoln, was a pleasure—and a mournful, wasteful thing.

*Falling upon them all, and among them all, enveloping me with
the rest,
Appear'd the cloud, appear'd the long black trail;
And I knew Death, its thought, and the sacred knowledge
of death.*

Temple pivoted off his cane and offered Gardner his hand as he moved toward the door.

"I also have photographs of the president's funeral," Gardner said.

"Not those, thanks," Temple said. "But can I borrow your horse?"

"Tied up on E, to the right when you go out downstairs. I'll need him back tomorrow afternoon."

They shook hands.

"Sic as ye gie, sic wull ye get," Gardner said.

"I'm Irish, friend."

" 'You'll get out of life as much as you put in.' One of my dearest Scottish phrases."

"Maireann croi éadrom i bhfad," Temple said.

"Eh?"

" 'A light heart lives longest.' A good Irish phrase."

"Then we've made a fair exchange this evening," Gardner said as Temple passed through the door.

CHAPTER SIXTEEN

THE TORCHES

Augustus sat by his window in the Shaw, watching the night deepen and following plumes of fog slinking across the yard around his house. Fiona and Temple would be returning through that fog, and he hoped it wouldn't thicken. There was little light as it was, and no moon out at all. But stars were painted across the purple sky in winding strokes, and Augustus looked up at them, satisfied—the Little Bear charged along, the Dipper on his flank, pinned to the heavens forever by Polaris.

I thought I heard the angels say
Follow the drinking gourd
The stars in the heavens gonna show you the way
Follow the drinking gourd

The constellations were so rich that Ursa wasn't alone. Virgo, Leo, Cancer, and Gemini waltzed beneath him. As summer came on, only Virgo would hold her ground, shunted to the side by Libra. Augustus remembered his mother now, telling him in Texas when he was a boy that she couldn't read books but she could read the stars; Polaris might help get the runaways north, but Libra—"Justice, son, justice!"—would be the only thing that would make the North a home. "That Libra's important, Augustus, more important than the others. Fix your gaze on it and remember."

Texas is far away from here, Momma, for certain, and the whole damn country just waged war for lots of reasons, and maybe justice was one of them; at least the war became about justice and emancipation once President Lincoln framed it that way and gave that fighting and that death and that horror a higher purpose. And certainly we are pushing for justice now in the Shaw and with the Freedmen's Bureau, pushing for justice ourselves. Yes, ma'am.

Half of a cigar rested on his windowsill, and Augustus thought about lighting it up and finishing it. His tins were inside a pocket in his coat and he thought about something even stronger, but he restrained himself, reaching for the cigar instead just as another series of sounds distracted him: hooves pounding the ground, dogs yelping in the woods again, more insistent than on other evenings. He went to his door, and by the time he opened it, Fiona was out front in a fine black barouche, looking like a woman who owned the entire District. Before either one of them said a word, they were both laughing.

"I will not even ask," Augustus said, chuckling.

"It's Mrs. Lincoln's carriage," Fiona replied, still grinning. "Your Mrs. Keckly and I are now friends, and we met with Mrs. Lincoln in Georgetown."

Augustus whistled, shaking his head. The driver looked down at him suspiciously, refusing to dismount to help Fiona out of the carriage.

"You're staying with this one?" the driver asked Fiona.

Fiona didn't reply. She held her hand out to Augustus, who helped her step down, then she reached back and pulled her bag from the carriage.

"I'll make sure Mrs. Lincoln is aware of your hesitations, sir," Fiona said to the driver, who, without responding, snapped the reins and led the four black horses into a brisk trot away from Augustus's house.

"Are you smoking again, Augustus?" Fiona asked.

Augustus flicked away the cigar, and he and Fiona walked inside; he poured two glasses of water and they sat down. The same candles from the evening before were glowing around the table.

"I was growing worried about you and Temple," he said.

"He hasn't been back yet, then," Fiona replied. "Well, he'll arrive. He always arrives."

"Tell me about Mrs. Lincoln!"

"I want to talk about Mrs. Keckly first, Augustus. I owe you an apology."

Augustus looked away, just as he had the night before when Lizzy first arose as a subject. He hadn't wanted to talk about her then, and he didn't want to talk about her now. Fiona placed her hand on his until he looked at her, and then she told him about meeting Lizzy in Lafayette Park, their journey to Georgetown, and Lizzy's son, George. Just the name George was enough to deflate Augustus, and he sank back in his chair.

"She thinks his death is my fault," Augustus said.

"She used to think that. I don't know that she does now."

"She said that?"

"She did. She wept, but she did."

Augustus pressed his fingers to his eyes and rubbed them.

"I was consumed with melancholy when George Keckly died," he said. "I could not sleep deeply; sometimes I could not sleep at all. I had no appetite, no interest in the everyday. It's a powerful thing for me to hear that his Lizzy is in a forgiving state."

"You are not responsible for George Keckly's death. As Lizzy made clear to me, her grief as a mother confounded her judgment. She lost her child. I do not believe she blames you for that any longer."

Augustus patted Fiona's hand and rose from the table, looking out the window and up at the stars.

"I thought that you and Lizzy had romantic feelings for each other," Fiona said, bursting into the same fit of laughter that overtook her when she arrived earlier in the barouche. Augustus turned back to her and began laughing, too. They let their laughter run a good long spell, until their moment was interrupted by the sound, yet again, of trotting horses.

There were far too many horses approaching the house this time for it to be Temple arriving alone. Augustus glanced out the window, and then he and Fiona hurried to the door. A group of ten men were out front, all of them mounted and carrying rifles that rested across their laps. Their horses were unusually steady, the fog wrapping their fetlocks in a fine mist that held its form because none of the mounts was skittish. One of the men spurred his horse and rode forward. He was a big, steely man, his hair and beard jet black, with a bandage spanning the top of his forehead, and he brought his horse close enough to Augustus and Fiona that its shoulder was just a few feet away from them. The rider leaned down from the horse with a flat, forced smile.

"Your husband recently stole my horse at the B&O, Mrs. McFadden. Would the man of the house be inside?"

"The man of the house is right here," Augustus said.

"She's not owned by any nigger, boy, so keep your lips from flappin'."

A few of the other riders advanced toward the house. There was a gun inside beneath a floorboard, and Augustus began to edge backward toward his door. Two of the riders trotted forward and blocked the path between him and his house.

"How dare you," Fiona said. "You have no decency about you."

"How dare I? Your husband took a very valuable package that belonged to me, then stole my horse after pummeling me with his damn cane, and then intruded upon my afternoon pleasures to inflict yet another of his beatings. How dare I?"

"Then you must be Lafayette Baker," Augustus said.

"Did I not say I want none of your chatter, boy?" said Baker, glancing at one of his men saddled behind Augustus; on cue, the man reached down from his horse and smacked Augustus across the side of his head.

"Well, Mrs. McFadden, I am guilty as charged. I am Lafayette Baker of our capital's National Detective Bureau, and these men are also public servants who work for me. Good men, each and every one of them. I take it that your husband is not here?"

"He is not," Fiona said. "And I don't expect him back this evening, either."

"Now, Mrs. McFadden, I'm hardly a fool. Of course he's on his way back here. Until he arrives, we will have to enjoy the pleasure of one another's company."

"Whenever he arrives, he will not like what he finds here. And he is not a man to be trifled with."

"I will give you that. By all standards, your husband is a wonderment. I was tasked earlier in my life to keep order on the streets of San Francisco. Later on, keeping my identity cloaked in the service of the Union, I tried to track Jefferson Davis himself in Richmond. And I spent twelve days chasing an enigma until my men corralled John Wilkes Booth in a burning barn. But goddammit, madam, I find your husband to be a unique and incalculable bother," said Baker, steady in his saddle. "Still, he is just a man, and I aim to get my package back. And my billfold. The fingerlicker took it off me last time. You married a common thief, Mrs. McFadden."

Baker dismounted slowly and then stepped over to Fiona, placing one hand on her throat and using the other to fiddle with the buttons at the top of her blouse. She grabbed at his wrists to pull his hands away from her but couldn't move his arms. She dug her nails into his arms, but Baker didn't flinch.

"Perhaps you and I should go inside while your nigger friend waits out here," he said.

Augustus cocked his arm, ready to strike Baker, but before he took a step, one of the men behind him cracked him in the back of his head with a rifle butt. Augustus dropped to his knees. The other man near the house got off his horse and opened the door, gesturing to Baker to cross the threshold.

"My men honor me with the spoils of our victory tonight," Baker said. "Follow me inside, Mrs. McFadden, or I will carry you in on my shoulder and dump you on the floor like a sack of field crops."

He grabbed Fiona's wrist and yanked her arm up, stepping toward the house and getting ready to drag her behind him if she resisted.

Fiona pressed her heels into the ground and began to scream, when a loud whistle from near the road caused her and Baker to freeze. Baker turned back, dropping Fiona's wrist, redirecting his energy and attention to something entirely new, a wrinkle in the steady progression of his plans.

The whistle had come through the night and the fog from a man atop a horse, galloping at a full clip up from the road. As the rider got closer to the house, he slowed, easing his horse into a steady trot. Man and animal, both shrouded in the darkness, were indistinguishable from each other, a hard-charging centaur. Fiona and Baker strained to see who it was that approached. As the rider emerged from the gloom and the mist with his cane across his lap, Fiona wrapped her arms around herself, exhaling as her eyes brimmed with tears.

Temple pulled back on his horse's reins as he got closer to the crowd arrayed in front of the house, and he found Fiona's eyes. Then he turned his attention to Baker.

"You should step away from my wife and my friend."

"You don't even carry a gun, McFadden," Baker responded, laughing. "I have my men and their rifles. I have my LeMat and my distaste for you. And I have your nigger and I have your bitch."

"You have twenty bitches, and my wife is certainly not among them."

"How's that?"

"I was merely correcting you."

Baker looked at his men, confused. Then the entire group began to laugh, a soft gloating that became a wave of loud guffaws; each of Baker's men remained uncertain about what Temple meant but was sure that he intended a joke of some sort. Temple sat silently atop his horse until the laughter subsided, then raised his cane and loudly whistled again. A torch caught flame in the woods behind Augustus's house, but no one in Baker's group noticed the first flash of fire.

"Look to the timber behind you," Temple said. "Your bitches are on their way."

In short order, twenty torches flashed in the woods, and all of them, like so many oversized candles glimmering in an unsteady, bouncing line in the dark, began moving out from the shelter of the trees and toward Augustus's house. The trunks of the trees and the undersides of the leaves above them were basked in a honeyed glow when the twenty torchbearers passed by and emerged into the open field. Each of them held a leashed dog in one hand, a torch in the other. And behind each of the torchbearers marched another man carrying a sawed-off shotgun or pistol in one hand and a heavy club in the other—forty men, twenty dogs, and the lot of them seemed readily inclined, even itching, to fight, as they would on almost any day of the week and for almost any reason. To be expected, Temple thought with satisfaction as the torchbearers tightened around Baker's men: they're Swampdoodlians.

"Meet my legions, here to own the night and protect the homestead," shouted Nail, stepping to the front of the pack and pulling back hard on his wolfhound, which was straining on its leash and up on its hind legs. "We're also here to offer you some choices, Baker, you scurvy pest."

As soon as Baker recognized that it was Nail leading the torchbearers, he turned on him with a snarl.

"We helped set you up, Flaherty. In all my living days, Wood and I helped set up your shitty little counterfeiting operation, and now you're here representing and defending this vermin," he said, gesturing toward Temple, Fiona, and Augustus, who was still on his knees. Temple dismounted and walked toward the group, placing himself between Baker and his wife and Augustus.

"Me cogniacs is me cogniacs," said Nail, a long vein beginning to throb on the side of his forehead. "But me friends is me friends. Ya got it?"

"I got nothing," Baker screamed, unholstering his LeMat. The gun had nine revolving chambers on top, attached to a long, slender barrel, and a second fatter and shorter smoothbore barrel beneath that could fire a single shotgun round. The upper barrel would have gotten a shot off quickly. But in the dark, with Nail a good thirty feet away, Baker chose to spray his fire; he flicked up a rod on the right side of the LeMat's hammer, readying the firing pin so he could discharge the 28-gauge shell acked in the lower barrel. Fiddling with the pin took only a moment, but the delay gave Temple as much time as he needed.

As Baker raised the LeMat, Temple whipped his cane against his wrist, splintering the bone. Wincing and swearing, Baker dropped the LeMat and, with his other hand, drew a Bowie knife from his waistband, raising it above his head and rounding on Temple.

Temple grabbed Baker's good wrist, twisting it up and away from his body so forcefully that Baker yelled in pain and dropped the knife. Baker strained, trying to resist, but Temple kept twisting his arm backward until he fell to his knees.

"You insulted my wife and my friend, Mr. Baker."

"Nigger lover."

Temple, as he had at Mary Ann Hall's, slammed his cane into Baker's head, leaving him unconscious on the ground. As soon as Baker dropped, one of his men wheeled on his horse, working the lever on his Spencer, cocking its hammer, and aiming the rifle at Temple. Nail set his wolfhound loose, and the dog bolted at the shooter, leaping and sinking its teeth into his leg. A cloud of gunsmoke erupted from the barrel of the Spencer as the rider screamed in pain. The .56–56 missed Temple, blowing instead through one of the windows of the house.

All of the dogs were barking now, and Nail's men spread out, steadily encircling the smaller loop of Baker's men.

"Listen here, boys," Nail shouted, raising his torch. "We can each go to it and make this bloody, mix it up, trade what we got. Or we can lodge sensicles, marvelations, and wisdoshiness into our heads and part for the night."

The shooter with the Spencer was swearing at Nail's wolfhound still hanging off his thigh. Nail snapped his fingers and the dog dropped off, blood dripping from its mouth, and trotted back to its master.

"What say you, boys?" Nail repeated. "There are forty of us and just a handful of you turnips. I'll give you about ten seconds to decide before we tear you up."

"We don't leave without Mr. Baker," one of the men said.

"Temple?" Nail asked.

"I want to keep Mr. Baker here for the night," Temple said. "We have matters to consider."

"Won't work," shouted one of Baker's men. "He's with us. And when Mr. Stanton hears of this, you'll have hell to pay."

Temple weighed it all—Augustus and Fiona, the men on both sides who'd get killed or hurt, the smell of the Spencer's powder still drifting in the air, the weight of the night—and nodded at Nail.

"Get your man, boys," Nail shouted to the group. "Horse him up and get him out of here. If any of you return tomorrow, the next day, the next month, whenever, we won't give you the consideration."

Two of Baker's men dismounted and lifted his body, carrying it over to his horse and getting ready to hoist him across the saddle.

"Leave Mr. Baker's horse here," Temple said. "I liked his last horse before it was shot out from beneath me, and I'm sure I'll like this one. I'm keeping his gun, too."

"You can't take a man's horse and his gun," said one of Baker's men.

"Get your arse moving," Nail yelled. "All of you should feel sainted that you're even making it back home tonight. Stop the palaver and move."

Baker's men loaded him across a horse and lined up on their own mounts, trotting down to the road and into the dark. Temple swept Fiona into his arms and then put an arm around Augustus's shoulders. Fiona slipped her arm around Temple's waist.

"You arranged for Nail to oversee Augustus's house?" she asked him. He nodded, and she pulled him down to her and kissed him.

"Now I know why I kept hearing dogs in the woods for the last week," said Augustus. "The guardian angels of Swampdoodle. I'm grateful, Mr. Flaherty."

"Nail's enough. We're familiars now."

Augustus nodded.

"Anyway, 'tain't nothin'," Nail said. "I'm going to send my boys back to the woods and then confer with Temple privately, if you and Mrs. McFadden don't take insult at that."

Augustus was bleeding from the back of his head where the rifle butt had hit him, and Fiona took him inside to dress his wound. Nail scooped the LeMat off the ground and examined it.

"I haven't seen one of these before, Temple. What is it?"

"It's a LeMat, a Secesh gun. Baker drew it on me at the B&O that first morning when I found the diaries, and I knew right then that he had to be tied into the army in some way. Confederate officers carried LeMats and other arms made by the Frenchies because they were cut off from our guns up here. But the LeMat was unusual, and I reckon that Baker got it when he was spying in the South."

Temple took the gun from Nail, holding the walnut grips closer to the torch so that he could look at them more closely. Etched along the bottom of one of the grips was the original owner's name: "Col. George S. Patton—Richmond."

"There you go—Baker either stole it or beat it out of this Patton fellow," Temple said. "Alexander Gardner told me he trained Baker as a photographer so that he could spy in Richmond. He obviously collected mementos there as well."

"Arsehole!" Nail crowed. "Toting a Secesh gun."

"You keep it," Temple said, giving Nail the LeMat. "I'm no good with guns, and you deserve it, saving us all here."

"You saved me twice in New York, Temple. Not once. Twice."

"Then you still owe me a rescue."

"Baker is powerful strong and vicious, but you drove him into the ground."

"Only because I had an audience. The audience I want, however, is with the war secretary."

"Will he want to meet with you?"

"I think not."

"Then you'll have to get his ear in a public place. Think on that. What's happening on Tuesday?"

"Of course. Inspired, Nail, inspired."

"Yep, the Grand Review. Straight down Pennsylvania, two hundred thousand troops, two days from tomorrow, marking the end of the war. Stanton is sure to be in the reviewing stand, since he ordered up the whole shindig. You should be there, too."

"Thank you again, Nail."

"Danger's going to charge harder at you now, Temple. Baker wants what you have and you've embarrassed him too many times. He's not one to up and go away."

"I know. We'll have to leave Augustus's house soon. Can you maintain us in Swampdoodle?"

"For a brief time, a week or two. Keeping a Negro in there for that time is a juggle, for certain. But I've always found whatever widdy I needed to pop a lock, and I can mentalate around this hurdle, certain. Understand: I don't have any worries about standing up to Baker and the rest of his amalgamation, but I can't hold him off forever."

"A week is all I'll need. And Fiona and I will both need clothing."

"Then you'll have both—and I have an extra gift in mind for you as well."

Nail's wolfhound was at his feet, and it jumped up by his side as soon as he began walking back to the woods. He wrapped the dog's leash around his hand and set off toward a ring of torches deep into the trees, where he could hear harmonicas, fiddles, and song, where he knew there would be drink, where he would sit down amid his lads and their dogs and their tales and their cursing and their time in the night, in this night, under the stars—the very same stars at which Augustus had gazed before Baker arrived and the lines were drawn.

CHAPTER SEVENTEEN

THE WHITWORTH

"Mr. Baker didn't know my name when we encountered each other at Mary Ann Hall's," Temple said to Augustus and Fiona as he tipped his chair back against the wall, allowing it to rock slightly. "But he came here tonight knowing I had a wife and knowing my last name."

"How did he find you out?" Augustus asked.

"I'm working on that."

Temple had shown them the pictures of Booth, and when he was done speaking about his conversation with Gardner, Fiona told Temple about her meeting with Mrs. Lincoln. All of them were weary to their bones, and less animated about their mutual news than they might have been on a different evening. But Temple was pleased that Fiona would have an entire train ride with Mrs. Lincoln, and Augustus was anxious to work some of the code from the diary.

"It won't be easy getting you on the train with Mrs. Lincoln," Temple said. "She travels in a private car."

"But I am her invited guest," Fiona said.

"You're also my wife, and some of those around Mrs. Lincoln are likely to know as much. Her son has retained Pinkerton for other work. If he's there—or if Baker appears—then you'll never make it onto the train. They'll make sure of that."

"I suggest we sleep well for at least a night. We can measure our approaches to our problems in the morning," Fiona said.

"A wise woman!" said Augustus, who rose, stretched, and opened a blanket on the floor. He had given up his bedroom to Fiona and

Temple but had borrowed a straw mattress from the Campbell Hospital and laid it on the floor of his sitting room. After Temple and Fiona left the room, he took off his boots and shirt and lay down to sleep.

In Augustus's bedroom, Fiona and Temple rinsed their hands, necks, and faces with water and a sponge that he had left for them in a basin on a table near the door. There was also a small tin filled with powdered Peruvian bark that he had mixed with myrrh, green sage, and white honey so that they could clean their teeth. After washing, Fiona lighted a candle and knelt by the side of the bed, opening her Book of Common Prayer. Her lips began moving silently, but Temple knew her prayer before bed and could hear it in his head.

> *Oh, Lord, our heavenly Father,*
> *By whose Almighty power we have been preserved this day;*
> *By thy great mercy defend us from all perils*
> *and dangers of this night;*
> *For the love of thy only Son, our Savior, Jesus Christ. Amen.*

There was a small window by the bed, and Temple could still see the torches glowing in the woods nearby and the silhouette of one man, fiddle in hand, dancing on one leg as he played. Temple stared out the window, thinking about the days ahead of them and all that was left to learn and do, and then he pulled the shade down. He turned to Fiona, who had changed into one of Augustus's shirts and was wearing it as a nightdress.

"You need to pray, too, my defective," she said.

"It's easier for you," he said. "You have faith and I have confusion."

He rested his cane against the wall and slipped off his boots. Fiona began unbuttoning his trousers, and he slipped his hand inside her shirt, pulling her onto the bed.

"I would like to have children, Temple."

"Tonight?"

"One day," she said, smiling.

"You'll tell me when that day comes?"

"I will."

THERE WERE BAKED beans, bread, coffee, and water on the table when they woke up. And on the road down the hill from Augustus's house there were long lines of Union infantry, cavalry, and artillery rolling past on their way into the District. Temple joined Augustus, who had awoken earlier, outside his house. Both of them were accustomed to seeing soldiers with the Army of the Potomac in and around the District, but these were William Tecumseh Sherman's men, the Army of the Tennessee, and they wore a jumble of different sack coats, frock coats, and shell jackets over their trousers—some were regulation blue, like the standard uniforms worn by Grant's men, but most were a hodgepodge of ragtag styles and hues. Mules and pack horses rode alongside the troops, loaded down with booty that Sherman's bummers had looted from Southern cities and plantations: huge saddlebags bursting with silver candlesticks and platters, glassware, swords, fine china, paintings, rifles, jewelry, and coins, and—strapped or tied across some of the animals' backs—clocks, chairs, and tables.

Temple put a hand on Augustus's shoulder as they both watched the troops march along.

"Nail says there's going to be two hundred thousand soldiers in Washington for the Grand Review to celebrate the end of the war," Temple said. "The Army of the Potomac parades on Tuesday and the Army of the Tennessee parades on Wednesday. What land could have an army of this size in its capital and not fear a coup? Europe could never have this."

But Augustus wasn't paying attention to the troops or the plunder or the sheer number of soldiers who were pouring into the city. Instead, his eyes were riveted on the former slaves trotting along next to the mules, Negroes whom Sherman's men had also captured in the South and brought North with them.

"What land honors its soldiers for a war of liberation while it parades former slaves as if they are spoils rather than human beings? General Sherman wouldn't let any black soldiers fight alongside him, and he ignored Stanton's calls to arm slaves," Augustus whispered. "Now it's said that Sherman makes light of Stanton's efforts to protect Negro voters in the South. So why does Sherman's army spool these slaves alongside their mules today? Are they trophies, or will they be given shelter, an education, and work?"

Fiona, coffee in hand, stepped out to join them.

"This is why the District needs you to teach and needs you to help steer the Freedmen's Bureau, Augustus," she said. "So that they aren't just brought here as trophies and forgotten."

Augustus shook his head, speaking past Fiona.

"It's not just the slaves they're trotting along that vexes me," he said. "They are not allowing a single Negro soldier to march in the Grand Review, either—soldiers who risked their lives alongside white soldiers. Not a single one."

Fiona placed her hand on his arm, but Augustus kicked the ground in front of himself, thrusting his hands into his pockets.

Temple looked across the field toward the woods, where Nail was also standing, watching the troops file past. His wolfhound was sitting by his side, and he was leaning on an Enfield, mesmerized by the number of men marching on the road. Temple stared at Nail until the other man looked over, then raised his hand to wave. Nail waved back quickly, then returned to looking at the troops.

"Augustus, shall we work on our cipher?" Temple asked.

The three of them went to a table inside, and Augustus pulled out a slat on the wall, where he had hidden the two diaries. Augustus handed Mary Todd Lincoln's diary to Fiona, who held it in her hands, unsure of what to do with it.

"You could read it and acquaint yourself with it before your train ride to Chicago," Temple suggested.

"And then I would be doing exactly that which the two of you have done: compromising Mrs. Lincoln's intimacies," Fiona said.

"So how shall you prepare yourself for conversations with her, then?"

"I trust that she will tell me whatever she cares to tell me about her husband, of her own accord. Not because I have loitered upon her twilight thoughts."

"That is well and fine, but there are reasons that Mr. Baker wants Mrs. Lincoln's diary, and we need to understand those reasons ourselves. Considering that, reading her diary is not a sin."

"Well, you have told me enough of what you found in her journal for me to understand what we need to inquire of her. But I still want to say to her with all honesty that I myself have not peeked inside her diary. Now, I need to bathe and pack for my journey tomorrow."

Inside a cramped enclosure next to the bedroom, barely larger than a closet, Augustus had placed a large cast-iron cistern that he used for a tub. Fiona took two large pails to the well outside and began filling them; it would take her more than a dozen trips to fill the cistern and then she would need to wait an hour or so for the chill to come off the water before she could bathe.

As she passed in and out of the house, Temple and Augustus pulled the Vigenère table from Booth's diary and reengaged with their puzzle.

"Look hard at this again," Temple said to Augustus, writing *MARKOFC* on a piece of paper. "This is our cipher for breaking the Vigenère table, and I've gotten no further than when you said you had it days ago," Augustus said. "I am at a loss for how to proceed."

"I would read Booth's diary again, and I would read it with the eye of a sleuth."

"Your eye."

"No, Augustus, entirely yours, opened in new ways so as to gaze upon new places."

Augustus took up the diary as Temple walked outside to watch more lines of soldiers march past the house. It was a perfectly clear day, warm and free of the fog and rain of recent weeks. As Fiona approached the house with two more pails, Temple took one from her and tried to keep it from spilling as he trudged back into the house on his cane. He poured the water into the cistern and went back outside to the well. The last line of troops had filed past on the road, and Fiona was pumping more water. Nail, his Enfield in hand, was walking back into the woods. Temple refilled his pail and, as he neared the house, heard Augustus shouting. He hurried inside and left the pail in the middle of the room just inside the door.

"Temple, I have it!"

Augustus was standing, reading aloud from the Booth diary:

Patriot has told Maestro that I am no traitor, I am sure. Patriot says that Maestro owns Lord War. Davey, George, and Lewis are all heroes also, even if they, too, share the mark of Cain. Those that find this, those that chase me, know the cipher, and the cipher is true. I do not care that I am made a villain among those who honor the Tyrant. He wanted nigger citizenship and I ran him through.

"And?"

" 'They too share the mark of Cain.' There it is, *MARKOFC*, embedded in that sentence. The cipher is 'mark of Cain.' "

"Congratulations, Augustus. The world turns and you, too, are now a detective."

Temple stepped toward the water pail and into a rectangle of sunlight that poured through the doorway, painting a patch of the floor a creamy yellow. As he bent down, he heard two gunshots—bursting quickly and nearly in tandem, like two small, brief thunderclaps—and a bullet flashed past his leg and tore though the metal pail, leaving holes on opposite sides that leaked onto the floor in crisp, arced spouts. Temple dropped down, away from the light, and waved Augustus to the floor as well.

"Fiona?" he shouted.

"I am here and I am fine," she yelled from outside. "Are you hurt?"

"Only our pail. What of Nail?"

"He is well, too. Come out."

Augustus helped Temple to his feet, and the first thing they saw as they passed through the door was a man's body hanging upside down by the legs from the lower branches of a tree across the road, a four-foot-long rifle dangling on a strap from his shoulder. Nail was running toward them from across the field, the blue ink stains on his hands and arms visible now as they hadn't been the night before, and he whooped loudly, thrusting his Enfield up and down above his head. Dozens of his men were flooding out of the woods behind him, and Fiona, her hand on her mouth, stood watching as Nail hooted, at a loss for words of her own.

"Let's go take a look-see!" Nail shouted to Temple and Augustus as he ran at an angle past them and zipped across the road, not stopping until he was almost on top of the dead body tangled in the tree. Augustus was right behind him and while they waited for Temple to work his way to them on his cane, Nail began scrounging around the dead man's body. Several of Nail's men pushed forward, too, but he swore at the group, ordering them back and peeling a pouch of bullets off the corpse's belt. Then he yanked the rifle off the dead man's shoulder and began examining it. By the time Temple and Fiona reached him, Nail was issuing a series of elated whistles as he scanned the rifle's stock, butt, barrel, and sights.

"Today, on the face of this good, green earth, and with witnesses in abundance, Jack Flaherty did himself pick off a Union sharpshooter tucked in the trees and intent on plugging his bosom friend Temple McFadden from a range of . . ." With this, Nail looked back at the house, gauging the distance. "A range of about a hundred and twenty-five yards. All here say: 'Aye, Jack Flaherty, marksman robusto and boodler supremo!'"

In unison, all of Nail's men did as they were told: "Aye, Jack Flaherty, marksman robusto and boodler supremo!"

Nail pulled Temple over to look at the rifle, and Temple couldn't recall a time when Nail looked happier. Nail pointed to an engraving on the stock: "1st Regiment."

"This dead soul fought with Hi Berdan's group in the war. They were the best sharpshooters in the army, and this rifle—ooh, this rifle—is a Whitworth, costing ninety-six dollars new and now mine by rightful appropriation! To get in with Berdan you had to be able—from two hundred yards out, mind you—to place ten shots in a ten-inch circle. If you couldn't do that, he wouldn't have you. And here is the loverly part," Nail said, opening up the pouch of bullets, "The Whitworth fires ungodly pricey rounds, all shaped like little hexagons, and our dead marksman had a full stash on him!"

"The loverly part, Nail, is that you got him before he got me," Temple said. "Now we are even."

"I'm not countin'."

"How did you know?"

"They put Baker's body across a riderless horse last night. Somebody snuck away, because they didn't ride up with an extra horse. Didn't even absorb into my thinkerings that they hauled him off like that till I started looking at those mules pass by this morning with Southern loot strapped to their backs. So whoever they left behind could try to hide in the woods behind the house, 'cepting we was there. That left 'em the hospital, but too many other people in there. Only other spot to hide in is the clutch of trees right here. When the soldiers began filing by, I stood there, making like I was enrapturated by them. But I was scanning the trees for revelations. At one point he wiggled, just a little, and a tingling of sunsplash sparkled on his barrel. So when the troops wound down, I playacted back into the woods and set up with my Enfield. Split that farker's head as soon as his barrel stuck its nose through the branches."

"He didn't miss me by much," Temple said. "I heard his shot and yours as if they were married."

"Fast and good, sure he was, but he's morbitized now and you are still breathing," Nail said, slapping Temple on the back.

Nail's men pulled the corpse from the tree, and it flopped down onto its back; a ruby-red splotch of blood was splattered around a fist-sized hole in the sharpshooter's head, pale shards of skull and gray flecks of brain matter oozing onto the ground. Fiona turned away, shaking her head, and walked silently back to the house.

"This here is a fanatical group Baker has around him, Temple. He's scoring Union sharpies and who knows who else," Nail said. "You got to get out of the house tonight. I think Baker will be back here in force by then. And, Augustus, I reckon they'll burn down your house once they find it's empty."

Augustus nodded and turned back to the house.

"I have a good cast-iron cookstove in my back room," he said over his shoulder to Nail. "If you've got a wagon, you are welcome to take it before Baker comes for my house."

Nail's men took off the dead sharpshooter's boots, picked his pockets clean, and then dragged him by his feet across the road and the field and into the woods, where they buried him.

TEMPLE WAS CARTING the dirty water from Fiona's bath and dumping it at the side of the house later that afternoon, when Sojourner crossed over from the hospital.

"There's a sight," she cried. "Police Chief McFadden."

"I'm not the chief of police, Sojourner."

"You are very chief, and I know my chieftains. I'll call you how I see fit. Now, we seen all you gathering and firing arms for a day and a half and none of us even thought about leaving the hospital until you were done with your ruckus. My concern is that Augustus and that sweet wife of yours ain't coming into harm, because I am certain nobody came here for the two of them."

"They're right as rain, and you should join us inside."

"Truth told, I'd be awful teary if anything happened to you, too, Chief McFadden, because you're stand-up. I worry less about you, though—your type maintains in rough moments. Augustus is our scholar and your Fiona has a heart, and I'll save my worries for them."

"They'll both be glad you're here."

Augustus had wrapped up the Booth diary in one package and Mrs. Lincoln's in another. Both were on the table next to an open carpetbag holding his clothes and a few books. The Colt he had retrieved from the floorboards was next to the bag, and when Sojourner entered, he was poring over a small stack of pages he had transcribed from the Booth diaries.

"Will you take this into the alleys for me and make sure it's safely hidden there?" he asked, handing her the Booth diary.

"Y'all right, son?"

"I am. And I hate to be full of requests, but would you have two spare suitcases in the hospital for Fiona and Temple to borrow for a few days? They've been out of their own home for some time and will be vagrants even longer now."

"Assuredly."

Fiona, brushing her hair in the bedroom, heard Sojourner's voice and ran out to meet her. They were embracing when Temple came inside.

"Fast friends," he said.

"Li'l piece of starlight here," said Sojourner. "And it looks like we're gettin' crowded."

Nail was at the door with two stacks of clothing and a leather billfold. He put them on the table, pulling his hat from his head and greeting Sojourner.

"Jack Flaherty."

"Sojourner Truth, and I'm departin' so I can do my chores for Augustus before the sun hides. Wishin' all of ya wellness," she said, holding the diary close to her chest as she began marching out the door.

Temple stopped Sojourner and bent down to whisper in her ear, pressing a note and some money into her hand as he spoke to her. She nodded, patted his arm, and went on her way. Temple then turned to the bundle of clothing Nail had brought him: two pairs of trousers, two shirts, socks, and long johns. Fiona's pile had two walking dresses, pantalets, a corset, and a corset cover.

"Mr. Flaherty, you are an invention!" Fiona said, delighted. "I find corsets a murderous strangulation and will have to ignore that gift, but these are the first fresh clothes I've had in days. My sincerest regards for your courtesies—and your protection."

"Nothing of it. One of them dresses is fancier than the other. Temple and I were thinkin' it might make sense for you to have a more fashionable cut, seeing that you're traveling with Mrs. Lincoln," Nail said. "We'll be back up here to fetch all of you in an hour or so, and then we'll make our way to Swampdoodle."

Fiona went into the bedroom to pack her clothes, and Temple sorted through the pile that Nail had brought him. Stuck between the shirts and trousers was a fat billfold, stuffed with about $2,000 in greenbacks. He held it up for Augustus to see.

"Cogniacs?" Augustus asked.

"I would never know," Temple replied. "So I will have to ask our boodler. If they are true, then we are well financed."

LATER THAT EVENING, a telegram for Allan Pinkerton arrived at the Willard just after supper, and a hotel clerk delivered it to him in the lounge, interrupting his brandy and cigar. He gave the clerk three Indian heads and stepped away from his group to read his message privately, as he did anytime he received a telegram:

> *Alexandria, May 21, 1865*
> *Meet me at the Marshall House at the corner of King and Pitt tomorrow evening at 6 pm. I have information about the Booth diary and McFadden. Come alone, with funds.*

Pinkerton smiled to himself and sat back down to enjoy his brandy, watching the Willard's lobby swell with visitors arriving to partake in the Grand Review.

CHAPTER EIGHTEEN

THE PULLMAN

Nail housed Temple, Fiona, and Augustus in a three-room shack abutting the warehouse where he made his cogniacs. There were two beds in one of the rooms, a single bed in another, and a common washbasin and some chairs in the third. Other than that, the shack was empty, soured by the stench off the Tiber Canal, an odor that crawled across every path and room in Swampdoodle. After spending Sunday night discussing their plans for the following days, they all fell into a deep sleep.

Temple awoke ahead of the other two early the next morning, and when he stepped outside, he found Nail sitting in a chair facing the shack, his Enfield resting on his lap. His legs were stretched out in front of him, and from the look of his eyes and the muss of his hair he had been keeping watch all night. He sat up as Temple walked outside, glad to have the company.

"Some folks are talking about General Sherman, saying Stanton was worried about letting him in the District with all of his troops," Nail said. "They aren't letting Sherman sit in the reviewing stand near the President's House on the first day. It'll just be Johnson, Grant, and Stanton: two drunks and a bully."

"President Johnson and Grant may be drunks, but General Grant is a leader. And Mr. Stanton is a complicated man."

"Well, to get your chance to speak with him tomorrow you're gonna have to get close to him. Have you thought on that?"

"I have. Still thinking. But until I arrive at the solution, I have something else for you. We've made more sense of some of the pages from the Booth diary, and I'd like you to look at them."

Temple first gave Nail a copy of the Vigenère table and the slip of paper with *MARKOFCAIN* on it. Nail eyed the cipher and smiled.

"Booth was rather taken with his own drama, was he not? Makin' his shatty little deed biblical."

Temple gave him four telegrams and Nail spread them out on the ground, putting rocks on each of them to hold them down. He read through all of them several times, murmuring as he did so and letting his finger slide along under each name, stopping at names that, while decoded, were still a mystery:

March 4, 1865
From: Patriot
To: Avenger
    There is a room for you at National. I am for Elmira and Montreal. Horses to Richmond when you have Tyrant.

April 5, 1865
From: Patriot
To: Avenger
    Maestro sends funds. Goliath and others will join you. Wise Man and Drinker should be taken with Tyrant.

April 11, 1865
From: Patriot
To: Avenger
    You will be allowed to pass at Navy Yard Bridge. Refuge at Tavern.

April 14, 1865
From: Patriot
To: Avenger
    It is Ford's. Praetorians send a Parker to guard Tyrant. He will abandon the door or let you pass.

Nail read the notes several times and became so enmeshed that he didn't notice that Augustus had awoken and walked out of his shack to join him and Temple outside. When Nail was done parsing the notes he looked up and nodded a hello to Augustus.

"It looks like they wanted to pack off with Lincoln originally—kidnap him to Richmond, maybe?" he asked. "They probably realized they could never get out of the District alive with Abe in tow."

"There could have been other reasons they decided against kidnapping him," Augustus said. "Perhaps they needed President Lincoln out of the way entirely."

"So we assume that 'Avenger' is Booth and 'Tyrant' is Lincoln?" Nail asked.

"Assuredly they are."

" 'Patriot'?"

"Not a notion," said Augustus.

" 'Goliath'?"

"Lewis Powell," said Temple.

"How do you know?"

"Alexander Gardner told me that Baker and others referred to him that way, because of his size," Temple said. "And Powell attacked Seward the night Lincoln was assassinated, so—"

"So 'Wise Man' is the secretary of state."

"Yes. And I imagine 'Drinker' is Andrew Johnson."

"So the night of the assassination they targeted the president, the vice president, and the secretary of state."

"But they don't appear to have Edwin Stanton, the war secretary, on their list," said Temple. "Why not?"

"Is he 'Maestro'?"

"Perhaps. Though elsewhere in the diary Booth mentions 'Lord War,' which may be Stanton. I'm unsure."

"Some of the rest of this is clear. On the night of the murder, Booth escaped from the District and into Maryland on the Navy

Yard Bridge; the papers said the Union soldiers guarding the bridge didn't stop him. The papers also said that the Surratt family had a tavern in Maryland that Booth may have been aiming for, so the April eleventh telegram isn't too difficult."

"The April fourteenth telegram I understand, too. The Metropolitan Police Department is, I'm sure, the 'Praetorians,'" Temple said. "They sent one of ours, John Parker, to guard the door outside Lincoln's box at Ford's. I know Parker. He's a drinker, loose with his gun. He left the president unprotected at Ford's so he could go find a damn drink. Booth got into the box through Parker's door, and the MPD brought Parker up on charges of neglect of duty. Someone got the case dismissed."

Augustus stared at his stove, which was secured with thick coils of rope in the back of a wagon. Then he squatted down next to Temple and Nail and tapped his finger on the March 4 telegram.

"Someone sent Booth money so he could stay at the National Hotel. And look, it doesn't say 'kill Tyrant.' It says 'when you have Tyrant,'" Augustus said. "In March it looks like they weren't contemplating an assassination. It looks as if they wanted to kidnap Mr. Lincoln and hide him in Richmond. Something changed their minds between March fourth and April fourteenth."

"Reality probably changed their minds," Nail said. "Stealing the president like a sack of potatoes is a mite bit of a chore."

"That could be true."

"Out of the way of what?"

"I don't know."

The three men sat back down on the ground, and Temple handed the pile of telegrams back to Augustus.

"We need to know who 'Patriot' and 'Maestro' are," said Temple. "We find them, we find everything. There are more telegrams for Augustus to unlock, but that will have to wait because he has an appointment."

"And you?" Nail asked. "Where are you bound for?"

"You mean 'we,'" Temple replied. "This evening, you and I are going to escort Fiona to the B&O so she can join Mrs. Lincoln on her six p.m. train to Chicago."

FIONA ARRIVED AT the B&O at five-thirty. Though the station wasn't far from Swampdoodle, Temple had put her in a carriage that traced a circular route across G Street and up Massachusetts, then on K back over to New Jersey and down to the B&O. No use anyone knowing where she was coming from, he told her before he kissed her, placed a wad of greenbacks in her bag, and helped her into the carriage.

The B&O was as busy as Fiona had ever seen it, even during the height of the war. Travelers were arriving from all points for the Grand Review, and each of the station's three tracks had a train on it. For all of the commotion, Mrs. Lincoln waited almost unnoticed with her two sons—a tiny, fidgeting woman slipping the bonds of a city about to celebrate the end of a war that had martyred her husband and left her isolated, adrift, and no longer tolerated.

Lizzy spotted Fiona and waved, walking forward to help her with her bag.

"Mr. Robert is angry with his mother for letting you join us," she said to Fiona. "He said our traveling party is big enough as it is. But Mrs. Lincoln hushed him and told him there was plenty of room on their train and that you and I were the closest of friends."

"I'm grateful, Lizzy, and our train is undeniably magnificent."

Abutting the platform were Mrs. Lincoln's private cars, a pair of long, black, gleaming boxes atop sixteen iron wheels. Gold lettering on each of the cars' sides announced them as the Pullman Pioneer, and black bunting hung from the rows of rectangular windows that wrapped the upper third of the cars. The bunting was a remnant from the Pioneer's only previous run, ferrying President Lincoln and his casket from Chicago to Springfield after his funeral train arrived from Washington. Now, at Mrs. Lincoln's request, and keen for the publicity that would accompany her journey, George Pullman had sent the Pioneer across the country from Chicago to bring the president's widow back home, too.

Fiona, like everyone else in the District, had followed Mr. Pullman's new company with interest. He was said to be building a fleet of elegant sleeper cars that would make rail travel the most modern of modern contrivances. The Pioneer alone cost $20,000 to build, almost seven times more than competitors' sleepers; it had plush lounge chairs, high ceilings with ventilation, crystal chandeliers, beveled mirrors, etched glass, and dining service in its parlor car, while washrooms, linen closets, and wide, soft beds carved from cherrywood graced the sleeper car.

A twenty-five-ton steam engine was separated from the Pioneer's cars by a wide tender piled high with chunks of firewood. A sweeping triangular cowcatcher turned the front of the engine into a massive, imperious arrow, and the locomotive's boiler was topped off with a two-foot oil-fueled headlight and a five-foot metal smokestack leaking a hazy stream of white vapor from its bonnet as the stoker opened his blower to keep the idling train's fire hot. At peak speed, the Pioneer could travel faster than twenty miles an hour. Even with stops to refuel or take on new passengers, it could sprint to Chicago from Washington in only fifty-four hours—a pace that boggled the imagination.

As the baggage masters loaded Mrs. Lincoln's trunks onto the train, she waved Fiona over with a series of quick flaps of her hand.

"Mrs. McFadden, these are my sons, Robert and Tad."

Robert Lincoln held out his hand, barely acknowledging Fiona's presence. Taking after his mother in stature and looks, he was slight and had fine features and eyes. A light sheen of macassar kept his hair pressed against his head, in the European fashion, and he had a delicate, neatly trimmed moustache. Like his mother, he was aloof.

"Mother, Mr. Pinkerton was to be here this evening to see us off," Robert said. "Have you seen him?"

Mrs. Lincoln simply shook her head in response, and Robert, after bowing slightly to Fiona, climbed aboard the train. For his part,

Tad, the twelve-year-old, held out a bag full of apples to Fiona, and she reached in and took one.

"Thank you so much, Tad," Fiona said. "Can you tell me how you got your wonderful name?"

"My father gave it to me when I was a baby. He said that my head was so large atop my little body that I looked like a tadpole! My real name is Thomas."

"Which name do you prefer?"

"I prefer Tad because it came from my father and he made me laugh."

Mrs. Lincoln was looking on blankly, barely aware of the conversation or any of the people around her. Lizzy helped Tad onto the train and then turned back to help Mrs. Lincoln with a small bag she was carrying herself.

"I am traveling efficiently today," the widow said. "I sent fifty-five boxes ahead to Chicago to T. B. Bryan's residence on Twenty-second Street. American Express handled the shipment for me, without a charge. Mr. Pullman is letting us journey to Illinois at his expense as well. You see, vendors are honored to make a sale with me, and I make it my practice never to impose upon their good wishes by paying."

The train's engineer rang the Pioneer's bell and one of the baggage men approached Mrs. Lincoln.

"All aboard, Madame President."

"It is the night before a commemoration of a war my husband prosecuted, and there is no one here to see me off but my family and a baggage man," the widow said. "I will not miss Washington."

Fiona pulled Mrs. Lincoln's diary from her bag and gave it to her before they boarded. The widow smoothed the brown wrapping paper covering the diary and then took Lizzy's hand to board the Pioneer. Fiona followed them up, and several minutes later the whistle blew as the train pulled away, its wheels and pistons starting to turn in rushed, breathy whooshes. Temple and Nail stepped forward from the shadows beneath one of the overhangs at the end of the platform and watched it slip past. Temple lifted his cane to Fiona, who gave him a small, surreptitious wave from her window.

"Nail," said Temple, "the greenbacks you gave me. They're authentic?"

"Some is and some isn't. I mixed it up."

"How can I tell the difference?"

"If you can't sort them out, Temple, then why fill your head with ruminations?"

"You jumbled them on purpose so I wouldn't give them back to you."

"Perish the thought."

AFTER SOJOURNER HAD taken Augustus's package to Tiber Island, she delivered the messages that Temple had given her. The first went to the furry, bad-tempered photographer who always, always cursed a storm, heaven forgive him. He met her in front of his studio and also asked her to convey a note of his own to Temple. The second message Sojourner had to pass on was for Mary Ann Hall at her "dirty li'l establishment" on Maryland Avenue—and Sojourner intended to have a word with Temple later about him asking her to tote notes to a cathouse. Lordy.

PINKERTON HAD TO cross the Long Bridge from Washington into Virginia in order to get to the Marshall House in Alexandria, and the journey was a powerful test of his patience. The bridge itself was a mile long and three carriages wide, and on the Virginia side the Army of the Tennessee had pitched camp to await its triumphant march into the District on Wednesday.

Beyond that was a toll road that would take him another eight miles or so—past swamps, ravines, and hillocks peppered with stunted pines and under the Cumberland Canal viaduct—to Alexandria. Normally he could get there in one to two hours depending on the condition of the roads. Today, with the Long Bridge stuffed with wagons, horses, and pedestrians swarming the District to attend the parades, his carriage moved at a crawl, and he had given himself more than three hours to travel so as not to miss his parley.

Three hours was raw sacrifice. Among their many disciplines, the Pinkertons functioned on proper time management. It was, as Pinkerton himself made sure to invoke time and again in tutorials he gave to his staff, the bedrock of their organization. A minute wasted could never be recaptured. Yet here he was, pulled along by a promise and a note into offering up the better part of an afternoon. Patriotism was a worthy end, too, however, and Pinkerton and his staff were Union men through and through. His day and his time lumbering along to Virginia could both be redeemed if he retrieved at the Marshall House what he needed.

As he entered Alexandria, Pinkerton found the town pleasing. It was orderly, industrious, and tightly controlled, as every good town should be. It had its houses surrounded by fine gardens, its stores in squat brick buildings, and its churches green with ivy on almost every square, and warehouses and wharves laced its riverfront. A town that once had proudly displayed secession flags from its custom house and its homes was now little more than a military outpost fortified with Union cannon.

The Marshall House was handsome, if modest: three stories and an attic encased in red brick. Pinkerton entered and inquired after McFadden. Yet another note awaited him, and he scanned it before crumpling it into a ball and rushing back into the street. As the note instructed, he made his way to a green carriage at the curb about a block up from the hotel. A woman's hand dangled from the window, a scarlet kerchief ringed in white lace hanging from her fingertips, just as the note had said.

"You've stolen something that belongs to me," Pinkerton said to the woman inside, quickly assessing her clothing, her carriage, and the unusual cosmetics that gave her lips and cheeks a deep red glow—a glow that most sensible or discreet women in Washington who shunned the use of face paints would label as "forward."

"You should join me in my carriage because the town of

Alexandria—wait, I'm being unfair—because the gentlemen monitoring the entrances to most of the fine establishments here won't
permit a woman entry if she's without a man," Mary Ann Hall said.

Pinkerton leaned into the carriage's window, seething. His hours
had been squandered after all, and he was forced to waste them on a
painted lady. He could have slipped into a full fury, but that would
have meant submitting to his emotions. He was a modern man and
a student of discipline, and he chose instead to alight upon a proper
strategy and pursue the information he needed.

He stepped away from the carriage, adjusted his jacket, and drew
a long and calming breath. The woman observed him, amused. He
paid her no heed and returned to the carriage, injecting just enough
force into his demands to convey that he meant to control the situation, but would do so as a gentleman.

"Tell me about the telegram you sent me from here, and about
the diaries that McFadden jayhawked," he said.

"I don't know a thing about diaries, Mr. Pinkerton. And I didn't
send you a telegram from here."

"You most assuredly did. Who else would know to meet me here
for this particular game and at this particular hour?"

"Temple McFadden, of course. He directed me to tell you that he
sent the telegram and that he asked me to meet you here to—"

"To try to seduce me?"

"I'm not speaking of bedroom entertainments."

"Don't you get uppity with me, you strumpet," Pinkerton fumed.
"I have good suspicion about how one like you makes your way in the
world."

His self-possession lost once again, Pinkerton stepped away from
the carriage and adjusted his jacket. He inhaled deeply and reminded
himself of his goals for the day.

He was interrupted by Mary Ann, who had stepped down from
her carriage and leaned in close to his ear. He could smell the laven-
der perfume in her hair and on her throat, and he backed away in
embarrassment, looking around in jerks to see if anyone was watch-

ing them. Mary Ann pressed in closer again, pulling Pinkerton toward her by one of his lapels.

"I have a message for you. Mr. McFadden said he would like to speak with you at the Willard tomorrow evening, also at six."

"That's all? I have been subjected to the Long Bridge and I missed an appointment to escort Mrs. Lincoln to the B&O so I could be here. And this is all?"

"No, that is not all. Mr. McFadden said he promises you that this will be the last time that you will be humbugged. Now I must absquatulate."

Mary Ann climbed into her carriage and rolled off into the evening while Pinkerton yanked his hat from his head and threw it in anger onto the ground, digging his heel into it after it landed.

From his perch on the second floor of a building across the street, Alexander Gardner was pleased with himself. Even at a distance, with unpredictable variables and a late afternoon light, he had been able to take one good photograph of Pinkerton's encounter with Mary Ann.

CHAPTER NINETEEN

THE GRAND REVIEW

Alexander suggested that Temple get to Pennsylvania Avenue early Tuesday morning, well before the parade began at nine. They planned to meet at 15th Street, in full view of the Treasury and catty-corner from the President's House, in front of which two large, canopied reviewing stands stood on either side of Pennsylvania. The stands would seat hundreds of military and political dignitaries who would observe and honor this final gathering of the army before troops were mustered out and sent home.

People were already jockeying for space on the sidewalks when Temple arrived, and Alexander was setting up his camera and other equipment on the top row of a small set of wooden bleachers that the government reserved for newspapermen and photographers covering the event. Temple, allowed entry by a soldier after he flashed the press pass that Alexander had given him for the inauguration months earlier, hobbled up the bleachers on his cane, balancing a thick bouquet of red roses in his left arm.

"My guess is that the posies aren't for me," Alexander said.

"Not today. They're for Mr. Brooks whenever he arrives."

"No insult taken. And I have a gift for you anyway."

Alexander handed him a clean, clear photograph of Mary Ann and Pinkerton outside the Marshall House. Temple slipped it into his jacket and patted his friend on the shoulder.

"Noah's over there," Alexander said. "Introduce yourself. Gently. He still feels Lincoln's loss."

Noah Brooks was sitting alone at the end of one of the bleachers, slowly fanning himself with a newspaper and letting his head flop back as he looked up into the trees. He had several other newspapers from different cities piled next to him, a notepad and pencil in his lap, and a bright white carnation that was inadequately pinned to his lapel and sagged forward from his jacket as if it were napping. Brooks was bald and bearded and was so lost in thought that he didn't appear to notice the occasional fly landing amid the small beads of perspiration on his forehead. By dint of a graceful pen and his frequent coverage of the president for the *Sacramento Daily Union*, Brooks had also become an intimate of Lincoln's—more advisor than reporter, critics said—as well as one of the most well-known, closely followed journalists in Washington.

Temple's cane knocked against the wooden bleachers, the sound preceding him as he made his way, and the tapping forced Brooks from his reverie. He looked at Temple, shading his eyes with his newspaper and tilting his head.

"Alexander's friend?"

"Yes, Temple McFadden," he said as he bent to put down the bouquet so he could shake Brooks's hand.

"No need for courtesies, you can just sit down," Brooks said, digging through the pile by his hip. "How'd you get the limp?"

"I was born in Ireland and had some poor luck."

"So Ireland caused it, or was it poor luck?"

"Both."

"Do you follow the papers?"

"Not nearly as many as you, I'm afraid."

"Here's an observation that will appear in tomorrow's *Daily Illinois State Journal* on the parade we are about to witness today, written by a colleague who has shared with me a preview of his disappointment with the color line: 'If Negro troops were in the vicinity and were intentionally excluded from the display, the fact should cause a feeling of shame to tingle upon the cheek of every loyal man in the land. The troops, who have met the common foe and assisted to vanquish him, had a right to be represented here as they were upon the field of battle.'"

"I had a discussion of the Negro soldiers' absence in the Grand Review with a friend of mine on Sunday," Temple said. "He is a Negro himself and deeply resents this inequity."

"As we all should. But we all don't. There is work ahead for this country."

"Mr. Brooks, are you able to speak about President Lincoln?"

"No."

"On a single subject, no more."

"And no, again. I have lost many of my words since he was murdered."

"Can you speak to me about the president and the railroads?"

"Mr. McFadden, you are intrusive and insensitive, which recommends you for a career as a reporter."

"I'll forward my case, then: what was President Lincoln's opinion of the railroads?"

"Both enthralled and dismayed," said Brooks, giving in and shaking his head. "He thought trains would knit the country together, increase prosperity, and propel settlement in the West. So he supported them. Later, near the end, I think he became worried about the financial and political power the rail barons were amassing."

"So he would—"

"Nothing more about President Lincoln!" Brooks said. "I can barely manage his absence. Enough of the man. Gardner said you were interested in something other than that."

"If I'm not imposing, I would like to get these to Mr. Stanton," Temple said, holding out his bouquet. "I assume that he would know you from your time working with President Lincoln."

"You want me to give flowers to the war secretary?"

"Victory roses. Yes."

"Mr. Stanton is going to be sitting with President Johnson and General Grant in the reviewing stand, and they will be surrounded by soldiers and guards. I have no hope of approaching him. But there's someone else who will get your bouquet to Mr. Stanton; trust me with that. It will happen once the parade begins."

"I am in your debt."

"The world turns on favors, Mr. McFadden."

Temple returned to Alexander's end of the bleachers and sat down, stretching out his bad leg to relieve the flash of pain he felt behind his thigh. He tugged at Alexander's sleeve when he spotted Mathew Brady entering the bleachers and hauling his own photography equipment, but Alexander refused to look at his former mentor.

"Yesterday *The New York Times* predicted that nobody would stand in the sun for several hours just to watch a never-ending line of soldiers," said Alexander. "It appears that that was a miscalculation."

Crowds were now lacing the mile-and-a-half stretch between the Capitol and the President's House, leaning out of open windows, lining rooftops, filling doorways, standing on sidewalks, and climbing trees. They were present in such abundance—greater in number than the crowds that attended the inaugural or President Lincoln's funeral procession in the District—that members of the cavalry had to keep the spectators at bay lest they pour into the streets.

The firehouse had sprayed down Pennsylvania that morning so that the dust wouldn't be kicked into clouds when the infantry and cavalry presented themselves. Hanging in the portico of the Treasury building was a flag from the department's own regiment, torn at the bottom where John Wilkes Booth's spur had caught it as he leapt from the president's box in Ford's Theatre after shooting him. And across the uncompleted façade of the Capitol was a large banner, proclaiming in outsized block letters, "THE ONLY NATIONAL DEBT WE CAN NEVER PAY BACK IS THE DEBT WE OWE TO OUR VICTORIOUS UNION SOLDIERS."

Beneath the banner, on the steps of the Capitol, a choir of about two thousand schoolgirls erupted into song as soon as General Meade's soldiers began their march down Pennsylvania. The schoolgirls had chosen "The Battle Hymn of the Republic," which Miss

Howe had published to great acclaim in the *Atlantic Monthly* three years before.

> *Mine eyes have seen the glory of the coming of the Lord;*
> *He is trampling out the vintage where the grapes of*
> *wrath are stored;*
> *He hath loosed the fateful lightning of His terrible*
> *swift sword;*
> *His truth is marching on.*

Meade and his staff led their troops on horseback, with the eighty thousand soldiers of the Army of the Potomac following them in a dark blue phalanx, row after row of thirty men abreast spanning the width of Pennsylvania Avenue, their bayonets raised at their shoulders and gleaming in the sun, bursts of purple-tinged white and yellow.

An hour or so behind Meade came General Sheridan's cavalry, who in turn were followed by the Zouave volunteers, dressed in bright red skullcaps and bespoke navy uniforms trimmed in crimson. Mounted artillery came next, pulling cannon by the hundreds, followed by tens of thousands of other infantry marching flawlessly in a rectangular, navy-hued block. A blizzard of flowers and flower petals swirled around the troops, flung from the sidewalks, rooftops, and trees by spectators; occasionally a woman would burst from the crowd and hang a garland around the neck of a horse as an officer passed.

When Sheridan's troops reached the reviewing stand at the President's House, a cry went up from the crowd as George Custer, the twenty-six-year-old war hero, approached on his stallion, Don Juan. Custer, the youngest general in the army and with his face and shoulders awash in a cascade of long honey-blond ringlets scented with cinnamon oil, was undeniably brave and an indisputable showboat. His leather jackboots were polished like mirrors, and he wore them over a pair of green corduroys; further departures from Union issue included a black velvet jacket edged in silver trim, a felt slouch hat with a broad brim, a billowy white sailor shirt boasting embroidered stars on its collar, and a crimson scarf that Custer kept loosely tied around his neck.

The ladies swooned.

When one of them burst off the sidewalk to hang a garland on Don Juan's neck, Custer's horse bolted away from his division, and the general had to maneuver to control him. He galloped past the reviewing stand before Custer got him under control, and only then because another officer rode his horse into Don Juan's path to contain him. As his stallion settled, Custer turned back to the reviewing stand, sweeping his hat off his head and bowing in the saddle as he passed Johnson, Grant, and Stanton. The crowd screamed his praises again.

As Custer circled past the bleachers to rejoin his division, Noah Brooks stood up and yelled to him. Custer, as attuned to reporters and publicity as he was to his clothing, trotted over to the newspaperman.

"Say, General Custer, I have a bouquet to honor Mr. Stanton," Brooks shouted. "Will you be so kind as to deliver it to the war secretary?"

"I shall, Noah, but you'll owe me an interview this evening."

"The bargain is struck, General."

Custer took the bouquet, turned his horse around, and trotted over to the reviewing stand. The only stars in the parade that were bigger than the pair on Custer's collar were those atop the reviewing stand, which were crafted from ferns and flowers, each of them about three feet high. Red, white, and blue banners hung from the roof of the stand and were draped across its front. Forty soldiers, in two lines of twenty, guarded the very center of the stand, where Johnson, Grant, and Stanton sat, while another eight protected the rest of the stand's expanse. As Custer rode up, the cluster of soldiers in the center simply parted, allowing the war hero to bring Don Juan to the very edge of the stand.

"I have a victory bouquet from an admirer of Mr. Stanton's, the renowned and incomparable journalist Noah Brooks."

Stanton stood up, the roses were passed up to him, and Custer tipped his hat and rode off. As the clapping died down, Stanton plucked a note card from the center of the bouquet and adjusted his spectacles as he read it:

> *Mr. Stanton: I am in possession of the misplaced diaries. Please ar-*
> *range a meeting today through Mr. Brooks or I will be forced to*
> *publicize what I have.*

Stanton sighed and exhaled, rubbing his fingers along the edges of the bloodred petals resting in his lap.

HUNDREDS OF MILES away from the Grand Review, Mary Todd Lincoln was adjusting to the ill effects of a fitful and sleepless night on the Pioneer. They had reached Pittsburgh earlier in the day, at six in the morning, and the twelve hours she had spent on the train before then had been filled with headaches and tears. In Pittsburgh they were forced to get off the train so that it could change tracks, and now, several hours further along, she was regaining her senses as she reclined in her bed in the sleeper car. Lizzy was rubbing her temples, while Fiona dabbed at her forehead with a moist cloth. Robert and Tad had spent most of the day in the parlor car avoiding their mother, playing checkers, and napping.

"I never should have begun reading that forsaken diary of mine last night," she said, the back of her hand pressed across her eyes. "Such turmoil."

"Just breathe deeply," Fiona said. "Try to distract yourself."

Snapping upright and pulling her sheets around her shoulders, Mrs. Lincoln accused Fiona of deliberately bringing the diary to cause her pain and slapping at the cloth that Fiona was using to wipe her head. Lizzy asked her to stop screaming, but she continued until her small, pale, fleshy hands were balled into fists.

Just as quickly as the widow had flown into a rage, she stopped.

"May I speak, Mrs. Lincoln?" Fiona asked.

"You may."

"I only returned the diary to you because it was rightfully yours. I had no other intention."

"I know, my dear, I know. I become . . . I become other than myself at times. Please forgive me."

"You have endured many burdens, ma'am."

"We nearly escaped our burdens, my husband and I. He wanted to build a home in California when we left the White House, but I insisted that Boston would be better for us. It would have been more genteel. He, of course, would have followed my wishes."

The widow broke down again, and Lizzy and Fiona let her weeping run its course this time. When she had recomposed herself, Mrs. Lincoln placed her hand on Fiona's.

"I would like to know more about you, my dear—what you do and where you are from."

"I was born twenty-one years ago in Oswego, New York, to extraordinary parents. They were abolitionists and freethinkers, and they raised me with an education and with opinions of my own."

"I was raised with an education, too, in Kentucky, but I was not encouraged to have opinions."

"Mrs. Lincoln, are you going to let Mrs. McFadden tell you her story or not?" Lizzy asked. "I recall you asked her about herself, ma'am."

Mrs. Lincoln fell silent as the train rumbled along, from Pittsburgh toward Youngstown and Akron on its way to Chicago, and Fiona spun her history. Her family owned an apple farm—they had cows and chickens on it, too—that her mother, Barbara, oversaw down to every last bushel of fruit and pail of milk; Fiona and her two sisters had worked on the farm as children until—magically it seemed—they no longer had to work. Fiona had been eight years old when her family's circumstances elevated. Her father, Arthur, a country doctor, had invested in land and, to his great delight, in a boring little shipping company at the port of Oswego. The port, and Arthur Linton's investment, boomed when the Erie Canal and the winding skein of railroads linked to the New York Central turned Oswego into a sprawling, bumping transportation hub.

Fiona remembered winters of cascading snowstorms and winds that whipped her wool leggings as she skated on the frozen canal; she remembered her parents' laughter and her sisters' games; and she remembered piles of books stacked in the corners and on the tables of almost every room in their house because the bookcases were overflowing.

Books were the family's only indulgence. Even after they came into money, the Lintons encouraged their daughters to live modestly, and the family never moved out of the simple frame house on a hill surrounded by orchards, the house where all of their daughters were born. They expanded two of the rooms off the back of the house and used them as study halls for the girls, who were instructed by the finest tutors the Lintons could hire.

"I was fortunate enough to grow up in a part of the state singing with reform," Fiona told Mrs. Lincoln. "The movement for abolition was strong, as was an open-mindedness about religion and the women's movement. We had a grand meeting for women's rights not too far from us in Seneca Falls when I was just four years old, and my parents insisted that I be taught and raised in an environment of equality and progress."

"I have little use for these women on the move," said Mrs. Lincoln. "I am from old stock and a noble culture that finds women more effective if they press their interests quietly and through the arts of the home and ministrations to their husbands."

"Mrs. Lincoln, ma'am, you're taking the conversation into your lap again," Lizzy said.

The widow fell silent, and Fiona continued on. Her parents, ascribing to the philosophy of Amelia Bloomer of the nearby town of Homer, had encouraged their daughters to wear comfortable clothing as young teenagers, so Fiona wore dresses only to social functions. As their education continued, Fiona emerged as the brightest of the three Linton girls. Her father told her she had a keen mind; her sisters teased that she was merely keen to have a mind. Such was her parents' commitment that when she was seventeen, they sent her to Syracuse Medical College so that she could train to be a doctor. The thirty-nine-week course cost $165, and Fiona threw herself into her studies, set on learning all that modern medicine had to offer.

After Fiona earned her certification, Arthur Linton had taken her into his practice, but father and daughter soon discovered that no matter how much upstate New Yorkers convened to preach the notions of equality, few of them were ready to place their faith and their health in the hands of a female doctor. Arthur convinced his daughter to playact at being a nurse, but as the months wore on, Fiona bridled at the arrangement. When she turned eighteen, she decided to be of service in the War Between the States, where the demand for physicians was so great that surely she could practice as a doctor, even if Oswego wouldn't have her.

One of her predecessors in college, and a mentor, Mary Edwards Walker, had followed this path and introduced Fiona to Dr. Gross, who helped train Fiona and found her medical work at the hospital fashioned inside the Patent Office in Washington. She'd had the joy of meeting her husband in Washington, but also discovered that the men leading the war effort were no more willing to embrace a female doctor than the good people of Oswego.

"What of your husband?" Mrs. Lincoln asked. "How did you meet him?"

"We were introduced," Fiona said. "We were both new to Washington and we both knew Alexander Gardner. He invited us to a dinner."

"Mr. Gardner was much admired by my husband. And what convinced you that your husband was someone you would marry?"

Fiona paused at this: a simple question without a simple answer. Although she was barely acquainted with Mrs. Lincoln, the moment offered her a chance to maintain and build upon this small bond. In ways, from what she heard tell of the president, he and Temple were similar men, though Mr. Lincoln was blessed to be without Temple's impatience and occasional furies. Each man had big, strong hands—the hands of workers. The president was taller than her husband by two inches, but Temple still usually towered over those around him. Like the president, he had knowing gray eyes.

Fiona remembered how pained Temple had been when word of the assassination first reached them, how the anguish had creased his eyes. He'd gone to his little shelf of books and come back to her with a ragged copy of *Julius Caesar,* flipping through the pages until he found the passage he wanted, which he read to her aloud.

> *When beggars die there are no comets seen;*
> *The heavens themselves blaze forth the death of princes.*

Still, similarities were not familiarities, and Fiona hesitated an instant longer before deciding to share her affections for Temple with Mrs. Lincoln.

"He gave me a sense of security and belonging that I never understood I hadn't had before in my life until I had it with him," Fiona responded to Mrs. Lincoln. "At his core he is true and good and resolute as an oak, yet kind to me beyond measure. He is a wonderful and patient listener, and he can fill me with laughter. I feel utterly well met and well matched in Temple. I am devoted to him."

"He has no flaws?"

"He does."

"Well, then?"

"I find it harder to discuss his flaws than his strengths, I'm afraid."

"Mrs. McFadden."

"Ma'am?"

"These men are all scarred. They bring their bad to us with their good—as sons and as husbands. The boardinghouse owner, she had a son."

"Mrs. Surratt."

"Yes, her. Her son is said to be a confidant of my husband's murderer, but it is only the mother they have imprisoned. And me, here now on this train and abandoned by my husband—the entire world feels like a prison to me. My son Robert aspires to keep it as such. I tell you, these men visit as many ills upon us as they do joys. Perhaps more."

"My husband gambles and is loose with money," Fiona said. "And I fear that he doesn't want me to bear him children."

"You are steady with your passions and with money?"

"I am far steadier with vice and with money than my husband, yes."

"You anchor him as my husband anchored me," the widow replied. "You and my Abraham have interior discipline. He grew weary of me many times. Are you weary of your husband?"

"No, I am not weary of him. I am unsure of him."

"Why does he not favor children?"

"He is an orphan. He also feels constrained by normal living."

"Yet you are bound to him."

"Am I?"

"We all are, my dear. Bound to men. It is the way of the world. What measures do you know of that he favors in you?"

"He said he was enthralled by my eyes and my love of medicine. He said I challenged him and that being with me gave him a sense of purpose. And he respected my opinions!"

"Yes, yes, yes. Opinions. Yes, yes. Oh, I fear my opinions were just a lashing for Mr. Lincoln. Yes, yes. Like a whipping."

The widow broke down crying again, pulling the sheet up to her face and moaning softly. Robert looked in from the parlor car, saw that his mother was sobbing, and closed the door.

As the door shut, Mrs. Lincoln stopped crying, pulled the sheet from her face, and glared at the spot where Robert once stood. Her voice steadied and she sat up, transformed into a woman so cool and deliberate as to be unrecognizable as the wailing, damaged creature huddling under her sheets only a moment before.

"The lawyer overseeing my husband's estate extends me only a hundred and thirty dollars each month for my living expenses. I stand to inherit almost forty thousand dollars, but until then I am entirely dependent on the character of our lawyer and Robert's support. And Robert," she said, turning toward Fiona, "wants that money for himself."

"Ma'am, do you really want to speak about money issues around Fiona?" Lizzy asked.

"I want her—I want everyone—to understand why I don't trust my son. I will speak of it on the streets if it suits me, and I will speak of it with perfect strangers."

"Ma'am, don't you—"

"I also have debts of seventy thousand dollars from my four years in the President's House. Decorating. Clothing. I have much to attend to. Yes, yes, yes."

"Were you happy in the President's House, Mrs. Lincoln?" Fiona asked.

"Only in the beginning, in the first months we were there. But we have other paths to occupy us now, and other things to talk about. Yes. Other matters. Tell me about your husband."

"I do believe that he is the best man I have ever met; he is my partner and I am his. And he is a detective with the Metropolitan Police Department."

"Is that how he came to possess my diary?"

Fiona explained the fighting at the B&O to Mrs. Lincoln and that amid the brawling, Temple had come upon her diary quite accidentally. The widow pulled her journal from beneath the blankets and began flipping through it.

"Did he read through all of this?"

"No, Mrs. Lincoln. I wouldn't have allowed that. He said there were many letters and entries in your journal that he did not explore once I raised the matter of your privacy with him."

"What are his interests in my diary?"

"I believe he cares about the railroads, Mrs. Lincoln, but beyond that I confess to not having a very complete sense of what exactly it is that he is pursuing."

"Railroads. Yes, yes, yes. We mustn't talk of railroads when Robert nears. My husband and he were divided over the railroad men. Our Robert began trooping them through the President's House like salesmen in our last year there."

Mrs. Lincoln sobbed again, and her head drooped into her bedding. Fiona slipped her hand into Mrs. Lincoln's, but the widow didn't seem to notice. A moment later Mrs. Lincoln began flipping through her diary, fanning the pages so rapidly that Fiona thought some of them might tear. When Mrs. Lincoln found the section she wanted, she plucked out a letter that had been pressed between two pages and was written in the late president's hand. She studied it at length, moving her head back and forth in small bursts and shaping the words she was scanning with her lips. She paused, read more, stopped, then looked at Lizzy and Fiona and began reading:

April 7, 1865
Dear Mr. Scott:

As the misery of this cruel war and our noble endeavor come to an end, I am, by the day, growing profoundly aware that the Republic may well bend to a force that the war itself has helped advance and institutionalize: the might of the railroads and of the great men that create and support them. Our railroads, as you and I well know, are a national treasure and I remain inspired by the promise they embody for a nation so recently divided. In my darker moments, however, I confess to worries that the money powers behind the railroads will seek to reinforce our prejudices and prolong our differences to further aggregate their wealth. Informed

by my anxieties, I would ask you and Mr. Stanton to meet with
me to consider our goals for the railroads during my second term.
Sincerely,
A. Lincoln

Mrs. Lincoln looked up from the letter, awaiting a response. None came. Fiona was uncertain what to say and looked to Lizzy, who was equally at a loss. As the train rumbled along, passing into the western flats of Pennsylvania, the widow stared back quietly at Fiona and Lizzy, then slapped the letter and her arms down on her lap.

"Don't you understand? It's to Mr. Scott!"

"But who is Mr. Scott?" Fiona asked.

"He is Thomas Scott. He works closely with Mr. Stanton as the assistant war secretary, and he was a railroad man before Mr. Stanton and my husband called him to Washington," she said, her voice slipping into a low, breathy whisper as she leaned forward in her bed toward Fiona and Lizzy.

Their lack of understanding appeared to send Mrs. Lincoln into a panic, and she plucked a squat brown bottle of laudanum off her bedside table. She poured the drug into a spoon and tipped it into her mouth, waiting for it to take hold before she began speaking again.

"Mr. Scott and my Robert are friends, you see. They are devoted to the rails, and Robert is devoted to creating his own fortune," she continued. "If it were not for my Tad, I would not want to be with Robert on this train or in Chicago. I will be betrayed. Yes, yes, yes. A house divided. Yes, yes, yes."

The door to the sleeping car slipped open and Robert Lincoln stepped inside, gazing at the three women huddled around the bed. He sat down on a small bench bolted to the wall between the beds that Fiona and Lizzy slept in, and he stared out the window as if accounting for every tree or small barn they rattled past. He rubbed his fingers against the glass and wiped them on his trousers.

"Even though it's warming up outside, the window is cool," he said. "Mother, I wasn't aware you were keeping a diary or that you had any of Father's letters."

Mrs. Lincoln stared down into her bedding.

"Do you know what people in the President's House called my mother, Mrs. McFadden?" Robert continued. "My father's secretaries referred to her as 'Her Satanic Majesty.' My father's physician simplified things—he just called her 'the Devil.'"

Mrs. Lincoln threw her diary across the car and it careened off Robert's head, drawing a faint line of blood near his eye before it fell to the floor. Her eldest son pulled a kerchief from his vest pocket to blot his scratch and bent down to scoop up the journal. He stood up and walked back to the door, turning to Mrs. Lincoln as he opened it.

"I think I shall acquaint myself now with your diary, Mother," he said, stepping back into the parlor car, where, through the gap in the door, the three women could see Tad on the floor reading a book.

Mrs. Lincoln fell back onto her pillow, pressing her lips together as she stared into the ceiling and began counting the lines and cracks traced in the walnut slats above her bed.

CHAPTER TWENTY

THE LODGING HOUSES

ugustus always avoided the District's lodging houses. He'd step into the street to avoid their entrances, his thoughts pegged to what his father had told him about the hotels: in the years before the war, some were transit points in the slave trade, offering their services to owners and buyers trafficking in healthy, productive, and valuable Negroes. Even being near the hotels could make him light-headed, as fears that had slopped around his imagination as a child—visions of grown men and women stuffed into cellars—awoke and gripped his chest and throat. That quickly, they could rise up and take hold of him.

Remember, his father told him, the President's House was built by slaves. Even Frederick Douglass was turned away from the mansion until Lincoln ordered him admitted. And the Charles Hotel once had six big holding pens in its basement—dark catacombs lined with iron cages where slaves were shackled in leg irons—that allowed owners to lodge upstairs, comfortable in the knowledge that their property was secure. The owners of the Charles had understood this to be a unique selling point and maintained a small billboard near the front desk to remind lodgers of the hotel's benefits: *The Proprietor of this hotel has roomy underground cells for confining slaves for safekeeping, and patrons are notified that their slaves will be well cared for. In case of escape, full value of the Negro will be paid by the Proprietor.*

So when Temple had asked him to visit Lucy Hale at the National Hotel on the second day of the Grand Review, Augustus needed time to accommodate himself to the notion. He'd tried to beg off from the venture, but Temple said he would be preoccupied on Pennsylvania Avenue and Fiona would be on Mrs. Lincoln's train. Besides, Temple reminded him, John Hale knew Augustus from the abolitionist movement and could arrange a meeting with his daughter. The Hale family had made the National their home, and as circumstance had it, Johnny Booth, inclined toward extravagances that mirrored the arc of his ambition and his sense of his proper place in the world, also kept a room at the National as well. And it was at the National that Lucy met and fell in love with the celebrated actor.

"The senator won't want this," Augustus had told Temple.

"Lincoln had just brought Hale back from Spain before he was assassinated," Temple had said. "The senator is in mourning for the president, and he will be sympathetic to our challenge."

"We have no reason to accost him so. Senator Hale's wife has already fled the District for New Hampshire to avoid public shaming."

"Augustus, his daughter knew Booth, knew his movements and whom he was consorting with. We need to know whom Booth was close to."

"We'll have no way to secure a meeting with her," Augustus had said. "Lucy Hale loved Booth and John Hale considers that a curse."

"His daughter was secretly engaged to Booth. He'll find this an embarrassment."

"And?"

"Gardner can help keep news of the engagement out of the papers for a time."

Hale was inside the lobby of the National when Augustus arrived, but Augustus waited outside, unable to move through the doors. The senator took Augustus's hesitation to be that of a Negro uncertain of his welcome in a Pennsylvania Avenue hotel and walked toward him, hand outstretched.

"You can come in, my friend," Hale said, before addressing the doorman. "Mr. Spriggs is a most well-received visitor."

The senator pulled Augustus through the doors and across the lobby, still misunderstanding his unease for anything other than a raw loathing of hotels. They ascended the stairs to the second floor, and as they walked down the hallway, Hale nodded glumly at room 228.

"Booth's," he said. "The murderer was just doors away from us."

"Senator Hale, I appreciate your help, but before we sit with Lucy, I have to share with you a troubling revelation."

The men stopped short of the end of the hallway where the Hales' two-bedroom suite was located, and Augustus lowered his voice. He told the senator that Temple had learned that among Booth's belongings were photographs of five women, Miss Hale being one of them; the assassin claimed engagements to each.

Hale absorbed this, shaking his head.

Augustus cleared his throat.

"I would not want to hurt Miss Hale in any fashion," he whispered.

Hale nodded. "She should know so she understands the measure of that despicable man. She was besotted. She invited Booth to attend the president's second inauguration with her, as our guest. At our invitation the killer was just feet away from Mr. Lincoln—even then, just steps away."

"Temple has told me that he can keep much of the information about Miss Hale out of the newspapers, if that's of any comfort, sir, but it won't remain unknown for very long."

"We are Hales and we will manage this on our own. You are after the president's killers, and I believe my daughter has information to impart."

Lucy Hale was perched on the edge of a settee in the middle of the suite's parlor. Her hair lay against her head in two thick braids, a clutch of ringlets dangling near her ears, and she wore a crisp navy blue dress. She was stout and plain, and rumor had it that Booth, who had his choice of the District's beauties, had targeted Lucy to gain access to her father's influential circle.

Lucy's eyes were bloodshot and she knotted a kerchief in her hands as she looked past Augustus and her father, her gaze settling somewhere on the wall beyond them. A neat stack of letters bound together with green velvet ribbon sat nestled in her lap, with a thick lock of brown hair tucked under the bow. Augustus cleared his throat but didn't say anything. Lucy's gaze wandered from the wall to Augustus, and she patted the letters in her lap.

"Johnny gave me these," she said. "These, and his hair."

She began weeping in heaves, pressing her kerchief to her eyes and rocking back and forth on the edge of the couch as the letters slipped from her lap and spilled onto the floor. Augustus wanted to leave and turned toward the door, but Hale pulled him back by his arm and then walked to his daughter's side. He retrieved the letters from the floor and placed them by her on the settee, patting her on the shoulder and stroking her hair until she calmed.

"He had large, dark eyes, and he was kind to me, and he could recite Shakespeare better than his illustrious brothers," she said, looking up at her father, her eyes still glassy.

"He was a murderer, Lucy," said Hale.

"Do not be a tutor to me, Father!" Lucy screamed. "He was my betrothed and my own."

Hale pushed away from Lucy and stormed into one of the bedrooms, slamming the door behind him. Augustus sat down on a stool near the settee, staring at the floor until Lucy spoke again. She pulled the letters back into her lap, dropping her kerchief and twirling the lock of hair in her hand.

"I could give you these, Mr. Spriggs, but they aren't of any value. They are Johnny's love letters to me. There is nothing here of plots or murder. You aren't the first to visit me, of course. Mr. Stanton sent a very threatening man, a Mr. Baker, to speak with me weeks ago. He read through all of my letters and didn't keep a single page."

"And that was all?" Augustus asked.

"They ransacked Johnny's room down the hall and said they found encrypted letters in envelopes bearing New York marks. Mr. Stanton's man suspected that my letters might conform with an inscrutable code they also found in Johnny's room. But all they found in his letters to me was love."

"Booth never discussed with you a fascination or an obsession with President Lincoln?"

"Other than his desire to be at the inauguration, he did not."

"Well. That is all, then."

Augustus rose from the stool, bowed to Lucy, and asked her to remember him to her father. When he reached the door of the suite, she stopped him.

"That is not all," she said. "Johnny did meet frequently with others at the Surratt boardinghouse. And as I told Mr. Baker, one person from that group hasn't been fully claimed by all of these investigators, police, and soldiers."

"And who is that person?"

"John Surratt. My Johnny and he were confidants. Where, I might ask, is John Surratt? Why has no one pursued him?"

"Good day," Augustus said.

"Good day."

Augustus left the National alone, the bellman and the doorman eyeing him as he passed through the lobby and onto Pennsylvania Avenue. He pulled at his collar to get some air and walked a block before pausing to lean against a building, clawing at his collar again. He could hear the sounds of crowds swelling to join the Grand Review. He felt penned in, ready to visit his dreams. His right hand was shaking and he covered it with his left, then swiped at his nose, which had started to run. He needed to visit his dreams. He needed to find some smoke.

THE WAR SECRETARY demonstrated his well-known pluck in the message he sent through Noah Brooks in response to Temple's request for a meeting: *Whoever you may be and whatever "diaries" you may possess, I will not meet with you without further proof of the true value of that which you claim to have.*

Temple responded: *Mars: I will leave a packet in your name at the Willard this evening at half past six.*

Allan Pinkerton was at a table in the Willard's lobby when Temple arrived. He was drumming his fingers, and his hip shook slightly in response to the frantic pumping of his left foot beneath the table. Pinkerton followed Temple as he made his way across the lobby, his pace hobbled by his bad leg and his cane.

"You look angry with me, Mr. Pinkerton."

"I am determined to conclude this very messy affair."

"And how do you propose to do that?"

"You will give me the diaries."

"I obviously won't. But you and your men will stop following me and my wife as of this evening."

"We'll do no such thing," Pinkerton roared, bolting up from the table and shoving his chair aside. "I have four of my men outside who will enter at my prompting and resolve this dilemma."

"My friend Nail and his acquaintances have disbanded your guards, Mr. Pinkerton. At this moment, they're being . . . transported. I also have a photograph of you in Alexandria consorting with the most well-known madam in the District. The picture can get into the newspapers and it can get to your wife. So sit down, Mr. Pinkerton, and be civil."

Allan Pinkerton subdued was like a man tied and gagged, struggling against the emotions binding him and rocking to and fro in search of an escape. Once Pinkerton settled, Temple and he came to terms: Pinkerton would disappear from the District.

"It was my men at the B&O confronting Baker's stooges, and it was my men who rescued you at the Center Market," Pinkerton said. "And for this you would have me exiled?"

"You came to my aid because you wanted the diaries. But how did you know I even had the diaries?"

"We tracked you from the B&O right behind Baker's team when they gave chase."

"What took you to the train station to begin with, Mr. Pinkerton?"

"Stump Tigani. He worked as a courier for Baker, and my network told me what he had."

"Which was?"

"The Booth diary and Mrs. Lincoln's journal. Was I wrong?"

"No, you weren't. But your men needed to slice open Tigani's throat to get them?"

"Tigani was a dangerous man. He wouldn't have parted with the diaries. As you saw at the B&O, Lafayette Baker was there to protect him."

"Why was Tigani traveling to New York?"

"That is a secret that only Baker and Edwin Stanton can unveil. I loved President Lincoln; I served him and General McClellan during the war—until Stanton removed me in favor of Baker. The diaries will serve as instruments for justice."

"Justice for whom?"

"That was what I was intending to discover when you interfered with my work, Mr. McFadden. I believe the journals will aid those seeking information about the assassination of the president."

"I'm sure none of your thirst for the diaries involves embarrassing Mr. Stanton. You're to leave the District, Mr. Pinkerton."

"What of your photograph of me in Alexandria?"

"You have my word that it shan't circulate and that the plate will be destroyed."

"I saved your life, McFadden," Pinkerton said as he stood again. "My goodwill would have me exiled?"

"By tomorrow afternoon."

"I doubt I can call off my people in Chicago in time. I'll send a telegram, but they're already waiting for your wife there."

"My wife is a capable woman. Good night and goodbye, Mr. Pinkerton."

Pinkerton held Temple's eyes for a moment, spat on the floor by the detective's cane, and then turned on his heel. After Pinkerton left the Willard, Temple reached into his jacket and pulled out an envelope bearing Edwin Stanton's name—with "Lord War" inscribed below it—and left it at the hotel desk with the concierge.

CHAPTER TWENTY-ONE

THE GATLING

dwin Stanton sent two cavalry officers to meet Temple in front of the Capitol on Wednesday morning, an hour before the Grand Review launched into its second day. The Union boys identified Temple by his cane and put him on a separate mount accompanying them. He was to be seated next to the war secretary as a guest in the reviewing stand.

Stanton, round as an egg and resolute as an ironclad, took Temple's measure as soon as he reached the reviewing stand, scanning him up and down and nodding slightly as he did so. He didn't extend his hand or ask Temple his name before they made their way to their seats, which would place the two men between Andrew Johnson and Ulysses Grant, both of whom had yet to arrive. Stanton moved deliberately, accustomed as he had become after long years of war and the burdens of his office to giving, rather than receiving, orders.

"There aren't many who know me as Lord War," Stanton said as he sat down. "Your diligence is impressive, Mr. . . . ?"

"McFadden. You also are known as Mars?"

"You've gotten inside a Vigenère table as well. Also impressive. But you're putting yourself in a very perilous and untenable place. Why?"

"I agreed to help uphold the law."

"Come now."

"It's the truth," Temple said, after considering—and deciding against—offering Stanton a more elaborate explanation. "I also deeply admired the president. It isn't any more complicated than that."

"Everything in the District right now is more complicated than it appears. Do you mean to do me damage?"

"I mean to find out why President Lincoln was killed."

Stanton worried about the risks he had taken allowing a stranger to sit so close to him, Grant, and Johnson so soon after the president's murder. He looked about for his guards, and mopped his brow with a handkerchief before turning back to Temple.

"I could detain you right now," he said. "Right here and indefinitely, for no other reason than I wish it so. The state has given me those powers, and habeas corpus is just a cloak that we lift and drop as we intend. You would vanish."

"You want what I have and you don't have it yet," Temple said. "If you wanted me arrested, you would have had it done when your men met me earlier at the Capitol. And you did not."

Crowds were swelling again along Pennsylvania, and with both the Irish Brigade and Sherman's troops set to march, the morning's festivities had already turned distinctly rowdy and snapjacket. Scuffles broke out on corners where people jockeyed for better views; some police meant to patrol Pennsylvania Avenue were already drunk; cheers and peals of laughter coursed through windows and from the rooftops of shops and houses; flags and red, white, and blue bunting hung from windows; and, with legions of Union soldiers moving down the boulevard from the Capitol, the sun painted the entire enterprise as if, for a moment, to cleanse it and keep it whole before ancient hatreds threatened to divide it all again in the nights that were to come.

Temple leaned toward Stanton to continue their conversation, but the war secretary ignored him, rising from his chair to meet General Grant and President Johnson as they arrived. Johnson sat to one side of Stanton and, after the war secretary shooed Temple down a seat, Grant sat on the other, leaving Temple perched next to the man who, after Lincoln, was the most popular hero in the North.

As on the day before, a band preceded the military procession, but today the musicians were playing the anthem that had come to symbolize Sherman and his Army of the Tennessee, "Marching Through Georgia." As the band's refrains boomed louder, the throngs along Pennsylvania began to sing along with the music:

> *"Sherman's dashing Yankee boys will never reach the coast!"*
> *So the saucy rebels said and 'twas a handsome boast*
> *Had they not forgot, alas! to reckon with the host*
> *While we were marching through Georgia.*

The song was a preamble for the appearance of Sherman himself, who sat tall on Lexington, his chestnut stallion, and rode in a new uniform before sixty-five thousand of his men, including some of the same bummers and free Negroes who had passed along with their ragtag gear and plunder in front of Augustus's house. The mounted infantry of the Ninth Illinois rode ahead of Sherman and cleared a path for the general and his troops as crowds surged toward the war hero, offering him wreaths and gifts. "The Battle Hymn of the Republic," which Sherman's army had played as they left a gutted, ravaged Atlanta the year before, replaced "Marching Through Georgia," and Sherman bowed in his saddle toward the crowd. All of the onlookers roared in response, clapping and calling out his name.

When Sherman passed the reviewing stand, he saluted President Johnson with his sword, dismounted, and climbed the steps up to the platform. Sherman and Stanton harbored a well-known hatred of each other; Stanton suspected Sherman of having designs on the presidency and loathed his insubordination, while Sherman saw Stanton as overly sympathetic toward the Negro and in too much of a rush to reconstruct the South in the image of the North. When Stanton extended his hand to Sherman, the general ignored it and shook hands with his good friend Grant instead. Temple was asked to move down yet again so that Sherman could sit beside Grant.

A minister on the platform, observing Sherman slighting Stanton, rose and shouted: "Edwin M. Stanton, savior of our country under God, rise and receive the greetings of your friends!" When

Stanton refused to stand, the minister repeated himself: "Edwin M. Stanton, savior of our country under God, rise and receive the greetings of your friends!" As waves of applause rolled out from the same onlookers who had cheered Sherman earlier, Stanton stood up and received the ovation. Sherman, refusing to acknowledge the moment, leaned in toward Grant and whispered in his ear.

The generals took no notice of or interest in Temple, and for the rest of the day he would occasionally lean out from his seat and look down the aisle to scrutinize Stanton, taking stock of his comportment, his demeanor, and his reactions to the surges of emotion that accompanied the crowd's response to each new military regiment as it passed by for review and with each thundering volley of rifle fire that sounded up and down Pennsylvania. When Temple's friend Michael Gleason, a captain in the Irish Brigade of Illinois, rode by with his sword raised, Temple cheered him, and he noticed Stanton cheering heartily as well. But such outpourings were rare from the war secretary, who was almost regal in his self-possession and who took in the last hours of the Grand Review as a man entranced by the human spectacle and made somber and weary by the sacrifices that gave rise to it.

When the parade ended at three-thirty, the reviewing stand emptied quickly as the dignitaries tried to escape the crush on Pennsylvania. Crowds encircled Sherman, who lost his temper as he and his wife were besieged; he screamed, "Damn you, get out of the way! Get out of the way!" Temple noticed that Sherman's protests drew a faint smile from Stanton, but the war secretary knew better than to let himself be caught gloating. His lips re-formed into a thin line and he turned toward Temple, finally ready after several hours to converse. The two of them, and Stanton's contingent of four bodyguards, were the only ones left on the platform.

"An entire army, the mightiest and deadliest ever assembled, marches through Washington in two days and then disappears forever into the citizenry," Stanton said. "A million men of war turned into men of peace in only forty-eight hours."

"Four *years* and forty-eight hours," Temple said. "With the Union preserved."

"The South is subdued, not conquered. There is still mighty work to be done to bring our Southern brethren into the fold, and it will be all the more daunting with President Lincoln away from us."

"Pardon my impatience, Mr. Secretary, but why have you kept me here for so prolonged a time? Isn't our business straightforward?"

"In good time, Mr. McFadden, all will become apparent. I want you to consider what stands between the end of this war and a reconstructed South of a fit with the nation that surrounds it. What stands in the way, sir?"

"The Southerners themselves, I would imagine."

"To a point. They will stand in the way of the Negro and the rights of the freedmen. They will resist rule from the North. They are bitter and will be so well into the future. There is all of that. But there is also our new class of industrialists in the North made robust and wealthy by the engines of this war and the inventiveness of our citizenry. They have designs on the western territories, and they would be content to force our politicians to bargain for fewer concessions from a defeated South—if the Secesh are willing to cede the expansion of the West to the railroad interests, and to permit a new railroad to be built through the South and Texas."

"I am at a loss as to how this involves my letter to you," Temple said. "I have abided this delay today in the hope that I would gain more than a tutorial."

Stanton shook his head. He was a man whom the war had made rough as bark and who had come to understand things he had never wanted to consider. He reached into the pocket on his vest, made tight by the pressure of his girth, and withdrew the note Temple had left for him at the Willard. He unfolded it, then waved away his bodyguards as he read from it in a whisper that only he and Temple could hear: " *Dear Mars: The Booth diary speaks of you, in conjunction with Patriot, Avenger, Tyrant, Goliath, Wise Man, and Drinker. Mrs. Lincoln's diary speaks of misery, of course, and of the railroads. I would like an interview with you. Please send your men to fetch me tomorrow morning in front of the Capitol building. I am identified by my cane, my wayward hobble, and my height. If your men do not arrive for me I will register you as uninterested and go on my way.'"*

Stanton folded the note again and slipped it back into his vest pocket.

"You have a strong, confident script. It speaks well of you."

"Who are these people, Patriot and the rest?" Temple asked.

"Mr. McFadden, I have chosen not to answer your questions today. My men here are going to take you into custody."

"I don't have the diaries with me."

"I've kept you here these long hours today so you wouldn't cause any interferences in Swampdoodle, which is where, I believe, the diaries are, yes? In safekeeping with Jack Flaherty—'Nail' to his friends and to you, but a boodler and a thug to the rest of us. You are a worthy man, but you're interfering and in an arena beyond your scope and abilities."

"You're wrong about the diaries."

"About one of them, you mean? Of course. Only one is in Swampdoodle. The other is with your wife and Mrs. Lincoln on her private rail cars to Chicago."

Temple stumbled back a step, dizzied, trying to calculate how long it would take him to get back to Swampdoodle. And where, between Chicago and here, Fiona might be. His breathing started to come in rushes and he tightened his grip on his cane, looking away from Stanton and trying to decide where on Pennsylvania Avenue he could secure a horse.

"I can see your thoughts revolving, but there isn't any time left for you on this. Robert Lincoln will intercept his mother's diary, and no one is going to take the widow at her word about her scribblings in a journal. Everyone considers her quite mad. I imagine Robert will have to have his mother institutionalized on some coming date," Stanton said, shaking his head. "And, as I'm also sure you know, Lafayette Baker has a long list of resentments and injuries cataloged against you and Mr. Flaherty, and he has shared them with me. You've seriously injured a number of his men and embarrassed him in the fields around Augustus Spriggs's handsome new home, and Mr. Flaherty even shot one of Mr. Baker's marksmen from the trees. These men were and are agents of our government, and you have intruded upon their work. Mr. Baker has ventured into Swampdoodle today and I am sure shots have been exchanged, but with all of the rifle fire accompanying our parade, I doubt anyone heard them. I am sorry this has taken such an ugly and unfortunate shape. I truly am."

Temple saw regret trace its way across Stanton's face, but he had no time to consider the matter further. He pivoted on his cane, his mind spinning as he skittered down the aisle, away from Stanton. The war secretary nodded to his guards, who closed in on Temple from either side. Temple cracked his cane across the knees of the first soldier and then clubbed him in the jaw as he dropped. The soldier behind him had his bayonet drawn, but Stanton ordered him to take Temple alive; the soldier hesitated, and Temple turned on him and sliced his cane into the side of the man's head and then butted him in the stomach with it as he collapsed. But Temple never saw the two guards vaulting over the bleachers toward him from several rows above, and when they reached him, one of them threw his arms around him in a bear hug. The other slammed his gun into Temple's head, snapping his neck sideways and causing his vision to blur.

> *Comrades mine, and I in the midst, and their memory*
> *ever I keep for the dead I loved so well;*
> *For the sweetest, wisest soul of all my days and lands . . .*
> *and this for his dear sake;*
> *Lilac and star and bird, twined with the chant of my soul,*
> *There in the fragrant pines, and the cedars dusk and dim.*

Temple slumped back unconscious, a fine tendril of blood spiraling down from his scalp.

"Take him to the Old Capitol Prison," Stanton said.

A FEW HOURS earlier, Nail was napping in his warehouse, fresh ink stains on his hands and forearms and fresh sheets of cogniacs drying and gently flapping on the wall above him, when a series of rifle shots awoke him. It must be the Grand Review, he thought before rolling back on his side. But a scattered round of subsequent shots were not at all like the measured rounds of a military volley, which would have charged off in sequence: pause, fire, pause, fire. No, not like that at all. This was a gunfight. A battle.

The noise he heard next was new and strange. It sounded like a series of metal hammers pounding away at a wall and creating little explosions each time they landed. He heard screams of the sort he had never heard in Swampdoodle before. He heard fear.

Nail pulled one of his shotguns from beneath his cot and grabbed a pistol lying on a nearby table. They were both always loaded, but he checked again to make sure. Before he got to the front door of the warehouse, it was flung open in front of him. One of his men, bloodied across the front of his shirt, was staring at him wild-eyed. He was stuttering, unable to speak, and pointing with a forefinger back over his shoulder.

"What is it?" Nail shouted.

But the man couldn't get a word out. Nail slapped him hard across the cheek, and the man corralled himself.

"There's a good one hundred of them, and they came right over the bridges with guns. They killed the women and the dogs at the entrance to Swampdoodle, and they rolled over any of the children who got in their way. And then they just mowed the men down, Nail, with a horrible thing. Three of them. Horrible and large."

"Three men?"

"No, three guns. They spin and they spit bullets and they're a terror."

By the time Nail emerged from the warehouse, a wide semicircle of his men, forty to fifty strong, had formed in front of the warehouse, armed with clubs, guns, and knives. The noon sun was high over their heads when the first of the three wagons appeared—huge wooden arks, each pulled by two horses and arriving in single file. Drivers sat atop the wagons, and behind each of the drivers knelt three sharpshooters. They began picking off Nail's men, one by one, to protect the drivers until all three wagons had passed across the rickety, splintered bridges and into the expanse before the warehouse.

Behind the wagons marched five-score men, all wearing the long black frock coats common to Lafayette Baker's men. As the group moved in, the drivers wheeled the wagons around so that their blank backsides faced the warehouse and the horses now faced Baker's own men, an oddity that caused some of Nail's people to look back at him, puzzled. He shrugged, unable to provide an answer.

As the wagons settled, Baker shouted out to Nail from behind one of the wagons. "Give us what we came for and this needn't be bloodier than it already has been."

"If it had been a rainy day, you never would have gotten those wagons across our swampland," Nail shouted back from the steps of the warehouse.

"It's not a rainy day," Baker replied.

Nail lifted his pistol and shot one of the wagon drivers through the back of his head. Before he could lower his arm, a sniper's bullet tore through his shoulder and his gun fell from his hand. The sniper took the reins of the wagon from the dead driver as Baker shouted out again.

"Last chance, fingerlickers. Drop your arms and give us what we came for."

"Answer him, men!" Nail shouted.

A round of fire erupted from the semicircle, and splinters of wood blasted from the sides of the wagons. Two of the marksmen fell from the wagons, and some of Baker's men behind the wagons dropped.

Nail's men roared, raised their clubs, and began to charge across the thirty yards separating them from Baker's private army.

Tall, thick doors swung open on springs in the back of the wagons, and from each of them three long, chubby, gleaming steel guns emerged. Each bore six barrels that rotated around a central shaft, spun by a man turning a large wood and metal crank while another fed rounds into a hopper above the contraption. Each of the three guns began firing six hundred rounds a minute—sounding just like a series of metal hammers pounding explosively at a wall, Nail thought—and they shredded his men like paper dolls in front of his eyes. Bone fragments and chunks of flesh showered the field, shrouded in eruptions of blood and laces of red mist. Those who weren't killed were left writhing and screaming on the ground, pieces of jaw and cheek missing, limbs chewed into strands, fist-sized crevices where eyes had been, parts of heads sheared off. When the guns stopped, Nail stood alone on the steps, everyone else around him dead.

Baker stepped out between two of the wagons. The bandage covering the wrist that Temple had broken was as white as snow in the sunlight. In his good hand he was dragging two of Swampdoodle's boys by the scruff of their necks.

"My guns are a wonder, aren't they?" he shouted to Nail. "Developed for our army by Richard Gatling and ready to go into service sometime next year. A killing machine, as you can see."

Nail hopped down the steps, choking back dust and bile, and raced toward the wagons, hoisting his shotgun with the only good arm he had left.

"Take him down," Baker commanded.

Three shots rang out from the marksmen; one separated Nail's left hand from his shotgun while the others spun into each of his legs and forced him to crumple. He flopped forward onto his chest and face.

When Baker reached Nail, he kicked him in the side and rolled him over on his back, then turned Nail's head toward him with his boot. Baker let go of both boys—neither was more than five years old—and the pair stood there shivering with fear. He pulled his LeMat from his belt and pounded the butt against the head of one of the boys, toppling the child across Nail's torso.

"I'll kill both of these tots unless you tell me where the diary is."

Nail spat onto Baker's boot, and Baker shot him through the shoulder.

"Tell me. I have plenty of men here and they'll search the place once you're dead. Tell me."

Nail began laughing.

"It wasn't here more than a night, and we've moved it. You'll never find it, and whatever you do to me won't matter, you silly, buggering arsehole, because my friend Temple is smarter than all of you."

"Your friend Temple isn't likely to last the day, either."

Nail spat at him again. Baker put his Colt to Nail's head and blew his brains out the back of his skull in a moist pile of bone splinters and flesh that turned the ground crimson.

Baker brushed droplets of blood off the front of his coat and stuffed the LeMat back into his belt. He dragged the first boy off Nail's body and stood him next to the other; the pair looked away from him, quivering.

Baker reached down and patted one of them on the cheek.

"I'm not the kind who would kill either of you boys. You're both going to grow up in a country that has a little more order to it. Run along."

He watched the pair stumble away from Nail's body and then break into a slow, winding trot as they headed back into the shacks of Swampdoodle.

"Move out across this shithole now," he shouted to his men. "We're hunting for a diary."

PART THREE

MAESTRO

CHAPTER TWENTY-TWO

THE HANDOFF

Swinging her arms until they felt like they would loop back upon themselves, Fiona tossed the only piece of leather luggage she had ever owned from the back of Mrs. Lincoln's train shortly before the locomotive rumbled into Defiance, Ohio.

Buckles on the bag's sides flickered in the sunlight as it tumbled end over end into a mound of grass alongside the tracks, ten feet away from Fiona, then twenty, then thirty, as the train, exhaling clouds of steam from its underbelly and barking three shrill blasts from its stack, slowed to a stop. Fiona made a short leap from the last step on the back of the train, clutching her medical bag under her right arm and extending her left to catch her balance as she landed.

Her luggage—scuffed and shrouded in gravel powder—rested reliably, indeed loyally, she thought, beside a blackened steel rail. The train had made the same brief, odd pause in Defiance as it had in every other station along its route so far. It took on no passengers and had no need to stop anywhere at all given the unusual and celebrated trio still riding inside it, yet at each station its engineer paused only long enough, it seemed, for local onlookers to marvel at industrial progress paying a noisy and unexpected visit.

Mrs. Lincoln's train departed Defiance within minutes. As Fiona bent down to retrieve her luggage, she cocked her head sideways to contemplate the train's caboose growing ever smaller in the distance. She was certain Robert Lincoln would be the first to notice that she was missing from the train. He would notice long before Mrs. Lincoln, who had barely emerged from the delirium she had so unfortunately entered after pitching her diary at her son. And she believed that Robert Lincoln would notice her absence even before Lizzy Keckly, who had been monitoring Mrs. Lincoln by her bedside with unwavering and steadfast attention.

Fiona had wanted to give Lizzy a proper and grateful farewell, but Temple had told her not to pass beyond Defiance and by no means to continue on to Chicago because, sure as the day was long, there would be men waiting for her there. They would be men, Temple surmised, in league with Robert Lincoln and without sympathy for his mother. They would want the diary and they would want Fiona, and they would do whatever was necessary to extract any information they needed from her.

He had made it clear: leave the train in Defiance.

Fiona knew a train would be bound east from Defiance only thirty minutes to an hour after the Lincoln cars pushed through, and so she would be on her way back to Washington before Robert was any the wiser. Should he want to raise an alarm, his best bet would be to get off at the next station, Auburn Junction, to telegraph his handlers in Chicago and Washington—if in fact there was a telegraph in Auburn Junction. If he managed to do that, then all would still be well, because Fiona would be changing trains one more time on her return to the District, in Wheeling, from which she could then travel to Cumberland. In Cumberland, Alexander would meet her with horses and they would eventually slip back into the District at night. Temple had mapped all of this out with her before they ever went to the B&O to board Mrs. Lincoln's train, and now, standing with her luggage in her hand, her medical bag under her arm, and a light veil of perspiration on her forehead, Fiona was ready to turn back toward home.

The station was a humble and empty clapboard assemblage, nearly as passive and commodious as a warehouse. Only two people were in sight, and neither of them paid mind to Fiona, just as they had not even furrowed a brow when her luggage arced out from the back of the imperious mass of iron, smoke, and speed that was changing and absorbing the good people of Defiance despite their best efforts to preserve—in their town, their churches, their homes—what they had always preserved.

A faro dealer peeled out cards onto an empty table in front of him, waiting and preparing for a small group of optimists who would inevitably gather around him later in the day so that he could empty their pockets. As Fiona mounted the platform, he eyed her curiously but made no effort to bring her into his game. A young, chestnut-haired woman with a lovely cerulean petticoat peeking out from beneath her skirt sat on a bench minding her knitting and saying nothing as her hands bobbed in and out of her skein, the edges of a blanket forming around her needles. Just two people and utter silence, save for a breeze winding among the leaves at the top of a nearby row of buckeyes and inciting them to applaud gently. Or perhaps the buckeyes were snickering? Fiona thought on that possibility but chose to ignore its implications and strode with purpose to an indoor waiting room on the side of the station.

When the door swung outward from the waiting room, well before Fiona had gotten near enough to open it herself, she knew she was caught. She knew it because she knew the navy sleeve on the arm opening the door belonged to a Union soldier; she knew it because that same soldier was visibly pleased with himself and smiled at her with the satisfaction of someone who had been waiting patiently—hours and hours—to fulfill his duty and had, as a reward for his patience, just fulfilled it; she knew it again when two other soldiers crowded out from behind him through the doorway, making room for a short, mustachioed man fingering the top of his sword and wearing a uniform embroidered with gold braid at the shoulders that conveyed his rank over the three men in front of him; and she knew it with certainty when he smiled at her with the same satisfaction that had brightened the face of the first soldier, the one who had opened the door.

"Mrs. McFadden?" the officer purred.

"I am," she said, having decided in the milliseconds available to her that lying was pointless. There were several horses—six if her count was right—tethered to a rail in the yard beyond the waiting room, but they offered no hope of escape.

"Mr. Stanton, at Mr. Baker's behest, dispatched men to every station along this line, and it does appear that we are the lucky ones to have encountered you, ma'am. The war secretary is a forward-thinking man."

"I have heard as much of him. Are we to wait here together?"

"Yes, and we shall escort you on the train to Washington—after we have a moment to examine your luggage, ma'am."

"Examine for what, pray tell?" Fiona asked.

"For a leather-bound diary penned in Mrs. Lincoln's hand. Mr. Stanton would much like to have it."

"Your name, sir?"

"Major Bufus Ragland."

He reached for Fiona's luggage, but she stepped back. He reached again, but she swung the bag away from him, so he stepped forward and smacked her across the cheek with the back of his hand. The blow staggered her and drew a welt out on her cheek. She dropped her luggage but held her medical bag close. The pair of travelers who had been sitting at the side of the station now stood up to stare, but neither spoke up. A woman traveling alone had questionable morals, and if four members of the Union army also found something amiss with her, then it was not up to anyone in Defiance to interfere.

The major grabbed Fiona's arm and pulled her into the station. He slammed the door behind him and gestured to one of his men to close the shutter on a window that looked onto the opposite side of the station and yet another row of buckeyes. Yes, Fiona decided, the buckeyes had been snickering. She rubbed her cheek and examined her surroundings. Even at midday, the sealed shutters plunged the station's bare interior into murk accented with the lingering, stinging odor of cheap cigars. One of Ragland's men struck a match and lit a small, squat candle sitting on a table next to a bottle of liquor and several glasses. Fiona stared at the liquor, gathering her thoughts and feeling her breath begin to quicken.

"It's whiskey," Ragland said. "Pour us all a glass, Mrs. McFadden. We've been waiting for more than half a day in this shithole and we're in need of . . . diversion."

Ragland laughed, and the other men in the room joined him. Fiona placed her medical bag on the table. She pressed her fingers to her eyes to avoid thinking about the pain in her cheek while Ragland strolled across the room and picked up her luggage, the heels of his black boots knocking against the floorboards before he sat down.

"We have been told—"

"By whom?" Fiona snapped, interrupting him.

"By the war secretary, Mr. Stanton, himself."

"And he told you what? I have nothing to do with the war secretary."

"He told us that you were riding on the widow's train, madam. We have no time for you to be an intemperate bitch. I'm sure you know what we've come for."

Fiona kept her back to the room, arranging the glasses and uncapping the whiskey. She shook her head. No, in fact, she didn't know.

"Well, say what you will. I imagine what we want is right in here," Ragland said, unclasping her luggage and rummaging around inside. The other three men gathered close to him, peering into her luggage as well. Ragland pulled out a pair of blouses, a hairbrush, two books, some hairpins, a pair of socks, a Bible, and a Chinese fan, dropping all of it on the floor as he picked his way along. He began plucking things from the bag faster and faster, swearing under his breath until he cast the luggage aside.

"Put her on the wall," he snapped at one of his men. "There's no diary in here."

A short, stocky soldier with a red beard spun Fiona away from the table and slammed her into the wall, pressing his hand to her breast. He circled his other hand around her neck and squeezed until her face flushed red and she gagged, a small stream of spittle leaking from the corner of her mouth. He squeezed harder and she thought she would faint.

"Wait," Ragland said. "Look in the small bag on the table first."

The soldier yanked his hand from Fiona's throat and she doubled over at her waist, coughing and sweating. He turned back to the table and opened her bag.

"It's all bottles and vials," the soldier said, confused. "Medical supplies."

"Mrs. McFadden," Ragland asked, amused, "are you a conjurer?"

"I am a trained medical professional," she rasped, forcing herself up and staring at Ragland with as much confidence as she could muster.

"There is no diary in this bag, either," the soldier roared, and he pounced on Fiona in a fury, forcing a hand between her legs and latching the other to her throat. She sputtered as the air rushed out of her mouth, both of her hands reflexively but uselessly grabbing hold of the soldier's arms as her pressed her back into the wall again.

"Wait!" Ragland shouted.

The soldier released her.

"She does not have the diary on her person, and we need to ask her some things before you feel her up any more, goddammit."

Ragland stood up and pulled his jacket down at his sides, composing himself.

"Bring us our whiskey and we will interview Mrs. McFadden properly."

The soldier, still hovering over Fiona, pressed both of his hands back against his chest and arched his eyebrows.

"Yes, you arsehole. Get the whiskey," Ragland said. "You've left the woman gagging, and she's in no position to serve whiskey to the four of us. So serve it."

The other two soldiers chuckled and sat down at the far end of the waiting room, near a wall with a blank surface except for the faint rectilinear slats of sunlight creeping in around the edges and straight down the middle of the shutter framed in its center. They stretched out their legs and waited for their drinks.

Four glasses were poured and brought over. Each of the men tipped his head and shot back the whiskey.

"It's bitter," one of the men complained.

"I bought it," Ragland replied. "You'll drink it."

After a second and third pour went around, Ragland stood up and walked slowly over to Fiona, whose hands were clasped in front of her waist. A yellow tongue of candlelight played across her cheeks, giving her eyes a wider and deeper cast.

"You are a fine-looking woman, Mrs. McFadden," Ragland said, fingering her cheek. "Under different circumstances I do believe we would enjoy sharing each other's company more intimately."

"Major Ragland, I cannot imagine any circumstances in which I'd take pleasure in your company," Fiona said, batting his hand away from her face.

Ragland stepped away, slipped his hand inside his belt, and withdrew a small silver knife with an ivory handle and a short blade. The edges of the knife picked up the light from the candle, and Fiona could see a locomotive etched in fine black lines across the length of its blade.

"You're a spirited woman, but I'm afraid I don't have the time to amuse myself with your banter," Ragland said, stepping forward and pressing the tip of his knife into Fiona's throat, drawing a tiny burst of blood. She tried to back away from him, but the wall behind her stopped her.

"You are wanted by the government of these United States for theft of its property, and I will do whatever is necessary to ensure that you tell me where that property is located," he said, drawing closer and whispering into her ear.

She could smell the whiskey, thick on his breath. He, too, fondled her breast, before slapping her again with the back of his hand and knocking her to the ground. Tears burned in her eyes, but she blinked them back and stood up. The air in the waiting room felt dense now and pressed down upon her from the rafters. Cigar smoke, whiskey, probing hands, questions.

O Almighty God, who art a strong tower of defense to those who put their trust in thee, whose power no creature is able to resist, we make our humble cry to thee.

"I have no diary upon my person," Fiona said. "Mrs. Lincoln is now in possession of a diary that rightly belongs to her and to which no one else has claim."

"There's a second diary."

"I'm not aware of it."

He hit her again, harder, and she fell to the ground, nearly fainting from the pain that drew tiny pinpoints across her skull. Ragland dropped to one knee, took Fiona's skirt in his left hand and pulled it taut, then cut straight through it with his knife, until the blade was inches from her nether areas.

"I will slice your pudenda, Mrs. McFadden, unless you give me the information I need."

He was close to her face again. Cigar smoke, whiskey, probing hands, questions: this is all you smell and hear when you die away from home, Fiona thought. Maybe I'll simply close my eyes as it happens.

Fiona braced for the cut, pressing her back into the wall as firmly as she could, but Ragland's head snapped away from her, his lips pursing in rubbery circles that gave his mouth the cast of a palsied bass beached at the edge of Black Lake. No sooner had Ragland's lips started dancing than his throat began pulsing in thick spasms and he gasped more furiously for breath, his eyes caught between surprise and horror as he tried to focus on Fiona, a wall, the ceiling, whatever he might stare at as he wrestled fruitlessly with his own body. A moment later his arms began twitching and his hands shook violently enough that he dropped his knife into Fiona's lap, scuttling backward from her on legs moving so rapidly and randomly that she no longer thought of him as a stranded fish but as an oversized, pan-icked crab. His grimace hardening, Ragland repeatedly chopped at his swelling throat in scattered, violent swipes. As the furies cascaded across his body, Ragland's sword and scabbard clattered repeatedly against the waiting room's floor, swinging off his hip in ever longer slices as his body began a final permutation: with his head nearly touching the floor and his face forced upward, Ragland gagged loudly and plaintively as his back bowed and his torso arched toward the ceiling, gold officer's braid dangling down from his shoulders.

And Ragland was not dying alone. His three men were seized with conniptions of their own—choking, straining, and caterwaul-ing about the room in crazes that left them bouncing from corners and rounding off one another in crooked, frenetic cartwheels, their shadows intertwined and thrown into relief on a ceiling highlighted by the dull yellow glow of the single candle still lighting the room.

Fiona had covered her eyes and stopped watching the soldiers' final moments when the last of them finally fell, choking and fidget-ing, into the table. The candle and the whiskey bottle flipped off the table, leaving Fiona's medical bag teetering on the edge. As it had been shortly after the soldiers and Fiona entered, the waiting room was now illuminated only by thin lines of sunlight splitting the bor-ders of the shutters covering the windows. There was a soft moan coming from one of the men on the floor, but in the darkness Fiona couldn't tell which one it was. She resisted the urge to vomit and began to slide across the floor, away from Ragland's corpse and toward her medical bag. She was just beginning to stand when the door to the waiting room opened.

The chestnut-haired woman who had been knitting on the plat-form stood in the doorway, light pouring in around her. The faro dealer peered in behind her, wide-eyed. She turned to him and pulled several greenbacks from her bag, pressing them into his hand.

"The men on the floor in here are all drunkards and they have tried to violate the honor of this poor woman," the woman said to him. "Please respect her privacy as I attend to her."

"What was all the banging and shouting, then?" the faro dealer asked. "And none of them look ripped up to me. They're all smiling the monkey smile. I 'spect they're conversing with their Maker right about now."

"As I said, they are clearly a rambunctious lot," she reiterated, and gave him two more bills. "If you return to the platform, there will be more money for you when we depart."

The faro dealer turned back toward the platform, and the woman closed the door, then pulled on a lever along the doorjamb to prop open the transom above it, allowing her to leave the shutters in place on the windows while illuminating the slaughter on the floor in front of her. The four men all lay akimbo, their limbs splayed at odd angles from their bodies, frozen in rigor mortis.

She surveyed the room and then walked to the corpse nearest her, crouching down to examine whatever aromas still lingered around his mouth.

Fiona thought: Cigars, whiskey, death.

"They were all drinking whiskey," she told the woman.

"And the whiskey did this to them?"

"I'm at a loss as to what prompted their passages," Fiona said, standing and walking to her bag. She still felt dizzy, and her cheeks were throbbing. One of the men on the floor wheezed, still struggling, however faintly, for breath.

The woman walked to him and crouched down. She pulled the ball of yarn from her bag and pressed it over his mouth and nose to block any more air from entering. The soldier's heels rattled briefly against the floor before he expired.

"Who are you?" Fiona asked, leaning on the table for support.

"Kate Warne of the Pinkertons, Mrs. McFadden. At your service."

TWO OF THE horses in the yard were Kate Warne's; the rest belonged to the dead soldiers. Warne and Fiona were on their way in minutes, their bags strapped behind their saddles and hanging from their pommels. As they circled the yard, the faro dealer tipped his hat to them and smiled.

"He will give us over to the first curious person who comes to the station, so we have little time to waste," Warne said. "But I have a query of you first: strychnine?"

"They were drinking whiskey, which was fortuitous. It masked part of the strychnine's bitterness. I had a moment to taint the entire bottle, and I did."

"Because you routinely carry poisons in your bag."

"I don't know if I would have left that room alive had I not done what I did. I am a healer first and foremost," Fiona said. "Along with my God, my medical bag is my armor and my cause, Miss Warne, and in all of my adult years I haven't traveled without it. Now I have a question of you."

"And I will listen and respond, but only after we have put considerable distance between us and Defiance. Until then we don't have the luxury of extended chatter."

Warne snapped the reins, and her horse broke into a gallop. Bruised and still numb, Fiona followed suit, and the pair rode at speed away from Defiance, southeast along a post road that Warne clearly knew from memory.

Five hours later, their horses in a lather, Fiona and Warne arrived at a trim, well-maintained farmhouse where two fresh horses were waiting. Fiona hoped they would stop there, but when a lanky old man in coveralls marched out of the house with a bag of apples and a large pail of water, she knew they were simply exchanging horses.

"The Pinkerton network," Warne said, giving the man an envelope she pulled from her bag.

"The Pinkerton network," the old man replied, swatting at several flies that circled his head and giving Warne an envelope of his own.

They drank and ate, and within minutes they were off again, Warne nodding in gratitude but saying nothing more to the old man as they left.

Two hours later, with dusk pressing in, they arrived at yet another farmhouse just outside Columbus.

"We can stay here tonight," Warne said. "In the morning we will find our train back to Washington."

The same exchange occurred again. Warne identified herself as a Pinkerton, and the owner of the house—a middle-aged woman with two children who sat and stared from a corner of the kitchen—replied in kind and showed them inside. The owner had laid out two night-dresses for them in her bedroom, and Warne and Fiona went there to change and freshen themselves from a shallow basin of water set on a chair by the bed.

Warne peeled her petticoat away, revealing several pouches sewn into her corset. Two derringers were tucked into a pair of the pouches, the handles of the pistols curling out like commas. Three other pouches harbored knives.

"How do you bear a single day in a corset, much less a corset or-namented with weaponry?" Fiona asked.

"My breaths get squeezed," Warne said. "But it is all part of my work, and I enjoy my work. I have seen things in my work. My work defines me. I am a Pinkerton, and the only woman Mr. Pinkerton has hired. I helped him get Mr. Lincoln safely through Baltimore and into Washington after he was first elected, you know."

"Then I should be honored that you have escorted me to safety as well, but I don't know how you found me or why."

"Your husband managed to force Mr. Pinkerton to leave Wash-ington, but his contacts are vast and he didn't see fit to end his inter-sections with you and your husband just yet. He knew you to be on the train with Mrs. Lincoln, and he ordered agents to wait along the line to Chicago. I hadn't expected to see Mr. Stanton's soldiers in Defiance, however."

"I had not expected them, either," Fiona said, stroking her cheeks.

"You'll be deeply bruised about your face for a few more days," Warne said, slipping into her nightdress.

"What are your plans for me?"

"Mr. Pinkerton said you are a handoff, nothing more. Whoever encountered you between Washington and Chicago was to ensure your safe passage back to the District."

"Nothing more than that?"

"If we were to find a diary upon you, we were to take it."

Fiona, still half dressed, stood up.

"Please sit, Mrs. McFadden. I imagine your interlude with the soldiers in Defiance would have been briefer if the diary Mr. Pinkerton wants was still in your possession. I don't have you here to assault you. You remain a handoff, and I will get you back to Washington."

After both had changed into their nightdresses, Warne and Fiona folded their own clothing atop their bags at the foot of the bed. The owner of the house escorted them through the main room to a short, six-rung ladder propped against a loft built into a corner of the farmhouse's roof. There was a small featherbed atop the loft, and Warne and Fiona shared it for the night.

THE NEXT MORNING they washed again and then made their way to Columbus, where Fiona decided, in a burst of extravagance she felt was well deserved, to spend $15 on a new dress and another $3 on fresh undergarments that she bought on the High Street near Union Station. Her old clothing still smelled of cigar smoke—or at least she believed the odor still lingered, and in that moment she recognized that quite possibly for the rest of her life the smell of a cigar would weaken her knees or cause her imagination to race and strain against an unseen fear.

At 11:15 A.M. the women boarded the CC&C to Cincinnati, where they would pick up a spur of the B&O that would then take them through Parkersburg, Grafton, Cumberland, and Harpers Ferry before they reached Washington. Fiona would also miss her rendezvous with Alexander Gardner, but for now there was little she could do to remedy that.

CHAPTER TWENTY-THREE

THE PRISONER

"*Step back and dodge the fist,*" Dr. McFadden shouted. "*Dodge it!*"

"I can't step back."

"*Learn to step back, even with your leg. You'll need that skill.*"

Temple was no longer crossing the Atlantic aboard the *Washington* when he dreamt. On firm land now, in Manhattan, he was a teenager whose father was driving him as hard as he ever had.

"You are an Irish immigrant in a hostile land. My money won't protect you from that. Improve yourself. Defend yourself."

A private tutor for math, science, and literature. Endless books and lessons. The silliness with his cane that began on the ship had become a regular affair, three days a week; a fencing master would come to their rooms near Union Square and train Temple to defend himself with his cane. And now training in fisticuffs, also three days a week.

"Dodge the fist!"

Temple would sometimes sulk, worn down by the schedule.

"I'll run away."

"You'll never run away," his father would reply, laughing and pulling him close.

And he wouldn't. He was content and felt safe near his father. On days when he did complain—and the complaining came from the rigors of his work rather than simple whining—he knew what would follow: a trip with his father to Barnum's American Museum to see Tom Thumb and the Feejee Mermaid, a visit to the Astor Library on Lafayette Street to find poetry, an outing to the far northern edge of the city at 40th Street and Fifth Avenue to walk on the ramparts of the Croton Reservoir, vaudeville at Niblo's Garden, or—the best treat of all—a trip across the river to Hoboken to watch the Emmetts and the Sarsfields go after each other in a hurling match.

Dr. McFadden also took Temple for visits with Archbishop Hughes, the man his father simply called "Conscience." The doctor burst with pride that the Catholic prelate was remaking the city with schools for boys *and* girls, with threats to dispatch his burgeoning flock into the streets and turn all of Manhattan into a "second Moscow" if Protestants torched any more churches, and with the creation of a bank that catered to the Irish. The archbishop was doing all of this, Dr. McFadden noted, with a deep and hardy love of the Lord Almighty—an apparently vengeful God who, Temple reflected, forgave the prelate's eye-for-an-eye enthusiasm for arson.

In time, Temple came to love the archbishop even as he abandoned the Church itself. The prelate had impressed upon Temple the need to learn how to "navigate," as he put it, and to that end encouraged him at the age of sixteen to look in on the meetings at Hibernian Hall on Prince Street, where, the archbishop advised, Temple might get to know the Irish political leaders and ward heelers beginning to assert some control over the city.

Cards and dice were as prevalent as politics at the Hibernian, and it was there that Temple first learned how to play faro, and where he first discovered the hungry, sexual throb of watching and betting on how dice spilled across the end of a table. He came to love the feel of the dice in his hand and the uncertain moment that came between rolling them in his palm and casting them into the air like doves, waiting for them to fall, turn, and tell him his fortune.

It was also at the Hibernian that he met George Matsell, New York's police commissioner, who convinced him, on his nineteenth birthday, and much to his father's unremitting dismay, to become a patrolman.

"You can be a man of letters or a professional. Why the police?"

"It feels real to me, Father. It's close to things."

"Diogenes."

"Your son."

Within months, Matsell, having recognized the unique constellation of skills, insight, and stubbornness harbored within the McFadden boy, promoted Temple to detective and boosted his salary to $50 a month. In a city half a million people strong and littered with murder, robbery, and graft, Temple had a gift for unraveling the tangled ends of calamities and violent disagreements.

"You have to love Manhattan," Matsell would say. "Every block. You have to love it because most of the time this city will not love you back."

Often Temple just worked harder than the rest of the scoffs in the department, but he also had an affinity for the work. He could cultivate the person who saw something untoward or amiss, and find the right crevice or melody in the conversation that offered more than the person knew or felt able to tell. At crime scenes, he spotted the torn piece of fabric or the broken bracelet that had the most promising provenance; he probed wounds to date their vintage and cause; he learned about the gangs and the pols and the swells and the whores and the merchants and the entertainers and the workers, becoming a part of the city's tapestry; he learned where points and people intersected—at what hour, in what place, on which street—and kept that map in his mind whenever he was called on to lend his eyes and ears to an investigation.

When esteemed phrenologists encouraged the department's budding contingent of detectives to examine the shapes and sizes of suspects' skulls, jaws, and brows to determine their propensity for committing crimes, Temple dismissed the training as quackery, pointing out that all he and his cohorts needed to do was examine the scene and the circumstances.

So it was that when one of the biggest fires on Pearl Street was blamed on a band of four disgruntled black dockworkers from Fulton and South, Temple spent hours inside what remained of the van der Donk Glass and Furnishings Emporium. After picking through the scorched rubble and splintered, pitch-black beams inside, he discovered several singed tin canisters ornamented with sets of small initials, A.P.G., around their rims. A thin trace of kerosene still swam in the bottom of one of the tins. While many buildings in Manhattan were converting to kerosene and even gas for lighting, the van der Donk works were still being illuminated traditionally, with whale oil. An abundance of kerosene in the building was an anomaly. And next door to Ilspeth van der Donk's family office in the Merchants' Exchange Cellar on Front Street was Roscoe's, lower Manhattan's largest purveyor of kerosene, turpentine, and other highly flammable lighting fuels, all of which the company distributed in distinctive tins that Roscoe's believed helped distinguish its enterprise from more downmarket competitors. The tins were stamped with the initials of Roscoe's Canadian partner, Abraham Pineo Gesner, who held a patent on refining kerosene and had set up a separate and thriving Long Island facility, the North American Kerosene Gas Light Company, to produce it.

Barton Roscoe noted when Temple interviewed him that Ilspeth van der Donk himself had purchased an unusually large supply of kerosene just days before the fire. Roscoe said that his company had loaded at least three-score tins on the back of a van der Donk supply wagon. After much to-ing and fro-ing, Ilspeth confessed to Temple that he had used kerosene to set fire to his store in order to collect upon an insurance policy he had secured on the property months before.

It was a highly publicized case that endeared Temple to New York's abolitionists, particularly the influentials at the Anti-Slavery Society, who began courting him and, in short order, converted him to their cause. For many of them, Abraham Lincoln was a hero—flawed and not always reliable, to be sure, but a hero nonetheless.

I do order and declare that all persons held as slaves within said designated States, and parts of States are, and henceforward shall be, free.

As time went on and Temple spent more evenings socializing and circulating among the society's members, he absorbed their adoration of Lincoln.

We here highly resolve that these dead shall not have died in vain—that this nation, under God, shall have a new birth of freedom—and that government of the people, by the people, for the people, shall not perish from the earth.

The van der Donk case also earned Temple the devotion of Tommy Driscoll, the police department's veteran sleuth, who noted to anyone in earshot that "young Temple McFadden is a prodigy and a wizard, goddammit." The case also put him at odds with the business class and right-minded gentry in Manhattan, who found Temple's dedication to the Negro to be an overly enthusiastic intrusion upon their desire that the police force simply serve their needs.

The police force that Temple joined was a motley and loosely corrupt band of hooligans, one of out of five of whom were Irish. They had no uniforms, enforced order (or administered random and often questionable beatings) at the end of a billy club, and paid more attention to the prerogatives of the city's network of neighborhood aldermen than to Matsell or anyone else in the department's hierarchy. Matsell, a Brit, said he wanted to model New York's police force on the English constabulary put in place by Sir Robert Peel, but the bobbies were meant to be a quasi-military presence on London's streets. Americans, Matsell well knew, would never stand for a police presence that so closely resembled and reminded them of a standing army. Thus, a lack of order, hierarchy, and purpose prevailed in New York's fledgling police department. Thus, a lack of rules and restraints.

Temple learned to navigate the workings of the police force alongside the political dynamics inside the Hibernian Hall as well, avoiding the "standard practices" common among the other policemen with whom he worked. He never took a bribe, never carried a billy club or administered pell-mell beatings, and rarely even lost his temper. He just studied things—a puddle of blood, a shard of glass, a dent in the wall, the words of witnesses, the arch of an eyebrow, the unexplained relationship—and made arrests. Then he went back on the street and did it again and again, cultivating informants, confidants, and supporters across the city.

Policing also distracted him from the series of rejections he received when he tried to enlist in the Union army. Three times in, three times rejected, all at a time when the army was taking the shaggiest and most scurvy of conscripts. *Damn my leg.*

In the wake of those rejections Temple threw himself more deeply into the society's effort to move escaping slaves through New York and up into New England and Canada on the Underground Railroad.

None of it amounted to serving in the Union army. Still, as a detective on the streets of New York, Temple felt engaged. It was the happiest he had ever been.

Which may have been why his new profession got so miserable so quickly. Happiness, he decided, always had a way of eluding him.

The cleaving came several months into Temple's first year on the police force, when New York erupted. The city had begun percolating earlier when locals learned that Lincoln planned to arrange a draft and that officials would publicly draw numbers to decide who would be conscripted. New York had already sent a substantial contingent of volunteers to the war, and the first day of the drawings went quietly enough. Word then began spreading that anyone with three hundred dollars could avoid conscription by paying that amount to have someone serve in their stead. Temple was near Union Square when he first read of the provision, in a story with a headline declaring, "Rich Man's War, Poor Man's Fight." Another story in the same paper pointed out that "$300 Men Are Worth Less Than $1,000 Slaves."

Tinderbox, Temple thought. Tinderbox.

The Hibernians and their like stoked it, warning Irish lads and other laborers that free Negroes would pour up from the South and steal their jobs. Temple watched this play out at Hibernian Hall and elsewhere and warned Matsell and Johnny Kennedy, the police superintendent, that it would come to a boil. Watch the firemen and watch the gangs, he told them. When things started to tip, it was the smokies who stirred it up first, with the crew from the Black Joke, Engine Company 33, stoning and then setting fire to the draft office on 47th Street. Johnny went up there for a look and, even without his uniform on, got thumped to within an inch of the abyss by Marty Sheehan's firemen.

Temple and others had rousted enough policemen downtown to help hold back the rioters there, though several from the Hibernian spat at him and labeled him a traitor. Uptown, however, a bloody and unforgiving riot ensued, snaking around the streets in angry, malicious waves. White rioters openly beat Negroes in the streets; they chased one into an alley, beat him, and then hung him from a tree limb and set him on fire. They lynched ten others as well, one from a lamppost. They burned and looted the Colored Orphan Asylum on Fifth Avenue, though the police there helped evacuate more than two hundred children out of the back of the building without harm. Chasing down two white women who had married Negroes, a crowd beat them with clubs and bricks, leaving placards on their unconscious bodies that labeled them as "amalgamationists."

Downtown remained largely safe, except near the docks on the East River. White longshoremen and black dockworkers there engaged in an epic set-to not far from the van der Donk building. Longshoremen destroyed bawdy houses, taverns, and tenements that served or housed Negroes and then stripped the clothing off the white owners of those establishments and paraded them through the streets naked.

In the end, the military entered the city and fired on the crowds, quelling the riot. The day it finally subsided, Temple was guarding the door of Daniel Lane's dance house on Walnut Street in Corlears

Point, where three Hibernians had come to thump Mary Burke, a white adventuress who specialized in servicing Negroes.

"Come through the door, then you've got to come through me, boys," Temple said to them.

Temple was known on the streets as a dangerous and perplexing brawler—for the unpredictable use he made of his cane and a prodigious strength unexpected in someone so lanky—and the group considered his warning and turned. On their way back down Walnut Street they waved their clubs and swore at him in a streak of creative obscenities that Temple found to be almost poetic and, at a minimum, musical. One of them cupped his hand to his mouth and emitted the long, plaintive howl of a dog. Temple decided there and then never to visit the Hibernian Hall again.

After he got Mary onto a horse and out of Corlears, he headed over to the docks to look in on the boardinghouse where some of the Negroes falsely accused in the van der Donk case lived. When he arrived, there was a crush of rioters at the door of the boardinghouse—hundreds more than had been in Corlears—and they were dragging screaming Negroes into the street. Two already hung dead from streetlamps, their feet bloody and dripping. Temple paused less than a quarter block away from the boardinghouse, uncertain of what to do. The rioters were as fearsome a lot as he had ever encountered, their eyes bulging and their voices bristling with rage. A wave of apprehension rippled through Temple's chest and broadened into an immobilizing fear that he had never felt in his life until that moment. He imagined himself pounced upon by the mob, his head pounded into a pulp, and he stood rooted to his spot as the violence continued to unfold in front of him.

Cassius Marks, one of the Negroes who walked from jail a free man in the van der Donk case due to Temple's handiwork, was hauled from the boardinghouse by two men, one of whom pounded Cassius's back with a club. Cassius leaned back on his heels and tried to pull away as he was dragged deeper into the mob, but two other men grabbed him around the waist and pulled him into the scrum. His eyes darted about as he looked for help from someone, and in a brief flash his eyes locked on Temple. A glimmer of hope washed across Cassius's face and he nodded to Temple, leaning back again from the tugs of the mob. Two people tore his pants from his waist, but he remained fixated on Temple, nodding but unable to speak.

Temple couldn't move.

Rioters knocked Cassius to the ground and swarmed around him, tying a rope around his scrotum and dragging him through the streets by it until he was unconscious; a fourteen-year-old boy then knelt on Cassius's stomach and plunged a knife into his chest.

Temple never moved.

The mob swelled uptown from the docks, leaving blood smears, bits of clothing, and several bodies, including Cassius's, scattered about the streets. After they had gone, Temple walked to the piers, leaned out over the East River, and vomited.

He spent the next two weeks gambling, drinking, and sleeping during the day. On two nights he awoke to find Cassius sleeping next to him, bleeding and looking at him with the same soundless, plaintive stare he had given him at the docks. One afternoon, as a runaway horse bolted down Broadway and galloped past Temple, Cassius bounced along on his back at the end of a rope tied to the stallion. Cassius stared at Temple again, looking for help.

Toward the end of his bender, after a night of faro on Bond Street, he stopped by his father's one morning for breakfast. When his father didn't answer, Temple let himself in and made his way to the small room his father had converted into a study and where he read the newspaper each day. He found his father slumped in a chair, with a bullet hole in his head and the gun he had used to kill himself on the floor by his foot. The muzzle was still warm and Temple could smell gunpowder. There wasn't a note or any other explanation for his father's suicide, and Temple collapsed on the floor, burying his face in his hands.

About a week later, when word arrived that President Lincoln needed New York detectives to populate his newly formed police department in the District, Temple contemplated his current disgust for Manhattan and pursued the request. His handlers at the police department all approved the move, and in short order he was off to Washington.

His dreams never journeyed closer to the present than after the moment when he separated from New York and the riots and Cassius and found his way to Washington and Fiona.

And his dreams of New York, lately, were always dreams of his father.

Step back and dodge the fist, Temple. Dodge it.

Slap.

He couldn't dodge it.

Slap. Slap.

Temple awoke in a cell, his arms bound behind him to the chair he sat upon, facing a small man covered in clouds of white whiskers and white hair who was slapping him to get him to stir. Slapping him hard.

"Stop!" Temple shouted.

The man grinned from within his whiskers, his teeth tangled and yellow.

"We have the mick's attention," the man said, nodding to a Union soldier who stood behind him in the cell. "You are in my prison at the wishes of the war secretary and we mean to have chats with you, sir. I would have you understand that we take these matters seriously and that our time is limited."

Temple pressed his wrists outward, testing his coils and the strength of the chair. There was little give in the rope and the chair was thick and sturdy; breaking it was going to require acrobatics and would be noisy, so that wasn't for now. He was, for the time being, a prisoner.

"I have met too many a new person in these recent days and

weeks and I am dizzied with names. What might yours be and where am I?"

"William Wood. Old Capitol Prison."

Temple knew the name, if not the man. Nail had occasionally mentioned Wood as one of his handlers during the war, when Nail was drafting cogniacs of Secesh currency. Temple also knew now that his cell was inside the District's most infamous prison.

Several stories of brick and bars, its bottom third painted with a heavy white band, the Old Capitol was a former boardinghouse now serving as a lockup for Confederate officers and other high-value prisoners. Two of those accused of conspiring to assassinate President Lincoln were being held there: the widow and boardinghouse owner Mary Surratt and Samuel Mudd, a doctor said to have attended to John Wilkes Booth's broken leg and given him shelter at his Maryland home after the assassination.

The Old Capitol had also been a stronghold for the Union's spy services during the war, and the men who worked in the building carried out Edwin Stanton's directives against enemies in the South and those closer to home, in the streets and salons of Washington. Nail and Alexander had both told Temple that William Wood was an intimate of the war secretary's and the steward of the Old Capitol—and therefore one of Lafayette Baker's overseers.

Temple looked about his cell, which was cramped and furnished only with his chair and a simple plank bed. The ceiling was high in the middle and sloped at a sharp angle where it joined a short, three-foot wall on the other side of the floor; they had him on the highest floor of the prison right beneath the roof. There was a single window in the room, more than halfway up the cell's largest wall, and it was fitted with four thick iron bars. His boots and cane were in a corner.

"Yes, we had the courtesy to remember your cane," said Wood, following Temple's gaze around the room. "We are benevolent men who do not want to overlook your severe handicaps, Mr. McFadden."

Temple didn't respond.

Wood sat in silence, too, staring at him. He raised his right hand and snapped his fingers, prompting the soldier in the room to leave. The metal door clanged shut behind him.

"We are alone now and we can speak with each other directly, as men. I would loosen your bonds, but I am told that despite your limp and your distaste for guns, you are a singularly dangerous man. That you have even kept Lafayette Baker at bay, and he is an individual not to be trifled with."

Temple remained as he was, staring down at the floor.

"Mr. McFadden, you must have respect for our needs and priorities. We have successfully prosecuted a war. The country will be remade and the South will be absorbed into the national plan. President Lincoln has been cruelly and unjustly murdered and we have his assassins incarcerated. We want completion. We want to move forward. Why do you insist on standing in the way?"

Temple didn't look up.

"I once worked with your friend Jack Flaherty. Then he changed. He stood in the way. He was killed yesterday, while you were harassing Mr. Stanton at the parade."

Temple's head snapped up and he strained against the ropes.

"Ah, some emotion from you at last. Yes, Mr. Baker saw to it that your friend Nail was gunned down. He did so most efficiently, with our new Gatlings. In a way, you're responsible for Flaherty's death. He would still be counterfeiting greenbacks among that motley tribe in the swamps had you not swept him up into this folly. Really, consider yourself and consider your circumstances. What are you trying to accomplish? Do you want to see your wife dead, too?"

Temple roared, stooping forward and raising the chair off the ground behind him as the ropes around him dug into his arms, chest, and wrists. He swore aimlessly, spittle flying from his mouth, but without his cane he couldn't take the weight of his body or the chair, and he spun in a half circle before tumbling backward onto the floor. The ropes hadn't loosened, the chair hadn't cracked, and Wood stepped into the space above him, his head framed by the beams on the ceiling.

"Lafayette Baker searched Swampdoodle for the Booth diary, upending floorboards and beating several residents for information. But he couldn't find it. I want that diary," Wood said, looking down at him. "I understand you have Mrs. Lincoln's diary as well, but the widow is of no threat to us. Her son Robert has already promised us that he will see his mother committed to an asylum in Illinois. She is quite mad, and no one takes her claims and howlings seriously anymore. Whatever case you fancy yourself building regarding the president's assassination will not rest upon his widow's proclamations."

Wood lifted his right hand again and snapped his fingers. The metal door swung open and the soldier stepped back in.

"Sit him upright," Wood said. "And get him some water."

After the soldier hoisted him back up, Temple returned to form, staring silently at the floor.

"I want to know where the Booth diary is, and you won't be leaving here until I have it," said Wood. "I know much about you, Mr. McFadden. Your father, for example, the immigrant doctor. He put a bullet in his head two years ago, shortly after the draft riots in New York, did he not? I assume you're wrestling with similar demons, which makes you a threat to society."

Wood turned away and walked to the door. As he yanked it open, Temple cleared his throat, and Wood froze in the doorway. Then Temple spoke for the first time.

"Who is Maestro?"

Wood bowed his head for a moment, then stepped out, slamming the door behind him.

THE GUARDS LEFT Temple tied to his chair for the night, and that was the condition in which Edwin Stanton found him when he arrived at the cell the next morning. Stanton turned on his heel in a fury and called in the guards to unbind Temple. They protested, pointing out that they were merely carrying out William Wood's orders and that Mr. Wood urged caution given the prisoner's strength and cunning. Stanton exploded again, telling the men that they could stand guard in the cell, weapons at the ready, and were free to fire should the prisoner attempt an attack or an escape.

"I'm sorry to find you like this, Mr. McFadden. It is not my preference that you be treated so."

Temple said nothing. After his ropes were loosened, he brought his arms in front of his body, slowly and painfully, for the first time in more than a dozen hours. He stretched his legs toward the wall, but didn't look up.

"You are inserting yourself into issues and among men that will only pollute you," Stanton said. "There were mighty forces circling around President Lincoln, and I regret that I did not see them sooner, but I know them now. I beg of you, do not pollute yourself further in this entanglement."

"The sun, too, shines into cesspools and is not polluted," Temple said.

"All you need to do is tell me where the Booth diary is. Speak up and I will get you out of here."

"We have two ears and one tongue so that we would listen more and talk less," Temple replied.

"You are going to stay in this cell barking platitudes at me—platitudes from a failed and homeless philosopher—while your wife and friends remain at risk?"

"I have nothing to ask of you, Mr. Stanton, but that you would remove to the other side, that you may not, by intercepting the sunshine, take from me what you cannot give."

Stanton shook his head and removed his spectacles. Temple thought it again: this was a weary man, bent by the weight of having prosecuted a bloody and uprooting war.

"You must understand that I thought President Lincoln to be a miraculous and extraordinary man," Stanton said. "I did not hold him in high regard when I first encountered him as a lawyer in Ohio, and I certainly did not hold him in high regard even when he invited me into his administration. Perhaps none of us did. But I came to love, admire, and respect him as the greatest man I have ever met. I would have made any sacrifice to protect him."

Temple stared at the floor.

"I will give you until tomorrow evening to make up your mind. Mr. McFadden, we will kill all of you if we have to, but we will have that diary."

As he departed, Stanton ordered the guards to leave Temple unbound, find two extra men to escort him to and from the latrine in the prison yard, and then bring him food, water, and a pitcher and towel to clean himself.

Temple interrupted Stanton's departure with the same question he had asked of Wood.

"Who is Maestro?"

Stanton looked at Temple and shook his head, sighing as he left the cell.

THAT EVENING, WOOD ordered his prison guards to move Temple, as well as Mrs. Surratt and Dr. Mudd, from the Old Capitol Prison to the Old Arsenal Penitentiary.

The Old Arsenal was a massive brick fortress several times larger than the Old Capitol and was home to none of the spycraft and intelligence gathering that had made its sister institution so noteworthy. Instead, the Old Arsenal, closed for years and reopened only recently at the war secretary's command, was dedicated solely and enthusiastically to a single mission: incarcerating the assassination conspirators and diminishing them as they awaited trial.

Dominating the tip of Greenleaf Point, where the Potomac and Anacostia rivers flowed together, the Old Arsenal featured heavily guarded, twenty-foot rampart walls that enclosed a sprawling, open yard baked by the sun. Inside the courtyard, a large brick building housed workrooms and dining rooms. The entire northern side of the penitentiary was a three-story brick slab lined with cells for prisoners, flanked on one end by the warden's residence and a chapel and at the other end by the deputy warden's quarters. Two squat, white wooden guard towers, topped by domed roofs and rounded like gazebos, loomed over the southeastern and southwestern corners of the entire structure and were manned by two lookouts and two marksmen from the military's rifle corps. The military was ordered to run the Old Arsenal with an eye toward Secesh sympathizers attempting to free the conspirators. Stanton mandated that Jack Hartranft, a Union general whom President Johnson had appointed to run the penitentiary, should keep the Old Arsenal in a state of lockdown—no one in, no one out, unless they had written orders from the war secretary or William Wood.

The Old Capitol guards herded Temple, Mrs. Surratt, and Dr. Mudd into the back of an enclosed wagon around midnight. It was the first time Temple had seen either of them. Two guards hoisted Mrs. Surratt into the wagon, and she sat down on a narrow bench lining one of its walls. Her dark hair was parted in the middle and swept into a tight bun, and her wrists, like Temple's, were bound by a pair of handcuffs fitted with six inches of chain. A rosary dangled from her hands and she kneaded its beads between her thumbs and fingers, her lips moving in silent prayer from the time she was stuffed inside the back of the wagon until they reached the Old Arsenal.

Guards placed Temple aboard next, and then they lifted Dr. Mudd into the back of the wagon. Almost bald and with a heavy moustache and goatee, Dr. Mudd looked just as listless and tired as Mrs. Surratt. His handcuffs, however, were unusual—a pair of Lilly irons that were several inches thicker around the wrists than the pairs binding Mrs. Surratt and Temple. Rather than being connected by a chain, Dr. Mudd's handcuffs were linked by a pair of flat, almost planar, iron slats that fitted over each other and then were locked together with a custom deadbolt. Temple had seen Dr. Mudd's handcuffs only in photographs that Alexander Gardner had taken of the prisoner camps; Union soldiers used them to hold Secesh and other prisoners of war. It was impossible for the doctor to move his hands, and he rested them in his lap.

"Mrs. Surratt, I would like to introduce myself," Temple said. "I am a detective with the Metropolitan Police Department and I would like to help you."

She kept on praying, her lips expanding into occasional O's and then flattening into efficient, thin lines as she continued murmuring into the night. Temple introduced himself again, but she ignored him.

He also tried to start a conversation with Dr. Mudd, whose eyebrows were arching and curling in a fashion so rapid and odd that Temple could only conclude that the doctor was panic-stricken.

"Doctor, might we have a word, I—"

"Why are we here?" he snapped back.

"Well, that's exactly one of the things I would like to know, Dr. Mudd. Why are we in this prison?"

"Why are we here?" the doctor said again, not heeding him.

"I believe we are because we stand accused."

"I know we are accused, you fool. I want to know why we're here, in this wagon at this hour. If you can't tell me, then please do not accost me any further."

The rest of the ride from the Old Capitol to the Old Arsenal was made in silence. But when they reached the Old Arsenal and were pulled down off the back of the wagon, Mrs. Surratt burst into a long, low cry, one that stretched into the night like a mother mourning for a child. Stumbling away from the wagon, she pointed at six men lined up near the prison's gates, and she began shrieking and sobbing even louder.

Each of the men, all of whom were also alleged to be involved in the conspiracy to assassinate the president, wore white canvas hoods that gathered tightly around their necks with small, laced gaps for their mouths and no other openings, even for their eyes. Each wore a pair of Lilly irons on his wrists and across his ankles; the devices securing the men's legs were also chained to seventy-five-pound iron balls.

Mrs. Surratt collapsed to the ground, still pointing at the men while she rolled the beads of her rosary in her left hand, her screams tracing the Old Arsenal's walls and echoing in the courtyard beyond the gates.

"You better shut it now, you dirty bitch, or we'll shut it for you," one of the guards shouted.

The guard lifted the butt of his rifle to strike her down, but Temple stepped in between her and the soldier, wrapping up the rifle's stock in the chains of his handcuffs and then spinning the entire weapon up and out of the guard's hands.

As the rifle clattered to the ground, it discharged with a burst of fire and a clap, sending a bullet whizzing into a wall thirty yards away. The shot silenced Mrs. Surratt, who kept pointing at the hooded conspirators until she fainted a moment later. Another guard stepped over and slammed his gun into the back of Temple's head, knocking him out.

WHEN TEMPLE AWOKE the next morning, he was lying on a lumpy shuck mattress on the floor of a cell. His cane was propped in the corner, but other than that there were no other objects in the room.

A faded sheet of paper hung inside a frame on the wall of his cell. It was inscribed with a list of rules that had been prepared many years before, when the Old Arsenal was a fortress still devoted to reform and when the prisoners were meant to cultivate a set of civic principles that they could take with them into proper society when they were freed:

1. You shall be industrious and labor diligently in silence.
2. You shall not attempt to escape.
3. You shall not quarrel, converse, laugh, dance, whistle, sing, jump, nor look at nor speak to visitors.
4. You shall not use tobacco.
5. You shall not write or receive letters.
6. You shall respect officers and be clean in person and dress.
7. You shall not destroy or impair property.

The list reminded Temple of similar rules at his orphanage in Dublin. All that distinguished this place from the prison of his childhood were bars.

THE SAME DAY, Stanton visited Wood in his office at the Old Capitol to ask why Temple had been transferred to the Old Arsenal along with the conspirators.

Wood rocked back on his chair, considering the question. Together he and Mr. Stanton had navigated all of the difficulties of waging a vast and complex war, as well as the messy, untoward business of supervising the District and rooting out spies and other miscreants. Mars, as Mr. Lincoln had so fondly nicknamed him, had never found need to question Wood's judgment in such matters before. Even so, the war secretary wanted an explanation of McFadden's relocation, and Wood was pleased to oblige.

"Those conspirators are going to hang, Mr. Stanton."

"So we hope they will. They are murderers, each and every one of them."

"And when they hang, they will hang in the courtyard of the Old Arsenal," Wood continued. "We will make sure that when that day comes, Mr. McFadden will be seated with a view so he can see each of them swing. That, Mr. Stanton, is sure to loosen his tongue—if, of course, whatever we do in the meantime fails to produce the information we need."

CHAPTER TWENTY-FOUR

THE PRIEST

iona and Kate Warne arrived in the District by train in the early evening. Warne told Fiona to remain on board and then walked the length of the platform in the B&O and looked into the station's main concourse to see if there was anyone waiting for them. Robert Lincoln would have had ample time to telegraph that Fiona had left the Lincolns' Pullman car well before Chicago, but the B&O appeared to hold no surprises. Two teenage Union soldiers were guarding the doors separating the platform from the depot's concourse, and passengers and baggage handlers were milling about—nothing and no one out of place. Twice, as she returned to the train, Warne spun around to see if she could catch someone observing her. Not a soul.

When Warne returned to the train, Fiona was gone. A peach-hued piece of paper rested on the seat that Fiona had occupied: "Thank you for escorting me."

Warne stepped off the train and scanned the platform again, but Mrs. McFadden was not to be seen. Most likely she had gotten down onto the tracks at the rear of the train and followed the rails out the station's side and onto D Street. Smart girl, Warne thought to herself. Smart girl.

There was no need to chase Mrs. McFadden. The handoff had been made, and Warne had fulfilled Mr. Pinkerton's orders. She went back on the train to collect her luggage.

AUGUSTUS HAD PLACED on a table the decoded entries he had transcribed from the telegrams inside the Booth diary, then slid a candle between the two columns of paper to better read them in the fading light. For two days, since Alexander had sent word of Nail's murder and Temple's imprisonment, Augustus had slept and eaten little. He didn't know if Fiona was safe, and he wasn't sure what he should do with the diary if he remained its primary guardian—if, in the end, Temple and Fiona were unable to come back for it.

Alexander had disappeared in search of Fiona, and Pint had all but evaporated. Temple had said not to respond to any messages from Pint but wouldn't say why.

Augustus pressed his thumb into the cover of the diary, and a shallow depression appeared for a moment before the red leather sprang back up and the dimple vanished. He peered inside again at Booth's writing, at sentences drawn in tight, neat lines and occasionally extravagant loops, the script tethered by incredulity and rage.

After being hunted like a dog through swamps, woods, and last night being chased by gunboats till I was forced to return wet, cold, and starving, with every man's hand against me, I am here in despair. And why? For doing what Brutus was honored for. What made Tell a hero? And yet I, for striking down a greater tyrant than they ever knew, am looked upon as a common cutthroat. My action was purer than either of theirs. One hoped to be great himself. The other had not only his country's but his own wrongs to avenge. I hoped for no gain. I knew no private wrong. I struck for my country and that alone. A country that groaned beneath this tyranny, and prayed for this end, and yet now behold the cold hands they extend to me. God cannot pardon me if I have done wrong. Yet I cannot see my wrong, except in serving a degenerate people. The little, the very little, I left behind to clear my name, the Government will not allow to be printed.

It was a slender thing, this assassin's journal, full of meanderings and self-regard, and now so much revolved around it. Augustus held it up as if it were an artifact, trying to appraise its value. Sojourner had returned the diary to him the morning of Nail's murder, and Augustus wasn't sure he wanted to be near its scribblings and bile anymore. There were parts of the diary he couldn't escape, and some of its sentences repeated themselves in his mind, pursuing him around the District.

The little, the very little, I left behind to clear my name, the Government will not allow to be printed. After leaving the National Hotel on the second day of the Grand Review, Augustus had avoided Pennsylvania and its crowds. Temple had asked him to meet at the canal entrance near Godey's Kiln at five o'clock that afternoon, but Temple had never appeared.

Augustus sent the diary back into the alleys with Sojourner that evening and then called out the damn journal again when he heard about what had happened to Nail and Temple. He could have done many other things that night; Augustus knew it wouldn't be safe for him to return to his house, and perhaps it would never be safe to go there again. He thought that it might be best to leave the District. Surely if the war secretary had caught Temple, then the war secretary would catch Fiona and himself.

But the Booth diary also exerted a pull of its own and had become more than a puzzle. It was the basis for an accounting, a reckoning, and he aimed, like his friends, to see that the diary's own peculiar paths were identified and followed.

"If you're ever fearful of being followed, change houses frequently," Temple had told him when they moved runaways through the Underground Railroad. "The more trails there are behind you, the harder you are to find."

Augustus found a series of havens, first in a backroom at Myrtilla Miner's Colored Girls' School, then at the Wayland Seminary, and finally at Alfred Lee's home on H Street. Alfred was one of the richest black men in the District, and the rumor was that in addition to his feed business he had almost $19,000 worth of real estate. Alfred had been a generous sponsor of the Underground Railroad and owned enough property that Augustus felt he could secrete himself within the network of Lee's buildings and not be found. Sojourner and Alfred were the only people who knew where he was, and Alfred once had claimed that he feared Sojourner's wrath more than the law.

"As it should be," Sojourner said when she heard this, amused. "Alfred's in his right mind."

Augustus had set to work in a bedroom at the back of the house, so no one could look in from the street and discern that someone inside was toiling away over a series of unintelligible diary entries and telegrams that had upended the District's sense of order. The Colt rested lengthwise across the top of the table, within easy reach. He looked again at the twin columns of transcribed messages he had placed on the table below the gun. On the left side were several Booth had already decoded or that he and Temple had worked through earlier:

March 4, 1865
From: Patriot
To: Avenger
      There is a room for you at National. I am for Elmira and Montreal. Horses to Richmond when you have Tyrant.

April 5, 1865
From: Patriot
To: Avenger
      Maestro sends funds. Goliath and others will join you. Wise Man and Drinker should be taken with Tyrant.

April 11, 1865
From: Patriot
To: Avenger
      You will be allowed to pass at Navy Yard Bridge. Refuge at Tavern.

April 14, 1865
From: Patriot
To: Avenger

It is Ford's. Praetorians send a Parker to guard Tyrant. He will abandon the door or let you pass.

On the right side of the table, in the second column, were several new messages that Augustus had also transcribed:

January 26, 1865
From: Patriot
To: Avenger

I have been at Tavern with mother. She has concerns about our group and our goals but knows nothing of our cause. There is support here from others, including the doctor. Maestro believes that USG might be best target.

February 2, 1865
From: Patriot
To: Avenger

Is murder our course? I am not troubled by this. Maestro says we must kill the head of the snake for our cause to survive. Is murder our course, then?

February 9, 1865
From: Patriot
To: Avenger

I am heartened by your response and honored that you are part of our cause. When Tyrant is gone, you will be remembered as a brave and honorable servant of a just campaign. Maestro asks for an audience with you in New York after your triumph.

February 14, 1865
From: Patriot
To: Avenger

The war is now against us. This makes your duty more paramount. We have recruited a Rebel soldier for you. You will know him as Goliath.

February 23, 1865
From: Patriot
To: Avenger

Maestro had Conductor intercede with the Bully. Tyrant is not safe and he will not survive us.

Augustus hadn't encountered "Conductor" or "Bully" elsewhere in the telegrams or in the diary. He flipped ahead in the journal to the page that he and Temple had used to unlock the Vigenère table:

Patriot has told Maestro that I am no traitor, I am sure. Patriot says that Maestro owns Lord War. Davey, George, and Lewis are all heroes also, even if they too share the mark of Cain. Those that find this, those that chase me, know the cipher, and the cipher is true. I do not care that I am made a villain among those who honor the Tyrant. He wanted nigger citizenship and I ran him through.

Augustus rubbed his eyes and stood up, reuniting the telegrams into one stack and stuffing them back inside the diary. He wrapped the diary in its brown paper bundle, walked down the hallway, and placed the package between the wall and a large oak bookcase in his bedroom.

The little, the very little, I left behind to clear my name, the Government will not allow to be printed. He used his candle to light a cranberry-colored oil lamp in the hallway outside his bedroom and then snuffed the wick of the taper between his thumb and forefinger. He was watching a faint gray tendril of smoke rise off the wick when he heard a horse trot up in the street outside Alfred Lee's home. He turned back to the oil lamp and wound down the wick until the yellow light disappeared from its tubular glass chimney, plunging the hallway into darkness.

The Colt was on the table in the room at the end of the hallway and Augustus moved toward it, sliding his hand along the wall to guide himself forward. He bumped into a chair, sending it sliding along the narrow floor with a brief wooden croak that echoed against the ceiling and walls around him. He froze, waiting, but heard nothing more from outside. He stepped forward again, dodging the chair and reaching the end of the hallway, his hands out in front of him and his fingers splayed as he swung his arms back and forth in the space across from his chest, blindly and frantically searching for the table.

Augustus heard the footsteps, distinct and with a series of creaks, as they mounted the wooden staircase at the front door. There were at least two people on the stoop, he guessed, and he began to wave his right hand wildly until he grasped the edge of the table. Then he slid his hand along the top and found the Colt. He considered cocking back the hammer but feared the sound would give him away. So he stood by the table and waited.

There were short raps on the front door, and he stepped forward into the sitting room to try to peer into the foyer. Two long vertical windows crisscrossed with slender muntins were at the front of the sitting room, but he was too far back in the house to see anything through the windows other than several blank town houses framed by a purple sky.

There were two more raps at the door. He pulled back the Colt's hammer with the palm of his left hand, and it locked into place with a loud snap.

"Don't you dare," he heard through the door. "Don't you dare cock a gun at me, Augustus."

He exhaled and pushed the hammer forward.

When he opened the door, he found Sojourner staring up at him in irritation and nearly dancing a jig. Standing next to her was Fiona.

FIONA'S CHEEKS WERE BRUISED, her hair mussed into a brown tumbleweed. Augustus had never seen her so out of sorts and thought she looked almost like one of the ragamuffins who frequented the Center Market. Then her eyes, resolute and blue, flashed back at him. He reached out to her, sweeping her into his arms.

"Lordy, stop that and stop that now!" Sojourner demanded in a voice several registers above a whisper but still several more below a yell. "Anybody, just anybody, look out their window round here and see a black man embracin' a white woman? I don't need to tell you the consequences if word of that begins to get around the District, my children. Inside!"

When they were in the house and a candle was lit, Augustus led them to the back room again to avoid being seen from the street.

"Nail is dead and Temple is in a cell at the Old Capitol Prison," Augustus said right away, mustering as much level-headed courage as he could to share the news with Fiona.

She sat down and stared off at a wall for several minutes, occasionally nodding in response to her own unspoken questions. She then asked Augustus for more details about how Nail had died and how Temple had been taken.

"Temple told me what to expect on that train, and he kept me from staying on it all the way to Chicago," she said, breaking a long silence. "We're going to have to get him out of that prison."

Augustus lurched back in his chair.

"It's the Old Capitol," he said, shaking his head and reconsidering Fiona's eyes to see if he could spot any demons there that might have shaped the notions spilling out of her mouth. "They take people in there and keep them for as long as they want. No one just gets people out of there."

"We are going to help him escape," Fiona said.

She fumbled for her bag, took a brush from it, and began pulling the bristles through her hair in long, determined sweeps. Augustus brought bread, jam, and water from the kitchen and put it on the table.

"Poor Mr. Flaherty," Fiona said to no one in particular. "He was a good man."

"He was that Irish man from Swampdoodle, the blue ink cascading all over his hands?" Sojourner asked.

"He was."

"Wild one, that man."

They ate, and Fiona shared her interactions with Mrs. Lincoln and her sons on the train.

"Did you know that Mrs. Lincoln spent two thousand dollars on her gown for the president's first inauguration ball?" she asked them.

"Southern senators made much of that, actually," Augustus said. "In the Congress and in newspapers, Mrs. Lincoln's debts were fodder for many a conversation. People knew."

"Well, I didn't know," Fiona said. "Two thousand dollars. That was four years of Temple's pay in New York."

"The senators from the South had a different benchmark," Augustus said. "They pointed out that Mrs. Lincoln's two-thousand-dollar gown was the same price as two able-bodied slaves."

"Mercy," Sojourner said.

When Fiona told them about her encounter with the soldiers in Defiance, both Augustus and Sojourner shook their heads in disbelief. Sojourner reached over and stroked one side of Fiona's face, cooing softly as she traced the outlines of the welt still faintly visible on her cheek.

Fiona told them of the cigar smoke and the knives and the strychnine, her voice straining against the recollection. Augustus and Sojourner were mute, listening to her tale and absorbing what had occurred in Defiance. Sojourner looked at the ceiling and pursed her lips, rocking back and forth in her chair.

"Well, child, we live in a complicated time," she said to Fiona. "The good Lord works through all of us in mysterious ways. I suppose that if God hadn't wanted you to use that poison in that very moment, he wouldn't have given you a sharp mind to learn about such things in the first place. And them soldiers were devils, no doubt."

Augustus patted Fiona's hand, nodding in agreement with Sojourner.

"The endless resourcefulness of Mr. and Mrs. McFadden," he said. "But why was there a Pinkerton in, of all places, Defiance, Ohio?"

"A female Pinkerton, mind you," Fiona said.

"Women are gettin' in all the trades," Sojourner said. "Just a matter of time, just a matter of time."

"It would appear that despite the fact that my husband convinced him to leave the District, Mr. Pinkerton has a separate agenda."

"The diary?" Augustus asked.

"Yes, but his agent did me no harm when I told her I didn't have it; indeed, she escorted me through their network and onto a train back to Washington. They want more than just the diary, I assume."

"And you found me through Sojourner when you got back to the District?"

"Temple told me that this would be the way to reorient when I returned. He said it wouldn't be wise to return to our boardinghouse and that if I couldn't go to Alexander's, I should find our dear Sojourner. So I did."

Sojourner stood up, took the brush off the table and began pulling it through Fiona's hair herself.

"Why didn't you go to Alexander's?" Augustus asked.

"Because poor Alexander is somewhere on the railroad looking for me. I was supposed to meet him in Cumberland, but then I had my adventure in Defiance. I wasn't sure where he would be, so I looked for Sojourner."

Sojourner yawned, put the brush down, and told them she was wandering off to bed. Augustus and Fiona ate some more, and then he pulled out the Booth diary from behind the bookcase. They spent an hour looking at the telegrams Augustus had transcribed, sharing thoughts about what they might reveal.

Augustus also told Fiona of his visit to the National Hotel during the Grand Review and his conversation with Booth's betrothed, Lucy Hale.

"She said that John Surratt, the son of the boardinghouse owner, was a close confidant of Booth's—and yet the government and the police have largely ignored him."

Fiona turned the discussion back to the Old Capitol Prison.

"Temple is not the only person they have there, Augustus."

"Of course he's not."

"Two of the conspirators are there, those accused of plotting the president's assassination."

"Mary Surratt and Samuel Mudd."

"Yes, and Mrs. Surratt's priest visits her there regularly, according to the papers."

"I don't understand."

"The priest, Jacob Walter, has a Catholic church here in the District on F Street—St. Patrick's. He also runs an orphanage there," Fiona said, smiling faintly at the memory of how that particular geography discomfited her husband. "Temple hates orphanages and would have avoided F Street for that very reason—except that the Patent Office is on the same block."

"Where you work."

"Where I work!" she said. "My poor, brave husband was reduced to a sack of nervous bones whenever he came to fetch me at the Patent Office's makeshift hospital, because there was an orphanage nearby."

"Fiona, I'm lost in this, I'm afraid."

"Temple was trapped in an orphanage in Dublin as a child and was bullied there. He fell from a window, and the fall split his leg."

"He never shared that with me. Hence his trepidation concerning F Street."

"Yes, he has been uncomfortable on F Street. And on the day that all of this began, when he was being chased from the B&O with the diaries, he was forced to ride down F Street. Temple told me later that he nearly tossed away the diaries and let his pursuers have them because he found himself riding right past that frightening orphanage!"

They both began laughing at this in a full, rounded way, like neither of them had laughed in days.

"I still don't understand what use we can make of this now, Fiona," Augustus said.

"Temple said he remembered as he passed the orphanage during the chase that Father Walter was Mrs. Surratt's priest. Temple knows Father Walter. When Temple first came here from New York, Archbishop Hughes gave him a letter of introduction to the priest."

"And?"

"And as I said, the newspapers report that Father Walter is allowed to visit Mrs. Surratt at the Old Capitol Prison."

"It is still a formidable pile, that prison," Augustus said, nodding.

"It is," Fiona acknowledged. "But as you said, the McFaddens are resourceful."

She rose from the table and then cupped her elbow in her palm, bringing her hand up to her face and hunching over. In a moment she was standing upright again, her composure intact.

"I miss him in a way that consumes me, Augustus."

Augustus stood up to comfort her, but she waved him away, saying good night instead and finding her way to one of the bedrooms.

"I'll sleep on the sofa in the sitting room, and I'll have the Colt on the floor beneath me," Augustus said to her as she walked down the hallway.

"Thank you, Augustus," she replied, stopping and turning back to him. "You are our dear, dear friend."

Later, lying on her side in bed and running her fingers across her face to measure the swell of her welts, she longed for Temple even more than she had earlier while imagining him in a cell at the Old Capitol; she longed for him so intensely that the tug in her bosom drew deep, like something overflowing on the end of a rope at the bottom of a well. She began crying as she pulled the sheet up to her chin, and eventually she fell asleep.

"WE'VE BEEN HERE a very long time, seventy years, founded to look after the spiritual needs of the lads building the Capitol and the President's House, yet you and your husband have never once visited us nor joined us to celebrate a mass."

Father Walter, sitting on the edge of an old oak desk in an office wedged between the vestry and a storage room behind St. Patrick's sacristy, gazed at Fiona from beneath a pair of bushy gray eyebrows. His black cassock draped in folds to the top of his feet and a heavy silver crucifix hung from his neck and spread across his chest, as much a part of the priest's own architecture, Fiona thought, as it was a symbol of his devotion.

That morning she had washed her hair for the first time in more than a week and changed into fresh clothes Sojourner had retrieved for her from a trunk that Lafayette Baker's men had torn through but not soiled near Nail's shattered, smoldering warehouse in Swampdoodle. Then she made her way from H Street and down 10th to St. Patrick's, pausing briefly to look down the block to Ford's Theatre before she entered the empty church.

Father Walter had large, ruddy hands, and he clasped hers between them in a gesture she would have found overly familiar from anyone other than him. A Bible he had been reading when she knocked on his door was spread facedown on the desk, its brown leather binding worn and cracked. He followed her eyes to the Good Book.

"Colossians, chapter three, verse thirteen," Father Walter said. "I was reacquainting myself with it before you arrived." He pulled the Bible across the desk and into his lap, turned it over, and began reading the passage to Fiona. " 'Bear with each other and forgive whatever grievances you may have against one another—' "

Fiona interrupted him and completed the rest of the passage: " 'Forgive as the Lord forgave you.' "

"You have read your Scriptures," Father Walter said, putting the Bible back down on the desk.

"Matthew, chapter eighteen, verses twenty-one and twenty-two," she replied. " 'Then Peter came to Jesus and asked, "Lord, how many times shall I forgive my brother when he sins against me? Up to seven times?" ' "

" 'Jesus answered, "I tell you, not seven times, but seventy-seven times," ' " Father Walter responded, completing the passage. "Tell me, Mrs. McFadden, your husband came to the District well recommended by Archbishop Hughes, and yet he is a stranger to our parish. Is he as conversant in Scripture as you?"

"My husband fills his head with poems, I'm afraid. He admires poets and has an affinity for Walt Whitman's verse."

"Walt Whitman is a heathen."

"Father, I have seen Mr. Whitman at work in the hospitals ministering to the wounded, sick, and dying. Whatever his beliefs may be, I think he does the Lord's work."

"I understand he is an atheist."

"The war that all of us just endured made many men and women question their faith, Father."

"And yet you do not."

"I question the injustices that surround us, but I am a woman of faith."

"So we all must be in times like this," Father Walter said. "Forgive my bluster over Mr. Whitman."

"You are much concerned, it would appear, with forgiveness, Father."

The priest looked down at his Bible again and rested his hand atop it.

"I think that the true Christian is a forgiving Christian," he said, pulling the Bible back into his lap. "This has been a time of turmoil and blood and cruelty. Forgiveness is not the first path some of our brothers and sisters will choose to follow. I fear mightily for the well-being of one of the most devout members of St. Patrick's."

"Mrs. Surratt."

"Yes, Mary Surratt."

"She is why I'm here," Fiona said.

"I assumed as much, although I would have been more pleased to encounter you here in search of your Maker."

Father Walter drew the Bible closer to his body, enveloping it inside his arms and the folds of his cassock and reciting yet another passage. " 'Do not judge, and you will not be judged. Do not condemn, and you will not be condemned. Forgive, and you will be forgiven.' "

"Luke, chapter six, verse thirty-seven," Fiona replied.

Father Walter suggested that they visit the garden outside his office, where a trio of bees buzzed around a large wisteria arbor and several rosebushes. A magnolia tree, a black locust, a host of marigolds and lilacs, and clusters of purple hydrangeas were showing their buds or blossoming around a long wooden bench that spanned part of the garden's perimeter. Father Walter sat down and offered Fiona details about each of the flowers and trees before them: the wisteria vine's tendency to grow rapidly and out of control unless cut back frequently; the mix of soil and space around St. Patrick's stunting the black locust to thirty-five feet instead of the one hundred feet it could reach in the countryside; the magnolia tree's shabby appearance in the spring, with a gnarled trunk and limbs and brown, pockmarked leaves, soon to be transformed by an eruption of brilliant pink blossoms. He had planted the garden himself years earlier, he said, and nurturing it offered a respite from his concerns about Mrs. Surratt—and from his worry that forgiveness would elude her.

"I do not believe her to be guilty of playing any role in the conspiracy to murder President Lincoln," Father Walter said. "And I am not sure in my soul whether the men running our government and hunting these assassins have read or have taken to heart Colossians and Matthew. Mary Surratt deserves forgiveness, and I shall be vocal in asserting that on her behalf at the President's House and in whatever courtroom in which they try her."

Fiona paused a moment, considering her words, and then asked a question she had been wanting to pose since arriving.

"The press describes her boardinghouse on H Street as the haven for the conspirators—they all convened there, including Booth, and she presided over that house, did she not?" she asked. "And did she not provide the assassins with firing irons?"

"What else does the press say about her?"

"They describe her as a large woman, of the Amazonian style, with masculine hands and a swarthy complexion."

For the first time that morning Father Walter laughed, a staccato burst that rolled out from him with an abandon he rarely displayed in public.

"And you say that I have unfairly categorized the poet Whitman! Yes, you should meet with her and decide for yourself whether the newspapers are to be believed. I've told the authorities that Mary is innocent, and I've told them that if they hang her, that act will weigh heavily upon them for eternity."

He tilted his head back into the sunlight and closed his eyes, his fingers wrapped around a cross hanging from his neck. The priest sighed and opened his eyes again, pivoting away from his struggle to reconcile Mary Surratt's plight with his belief in the righteousness of the good Lord.

"Why do you desire a meeting with Mary?" Father Walter asked. "You must share this with me if I am to do anything on your behalf."

"We have a number of things, documents, that involve communications about the president's assassination. My husband has pursued this and is now in the same prison as Mrs. Surratt. I have spent time with Mrs. Lincoln, traveled with her, and have shared her intimacies. I would like to convey Mrs. Lincoln's thoughts to Mrs. Surratt. And I most desperately want to see my husband."

"The Old Capitol is a hard, bitter place, and if your husband has alienated our government to the same degree that Mrs. Surratt has, then I consider his incarceration an equal abomination," the priest said. "You must know you are on a perilous course. So, tell me: what do you fear?"

"Oh my, I fear many things. I fear aging, and death, and the loss of my husband. I fear a life without children of my own."

"I can say that I do not fear aging or death, but I fear evil in the world," the priest said. "I fear the injustices of mankind."

"I have come here to try to right an injustice."

"You can save Mrs. Surratt?"

"No, I don't believe I can."

A flock of red-winged blackbirds landed in a spiraling flutter atop the magnolia tree, shaking their wings and bouncing from branch to branch.

"Mrs. Surratt used to sit with me in this garden and tell me about a dream she often had," the priest said. "She would dream that one of the roses in the garden had grown thick and mighty as an oak, its stem swelling and swirling for hundreds of thousands of feet, climbing and climbing and climbing, until it reached to heaven. She would climb the stem of that rose, pulling herself up and around its thorns, cutting her arms and hands and legs all along the way, and praying to the good Lord to give her the strength she needed to complete her journey. At the end of her dream she always reached an enormous burst of silky red petals at the top of the stem. And then she would find her way to bliss."

The blackbirds stirred and flew up from the magnolia, trading places in tight little loops as they glided over one another on their way toward the Potomac.

CHAPTER TWENTY-FIVE

THE ALLY

Fiona left St. Patrick's through the garden and exited onto 9th Street, walking all the way up to New York Avenue and back down to 13th Street to see if she was being followed, checking over her shoulder and scrutinizing passersby until she was back at H Street again and the Lee house. When she got there, Alexander Gardner was seated at the top of the front porch waiting for her, a long blade of grass in his mouth. He had a broad-brimmed straw hat on for the sun, and wide crescents of sweat soaked his shirt at the armpits. Alexander stirred at the sight of her, sitting upright and spitting the grass from his mouth.

"You stranded me at the train station in Cumberland," he said to her. "But I have to admit that seeing you back in the District soothes the nerves."

"You would be less uncomfortable in the heat if you shaved your beard," she said, waiting for him to move so she could climb the stairs. "Then again, a man with a brogue like yours needs a beard, I suspect. I trust you made your way back without incident."

Alexander held Fiona's eyes and tipped his head over his left shoulder toward the corner of 12th Street, guiding her view down the block to where a small group of soldiers were gathered. Fiona hadn't seen them thanks to the path she took from St. Patrick's, and now she cursed herself. The Surratt boardinghouse was only several blocks away, down near 6th Street, and of course there would be soldiers circulating in this neighborhood. Why hadn't she considered that earlier? Why hadn't Augustus? Temple would have spotted this the first moment in. Empty-headed. Alexander saw the anxiety sweeping across her face and leaned toward her, patting her hand.

"I don't think you need to worry, Fiona. There isn't a chance on this green earth that those boys are going to notice you. Take a harder look at them."

None of the four Union soldiers gathered at the corner was scanning the street or even seemed to have a destination in mind. Instead, they had formed a small, tight circle and were facing one another as if they were on the verge of performing a sacred ritual or exchanging the passwords of a secret society. Their rifles were lying in a scattered heap by the base of a town house, not propped against a wall in a trim line as they would be normally. In their right minds, following training and orders, they would never be so jumbled of wits as to make a pile of their weapons. The Union boys' dynamic revealed itself to Fiona in the rhythmic swaying of their entire group. They were rolling slowly forward and then back again on the balls of their feet, a subtle wave of blue uniforms. Fiona couldn't see any detail in the soldiers' faces at this distance, but she was certain that if she could, she would find all of their eyes to be moony and unfocused.

"They're addicts," she said.

"Through and through," Alexander replied. "Opium."

Fiona had already seen ready evidence of this scourge in the military hospitals. Soldiers, many of them barely older than boys, had endured such unbearable pain from a bullet wound or the gouging of a bayonet that they were given large and frequent doses of opium to blunt the trauma and soothe their nerves. Morphine addiction was common enough, too, particularly because the army gave soldiers doses to take home with them. Now, thousands of war veterans— perhaps even tens of thousands, if the most dire of calculations were true—had the "army disease." With the war over and soldiers only starting to separate from their units to return home, groups of Union boys were seeking out one another to share opium and morphine.

Whether they were doing so as recreation or self-medication didn't really matter. The fact was, a good number of the soldiers had mentalities so wallpapered by drugs that they weren't much better than bummers.

While it wasn't uncommon for the soldiers to share their addictions in camp or in taverns near the Potomac docks, it was more than passing strange to find them openly enjoying or riding out their latest medicinal spree—and in their uniforms, no less. No more than bummers with rifles, she thought.

Alexander could barely contain his disgust with the group, as was his wont lately. He had started the war with great enthusiasm for the entire vast enterprise and for his role in chronicling its realities, idiosyncrasies, heroes, and heroics. But the battlefields had carved their own peculiar and wearing places into his imagination, and he no longer wanted to train his lenses on whatever was going to be left behind as the war machine unwound itself. Lincoln's murder had only furthered his bitterness.

"I am so tired of the District," he said to Fiona, his eyes fixed on the group of soldiers down the street. "I want to trail and photograph the Comanche and the Lakota, and I want to photograph the railroads. I want to leave here and find my fortune in the West."

He stood up. "We should go inside," he said. As he pushed open the door for Fiona, he stopped to confide in her. "There was a Pinkerton agent in Cumberland."

"Fancy that. I encountered my own Pinkerton in Defiance, Ohio."

"But I had *the* Pinkerton. Allan. I wasn't going to tell you because of the trepidation I was worried you might feel about the Pinkertons' return. More aggravation for you," he said. "Temple went to very elaborate and fruitful ends to convince Pinkerton that the time had arrived for him to leave the District. We thought we were successful in that regard."

"What did Temple do to intimidate him?"

"Photographs."

"Of whom or what?"

"Of Pinkerton and a woman of ill repute together in Alexandria."

"I don't imagine I'll ever meet the enterprising photographer who managed to take those photographs?"

"I imagine he's quite talented," Alexander said.

The house was silent.

"Is anyone here?" Fiona asked.

"Augustus."

"Where is he?"

"In his room."

"Is he sick?"

"Of a fashion."

A large pile of Nail's counterfeited greenbacks had been scattered on a table in the parlor, and Augustus's jacket hung on the back of a chair. Two tins were open on the table, one of them containing a few brown, tarry wads of opium that were the size of Fiona's thumb. She followed the sweet, pungent smell of the smoke into Augustus's room and found him there, sprawled on his bed, glassy-eyed and adrift.

FIONA AND ALEXANDER were sharing a loaf of bread, jam, and a small pot of coffee when Augustus awoke late the next morning and came into the kitchen.

"So you found me and my tins," Augustus said to Fiona.

"You put yourself and all of us in danger with your addiction," she said, refusing to look up at him. "You chose a safe house for us that was convenient for you and your drugs."

"I don't need nor do I want your lectures. As I've told you before, I am not your husband."

"You are my friend. Is this why you needed money from your scheme at the B&O with Temple and Pint? To fuel your addiction?"

Augustus ignored her and searched for his money and the opium, becoming frantic when he failed to spot them.

"You've taken my things," he said to Fiona, his anger rising.

"Temple is in prison and this will not continue on your part."

"I want my things," Augustus said, shaking his head. "Alexander's gotten word about Temple, and he knows what we're up against now."

"Yes, I know—he's been imprisoned at the Old Capitol," Fiona said to Alexander. "And we have much afoot in that regard. We intend to free him."

Alexander stood up from the table and drove his hands into his pockets, turning away from Fiona.

"Not entirely accurate anymore, I'm afraid," he said to her. "Temple's imprisoned, true, but not at the Old Capitol. Pinkerton told me that they've moved him to a very different compound—the Old Arsenal Penitentiary."

"Different in what way?" Fiona asked.

"We may have had some faint hope of getting Temple out of the Old Capitol," Augustus said, looking in closets and on shelves for his tins. "But we will never, ever, remove him from the Old Arsenal."

Alexander revisited matters with Fiona: his encounter with Pinkerton in Cumberland, their joint return to Washington, and the information Pinkerton had gathered about what had happened to Temple. Pinkerton had suspected that Fiona would never stay on Mrs. Lincoln's train all the way to Chicago and had decided to trail Alexander. Pinkerton told him that he didn't believe Stanton knew of Alexander's friendship with the McFaddens, but that Stanton didn't remain unaware of much in the District for very long.

The most significant aspect of his unexpected encounter with Pinkerton in Cumberland, Alexander said, was that Pinkerton had offered up a bounty of explanations for why the diaries meant so much to him.

"Mr. Pinkerton made his motivations very clear to me—why he intervened at the B&O to get the diaries to begin with and why he rescued Temple from Baker's men at the Center Market the same day," Alexander said. "Pinkerton is not hesitant to talk about it, and he acts like a desperate man, as if he's about to lose one of his tethers to the world."

"I have been intimate with that same emotion in recent days," Fiona said, watching Augustus continue to cast about for the tins and the money. "But I am powerfully hesitant to put any faith in Mr. Pinkerton."

"Pinkerton said he stands in opposition to Stanton and Baker. He planted his operatives along the major rail stops west of here to Chicago to protect Mrs. Lincoln from Baker, Stanton, and her very own son," Alexander said. "He was concerned something might befall the widow, and he began putting his people into position well before you even schemed to be on the train with—"

"Schemed?" Fiona asked.

"Pinkerton's terminology, not mine. Pardon. He had people along the tracks, and he was able to get word to them from Alexandria the same day that we entrapped him."

"And he looks upon us with benevolence now because of what?"

"Because he believes that the murder of the president needs to be avenged and righted and that those responsible must be forced to meet the noose. We have the Booth diary, and he wants the diary to be in his possession and to be made public."

"We can publicize the diary just as easily as he can."

Augustus gave up his search and sat down at the table next to Fiona, his leg bouncing up and down and his nose running.

"I don't think we can reasonably entrust Pinkerton with the diary or anything else," he said. To Alexander he added, "And how do you know that Pinkerton hasn't followed you here?"

"I was careful returning to my studio, and I met with Sojourner discreetly when I left there," Alexander replied. "She was concerned about Pinkerton, too, and before she would give me this address made me hire a carriage and travel in loops for nearly an hour. Sojourner can be a commanding presence when she sets her mind to it."

"Anyone who can meet with Sojourner discreetly has my admiration," Augustus said, shaking his head.

"How do you know that Stanton hasn't had people following you and Sojourner?" Alexander asked.

"Unlike you, there are not abundant photographs of us," Augustus said. "And Temple revealed himself to them at the Grand Review. Until then, I don't believe they knew what he looked like or even who he was. I think they know of us, of course, but they would be hard pressed to identify us."

"They didn't follow you to Mary Lincoln's train, Fiona?"

"Temple and Nail were watching the station and never balked. Stanton and the military could have arrested me at the B&O and taken Mrs. Lincoln's diary if they had wanted. They could have just shut down the station and surrounded it with troops and done that if they knew. But they didn't, which leads me to believe that while we are perhaps known to them now, we are still largely anonymous."

Augustus sprang up from the table again and began pacing. Alexander stopped him and put his arm around him. Fiona stood and put her hand against Augustus's cheek. Augustus left the kitchen and went back to his bedroom.

"Anonymity has many virtues," Alexander said, picking his jacket up off the back of a chair and fishing around in one of its pockets, producing a thin metal tube that was hinged in the middle. He held it up between his thumb and forefinger, showing it to Fiona. "I'm certainly for the idea that we cannot be harmed if Allan Pinkerton managed to dig inside himself and discover that the right path was in allying himself with us. To that end, he has given this to us as a demonstration of his goodwill. It is meant for Temple, but the trick will be getting it to him inside the Old Arsenal."

Fiona craned her neck so that she could examine the metal tube more closely.

"If this little tube is all that we have to deliver to Temple, then the scale of our challenges has shrunk," Fiona said, taking it from Alexander's hand. "We can get this to Temple, I'm confident of that. It's getting Temple himself out of the Old Arsenal that still leaves me confounded."

"Well, I believe Pinkerton has his own thoughts about that side of our problem," Alexander said, opening the metal tube at the hinge and revealing its contents.

CHAPTER TWENTY-SIX

THE NUN

William Wood was amused.

He knew that he should have been inspired, probably, by the priest's dedication and will. He certainly knew that he should have found it spiritually uplifting, yet another demonstration of the mighty hold the Catholic faith held on its flock. But he had little regard for the priest, his ancient European rituals, and his devotion to a prisoner and a conspirator.

He was simply amused.

"And why, Father Walter, do you feel the need for yet another visit with Mrs. Surratt? Surely she has had her fill of you by now and can find her own way to her Maker."

"I remind you, Mr. Wood, that Mrs. Surratt has yet to be found guilty of any crime that would recommend the notion that she'll be visiting with her Maker in the near future. A trial still awaits her," said Father Walter. "I also retain an inexhaustible interest in Mrs. Surratt as a member of my church and a woman desirous of spiritual guidance. Despite your observations to the contrary, I believe her need for my presence has yet to be fully tapped, Mr. Wood."

Wood wondered whether he should press the priest any further. He enjoyed toying with him and found his presence annoying, but he had more urgent matters at hand, including helping Stanton and the others prepare the case against the conspirators. Summer was upon them and the Old Capitol was musty, its walls already licked by the heat that made him loathe the District. His office began to strangle him once the heat set in, and the more he thought about that prospect, the more he felt that it was already upon him; he got up from his desk and opened the room's only window. Two small stacks of books were piled by the window, and a Colt, a box of bullets, and a Bowie knife sat atop them.

"You realize, of course, that you're greatly inconveniencing me," Wood said, turning his attention back to Father Walter. "Mr. McFadden has been moved with the conspirators to the Old Arsenal Penitentiary."

Wood paused, allowing the revelation to gain traction.

Father Walter simply returned Wood's stare.

"I said that they've been transferred to the Old Arsenal. It has only been a day and very few people are aware of this, even in the government. Yet you don't look surprised."

"I am surprised."

"But I will say it again: you don't look surprised."

"I am surprised to hear this," Father Walter said. "But I am more saddened than surprised. You have remitted these people to an even crueler detention."

"Tut now, Father. Tut tut. They are criminals, each and every one of them. Treated with discipline, citizens respond with discipline. Treated with kindness, citizens respond with treason."

Wood searched the priest's face again, satisfying himself that sadness was in fact residing there and that he was mistaken to be suspicious of anything else about Father Walter's response. He turned his attention to the nun seated next to the priest, scanning her up and down, then up and down again. The District can become a furnace and yet these people cloak themselves in thick black cloth, he thought; even the women are sheathed in blankets as if a frost were coming.

"This is the first time that you will be visiting Mrs. Surratt with someone else in tow," Wood said, gesturing toward the nun. "I suppose that she, too, is saddened by the conspirators' incarceration."

"I believe Mrs. Surratt may be more comfortable sharing some of her concerns and fears with another woman, so I have burdened Sister Grace with my request that she join me on my visit with my parishioner."

"Ever been in a prison before, Sister?"

"No, I haven't, never," the nun responded, her face barely peeking out from within the wimple that covered her cheeks and neck. The stiff white brim of her coif, snug beneath the bandeau covering her head, cast a small shadow across her eyes. Black crepe also hung down around her face, dropping in folds around her shoulders and chest, before it became lost in the darker and heavier folds of her habit.

"Well then, Sister Grace, are you certain that you're prepared for a visit to the Old Arsenal? It may be one of the most unforgiving hellholes you will ever see."

"I trust that the good Lord will watch over me."

"Of course you do, dear. Of course you do."

She was rather fine-looking, Wood thought. She had beautiful, translucent blue eyes and full lips. Why, if he weren't a guardian of the law he might just take her right here on his desk. Yep, take her on his desk and teach her the meaning of salvation.

Wood yanked two pieces of paper from his desk drawer and dipped the nib of his quill into the umbrella-shaped ink well by his right hand. He dated both sheets and noted that their bearers had his authorization to visit the Old Arsenal that afternoon to interview Mary Surratt. He dipped his quill again, signed both sheets, and then waved his hand over them to help the ink dry.

"You are both lucky that I am in a magnanimous mood today," Wood said. "I don't think I shall permit any visits with the conspirators after this. I think I have already given them more liberties than they deserve."

"I have come to understand that you have them in hoods, with their heads completely covered except for a small opening for their mouths," the nun replied. "Surely there is little more you could do to strip away their dignity than that."

Wood's hand stopped moving over the sheets of paper, and Father Walter turned in his seat to look directly at the nun. Wood laid the quill down on the desk and folded his hands together in front of himself. His eyes rose and locked on the nun's.

"In fact, there is quite a bit more I can do to disrupt their sense of themselves, and I feel absolutely no remorse or moral confusion about any of it," Wood said. "These people killed President Lincoln. They are murderers. They don't deserve dignity."

Sister Grace looked away from Wood and let escape a breath she had been holding in her chest. She turned back to him, avoiding his eyes.

"I understand your position. Forgive my insolence, Mr. Wood," the nun said, bowing her head and blessing herself with a brief sweep of her hand across her face and shoulders.

Wood resumed fanning the pages in front of him and then slid the two sheets of paper across his desk to Father Walter. Clearing his throat, he called in the guard standing watch outside his door.

"Show both of these people downstairs to the courtyard and have them escorted to the Old Arsenal as soon as a military transport can be arranged. They have my authorization to visit the penitentiary and are carrying permissions from me to that effect."

The nun and the priest took the sheets of paper and began to leave Wood's office. He stopped them as they reached the door.

"Father Walter."

"Yes?"

The priest turned around.

"You left your rosary on my desk, Father."

The priest stepped forward and took the rosary, rolling it into his hand and sliding it into the sleeve of his cassock.

"God bless," Wood said as the tired old priest and the little harpy he'd dragged in with him finally departed. "Yes, that's right. God bless. God bless and go rot."

ABOUT AN HOUR after leaving Wood's office in the Old Capitol, Father Walter was in the back of a carriage with Sister Grace, accompanied by a cavalry officer on horseback who rode along behind them as they made their way to the Old Arsenal. Surrounded by soldiers, the priest had said little to the nun outside the Old Capitol; alone with her in the carriage, he struggled to contain himself.

"How did you take it upon yourself to decide that the time was right and proper for you to be a critic of Mr. Wood's treatment of the prisoners?" he asked her. "Particularly when we were already going to be beholden to him for the documents he provided certifying our eligibility to enter the Old Arsenal?"

"I apologize, Father. It was insubordinate and rash of me—I just found the man's certitude to be impossible to countenance. There was also something so horrifying about his comportment. And to think that the war secretary puts such stock in a man like that."

"Your behavior put us both in danger."

"I'm sorry."

"Remember, please, you are playing a role, Mrs. McFadden. That means that you aren't entitled to be yourself."

"I don't know that I've been myself at all for the past weeks."

GENERAL HARTRANFT AND a pair of soldiers escorted Father Walter and Fiona into the Old Arsenal's main cellblock, a yawning, three-story warehouse of dense masonry that was empty except for four tiers of narrow, seven-foot-high cells that spanned one of its walls. Iron walkways, accessed by stairwells on either end, ran the length of the three upper tiers. Each cell had an iron door topped with a lattice of metal that allowed a modicum of light and air to creep inside. Although the cellblock could hold eighty prisoners, its only occupants were the eight conspirators about to be tried for assassinating the president and a man the penitentiary's stewards knew to be a disgraced police detective and honeyfuggler with a pronounced limp who had conspired against the government in a separate and unctuous affair.

"We have another cellblock here that can hold sixty-four women, Sister Grace, but we elected to keep Mrs. Surratt with the men because there is ample room at the inn," said Hartranft. "But I refused to put her in one of those hoods the men are forced to wear, and she is also free from leg irons and handcuffs. Perhaps those are small concessions, but we are trying to respect her womanhood."

"Father Walter and I are eager to meet with her, General, and your considerations for our parishioner will not be forgotten."

"One of my men will escort both of you to her cell, then. My understanding is that you have an hour to visit with Mrs. Surratt. I will return and see you out when your time has expired."

"General, if any of the other prisoners wish to visit with us as well, are we free to minister to them?" Father Walter asked.

"Indeed you are, Father, but you will still only have an hour here."

Fiona fell into line behind Father Walter as the guards brought them upstairs to the second tier of cells. The first cell they passed was empty; a rat scurried past their feet as they drew near the second.

"The bitch ain't in this one, folks," said a voice from inside the cell. "You just keep movin' along now."

"Who is held in here?" Father Walter asked one of the guards.

"It's Lewis Powell, and I don't think he cares a jot for whatever generosity you're bringing here today, Father. He's the one who sliced open the secretary of state's face, and he's the damnedest one among them."

"Damned for all time and proud of it. Damned for being a cut-ter," Powell said, his thick frame filling the metal screen at the top of his cell door as he pressed into it. His mouth was visible through a single opening at the bottom of the white canvas hood enveloping his head. "Mmm-hmmm, I say, mmm-hmmm. I can almost smell it. I know we have a fine specimen of femininity in our midst today."

As they continued moving along, Powell pushed up against the weight of the shackles on his wrists, curled his fingers through the screen on the door, and stuck his tongue through one of the gaps as he licked the bars.

"Get the sister inside my cell to save my mortal soul," he said, cackling. "Get her in here and I will make her mine."

The next cell was empty, in keeping with Hartranft's orders that the prisoners had to have gaps between their cells to prevent them from communicating with one another. The guard stopped at the fourth cell and raised a key to the door.

"She's in here," he said.

The door offered a low, heavy grunt as it swung back on its hinges, and the block of light that fell into the cell illuminated the legs and feet of its occupant, who was seated on a wooden plank that also served as her bed.

Mary Surratt didn't speak or stand up as Father Walter and Fiona entered the cell.

"May we visit alone with Mrs. Surratt, please?" the priest asked the guard. "Her spiritual needs are a private matter."

"I'll need to lock you in with her, then, Father."

The guard slammed the door shut again, leaving the cramped cell almost completely dark save for the patchwork that came through the top of the door and drew a faint checkerboard on the far wall. There wasn't enough room in the cell for the three of them to move, and neither the priest nor the nun could see Mrs. Surratt's face. But they could hear the soft whimpering spilling out of her in breathy arcs.

"Mary, I've brought someone special to see you today."

"I am going to die in here, Father Walter. I swear, all that I can be certain of anymore is that I am to die in here."

"Your family and I are working night and day to compel President Johnson to consider the charges against you and to free you. I am putting my faith in the Lord that you shall soon be free of your tormentors."

"My family can't do a thing to help me, not a thing," Mary said. "And the one who might be able to come to my aid—my own son, my Johnny, my flesh and blood—has abandoned me."

"I think Sister Grace here might be able to lighten your burden. I have brought her with me so that you may have a woman to confide in."

Mary began whimpering again, rocking back and forth on the

plank until it squeaked in protest. Her whimpers gave way to a soft cry, and when the priest stepped over and put his hand on her shoulder, she took his other hand and kissed the back of it.

"Thank you for your many and varied kindnesses, Father Walter," she said, sliding off the plank and kneeling in front of him, her face still obscured in the darkness.

She and her priest prayed together for several minutes, and when they were done, Father Walter bent down and whispered into her ear.

"I'll come back soon," he said to her as he stood back up and called to the guard, asking for an escort to see if other prisoners sought spiritual counsel. The guard consented to leaving the door to Mrs. Surratt's cell open so that she and the nun would have more light, but insisted on another guard standing watch at the end of the walkway.

"May I sit next to you?" Fiona asked.

"Father Walter has told me why you are here," Mary said, sliding down to one end of the plank and into the light, revealing her face to Fiona for the first time.

Mary was sturdy and plain, her brown hair parted in the middle and swept into a simple bun. Her warm gray eyes floated above crescent-shaped pouches darkened by a lack of sleep, and she had the stubby, chafed fingers and thick nails of a woman who had worked with her hands her entire life. She was not a beautiful woman, but she was not of the Amazonian sort, as the papers would have had it. She was, like Mrs. Lincoln, thrown off kilter by the disappointments in her life.

Mary bent toward Fiona and whispered into her ear. "Father Walter said you are a confidante of the president's widow."

"An acquaintance, not a confidante."

"I must tell you that I hated her husband and I have no joy in my heart for the niggers," Mary said. "But never in the world, even if it was the last word I have ever to utter, was I part of a plot to kill Abraham Lincoln. Never."

Fiona drew away from her for a moment and then leaned back toward her.

"Your son?"

"What of my son?"

"Has he any complicity in this?"

"He was John Wilkes Booth's partner in many things, but he never spoke to me of murder."

"What did he speak of?"

"My son is an enthusiast. He is enamored of many things—except for his mother."

She balled her hands into fists and dug them into her eyes, her back convulsing as she sobbed. The guard came down the walkway and peered in for several moments before leaving the women alone again.

"To have birthed a son, to have raised him and fed him and dutifully brought him into the embrace of the Church, only to have him abandon me," she said, trying to bring her voice down as she continued to sob. "I do not know Mrs. Lincoln, but I do know that gossip in the District had it that she, too, shares the curse of an ungrateful and spiteful son. And I am imprisoned here in his stead, I tell you. I barely knew Mr. Booth, but my son consorted with him regularly. Yet he is not to be brought into this manhunt rather than me?"

She drew a carte de visite of a slender, pale young man from inside her blouse and began to tear it in half.

"Wait!" Fiona said. "Is this your son?"

"It is, Sister Grace. He is a demon to me now."

She threw the image to the floor. Soldiers had begun drilling in the courtyard outside, and the sounds of their boots hitting the ground in unison wafted into the cellblock.

"What were your son's enthusiasms?" Fiona asked.

Mary pushed the tears off her cheeks.

"He loved Dixie, for certain. And the Church. And Elmira."

"Elmira?"

"Elmira, New York. There is a Union prison camp there where Confederate soldiers are held. He was there frequently, plotting to free the soldiers. I have told the authorities this. I and many other sympathizers gave him money to support his activities there. I have told this to Mr. Stanton's investigators as well."

"Did he live in Elmira?"

"No, he did not. He stayed in Manhattan whenever he went up there."

"With whom did he stay?"

"A benefactor. Someone of ample means."

"Do you recall his name?"

"John never spoke his name to me."

"How is it that you came to know of a wealthy benefactor, then?"

"On two occasions, deep into his drink, he said his friend in New York could book him free passage on the trains anytime he wanted to go to Elmira. He also said this man was a colossus who was going to change the world."

"That is all that he ever said about him?"

"He referred to him as Maestro."

THE GUARD AND Father Walter found Mrs. Surratt on her bed, doubled over and sobbing again, when they returned to the cell. Fiona was next to Mary, rubbing her back.

"Sister Grace, we have little time, I am afraid. Only fifteen minutes or so," the priest said. "There is a prisoner on the block above us whom I think we need to encourage to pray with us. None of the others here say they have the need."

Fiona got up from the bed and scooped the carte de visite from beneath her foot, slipping it inside her habit.

Father Walter put his hand on Mary's head, telling her he would try to return the next day, and Fiona patted her on the shoulder, following the priest out of the cell. As the guard turned the key and the bolt slid back into its place, Mary stopped crying and rushed to her side of the door.

"Sister Grace, wait," she shouted.

"Yes, Mrs. Surratt?"

"You must never, ever have children. They will betray you."

The guard guffawed.

"She's losing her mind now, ain't she?" he said as they neared the stairway. "Thinking nuns are going to have babies."

"Imagine," Fiona said softly.

THE GUARD STOPPED at a cell in the middle of the third tier and rapped on the door.

"The priest is back for a visit, McFadden," he said. "Last chance."

"I'll keep watch over my soul myself," Temple replied through the bars. "On your way. I'll be fine."

"But you can't do it by yourself, Diogenes," Fiona said.

"What?" the guard asked.

The planks on Temple's bed creaked as he stood up inside the cell. He cleared his throat and shuffled. He cleared his throat again, trying to find his voice and struggling to keep his excitement at bay.

"It sounds like you don't just have a priest out there."

"No, there's a nun, too," the guard said.

Temple shuffled closer to the door, pausing for a moment. The chain on his handcuffs clanked and he caught his breath. My angel. My guardian angel.

"Right, perhaps I do need a hand in prayer," he said. "Show them in."

"You sit down on your bed until I have this door open."

Temple shuffled back and the guard turned the key. Fiona entered the cell and Father Walter stepped in behind her, filling the space between her and the guard. Fiona slipped her hand inside her sleeve and withdrew the metal tube Alexander had gotten from Pinkerton and dropped it into the top of Temple's boot.

Temple held her eyes with his as she straightened up and smoothed her skirts.

Like a windstorm
Punishing the oak trees
Love shakes my heart

"My guests, I have to inform you that your hour has run its course," Hartranft shouted up from below.

The general had returned, accompanied by two guards. Mary Surratt began wailing at the sound of his voice, her cries echoing into the corners of the ceiling that spread across the top of the cellblock.

"Goddammit, bag her head, too," Powell screamed from his cell. "Bag her fuckin' head and shut her up."

Father Walter came out of Temple's cell, and Fiona held her husband's eyes for a moment longer before leaving as well.

"I haven't had a chance to pray with this one yet," the priest shouted down to Hartranft.

"One blessing," the general responded.

Father Walter stepped forward and traced a cross on Temple's forehead.

"For your sins, the Lord forgives you," the priest said. "For the challenges that lie ahead, the Lord supports with his strength and wisdom."

Father Walter backed out of the cell again. As the guard forced the iron door shut, Fiona faced Temple through the narrow opening as it shrank, still holding his eyes with her own. Before the door closed, she brought her hand up over her heart. The chains on Temple's handcuffs clanked again as he pressed both of his hands against his chest in response.

Hartranft ordered two cavalry officers to escort Father Walter and Sister Grace's carriage from the Old Arsenal to St. Patrick's, and they set out from the penitentiary just as the sun began to set.

CHAPTER TWENTY-SEVEN

THE SPILLAGE

Temple lay back on the bed planks and raised his left leg high, shaking it until the metal tube that Fiona had given him dropped onto his stomach. He pressed inward on the hinge in its middle to open it, and a long metal lock pick fell into his lap, along with three tightly rolled sheets of parchment. He slid the papers off his lap and spread his hands apart; there were only three links in the chain holding the cuffs together, and he could barely get the angle and the leverage he needed to jimmy the pick into the lock at the bottom of the left cuff. But he managed to slip it inside, and after fiddling for a moment he was able to pop open the cuff. He slipped it off his wrist and picked the other lock, shaking the cuffs into his lap and rubbing his wrists to let the blood circulate.

They had given him a small map and two notes, one from Allan Pinkerton and another from Fiona. He memorized the map, which displayed the layout of the Old Arsenal, and then read and reread each of the notes. When he was done, he tore up all three documents, stuffing them slowly into his mouth and washing them down his throat with a gulp of dirty water from the basin he used for his hands. He pulled a blanket up to his mouth to muffle his gagging while he swallowed, and when he was done put the pick back into the capsule, dropped it into his boot, and snapped the handcuffs back onto his wrists.

The next night, Temple would be leaving the Old Arsenal.

PINKERTON, BEING PINKERTON, had made it his business to find out the rotation of the soldiers at the penitentiary. After eleven-thirty each night, the cellblock had one guard who replaced the four that patrolled it during the day. So, he wrote in his note to Temple, they would wait until after eleven-thirty the next night, when there wouldn't be a moon, and Temple would have one hour to follow the instructions that Pinkerton had laid out for the escape. It could only be an hour, Pinkerton emphasized. Sharpshooters in the two towers atop the corners of the penitentiary's ramparts would be likely to spot them the longer they lingered in the area.

Throughout the next day, Temple wondered where he would actually end up at the end of the night and why Pinkerton had returned. At midday, the guards stirred the prisoners and let them sit outside their cells for half an hour. Temple and Mary Surratt were the only two of the nine without leg irons, and the guards let them walk in the courtyard outside the cellblock. The walls surrounding them had begun to bake in the sun, and the bricks had become almost too hot to touch. Mary stood in the shade by one of the storage rooms, staring at the ground and mumbling. Temple walked over to her to begin a conversation, but the guards waved him off.

When Temple and Mary returned to the cellblock, the seven other conspirators were all back in their cells save for Lewis Powell, who sat above them on the second tier singing quietly. As they climbed the staircase, the guards had Temple wait on the second level while Mary was put back in her cell. Powell didn't move as they walked by. He was large, with a thick neck and long, muscular arms, and his wrists and ankles were shackled in heavy irons. The laces on his canvas hood hung below his chin, and after Mary passed, he rolled his head to the left and spoke to Temple through the gap in the hood surrounding his mouth.

"Mighty injustice that Lewis Powell is in here, don't ya think?" he said to Temple in a thick Southern drawl. "I was a war hero, one of Mosby's Rangers, for chrissake. Nobody minded our killin' when we was shootin' Union soldiers. But go and take a piece out of William Seward and they call it murder, conspiracy, and a crime against the state."

"It is a crime," Temple said. "You deserve to be here."

"Aw now, don't begin lecturing me. Y'all is here, too."

"So I am."

"That's a sockdologer, ain't it?" Powell said, chuckling.

"Powell?"

"Yeah?"

"How'd you get involved in all of this?"

"Johnny Surratt. We were both in the spy services for Dixie. Dave Parr introduced us in Baltimore, and then Johnny introduced me to Booth."

"Why isn't John Surratt here?"

"Well now, that's a mystery, ain't it?" Powell said, chuckling again. "His mama's got rights to be perturbed. All she ever did was feed us at that shithole boardinghouse they owned. And Johnny's out runnin' around still. Wooey. But if I'm near that bitch the next time she starts her screamin', I'm gonna snap her fuckin' head off clean, got me?"

"Got you," Temple said as the guard came back and shoved him up the stairwell to the third tier of cells.

Late in the afternoon, Hartranft visited Temple's cell in person to tell him that William Wood would be at the Old Arsenal the next day or the day after and that they intended to take Temple into the abandoned women's cellblock for several hours of "persuasion."

"You should reconsider your obstinacy, Mr. McFadden, and give Wood whatever it is that he's seeking," Hartranft advised. "He intends to beat it out of you if you don't."

"I'll take your advice to heart," said Temple. "I'll do my best to avoid an unnecessary confrontation."

TEMPLE RETRIEVED THE PICK from his boot as soon as heard the soldiers rotating through guard duty at eleven-thirty and popped the handcuffs off his wrists. He massaged his arms, stretched his back, and then hobbled to the cell door to listen. It took several more minutes for the soldiers to trade places, and then he listened for the lone guard to begin his routine: a walk along the ground-level cells, then up to the second tier, and then to the cells on his level. After that, the guard would normally climb the stairs to the fourth level and sit there for most of the night because a series of windows ran in a line across the top of the opposing wall and they usually afforded a view of the moon. But tonight the sky was dark, and more than likely the guard would sit things out on the first level.

When the guard reached the second tier, Temple began coughing and gagging loudly enough to be heard through his door. By the time the guard was on the third level, Temple was gagging in full force.

"Dry heaves here, boss," Temple said to the guard, sputtering as he did so. "I could use a latrine visit."

"No latrine visits after seven P.M., you know that," the guard responded.

"Understood, boss, but then I'm going to soil my cell if you leave me here and one of you is going to have to clean that up in the morning."

That logic appealed to the soldier, and he ordered Temple to step away from the door with his back to him.

"You're keeping your cuffs on while you spew down at the latrine," the guard said, placing the torch he was carrying into an iron holder on the wall and slipping his key into the cell door.

When the guard opened the door and entered the cell, Temple spun on him and pounded a fist into his throat and another into his belly. The guard doubled over, gasping for air, and Temple brought a knee up into his jaw, dropping him to the floor. He took the handcuffs off the bed and clipped the guard's wrists together behind his back; he had already sheared into strips the single sheet they allotted him, and now he used the pieces to draw a tight gag through the soldier's mouth, tying it in a heavy knot behind his head. He considered taking the guard's uniform, but the man was a good five inches shorter than Temple, so he dragged him into a corner, picked up his cane, slipped out the cell door, and locked it.

As soon as Temple pocketed the key and grabbed the torch, Mary Surratt began to wail again, a low, wandering cry. None of the other conspirators seemed to be stirring. As long as Mrs. Surratt was the only one making a sound, the guards outside the cellblock wouldn't raise an alarm; her wailings had now become as routine as the crickets chirping on the riverbanks outside.

He limped down the stairs as quickly as he could and came to a door on the west wall separating the men and women's cellblocks. The door wasn't locked, and he passed through into the next cellblock; on the southern wall was another door, locked, that led to the penitentiary's washhouse. A soldier was seated next to the door snoring, his rifle leaning against the wall next to him. He was a six-footer, so his clothes would be a fit. Temple hobbled up to him and let out a low, flat whistle. The guard shook his head as he awoke and reached to his right for his rifle, but before he could focus on whatever or whoever it was that had roused him, Temple thumped him twice on the side of the head with his cane and put him back to sleep.

The key he had lifted from his cell worked on the washhouse door as well, and Temple went inside and waved the torch around the room just long enough to register everything that was inside it. There were more than a dozen caped, sky-blue Union greatcoats hanging from pegs on the wall. Several small metal washtubs sat on tables around the room's perimeter, and a round bathtub on a wooden platform dominated the center of the room—just as Pinkerton had said it would in his note. Temple grabbed a burlap bag from one of the tables, then dunked his torch into a washtub to extinguish it before the light became noticeable outside the washhouse's windows.

He dragged the unconscious guard into the washhouse, stripped off the soldier's trousers, shirt, coat, and hat, and stuffed them into the bag. The fifth greatcoat to the left of the door was the longest one hanging on the pegs, and Temple counted out each one until he came to it and then he stuffed that into the bag as well.

The next piece of this is where it all rises or falls, doesn't it, he thought to himself. Well, thinking of you always, Fiona.

Temple reckoned he had about ten steps to the middle of the room but when his right foot banged into the bathtub's platform, he realized it was only nine. Damn my leg, he thought. He paused a moment to catch his breath before laying his cane down against the platform and feeling underneath the tub for its drainpipe. When he found the pipe, he circled it with his right hand and put his left on the rim of the tub, lifting it up and off the platform until the pipe cleared. Keeping his weight on his left leg, he rolled the tub onto its side on the floor and then turned it upside down. He nearly lost his balance straightening up before he pushed against the platform to see how tightly secured it was to the floor. If the platform was nailed to the floor, he planned on using his cane like a lever to pry it up. But it moved slightly when he pushed its side, and when he pressed his shoulder into it, wincing from the flash of pain where his bullet wound was still healing, the whole platform slid aside. Beneath it, as Pinkerton had said there would be, was a large metal grate sitting above the sewage line that served the entire penitentiary.

Although it was one of the few that the District could boast of, the sewer beneath the penitentiary was a simple and haphazard affair. It started below the washhouse and ran beneath the prison yard and the kitchen—which had the only other sewer access point inside the Old Arsenal—and then tunneled out about three hundred yards beyond the penitentiary walls to a point where the spillage emptied into the confluence of the Anacostia and Potomac rivers. Temple raised the grate, put the burlap bag between his teeth, held his cane high, and dropped down about eight feet into the sewer.

He was nearly overcome by the stench once he began making his way down the sewage line, crouched over at the waist. The walls and floor of the sewer were made of bricks and timber beams, and because the ground in most of the surrounding area was little better than swamp, the walls oozed with water and a silty muck that hung in droplets in between the bricks. It will happen that quick—just blink your eyes, and then the bricks and the timber and the rats will all tumble in on me, Temple thought. Started out trapped in an orphanage and might end up facedown in slop beneath a prison. Other than Fiona, nothing to show for it.

Slogging beneath a narrow tube of light beaming down from an opening in the kitchen floor, he could hear several men above him playing cards, laughing, and conversing. Flies were crawling on his face, hands, and legs, and his feet got caught up in an ankle-deep pile of rotting meat and vegetables.

> *The thoughts we are thinking, our fathers would think;*
> *From the death we are shrinking, our fathers would shrink;*
> *To the life we are clinging, they also would cling—*
> *But it speeds from us all like a bird on the wing.*

He pressed his sleeve across his mouth and nose and moved on, using the burlap bag to knock off rats that were trying to climb his legs.

The end of the sewage line, which was about twelve feet above the water, appeared at first as a faint purple disk. As Temple got closer, he could hear the river running past. When he reached the opening, he was alone.

He slid on his back down the muck outside the sewer and onto the marshes by the riverbank, pressing his bag and his cane against his chest as a cloud of mosquitoes swarmed his head. It was so dark that he could barely distinguish the water from the shore, and he thought about whether to make his way up the Potomac or the Anacostia. A man with a cane, reeking of sewage and carrying a burlap bag, wouldn't go unnoticed, whichever path he took. But he turned his attention back to the river when he heard the faint slapping of paddles against the surface of the water.

"*Tssst, tssst,*" Allan Pinkerton whispered from the lead boat, which glided quietly toward the shore. Pinkerton and an oarsman were both hunched over in the skiff, trying to meld into the murk blurring the distinction between the night and the water. A second skiff was just behind Pinkerton's boat, and two people sat hunched over in that one as well.

Pinkerton put his finger to his lips to remind Temple to keep quiet, then reached out to help him climb up. Temple waded into the water until it was at his waist, then tossed his bag aboard. He gave Pinkerton his cane and grabbed hold of his arm and the side of the boat, hauling himself up and into the skiff.

A few lights from the Old Arsenal were visible in the distance, as were the inky outlines of the guard towers, where the sharpshooters were perched. The two boats separated in the darkness without a word. Pinkerton's went up the Anacostia and the other went up the Potomac.

CHAPTER TWENTY-EIGHT

THE ASYLUM

Temple was lying on his back in the middle of the boat. Once they were halfway between the banks of the Anacostia, Pinkerton leaned over him and whispered into his ear.

"You smell like shit from that sewer, Mr. McFadden," he said.

"The river itself smells like shit," Temple responded. "I want to clean myself before I see my wife."

"Won't be time for that because we're getting off this boat in about five minutes and I suspect we'll see her right off."

"We're not heading farther upriver?"

"No, we're not. And you're welcome."

"Thank you."

"For rescuin' your sorry ass I deserve more than just a thank-you."

"My wife rescued me, Mr. Pinkerton," Temple said. "You just brought a map and a boat to the effort."

Both men chuckled as the skiff glided another thousand feet onto the far bank of the Anacostia at St. Elizabeth's, in view of the Government Hospital for the Insane.

"You can sit up now," Pinkerton said. "Your escape is a success, and the drama of your rescue will be the talk of the ages."

Temple could still see the imposing pile of the Old Arsenal outlined across the river. If there had been a moon out, one of the sharpshooters in the towers would have been able to pick off him, Pinkerton, or their oarsman.

"Why was there a second boat?" he asked.

"Your doppelgänger. We have you headed up to the Long Bridge in that skiff," Pinkerton said. "You will arrive there with your cane,

damp clothes, and muddy boots—though not quite as, ah, pungent—
and there will be a horse waiting for you. There won't be many people to see you on the District side, but when you cross into Virginia,
you'll pass the army fortifications and the military will see you ride
by, cane and all. Tomorrow, when Stanton, Wood, and Hartranft
discover that you've abandoned their holding pen at the Old Arsenal, they'll notify all forts and officers asking if an unusually tall man
with a cane might have crossed any of the bridges late the night before. After they get a confirmation of your sighting at the Long
Bridge, those crackerjacks are going to send dozens of men into Virginia to ferret you out. But they'll never find you there. For all pur-
poses, you will have vanished."

"Where will I actually be?"

"Right here. The Government Hospital for the Insane. There are
large, comfortable rooms. Anyhow, an asylum is the perfect residence
for you."

"And why are we still so damn close to the penitentiary?"

"Hiding in plain sight. They'll never imagine that you're within
spittin' distance just across the Anacostia. Your wife arranged our
stay here, and the location was her inspired idea. Now, out of this
boat and up to the madhouse. Mrs. McFadden and Mr. Spriggs
await your arrival."

DOROTHEA DIX WAS at the entrance to the asylum, a large brass
ring with a heavily populated circlet of keys in one hand and a lantern in the other.

"You'll need to wash before you enter St. Elizabeth's, Mr.
McFadden. I run a clean and tidy establishment."

Temple welcomed her offer, knowing from what Fiona had once
told him that it was folly anyhow to argue with Dorothea Dix. As
superintendent of Union army nurses, she had won the devotion of
Fiona and other women who tended to the wounded and dying,
Confederate and Union alike. She was outspoken in her views of
proper medical care, and that put her at odds with the phalanx of

male doctors in the army who guarded their prerogatives. Removed from her position for insubordination and what the military characterized as a "generally disruptive and free-ranging running off at the mouth," she continued overseeing the asylum she had founded several years earlier.

Government funding had made the Hospital for the Insane possible, but it was Dorothea Dix who made it function and took an abiding interest in meeting the needs of the feeble-minded who had been committed there. It was she who had insisted that the hospital be known by the more anodyne name of the grounds upon which it stood: St. Elizabeth's.

Pinkerton took the burlap bag from Temple and went inside the asylum. Mrs. Dix led Temple around the side of the building to where a tall wooden stall was affixed to the facility's ochre-hued wall. A fresh set of clothing, a new pair of boots, and a large tub of water were inside the shed.

"Where did these boots come from?" Temple asked.

"Your wife arranged for them. She said you ruin your boots and your clothing."

"It's discouraging to be predictable."

"Predictability can be a virtue. You'll find a bar of soap in that tub, and I expect you to make good use of the towels. We plan to give you shelter and food here. But we can't have you trudging into our hospital smelling like a swamp rat."

FIONA WAS WAITING at the foot of a broad staircase in the entrance hall when Temple came inside, holding the burlap bag that Pinkerton had handed off to her. Temple's hair was still damp, and he pushed it back from his face, glad that he had washed before seeing her. He dropped his cane as he rushed to Fiona and nearly stumbled when he reached her, steadying himself on the balustrade behind her and burying his face in her neck. She put both of her hands on his cheeks and raised his face to hers so that she could kiss him, pressing her lips into his until she became short of breath. He leaned on her as they retrieved his cane, and then she led him by the hand up the stairs to their room.

AUGUSTUS AND PINKERTON were seated by a window in a corner of the dining room the next morning when Temple and Fiona came downstairs to eat. Augustus dropped his fork and leapt up to embrace Temple as he neared the table. Two patients at a nearby table clapped and giggled, then banged their forks against their plates. A short, pudgy patient with cuts on his arms and neck was spinning in a slow circle in the middle of the room, singing to himself in a soft, drooling mumble.

"Did you decide on this locale, Mrs. McFadden, so you and your husband would present more favorably in comparison to those around us?" Pinkerton asked.

"People with unhinged mentalities are cared for in our society by chaining them in jail cells with common criminals, Mr. Pinkerton," Fiona said. "Mrs. Dix has given these poor souls a refuge. You should have more sympathy."

"People need to be responsible for themselves and their own misfortunes," Pinkerton said. "We cannot always keep life's miseries from intruding upon the lives of our fellow man."

"For someone who has gone so far out of his way to aid us, you remain extravagantly hostile," Temple said, cutting into the ham on his plate and spreading jam across his bread.

"You deceived me in a graveyard, tried to blackmail me with a madam in Alexandria, and have withheld the diaries from me—even after I saved your life in the Center Market. I have reason to be hostile."

"Which is why I'm confounded about your assistance to me and my wife."

"If either of you should perish, I imagine the world would lose one or both of the diaries. Such an outcome would spare the war secretary, Lafayette Baker, and the others from greater scrutiny."

"But how do you know that?"

"Know what?"

"That the diaries have information that would implicate Stanton and Baker or anyone else. Had you read them previously?"

Pinkerton put down his knife and fork and pulled the napkin from the top of his shirt, balling it up and putting it on the table in front of him.

"I might remind you that I oversaw the Secret Service for a goodly amount of time before the war secretary relieved General McClellan and me of our duties. I had extensive lines of information in every corner of the District."

"Of course, you did, Mr. Pinkerton," Temple said, putting his own napkin on the table. "I hope you'll excuse my failure to recognize your prowess."

"Apology accepted. Now, might I see the diaries?"

"I think the time has come for that. But I need to confer with Mr. Spriggs. I have had an evening with my wife but no time with him, and he and I have much with which to reacquaint ourselves. Might I leave you in my wife's good hands and we can discuss the diaries later in the day?"

"I find your wife more pleasing company than you, and I look forward to conversing later in the day."

Temple and Augustus got up from the table.

"Mr. McFadden."

"Yes?"

"It is only just that I view the diaries. I am owed what I am owed."

"Indeed you are."

AUGUSTUS'S ROOM WAS on a floor beneath Temple and Fiona's, and the rooms near his were more active. A patient a few doors down the hall had built a tiny monument from a collection of small, speckled river stones and was diligently knocking them from their pile and reassembling them, again and again, without looking up from his work.

"Fiona said you got lost in your opium when she stayed with you," Temple said to Augustus.

"It has never been something I've hidden from you."

"Yes, but it was something you agreed to keep from her."

"It has gotten to a state in which it's impossible for me to hide it from anyone."

"Well, we won't have Pint to help us raise cash anymore. Maybe it's time to purge ourselves."

"I think that is an easier challenge for you," Augustus said.

"You have no idea how gambling can consume the soul."

Another monument of river stones toppled onto the floor down the hallway, and a patient in another room began cackling.

"Temple, we must not show anything to Pinkerton. He's not to be trusted."

"I know that. It wasn't only the war secretary who removed him and McClellan from their duties. President Lincoln ordered it as well. He had grown weary of McClellan, and he ignored Pinkerton's entreaties not to cashier him also. I don't think justice has anything to do with why Allan Pinkerton wants the diaries."

"Why does he want them?"

"I don't know, but I will be finding out soon enough."

"How?"

"I'll need to go to New York to do that."

"I think New York is a fine destination."

"And why is that?"

Augustus pulled the Booth diary from a desk drawer and opened it to the back pages, where another telegram from Patriot to Avenger sat next to a version of the same message that he had decoded onto a fresh sheet of paper. Augustus spread them open across the top of the desk and raised a shade to allow more light into the room.

Temple bent over the desk to look at the pages. A familiar sensation coursed through his body, the rush of excitement and anticipation he got when people and events overlapped.

Two addresses were in the middle of the page:

Brainard Hotel, Elmira, New York
212 Madison Avenue, New York, New York

"Augustus, is the name John Surratt familiar to you?" Temple asked.

"Lucy Hale made a point of mentioning him to me at the National Hotel. I suspect he is the Patriot to Booth's Avenger."

"Well done. Now, tell me why you don't trust Pinkerton."

Augustus pulled two more sheets of paper from the back of the diary. It was another telegram that he had also decoded on an accompanying page. Temple scanned it, nodding in recognition as he reread it.

February 10, 1865
From: Patriot
To: Avenger
    Maestro says Bloodhound asks to be a cinder dick.

"We should get back to Mr. Pinkerton," Temple said.

"I was worried about even leaving him alone with Fiona."

"Fiona and Mrs. Dix have the situation in hand."

PINKERTON, STILL FOGGED, stretched his legs to their limits on his bed and pressed his elbows outward, trying to test the boundaries of the straitjacket pinning his arms to his sides.

Temple opened the door to his room and stepped inside.

"Your wife is untrustworthy, McFadden. She and that other beast, Mrs. Dix, had two attendants hold me back at the breakfast table, and then your wife chloroformed me."

"I'm aware of that."

"Your wife also did this to one of my men at the Smithsonian. She burned his jaw."

"I'm aware of that as well. You're not burned. Be thankful."

Pinkerton rolled against his restraints again, but the leather straps surrounding his chest and crossing underneath his crotch stayed taut.

"Mr. Pinkerton, you yourself have women in your employ who are quite pleased to be aggressors."

"One woman. I have just one woman in my employ."

"She aided my wife, and we're grateful to her."

"Right now I think Miss Warne should have let your wife rot in Defiance."

"Did you ever seek employment from a railroad man in New York?"

Pinkerton stopped struggling against the straitjacket.

"I loved President Lincoln, Mr. McFadden," Pinkerton said.

"You've said this to me before, Mr. Pinkerton, and I don't doubt that you loved the president. Your work for the Underground Railroad was honorable."

"You know of that?"

"I supported the Underground Railroad, too. It rather conflicts with your blather that the needy must always fend for themselves, does it not?"

"I wouldn't equate emancipating slaves with tolerating the vagaries and inadequacies of nutters who need to be confined to asylums. The latter individuals have already demonstrated that they cannot contribute to society. The former were never given an opportunity to prove themselves."

Temple sat down on a chair next to Pinkerton's bed and laid his cane on the floor. Pinkerton turned his head toward him, his eyes creased with worry.

"So there is mention of me in the diary, then?"

"Which is why you wanted it in the first place, yes?"

"Surely."

"You never have read it, have you?"

"No, of course I haven't. I knew about it because Lafayette Baker's read the diary. He told me that if I got unruly in any capacity, he would make sure that the information came out in some fashion. But

I'm not one to simply absorb threats without taking action. It was why my men were at the B&O in the first place."

"Why would it be damning for you to have sought work as a cinder dick?"

"We have much to talk about, Mr. McFadden."

"Be that as it may, you'll have to remain here and bound by your new camisole for a few days, I'm afraid."

"Days?"

"Days."

"The man who got us here in the skiff knows where I am. He'll return if he becomes worried."

"You'll send a signed note to the door through Mrs. Dix that you're not to be bothered."

"Without the use of my damn hands?"

"Mrs. Dix has four men here who can help her, if need be. They'll unstrap you. As far as they know, you're just another patient. If you begin screaming again, you'll get chloroformed."

Temple leaned forward in his chair, patting Pinkerton on the arm.

"Now," he said, "let's talk about New York."

TEMPLE SPENT TWO more days at St. Elizabeth's, resting, eating, conferring with Augustus and Fiona, and waiting for the search for his double in Virginia to begin winding down.

He left just before sundown on the fourth day, wearing the uniform he had pilfered in the burlap sack from the Old Arsenal. The greatcoat was too heavy for late spring in the District, and he draped it across the neck of the horse that Mrs. Dix had loaned him, stashing his cane beneath it, tied to the pommel, so that it wouldn't draw attention when he crossed the river again.

Fiona reached up to rub her husband's bad leg as he sat in his saddle.

"You finally got to put on a uniform."

"War's over, Fi."

"You still wear it well. And that's another brand-new pair of boots you have on."

"I'll mind them."

"You come back home to me, Temple McFadden. We have a life to live together."

Temple put his hand on his lips and smiled down at her, then tipped his Union cap to the doorway, where Augustus and Mrs. Dix stood. His horse bucked and snorted as he trotted down the hill, away from the asylum. Temple patted the mount's neck, leaning forward to whisper in its ear, until it calmed down. The light began to fade from orange to violet as he made his way to Edwin Stanton's home.

CHAPTER TWENTY-NINE

THE VISITS

Franklin Square was quiet.

But even on quiet nights, Edwin Stanton's three-story brick mansion was ringed by soldiers, three out front facing K Street, three in the alley behind it that ran between 13th and 14th streets.

Stanton's wife was asleep upstairs when he arrived home, so he sat in his library reading through the notes the prosecution had given him for the trial of the president's assassins. Floor-to-ceiling mahogany bookcases surrounded him. He had first ordered them specially made for the room when he bought the property in 1859, but war shortages meant it had taken six years for him to get them finished. Nearly three thousand volumes filled the shelves, the entirety devoted to law, military strategy, and history.

He'd also once set his mind on buying custom Italian glass for all of his windows during President Lincoln's second term. He never had made the purchase, and now he wasn't sure he would keep the house at all. He gazed out of his library into the dining room, recalling the laughter that used to surround the table when the president spun yarns at meals.

A drumbeat of poundings on the front door reminded him that the mansion's bellpull was still broken, and when he swung the door open, two soldiers were standing there. The first was one of Stanton's regulars; the other stood outside the pool of light pouring from his hallway and onto the stoop. The man in the shadows had a cane.

"Yes, Private Leonard?"

"This one here says he has an urgent delivery for you, sir. Says he has photographs of John Wilkes Booth that you requested."

Temple stepped into the light.

"Right through the front door, is it?" Stanton said.

"Right through the front door."

STANTON BROUGHT TEMPLE back into the library.

"Your resourcefulness surprises even me, Mr. McFadden."

"I haven't much time."

"I want you to know something: I loved the president."

"I have heard that said frequently of late."

"I am not jesting with you, sir," Stanton howled, slamming his fist on the arm of his chair. "When I began with him I considered him the original gorilla, plagued by imbecilities. At the end I believed him the wisest, steadiest soul I had ever encountered, and I firmly believe God put him here to serve in this moment. No one else could have."

"Mr. Stanton, we have other matters to discuss."

"We will get to those. But I need you to understand my utter devotion to President Lincoln. I watched him expire. I sat by his bedside and watched him die."

Stanton began crying with a sudden, childlike force, pulling his spectacles from his face and burying his fists into his eyes, his chest and his shoulders convulsing. Temple looked away, waiting for the war secretary to compose himself.

"I want you to tell me about Thomas Scott."

"Mr. McFadden, you have very little weight in this standoff."

"I have the diaries and I have two photographs of Booth."

"As of an hour ago you no longer have the diary," Stanton said, pulling a kerchief from his breast pocket and wiping his eyes and spectacles. "Troops led by General Custer went to the asylum on my orders and brought your wife, Mrs. Dix, Mr. Pinkerton, and the diary back to the War Department. They are all only a few blocks away from us right now."

Temple blinked, trying to make sense of what Stanton had just told him. The old man had outmaneuvered him, just as he had when he arrested him in the stands at the Grand Review. Temple's mouth went dry. It was all over now. Stanton had what he wanted, and Temple could no longer bargain.

"How did you know?" Temple asked.

"The oarsman. Mr. Pinkerton believed him to be one of his, but he's my man and I've had him with Pinkerton for two years now. Pinkerton is a man to be watched, and my man watched him. After the oarsman dropped the pair of you at St. Elizabeth's, he reported back to me. Please be assured, I have no intention of harming your wife or putting her in jail."

"Why didn't you send troops to the asylum the evening I arrived? Or the next day?"

"Because you needed time to compose yourself after your inventive departure from the Old Arsenal, and I wanted to see to it that you had the time to do so. And I wanted Mr. Wood to busy himself in Virginia. He hasn't a notion about where you and the diary are right now, and that's just as well. He has his uses, but they aren't in order here anymore; the war is over, and it's time for him to recognize that and be less eager for bloodshed. In any event, you needed your rest if you were to continue on the path you'd chosen. I hope you understand that all of what has occurred here will never become part of a public dialogue. But justice still might be served."

"How do you see that?"

"You're determined to find a certain person, I take it. After great deliberation I've decided that's perfectly fine. What you're digging into will never go to trial, Mr. McFadden. You understand that, don't you?"

"You're content to see Mrs. Surratt hang?"

"I'm confident that Mrs. Surratt was deeply involved in a plot to kill the president. I'm confident that the sooner our fragile democracy moves beyond this murder, the better. The diary offers the possibility of a narrative that is . . . disruptive. President Lincoln was a pragmatist and would have understood."

Stanton moved to his windows and looked out on his guards, his fingers coursing through his beard. He turned back to Temple.

"Do you know who Maestro is?" Temple asked.

"I believe I know what Maestro has done, but I do not know who he is."

"How did you become aware of him?"

"Through the diary at first—just like you did, yes? Once I was aware of Maestro's presence in Booth's firmament, I began to think back to events, conversations with the president. That's how Thomas Scott came more fully into my view."

"For what reason?"

"Mr. Scott is an influential railroad man, an executive with the Pennsylvania Railroad. President Lincoln brought him into the War Department to oversee all of our rail lines during the war. He managed the transport of cargo and soldiers in an extraordinary fashion. On one occasion alone he successfully arranged the movement of some thirteen thousand troops and their horses by rail from Nashville to Chattanooga."

"What was his relationship with Maestro?"

"I am not entirely certain. But Mr. Scott is evangelical on the topic of railroads. He and a broader clique became quite intent on forcing President Lincoln's hand earlier this spring. They wanted him to use the powers of the federal government to support a national railroad that traversed the North and South and connected to the West. It would begin in Pennsylvania, connect in St. Louis, and terminate in San Francisco, with spurs throughout a rebuilt and revitalized South. Mr. Scott called it the Texas and Pacific Railroad. His Scottish apprentice, Andrew Carnegie, was very much involved. Mr. Carnegie, lest you're unaware, is an intimate of Mr. Pinkerton's."

"You and the president represented the railroads as lawyers and did very well on them. What was so troubling about the Texas and Pacific's plans?"

"The president was a railway advocate for much of his private career and for much of his presidency, certainly. He saw to it that the Railroad Acts bestowed large land grants and government funding on industry to speed the completion of a transcontinental railroad. But it all evolved into a force unto itself. There was corruption in the funding and construction of it, and there was corruption in the legislatures. The sums of money involved transformed people."

"So President Lincoln set out to block it?"

"Not the transcontinental railroad. Never. He said the ugliness around that was the price of progress. As I told you, he was a pragmatist. It was Mr. Scott he wanted to block."

"And why only Mr. Scott?"

"Mr. Scott and his group wanted to control all of the rail lines in the South. To do that, they needed cooperation from the Democrats controlling the region's legislatures. To that end, they wanted President Lincoln to withdraw Union forces from the South, to step back from securing the rights of free Negroes there and from imposing a new order on the Confederacy. The president, of course, dismissed this avarice, and I supported him fully. Only a week before he was murdered he had requested a meeting with Mr. Scott and others in his faction to make it plain to them that he would use every power at his disposal to stand in their way. Once stirred, President Lincoln was a mighty force."

"Mrs. Lincoln shared some of this with my wife."

"These men wanted to forsake every principle behind the war so they could pursue their fortunes. It was an issue that split the family. Robert Lincoln was allied with Mr. Scott and the others. I think that crushed the president, frankly. His own son."

Stanton began to wheeze heavily, and he peeled open the top of his shirt, slumping back in his chair. Sweat covered his chest and brow when he sat up again. His hands shaking, he drew deeply from a large cup of coffee on the table beside him.

"I struggle with asthma," Stanton said. "A symptom, my doctors tell me, of the depressed state of mind I have had since my childhood. They advise me that coffee will attack my malady. They have recommended tobacco as well, but I don't enjoy smoking."

"I still have the Booth photographs, Mr. Stanton," Temple said. "You are in no position to simply dictate terms to me."

"What do the photographs give you?"

"They clearly show that Booth had a journal in his breast pocket when his corpse was brought aboard the *Montauk*. The journal was never cataloged among his belongings. If the Congress were to be made aware of a missing diary, scandal would ensue."

"What do you want?"

"Safety for my wife and for Alexander Gardner. Mr. Gardner wants to give up his business and travel west to photograph the railroads and the Indians, and he will need a final, lucrative commission. Grant him an exclusive commission to photograph the conspirators' trial."

"I can see to all of that. I assure you, I am not a murderer, Mr. McFadden."

"You and yours killed my friend. That was murder."

"Mr. Flaherty was a criminal. A counterfeiter, a—"

"You made great use of his skills," Temple shouted. "If he was a criminal, why did your government employ him to make cogniacs out of Secesh currency?"

"Calm yourself, Mr. McFadden. You imperiled him yourself by hanging on to that damned diary. I have no regrets about trying to extract it from you."

"Or about sending Lafayette Baker into Swampdoodle?"

"I would do it again. I know that's not what you want to hear, but I would do it again."

"Why did you try to get the diary out of the District to begin with?"

"I had no idea that anyone was trying to spirit the diary away. I had given it to a judge for safekeeping and thought that was that. Lafayette Baker hired Mr. Tigani himself, and the madness at the B&O that morning surprised all of us."

"I want a guarantee of safety for my wife and friends. Including a

Negro whom General Custer apparently missed when he collected my wife at the asylum. His name is Augustus."

"Your wife and friends will be kept safe, I promise you that. I will have them moved into the Willard."

"I'd rather Mr. Pinkerton be kept under the impression that everyone is still detained. He's inventive, and he'll inevitably try to follow me. Keep him in a room at the Willard without a view to the street. I want safe and unencumbered passage for myself in the District and to New York."

"You will have those."

"If and when I return to the District, you'll have the Booth photos. If I don't return, the photos will pass on with me."

"Fine. Where are you bound for now?"

"I have one more visit to make in the District, and then I plan to go to New York."

"Will you be seeing Mr. Baker?"

"I will."

"Mr. Baker made much of the fact—to my face he said this, mind you—that the Booth diary conveys the notion that Maestro controlled me. There is no truth in that. I would never have betrayed President Lincoln for an outsider."

"But you still have a reputation to preserve. The diary has a power to stain people that goes well beyond the truth of whatever is written in it. So you have had ample personal reasons to keep it out of the public eye."

"You are free to believe what you want, Mr. McFadden. Be that as it may, the diary, in fact, will never become public. Now, here, read this."

Stanton walked to his desk and scooped two leather-bound dossiers from a shelf above it, passing them to Temple. Temple thumbed through both, pausing on certain pages and flipping more quickly through others.

"There are several copies of both dossiers," Stanton said. "You may take these two with you."

Temple took a quill from the inkwell on the desk and scribbled a note across the front of the first dossier, signing his name to it and blowing on it until it was dry.

"I'll need funds as well," he said.

Stanton removed a block of books from one of his shelves and pulled a strongbox from a hollow in the wall. He counted out $1,000, slipped it into an envelope, and gave it to Temple.

"I'll be off now. Good night, Mr. Stanton."

"Good night, Mr. McFadden."

After leaving Stanton's home, Temple rode to Noah Brooks's office and slipped the first dossier under his door.

"LIGHT A CANDLE," Lafayette Baker said.

"I can't find a goddamn candle."

"Then light your fuckin' hair on fire, but I want to see."

Baker's man fumbled about at a table, finally finding a candle and a match to brighten the room. Pint stood in front of Baker, "Fidelity Construction" stenciled in the glass that the candlelight illuminated on the open door behind them.

"Get us some whiskey in the next room," Baker told his man.

Baker waited in the doorway while Pint entered the offices of the National Detective Bureau and lit an oil lamp nestled in a wall sconce. A scrap of paper beamed up at Pint from a table under the lamp, and he bent down to read it: 217 Pennsylvania Ave.

Pint stumbled back from the table.

"What's got into you?" Baker asked.

A bottle shattered in the side room, followed by some scuffling and the heavy thump of a body slamming into a wall. Then quiet.

"What the hell is going on in there?" Baker said.

"Your man is down," Temple said, leaning on his cane as he stepped out of the side room.

"I am so fuckin' tired of you," Baker said. "You're supposed to be in a cell. Only a dozen people in the District know where this office is."

"Pint knows the address, don't you, Pint? You wrote it down on that scrap of paper I lifted from your pocket in Jimmy Scanlon's saloon."

"It's better to be a coward for a minute than dead the rest of your life," Pint said.

"You broke my heart, Pint. Why'd you do it?"

"Pinkerton wanted you at the B&O that morning. I told him I knew someone on the police force, and he paid me to get you there. So I ginned up the story for you and Augustus about my shipment of Secesh silk and silverware to get you to come along. Pinkerton just wanted a policeman there as a diversion. He never counted on you throwing yourself into this like a whirlwind. You're a surprise, Temple, a downright surprise. All he thought the presence of a policeman would accomplish would be to regulate old Baker here, to keep him from getting violent in a public space when Pinkerton's men went for the diaries. Baker's a surprise, too, though. I'm surrounded by surprises."

"You sure are, you nuisance," Baker said, pulling his LeMat from his waistband and blowing off the bottom of Pint's jaw. "So quit your yabbering."

He fired another round into Pint's head as he crumpled to the floor, blood and tissue spraying against the wall.

"If I bribe the little bastard, he should stay with me, right?" Baker said. "I hadn't the foggiest that Pinkerton was also paying him. There's no more honor left in this town. Doesn't bother me that he was entrepreneurial, mind you. What bothers me is that he was walking around the fuckin' District with my address in his pocket. Can't have dimwits in the organization."

Baker turned to Temple and raised the LeMat again.

"And you and I are now officially finished," he said.

Before Baker could pull the trigger, Augustus stepped into the room from the hallway and put his Colt to the back of Baker's head, cocking back the hammer.

"Let go of the gun, Baker," Augustus said.

"If I just shoot the cripple here, then what?"

"Then your brains will be on the wall next to Pint's."

Baker let his arm go slack, and Augustus pulled the LeMat from his hand, stepping back into the doorway.

"Do you know who Maestro is?" Temple asked Baker.

"He's in the Booth diary, that's as much as I know."

"Liar."

"He is an unknown. Why would I really need to lie about anything to you? You're a nothing."

"How's the wrist?" Temple asked, tipping his cane at the bandage wrapped around the top of Baker's right hand. "Impressive that you can still heft that toy gun of yours with your left hand."

"You snapped my wrist at your darky's house, and I killed your friend in Swampdoodle. Feel worth it to you? Happy with the swap?"

Temple lunged forward and swung his cane into Baker's jaw, breaking it. Baker dropped to a knee, howling in pain. Circling behind him, Temple wrapped an arm around his neck, choking him.

"How does it feel, having the life squeezed out of you?"

Temple planted his left hand on the side of Baker's head, pushing Baker's skull against the weight and force of his chokehold so he could snap his neck. Baker began to scream as his broken jaw was turned. Augustus grabbed Temple by the shoulders, shouting at him to stop and pulling him off Baker.

"Don't turn yourself into him," Augustus said. "Don't turn yourself into a murderer."

Temple fell back from Baker and stood up, his arms shaking. He dug his heel into Baker's back and toppled him over. Crouching back down, he whispered into Baker's ear.

"Listen closely, Baker. Noah Brooks has a thick file on you prepared by Edwin Stanton's staff. You've been tapping into Sam Morse's National Telegraph line on the second floor of the War Department. You've been listening in on President Johnson's private correspondence and confidential Secret Service traffic. That's a crime. Noah's going to put this on his front page tomorrow afternoon, and Stanton's going to cashier you because of it. You'll be lucky if they don't send you to the Old Capitol as Wood's guest. At the very least, you're done in the District and you're done in the government. You're going to spend the rest of your days looking over your shoulder, afraid of who might be coming after you. Enjoy living with your ghosts."

Temple stood up and brought his cane down on the back of Baker's head, leaving him in a pile on the floor as he and Augustus departed for the Willard.

CHAPTER THIRTY

THE ENDGAME

Fiona brushed off Temple's jacket the next morning outside the Willard as he prepared to join the military escort taking him to the B&O on horseback. She squinted into the sun and peered up at his face, and he pulled her hand up to his lips and kissed it.

"You're always with me, Fi."

"And you with me."

Temple hugged Alexander and Augustus in turn, and Augustus leaned in toward Temple's ear.

"I should have stayed at the asylum longer," Augustus whispered.

"Had you done that, you wouldn't have been able to meet me at Baker's office."

"If I had stayed back, they might not have gotten the diary."

"They were Union troops. You saved my life. Had you not followed me, I'd be dead. If you vow to stay off your smoke, I'll vow to stop my cards."

The troops took Temple to the B&O, where, still in his Union blues, he boarded the train for New York. He transferred in Baltimore and arrived in Manhattan late that evening.

The following morning he bought a new pair of black trousers, a black jacket, and a white shirt for $10 at Moore & Sons, leaving his uniform neatly folded at the end of his bed when he left the St. Nicholas Hotel. A day later, he got a New York and Harlem train at Grand Street and then transferred onto the Erie in Piermont, heading north to Elmira.

. . .

AFTER RENTING A ROOM in the Brainard Hotel in Elmira, Temple spent the next three days downstairs at a table from sunrise until the doors were locked at night, eating, reading, and eyeing traffic in and out of the lobby until John Surratt finally arrived at the front desk to collect his keys.

Surratt was much taller than Temple had expected, and he was more emaciated than he appeared in the carte de visite that Fiona had taken from his mother's cell, his face so gaunt that his cheekbones formed fine ridges on either side of his face. A long, thin moustache drooped down on either side of his lips, and his hair was wispy and thinning. He was deliberate and calm as he went about his business, and he didn't bother to survey the lobby before going upstairs.

An hour later Surratt returned, and Temple followed him out the door, crossing the hurly-burly of wagons, horses, and people on Baldwin Street to the opposite corner so that he could observe Surratt as he walked down Water Street. Surratt lingered by the window at Schwenke & Grumme (LOUNGES AND LOUNGE BEDS MADE TO ORDER; HAIR, SPRING, STRAW AND HUSK MATTRESSES CONSTANTLY ON HAND; LOOKING GLASS AND PICTURE FRAMES READY FOR YOU) and then stopped at Preswick's Book Store at 16 Water. He unlocked and entered a side door leading upstairs. A sign above the second-floor window announced the enterprise nominally operating below: "J. Harrison: Land Surveys, Daguerreotypes, Ambrotypes, Photographs, Etc., Etc." A shade snapped down in the window a moment later.

When Surratt came back downstairs and headed toward the Brainard, Temple crossed the street, picked the lock at J. Harrison, and went upstairs. It was nearly empty in the office, save for a large drafting table in the middle of the room. On it were several maps and detailed sketches of the prison camp on the edge of town that, until recently, had been holding Confederate soldiers in conditions that the newspapers said were nearly as bleak and horrific as Andersonville. A number of reports, written in longhand and offering accounts of the conditions in the camp and in Elmira, were stacked neatly on the floor nearby. A knife bearing an elegant etching of a black locomotive across the length of its blade rested atop the papers, and in a lone box on a shelf was a stack of calling cards: "John Harrison, Surveys & Ambrotypes."

Temple went back downstairs and gave two Indian heads to a boy peddling apples on the corner, asking him to run into the Brainard and say he had a message that he was to deliver personally to John Harrison.

The boy returned and told Temple that the hotel had said Harrison was a recent arrival and was confining himself to his quarters for the rest of the evening. The message could be delivered in the morning, but before nine, because Mr. Harrison was departing for a train then. Temple patted the boy on the head and gave him another Indian head.

THE NEXT MORNING, Temple waited in the Erie Railroad station and then followed Surratt onto the train to Canandaigua, sitting three benches behind him. Surratt was smoking a cigar and wearing a richly tailored maroon Oxford jacket and a round-top hat, clothing that was a considerable price above what he had worn the prior day. He began counting out Canadian currency in his lap, just as calm and fastidious as he had been in the Brainard, and the sight of the money put Temple into a disagreeable spin. Surratt was planning on heading to Canada, most likely to Montreal, where there still was an active movement of Secesh and where he could evade American authorities. He was not on his way to Manhattan, as Temple had hoped. He leaned back in his seat, cataloging his alternatives.

A conductor came down the aisle collecting tickets, followed by a newsboy selling papers and cigars. Surratt put the Canadian currency in his breast pocket, bought a paper, and laid it on the seat. He then walked to the end of the car, slid open the door that connected it to the adjacent cars, and passed through. Minutes later, another man—tall, thin, and mustachioed—entered the car wearing Surratt's maroon jacket and hat. He sat down in Surratt's seat, picked up the

newspaper lying there, and began reading. None of his fellow passengers, save one, was any the wiser that he wasn't the same man who
had been seated there before.

Temple bolted up from his seat and hobbled down the aisle, passing into the next car and the car after that until he spotted Surratt
curled up against a window sleeping. He was wearing a simple gray
coat now, topped off by a floppy cotton cap with a wide brim. Temple
sat down at the opposite end of the car and exhaled.

When they reached Albany, Temple got off the train and watched
the man in Surratt's maroon jacket make a show of going to a ticket
window to inquire about the best form of passage to Montreal. Surratt waited aboard the Canandaigua train another fifteen minutes,
then stepped off and crossed the platform only minutes before the
departure of the train that would carry him south to Piermont and
then on to Manhattan. Temple followed him on board the train to
Manhattan, settled in behind him yet again, and then used the rest
of their journey together to contemplate the endgame.

AFTER BOOKING A ROOM at the Fifth Avenue Hotel for that evening, Surratt waited in Madison Square Park until a large black
brougham carrying a driver and two other men pulled up at the
northeastern corner of the square. Temple stepped back into the
trees and shadows behind the Worth obelisk, watching them. Surratt
didn't move until two men stepped from the brougham, canvassed
the immediate block, and then nodded to him. He scampered off his
park bench and into the carriage. Temple waited until the driver had
spurred his pair of horses before he stepped out of the trees, and then
he watched the brougham depart. A carriage Temple had retained
was waiting a block away and he stepped to the street to summon it.
He wouldn't need to follow Surratt too closely, because he knew exactly where he was headed.

FOUR DIFFERENT ARCHITECTS and three different contractors had
been retained to build the mansion at 212 Madison Avenue, and it

was said to be even more elaborate inside than out. In addition to rumors that the interior and its nine bedrooms were lined with gold leaf and marble, there was persistent chatter that the owner had spent nearly $50,000 on a glass and iron dome for the mansion, which in the end he decided to reject because it didn't conform architecturally with the rest of the estate. The entire home was outfitted for gas illumination—the first of its kind in New York—and the owner was said to have built a private railway depot adjacent to his basement.

Not in dispute was the fact that the owner had never been seen outside the mansion and had never extended an invitation to anyone in the neighborhood to visit him. Whispered in the most discreet fashion in what was agreed to be the most prestigious and expensive neighborhood in Manhattan was that the mansion's owner was most likely quite mad.

Had he cared to inform his neighbors or anyone else in Manhattan about his true preferences and tastes, the owner himself would have told all of them that he never would live in a home with marble walls and marble floors and that, instead, his estate featured mahogany, oak, and cherry so polished one could almost use the walls as looking glasses.

He also would have shown them, had they ever been welcomed inside, that in addition to modern gas tubing strung throughout the estate, he also had his own telegraph line; his own Otis elevators traveling between the mansion's basement and three upper floors on a singular system of pulleys, counterweights, and hydraulics; his own elaborate gardens; his own stable of horses; his own library of nearly forty thousand titles; two wine cellars, three Raphaels, and a Caravaggio; six carved fountains that he had imported from Europe, South America, and Russia; and a collection of gemstones kept in a room of their own alongside glass cabinets stocked with Ming vases.

He could catalog these holdings with the same ease that he could count the fingers on his hand. But he would never bother enlightening his neighbors about any of it because he had as little interest in their friendship as he did in their well-being.

"We are dedicated to serving only ourselves, are we not?" he said to his apprentice.

"That and nothing else, Maestro," replied Surratt, who was seated beside a medieval fireplace brought over, stone by stone, from Warsaw. It was large enough for seven men to stand inside it, but because of the summer heat it was unlit and yawned like a deep black cavern across most of an entire wall.

The owner sat in a high-backed dark walnut chair with rosettes carved on its frame. He had, in fact, installed over his office a glass and iron dome similar to the one he'd rejected, albeit smaller, never having intended to cap the mansion as a whole with such a thing, and during the day shafts of sunlight danced in bars around his desk. On nights with a full, lush moon such as this, a purple glow bathed the top of his head.

"I have arranged transport for you this evening on a steamship to Liverpool, and from there you are going to go to the Vatican and serve as a papal Zouave. The Vatican is a state unto itself, and our authorities have no power to pluck you from there."

"Thank you for arranging this, Maestro."

"Thank you for your service in Richmond, Washington, Elmira, and Montreal. We plan to pay you well for all that you have done."

Surratt stood up from his chair, measuring his words and his nerve as he listened to the sound of water trickling in the courtyard fountain outside. The low whir and rumbling of the mansion's elevators rose and fell as the cars moved inside the walls.

"I want railroad stock," Surratt blurted, rushing to get the words out before his legs grew rubbery again. "Judah Benjamin asked for the same when I met with him in Richmond in March. And he wired me in early April when I returned to Elmira to say that he had burned all records of the rail negotiations, as you wished. He said it was only right that he also receive a stock grant."

The owner cleared his throat, assessing Surratt as if seeing him for the first time. He appreciated men who could reduce discussions to money. If they were entitled to a claim, it made everything more rational. If they weren't, well, then they weren't and that, too, offered clarity.

"Of course you want stock," the owner said, holding out his hand to Surratt, who stepped forward tentatively to take it.

In a corner of the room beneath a gaslight that cast an amber shroud around him, a slender, graceful man uncurled like a cat from a high-backed, tufted leather chair and began to stand up. He paused, frustrated, because his left leg, broken when he'd leapt to the stage after killing Lincoln, still couldn't bear all of his weight.

He forced himself upright and reached back down to a tray by the chair to pull a cigar up to his mouth, chuckling and leaning against a wall to continue observing Surratt's negotiation. He had pale skin that gleamed in the room's half-light, large, sensual eyes, and a moustache and wavy hair the color of India ink. He waited until the throbbing in his leg subsided, then gestured with his cigar toward the middle of the room.

"I suppose, then, that I should request stock as well, Maestro," John Wilkes Booth said. "I'd like something that gives me a deeper taste, a true financial partnership that reflects all that we've accomplished together."

CHAPTER THIRTY-ONE

THE DOSSIER

Temple had used his time earlier in the evening to read through the second dossier that Stanton had given him at his home. Stanton's spies had assembled it and probably added information that Wood had beaten out of his prisoners. It offered the barest description of the mansion at 212 Madison, along with a floor plan, a roster of how many guards were around it and when they changed shifts, and an outline of the comings and goings about the house.

Of more interest was the skeletal biography of the owner, a man referred to in telegrams and correspondence as Maestro but with nothing more known about his real identity or past. It was unclear which banks he used or who his lawyers were. Tailors, food, furniture, and other deliveries came to the house, but guests rarely came and its owner never ventured out. He was believed to exercise control of a network of railroads and real estate, but his holdings couldn't be traced. He communicated freely with Thomas Scott, though their means of communication couldn't be discerned. He had a handicap, the result of an unknown accident: he had a prosthetic wooden arm capped with a steel hook to replace the one he'd lost.

Temple had circled this last point, read through the dossier another time, then torn it apart and stuffed it inside a sack of offal near the kitchen door at the back of the hotel. After watching Surratt leave Union Square and head north to Madison, he instructed the carriage driver he had hired to proceed to Lexington instead and head north to the luxury homes and rolling, open spaces around 35th Street. There was a small carriage house behind 212 Madison, and at this hour there would only be a single guard inside it.

He waited in the shadow of a small elm tree for about an hour until the guard came outside to piss. Temple recognized the guard as he stepped beneath a small, ornate gaslight shaped like the cow-catcher of a locomotive. He had been one of the men at the B&O the day that Stump Tigani got his throat opened up. He had stood over Temple with a metal bar and ordered him to give up the diaries. Temple hobbled over to the guard before he had finished emptying himself and dropped his cane on the ground.

"Remember me?" Temple asked.

The guard still had his hand at the opening of his trousers, and he jumped when Temple spoke.

"Do you?" Temple asked before taking the guard's head in his hands and twisting it like a top until the man's neck snapped. It sounded like a handful of dice being crushed by a wagon wheel. The guard was so startled, he didn't make a sound, other than a slight whimper right before his eyes went lifeless.

Temple pulled a set of keys off the guard, made his way through the carriage house, and let himself in through the back door of the mansion. The only noise was the whirring of some sort of mechanical device in the walls and the sound of three men speaking upstairs.

Temple climbed a huge circular staircase, pressing his back against the wall and trying to stay in the shadows that fell between the gas lamps above him. His bad leg throbbed, and he leaned on his cane when he reached the top of the stairs.

He was staring down a double-width hallway lined with artwork. The gaslight burned brighter in the hallway, and he recognized several of the pieces: "The New Jerusalem," by George Inness; "Peace Consoles Mankind and Brings Abundance," by Eugene Delacroix; "A Vision of the Last Judgment," by William Blake; three panels—each twenty feet wide—from John Banvard's "Mississippi River Panorama"; two marble busts of Caesar; a bronze mermaid; and a nine-foot bronze of Hephaestus, fashioned so that the Greek god's hammer rose a foot above his head and nearly touched the ceiling.

The floor planking gleamed and reflected the gas lamps as buttery smudges. Halfway down the hall a tongue of light spilled out from beneath two oversized mahogany doors, each of them fronted with elaborate scrollwork depicting cotton bushes with branches bending beneath the weight of bolls cast from thumb-sized pearls.

Temple crept to the edge of the doorway and waited by the statue of Hephaestus, listening. He leaned on the anvil tilting toward the god's knees and could hear the sounds of three men speaking again on the other side of the doors.

"You will not be given stock or any more cash, Mr. Surratt," said one of the men beyond the doors, his voice deep, steady, and Southern, and only loud enough to register that what he was saying was both an order and a warning, not a request. "You will have protection, and as long as you keep yourself removed and in Europe, you will be permitted to stay alive. I assume now that our discussion is over?"

"It is over," said Surratt. "Will you arrange transportation for me to the docks?"

"Certainly. Fetch one of my men in the carriage house to take you."

Temple stepped behind Hephaestus when Surratt yanked open one of the doors and burst through, barely concealing his anger. He scurried past Temple, swearing under his breath, and then rushed down the stairs.

Temple peered around the edge of the door.

One of the men inside was tall, thin, and blond, immaculately dressed, with a hook protruding from the cuff of his shirt. The other man stood in the shadows in a corner of the room, the tip of a cigar burning red in his hand.

From the shadows the other man declared—in a voice that Temple found theatrical—that he didn't give a damn what Surratt had settled for; he himself wanted railroad stock.

The blond man rose from a chair the size of a throne and stood by an ornate walnut desk, tapping it with the tip of his hook.

"Unfortunately, I don't partner with anyone in that fashion," he said. "I am a sole proprietor in every meaningful way. Moreover, you were a functionary in the assassination, not an architect."

The man in the shadows snarled at this, his voice rising to an operatic pitch.

"I am the Brutus of this nation! I spared our republic the rule of a dictator. I am no mere functionary. I will be praised through the ages."

He walked with a pronounced limp toward the blond man, his face now aglow from a thick candle that burned atop the desk. He placed his cigar in an oyster-shell ashtray on the desk and rubbed his thumb and forefinger together, grinding bits of tobacco leaf into the smoke rising up from the butt.

The man was small and unusually handsome, with round, coal-black eyes, black hair that fell around his face in lazy curls, and a carefully pomaded moustache.

Temple gasped, loudly enough that the two men swiveled from the desk to stare back at him in the doorway.

"Well, Mr. Booth, this is not Mr. Surratt in our doorway," the blond man said, amused. "It would appear we have a visitor."

John Wilkes Booth smiled.

Temple slammed the other door open and hobbled into the drawing room, his cane pounding the floor with each step he took toward the men.

"After all that we have evaded, someone decides to send a gimp after our worthy selves, Maestro," Booth said, snickering.

"Beware, Mr. Booth. I believe we are at last face-to-face with Temple McFadden, and he is not a man to be trifled with. I have had astounding reports about him from Washington. I suggest we conclude our business posthaste."

Temple swept a porcelain urn from a table and hurled it at both men. It sailed over the desk and crashed against the floor by the fireplace.

"Excellent, excellent," Maestro said, rapping his hook against the desktop. "A display of passion and anger. A man wedded to the moment. But I have grown weary of your annoyances. Take him, Edgar."

Another bodyguard had entered the room behind Temple and pressed the muzzle of a derringer into the side of his neck. It's cold, Temple thought to himself. The end of a gun is cold.

"I don't want him disposed of yet," Maestro said. "I have questions for him."

Booth considered Temple for a moment, then turned his attention back to Maestro.

"I am supposed to be cold and in the grave, sir," Booth said. "All I need to do is turn myself over to Stanton's people and explain your involvement. Your machinations and your use of me to carry them out will come to naught."

Booth waved his hand around the room. "All of this will be taken from you," he continued. "Unless I am given a portion of your empire. I aim to be a man with stock."

"Of course. Your reasoning is sound," Maestro said. "I would like your stay with us these past few weeks to end on more cordial grounds than this."

"Then it would appear that honor is restored and we have grounds for an accommodation."

"We most certainly do."

Maestro came around the desk to shake Booth's hand. As he neared Booth, Maestro swung his arm in a sweeping, upward arc across the actor's belly, drawing a thick red ribbon of blood that spurted from a gash in his vest and drained the color from his face. Booth looked startled, as if a flawless line reading had been overlooked, and pitched forward onto the desk. Maestro wrapped his hand in Booth's hair and turned his face toward him.

"You are neither Brutus nor an architect," Maestro said. "You are a functionary and a fool."

Booth slipped from the desk and fell to the floor in a pile.

Maestro took a handkerchief from his pocket and wiped the

blood from the metal hook protruding from his right arm. He bent toward Booth, waiting to see the life escape from his eyes, but was interrupted by a shriek from the other side of the room.

John Surratt stood in the doorway, eyes wide at the sight of Booth dying on the floor.

Edgar flinched when Surratt yelled, and the end of his gun slipped away from Temple's neck. Temple grabbed Edgar's wrist and turned it upside down and inward, squeezing Edgar's trigger finger for him. The bullet tore out the bodyguard's throat.

Surratt fled down the hallway, screaming.

"It is a shame for you that derringers house only a single round, otherwise you'd have me at bay," Maestro said. "But they are compact and elegant pistols. All of my guards have them. We gave one to Booth."

"So he could murder the president for you."

"How did you get in here?"

"I entered through the carriage house."

"And my guard there?"

"Dead."

"I have others here who can easily replace him."

"No, in truth you don't."

"The men on my front door?"

"Down. Tommy Driscoll slumbered both of them for me. Edgar was your last."

"Mr. McFadden, you are an amazement. You must come work for me. I can pay you twenty-five thousand dollars a year."

"Gold is good in its place, but living, brave, patriotic men are better than gold."

"You needn't cite Mr. Lincoln's bromides anymore. The man is dead."

"You arranged his murder. You're going back to the District in cuffs, and you're going to be hanged."

"Lincoln had but a marginal sense of enlightened progress; he couldn't grasp the totality of it. He fancied a mighty railway west to unite the coasts, and he even put the government's coffers behind the effort, but he somehow found it necessary to stand in the way of my interests in the Southern railroads. There is a new industrial order in this country, and it is establishing itself despite government intrusions. To the extent that the government becomes an obstacle it will be brought to heel or forced aside."

"Who are you?"

"I am capital."

Temple rested his cane against a chair, and Maestro leaned back against his desk, holding out his artificial arm and rolling up the sleeve so that Temple could see the extent of it.

"I was an orphan when a cotton gin near Memphis snared my arm; I like to think of it as my industrial baptism. You were a disabled orphan as well. I was born in Florence and you in Dublin. Now we are making our lives here. We have more intersections than you care to take into account, and it qualifies us as secret sharers."

"Prattle. I share nothing with you. Baker, Stanton, Scott, Pinkerton—do any of them know you?"

"No one knows me. I don't exist. They have only intimations of me," he said. "Baker arranged Booth's escape from the Garrett farm, but in his distressing thick-headedness he failed to empty Booth's pockets before putting his clothing on a suitable double."

"They also didn't want anyone examining the corpse too closely. The coloring around the bullet holes wouldn't have been right. People would have suspected a substitute."

"We bribed the doctor and dentist who went aboard the *Montauk* to identify Booth's body, and we thought that once Baker had resecured the diary, we would be done with this matter. But then you happened upon the B&O that morning and introduced chaos."

"What of Thomas Scott?"

"His interests and mine align perfectly, though he knows me only as a conduit for investments in the Pennsylvania Railroad. I am partnered with Warren Delano in the opium trade, but he doesn't know who I am. I have similar relationships with the Morgans in banking and Eliphalet Remington's sons in arms and munitions."

Maestro walked to the fireplace and pulled a long black poker from a brass canister sitting near the hearth.

"I'll miss you," he said to Temple.

"You're going back to Washington with me."

"I have absolutely no intention of doing that."

Maestro lunged around the desk at Temple, brandishing the poker. He swung once; the tip missed Temple but sliced across the candle on top of the desk, sending it end over end into the curtains. They burst into flame, and the face of a bronze cherub on a table next to the curtains glowed orange.

"I don't care if any of it burns," Maestro said. "There is always more to be had."

The flames raced up the curtain and spread in tongues across the ceiling. Maestro came at Temple again with the poker, and Temple blocked it with his cane. With a second thrust he flipped the poker entirely out of Maestro's hand.

Maestro dove at Temple and punctured the top of his hand with the hook. Temple screamed in pain and dropped his cane, snapping Maestro's head back as he grabbed his neck. The pair tumbled out of the room and into the hallway. Black smoke was pouring out of the drawing room.

Maestro was gagging at the end of Temple's arm and swung wildly with his hook, trying to impale Temple's arm or shoulder. They collapsed together on the floor, each of them kicking and punching as the flames spread around them.

Temple freed himself and lurched up, but Maestro kicked at his bad leg and knocked him back to the ground, pouncing on him and slashing at his face with his hook. Temple rolled his head to the side and the hook caught the plank where his cheek had been.

Temple brought his left knee up and pressed his foot against

346 · Timothy L. O'Brien

Maestro's chest, launching him backward into a rail that ran around the opening of the stairwell. The rail cracked and Maestro tilted over the shaft, spinning his arms furiously to keep his balance. Temple managed to get to his feet and charged Maestro, the pair of them plunging over the rail and down the stairs into the basement.

They both lay crumpled and exhausted on the floor below. Blood pooled near Maestro's ankle, where a piece of wood had punctured it.

"I won't go to a prison!" Maestro screamed as they unwound themselves from one another.

"Then you'll burn here," Temple said, slamming his right hand against Maestro's jaw.

A rafter split above them and fell from the ceiling, pinning one of Maestro's legs to the floor. He batted at it with his arms, trapped.

Temple got to his feet and scrambled on his hands and knees up the staircase and into the front hall. He pulled his jacket over his head to protect himself from the flames, then stopped.

Shouts rang up from the basement. Or just more rafters snapping?

He turned back, but the entire entrance to the stairwell behind him was engulfed in flames and impassable. Hephaestus loomed along the wall, in his element, before the floor gave way beneath the statue and it disappeared.

Temple hobbled through the smoke and flames in the hallway and out the front door, past the dead bodyguards, and into a small courtyard that fronted on Madison, where he collapsed.

Flames were bursting from every window on the first and second floors by the time the initial group of firemen arrived. Shortly after that, the entire side of the mansion collapsed.

TOMMY DRISCOLL WAS KNEELING over him, wrapping a bandage around his head and mopping his face with a wet cloth, when Temple's vision first came back into focus. The pounding in his head began to subside. Tommy had arrived at the mansion about fifteen minutes before the fire started, waiting outside for Temple, as Temple had asked him to do, regardless of what he saw or heard happening inside. After Temple spilled from the front door and collapsed, Tommy got him onto the back of a wagon before the press or the rest of the police arrived. He had flashed his badge to clear the way so that he could get Temple out.

"You could have done something besides fireworks to let me know you were back in New York, Temple," Tommy said, propping his friend's head in his lap in the back of the wagon. "You're lucky you survived that."

"Got any water to drink?"

"Nope. Whiskey."

"Give me some."

Tommy poured it down his throat, but Temple spat it back up.

"How many bodies, Tommy? How many bodies on Madison Avenue?"

"The entire mansion is burned down, and there's no way to identify anybody in there. There were three bodies outside."

"Any bodies where the drawing room was?"

"Two, but so deep-roasted, no one will ever know who they are."

"Any in the basement? With a hook?"

"With what?"

"A hook. An artificial limb."

"No, Temple, no hooks, from what I heard. Not a single one."

"How are my boots?"

"What of 'em?"

"How do they look?"

"They're all torn up. There are shards of glass in 'em."

"Dammit."

"Go back to sleep now."

Tommy took Temple to the St. Nicholas Hotel and left him in a room overlooking Broadway. In the lobby, Tommy sent a telegram to Fiona to inform her that Temple was alive and well but needed rest.

· · ·

ONCE THE POUNDING in his head subsided, Temple sat at a desk in his room and began to write a letter to Fiona, explaining the last days to her.

> *Dearest Fiona:*
> *I have become what I had loathed.*

He crumpled the letter into a ball and swept it off the desk. Later that day, he tried again.

> *Dearest Fiona:*
> *I have encountered Surratt, Booth, and Maestro at a mansion here on Madison Avenue. Surratt has escaped, but I believe that Booth and Maestro are dead.*

Nail is dead, too, Temple thought. Maestro could well be alive. Were the timbers in the mansion cracking in the flames or was I being laughed at?

He crumpled the letter again and dropped it to the floor.

> *My darling Fiona:*
> *I am unsure now of what we have accomplished. I am so sorry for involving you and Augustus in all of this. I am undeserving of you.*

He tore this sheet of paper in half, left it on the desk, and went to his window to stare at the throngs on the street below him.

THE NEXT DAY he went to the front desk of the St. Nicholas and paid for a telegram.

> *To: Fiona McFadden, Willard Hotel, Washington*
> *From: Temple McFadden, St. Nicholas Hotel, New York*
> *I'm coming home.*

Then he walked out into the city to buy a new pair of boots.

On the train for Baltimore later that day, he watched porters scramble on the platform for luggage, and then he settled back into his seat as the locomotive left the station, wheel upon rail, wheel upon rail, wheel upon rail.

AUTHOR'S NOTE

The literature and online resources surrounding Abraham Lincoln, his assassination, and the social, political, and economic upheavals of the Civil War era are vast and I can't cite everything that I read or dipped into online and off as I did research for this novel. But in addition to acknowledging digital and print records at the Baltimore & Ohio Railroad Museum, the Historical Society of Washington, D.C., the Library of Congress, the National Archives, and *The New York Times*, I'm particularly indebted to the following books: *Mary Todd Lincoln* by Jean H. Baker; *Alley Life in Washington* by James Borchert; *The Age of Lincoln* by Orville Vernon Burton; *The Irish in America* by Michael Coffey and Terry Golway; *Lincoln* by David Herbert Donald; *The Lincolns* by Daniel Mark Epstein; *The Secret War for the Union* by Edwin C. Fishel; *Reconstruction* by Eric Foner; *Freedom Rising* by Ernest B. Furgurson; *Team of Rivals* by Doris Kearns Goodwin; *American Brutus* by Michael W. Kauffman; *Behind the Scenes* by Elizabeth Keckley; *The American Irish* by Kevin Kenny; *Throes of Democracy* by Walter A. McDougall; *A Nation of Counterfeiters* by Stephen Mihm; *Police in Urban America, 1860–1920* by Eric H. Monkkonen; *Washington Through Two Centuries* by Joseph R. Passonneau; *Old Washington, D.C.* by Robert Reed; *The Grand Review* by Georg R. Sheets; *The Trial* edited by Edward Steers, Jr.; *Book of Poisons* by Serita Stevens and Anne Bannon; *Lincoln* by Gore Vidal.

A special thanks to Lieutenant Nicholas Breul of the Metropolitan Police Department in Washington, D.C., who gave me a primer on the history of policing in Washington and also gave me a copy of an 1893 history of the department, *D of C Police*.

ACKNOWLEDGMENTS

I hope every writer winds up with an editor as graceful, smart, genuine, and committed as Mark Tavani. I know they won't, because Mark is unique, but everyone deserves a creative partner like him. I probably didn't deserve him, but I got him anyway. This book would have been much shallower without Mark's involvement.

I landed in Mark's hands through the efforts of Linda Marrow, who descended upon this work like an angel, because she is an angel. As the world turns, Jim Impoco led me to Linda, as he has to many other good things.

Andrew Blauner has been my agent for fourteen years and a friend for even longer. He is unwavering and decent and manages to be so in Manhattan, where the hunger to be otherwise can sometimes run deep.

My friend Mark Alexander and my brother, Michael O'Brien, read and helped improve early drafts of this novel.

Other than Mark Tavani, my closest and most important reader was my wife, Devon Corneal, who always arrives, eyes shining, with gifts of every stripe, including laughter, children, patience, and warmth.

When I was ten years old, my father's uncle, Arthur Mahony, gave me Carl Sandburg's three-volume biography of Abraham Lincoln for my birthday, and that's where much of this began for me. A hat tip to you, Unc, with gratitude for teaching me early on that one of the best things I could do for my lovely sons, Jeffrey and Cooper, was to give them books.

Read on for a thrilling chapter from the next Temple McFadden adventure.

CHAPTER ONE

THE PATENT

Anderson, Adams & Young
Nassau Street, New York

March 4, 1869

Fancy law firm, Dish thought. Heavy, grand furniture and a dozen desks the width of hansoms lined up in tidy rows of six. Gas lighting, large windows, an entire floor three stories above the financial district. Fancy. None of that, though, is what brought him down through the roof in the rain, into the main stairwell, and then, pick, pick, pick, past that silly lock on the door in the hallway. What Dish was most keen on sat across from him in the corner, squat, heavy, and defiant.

He lowered his leather shoulder bag to the floor as if it were a baby and eyed the Milners' safe the way he always did when it came time for him to size up an opponent. The moon painted stripes of mottled light on the safe's black sides as it streamed through the rain on a nearby window. It also had a Bramah lock, goddammit. He sat down on the floor next to his bag and pondered the beast. He had a hammer and chisel in the bag and he could just be crude about the affair and be done with it—turn the damn thing on its side, expose its bottom, slip the chisel beneath the rivets holding the base to the sides, and pound the top off each rivet like he was popping buttons off a bodice. The bottom would open up, and out would spill the innards.

Dish was better than that, though, and he hadn't been brought across an ocean to stir a ruckus on Manhattan late at night. Police were in the area, and the pounding of a sledgehammer when everyone should be asleep meant mischief to coppers. He was here, at great expense and with ample planning, because he was an artist and a thoughtful man. Using the hammer wasn't elegant, and it was risky.

But the safe had a Bramah on it, and Bramahs meant work. You needed a scored cylinder to pop a Bramah, so the army of skeleton keys in his bag were useless. He slipped his hand into his bag and pulled out a small velvet sack filled with a collection of metal picks. He fiddled with the pile, pushing each pick back and forth across his palm with the index finger of his other hand, until he decided on two of them. They were the longest and most flexible of the lot, almost like a pair of springs, and he admired them as he tied the velvet sack closed and dropped it back into his bag. He stretched. This could take some time. He dropped two cushions onto the floor in front of the safe, knelt down, and slipped his picks into the Bramah, feeling his way around the pins inside. He moved past the first pin easily, but as his picks traveled deeper inside the lock, it got harder to keep the mechanism turned and the pins stacked properly. He'd lose the stack and the pins would all slip away from him again and again, tumbling back into place and leaving him where he'd begun. It was dark in the office, but he didn't need light. The dance was all in his fingers and ever so slightly in his ears. His eyes didn't matter.

Four hours later, Dish was still at it. His knees were sore, his fingers ached, and sweat was beading his brow. The sun would be up in a few hours. Only a few years ago he would have been in and out of

American targets in a snap, but now, with their bloody infighting done and the war long over, Yanks were minting money, and law firms like this could afford to import the best British safes. He needed to think harder on how much he was charging his clients. His work had become more demanding.

He felt the final pin move inside the Bramah. When the entire lock, propped on his two picks pressed flush against the front of the safe, moved in tandem, he whispered a little victory cry and let the air escape from his lungs. He sat back and pulled the door open. His handlers had told him that the envelope in the safe would be easy to find, even in the dark, and that was true. Most of what the lawyers had dumped into their safe were ledgers. There was just one envelope, and Dish plucked it from one of the shelves. He was told to make sure that there was a complex drawing inside the envelope, so he took it to the window and examined the contents up against the moonlight. Two pages were inside, and six finely sketched drawings filled one of the pages. The first sketch was of a locomotive, and the rest were confusing enumerated drawings of drums and gears, all of which were lost on the safebreaker. Even so, the other page had everything on it that Dish needed to feel a sense of completion. Under the Anderson, Adams & Young logo was a notification to the government that the firm was filing a patent application that included the drawings.

Dish put the pages back into the envelope and slipped it into his jacket pocket. He took a moment to look out the window and bask in his victory over both the Milners' and that tightfisted Bramah. He also knew, seconds later, that he didn't have the street to himself any longer. A copper was looking up at him from the curb. He stepped back, flustered, and waited. He stepped to the window again and looked below. The copper had vanished. Then the pounding began on the front door three floors below him. By the time he had his tools back in his bag he could hear footsteps mounting the stairway, which meant he couldn't exit back through the roof.

He raised a window sash and stepped out onto the broad ledge that wrapped around the façade of the building. He pressed his back against the wall and, as he had done so many times before, slipped along the ledge toward the downspout several feet away. He'd be on the street as soon as the copper got into the law office, then off he'd go into the night. The downspout wasn't fixed to the wall, though, and when Dish grabbed it, it peeled away from the building. He lost his balance for a moment, and his bag fell from his shoulder to Nassau Street below. Disappointing, but the real prize was still in his pocket, and he could always find more picks. He exhaled and moved toward the gutter again. A step more, a step more, and then he'd be there. But when the copper stuck his head out the window and screamed at him, Dish lost his balance again. If the ledge he was standing on had been dry he would have been fine, but the ledge was wet.

. . .

THE FIRST PRECINCT called in Tommy Driscoll to look at the body a few hours later, because the burglar took the plunge from Anderson, Adams & Young and because the burglar was clearly more than a burglar. It was a Driscoll corpse for certain, and Tommy got pissy when they didn't call him on these.

Driscoll studied the patent application and the drawings and put them back in the envelope, then glanced at the face of the body stretched on the floor of a cell in the back of the First.

"They always look surprised," he said.

Among the personal belongings Driscoll's men had taken off the body was a clutch of currency from the Empire of Brazil and a pocketknife in an ivory case. Driscoll opened the knife and rubbed his thumb across the locomotive engraved on the blade.

"Go find Temple McFadden," he said to one of his men. "Find him in a hurry."

TIMOTHY L. O'BRIEN is the author of *The Lincoln Conspiracy*. He is the publisher of *Bloomberg View*, an opinion and analysis platform about business, politics, and world affairs. He was previously the executive editor of *The Huffington Post*, where he edited a Pulitzer Prize–winning series about wounded war veterans. He has also worked as an editor and writer at *The New York Times*. He is a graduate of Georgetown University, where he studied literature, and Columbia University, where he did graduate work in history, journalism, and business.